These tales are easy to digest. . . .

BLOOD LITE III: AFTERTASTE

features

CHRIS ABBEY • KELLEY ARMSTRONG • L. A. BANKS
MIKE BARON • JIM BUTCHER • DON D'AMMASSA • STEPHEN DORATO
J. G. FAHERTY • CHRISTOPHER GOLDEN • HEATHER GRAHAM
BRAD C. HODSON • NINA KIRIKI HOFFMAN • SHERRILYN KENYON
KEN LILLIE–PAETZ • ADRIAN LUDENS • WILL LUDWIGSEN
E. S. MAGILL • LISA MORTON • MARK ONSPAUGH • NORMAN PRENTISS
DANIEL PYLE • MIKE RESNICK & LEZLI ROBYN • JEFF RYAN
DAVID SAKMYSTER • D. L. SNELL • LUCIEN SOULBAN
ERIC JAMES STONE • JEFF STRAND • JOEL A. SUTHERLAND
JOHN ALFRED TAYLOR

Publishers Weekly **praises the national bestseller** *Blood Lite*

"This **toothsome** anthology of twenty-one **funny-scary** stories from members of the Horror Writers Association arrives **just in time for Halloween**. On the **humorous** end, Matt Venne's 'Elvis Presley and the Bloodsucker Blues' re-creates Presley's voice with pitch-perfect swagger and sets the record straight on how he really died, while Charlaine Harris's 'An Evening with Al Gore' depicts a novel way to deal with environmental criminals; both tales are **truly outstanding**. In a **creepier** vein, Steven Savile's 'Dear Prudence' finds a conflicted man repeatedly revising a note where he details **gory** plans for his significant other, and Nancy Holder's 'I Know Who You Ate Last Summer' features **stomach-churning** 'rock star cannibals.' Big names like Jim Butcher and Sherrilyn Kenyon will have comic horror fans **grabbing this anthology off the shelves**."

The Horror Writers Association

— presents —

BLOOD LITE III: AFTERTASTE

AN ANTHOLOGY OF HUMOROUS HORROR STORIES

Edited by Kevin J. Anderson

Pocket Books

New York   London   Toronto   Sydney   New Delhi

Pocket Books
A Division of Simon & Schuster, Inc.
1230 Avenue of the Americas
New York, NY 10020

This book is a work of fiction. Names, characters, places, and incidents either are products of the author's imagination or are used fictitiously. Any resemblance to actual events or locales or persons, living or dead, is entirely coincidental.

First Pocket Books paperback edition June 2012

POCKET and colophon are registered trademarks of Simon & Schuster, Inc.

For information about special discounts for bulk purchases, please contact Simon & Schuster Special Sales at 1-866-506-1949 or business@simonandschuster.com.

The Simon & Schuster Speakers Bureau can bring authors to your live event. For more information or to book an event contact the Simon & Schuster Speakers Bureau at 1-866-248-3049 or visit our website at www.simonspeakers.com.

Manufactured in the United States of America

10 9 8 7 6 5 4 3 2 1

ISBN 978-1-4516-3624-6
ISBN 978-1-4516-3625-3 (ebook)

Copyright Notices

Contents

∾

BLOOD LITE III: AFTERTASTE

I Was a Teenage Bigfoot

JIM BUTCHER

There are times when, as a professional wizard, my vocation calls me to the great outdoors, and that night I was in the northwoods of Wisconsin with a mixed pack of researchers, enthusiasts and . . . well. Nerds.

"I don't know, man," said a skinny kid named Nash. "What's his name again?"

I poked the small campfire I'd set up earlier with a stick and pretended that they weren't standing less than ten feet away from me. The forest made forest sounds like it was supposed to. Full dark had fallen less than half an hour before.

"Harry Dresden," said Gary, a plump kid with a cell phone, a GPS unit, and some kind of video game device on his belt. "Supposed to be a psychic or something." He was twiddling deft fingers over the surface of what they call a "smart" phone, these days. Hell, the damned things are probably smarter than me. "Supposed to have helped Chicago PD a bunch of times. I'd pull up the Internet references, but I can't get reception out here."

"A psychic?" Nash said. "How is anyone ever supposed to take our research seriously if we keep showing up with fruitcakes like that?"

Gary shrugged. "Doctor Sinor knows him or something."

Doctor Sinor had nearly been devoured by an ogre in a suburban park one fine summer evening, and I'd gotten her out in one piece. Like most people who have a brush with the supernatural, she'd rationalized the truth away as rapidly as possible—which had led her to participate in such fine activities as tonight's Bigfoot expedition in her spare time.

"Gentlemen," Sinor said, impatiently. She was a blocky, no-nonsense type, grey-haired and straight-backed. "If you could help me with these speakers, we might actually manage to blast a call or two before dawn."

Gary and Nash both hustled over to the edge of the firelight to start messing about with the equipment the troop of researchers had packed in. There were half a dozen of them, altogether, all of them busy with trail cameras and call blasting speakers and scent markers and audio recorders.

I pulled a sandwich out of my pocket and started eating it. I took my time about it. I was in no hurry.

For those of you who don't know it, a forest at night is *dark*. Sometimes pitch-black. There was no moon to speak of in the sky, and the light of the stars doesn't make it more than a few inches into a mixed canopy of deciduous trees and evergreens. The light from my little campfire and the hand-held flashlights of the researchers soon gave the woods all the light there was.

Their equipment wasn't working very well—my bad, probably. Modern technology doesn't get on well with the magically gifted. For about an hour, nothing much happened beyond the slapping of mosquitoes and a lot of electronic noises squawking from the loudspeakers.

Then the researchers got everything online and went through their routine. They played primate calls over the speakers and then dutifully recorded the forest afterward. Everything broke down again. The researchers soldiered on, repairing things, and eventually Gary tried wood-knocking, which meant banging on trees with fallen limbs and waiting to hear if there was a response.

I liked Doctor Sinor, but I had asked to come strictly as a ride-along and I didn't pitch in with her team's efforts.

The whole "let's find Bigfoot" thing seems a little ill-planned to me, personally. Granted, my perspective is different from that of non-wizards, but marching out

into the woods looking for a very large and very powerful creature by blasting out what you're pretty sure
are territorial challenges to fight (or else mating calls)
seems . . . somewhat unwise.

I mean, if there's no Bigfoot, no problem. But what
if you're standing there, screaming "Bring it on!" and
find a Bigfoot?

Worse yet, what if *he* finds *you*?

Even worse, what if you were screaming, "Do me,
baby!" and he finds you *then*?

Is it me? Am I crazy? Or does the whole thing just
seem like a recipe for trouble?

So anyway, while I kept my little fire going, the
Questionably Wise Research Variety Act continued
until after midnight. That's when I looked up to see a
massive form standing at the edge of the trees, in the
very outskirts of the light of my dying fire.

I'm in the ninety-ninth percentile for height,
myself, but this guy was *tall*. My head might have come
up to his collarbone, barely, assuming I had correctly
estimated where his collarbone was under the long,
shaggy, dark brown hair covering him. It wasn't long
enough to hide the massive weight of muscle he carried
on that enormous frame or the simple, disturbing, very
slightly inhuman proportions of his body. His face was
broad, blunt, with a heavy brow ridge that turned his
eyes into mere gleams of reflected light.

Most of all, there was a sense of awesome power
granted to his presence by his size alone, chilling even

to someone who had seen big things in action before. There's a reaction to something that much bigger than you, an automatic assumption of menace that is built into the human brain: Big equals dangerous.

It took about fifteen seconds before the first researcher, Gary I think, noticed and let out a short gasp. In my peripheral vision, I saw the entire group turn toward the massive form by the fire and freeze into place. The silence was brittle crystal.

I broke it by bolting up from my seat and letting out a high-pitched shriek.

Half a dozen other screams joined it, and I whirled as if to flee, only to see Doctor Sinor and crew hot-footing it down the path we'd followed into the woods, back toward the cars.

I held it in for as long as I could, and only after I was sure that they wouldn't hear it did I let loose the laughter bubbling in my chest. I sank back onto my log by the fire, laughing, and beckoning the large form forward.

"Harry," rumbled the figure in a very, very deep voice, the words marked with the almost indefinable clippings of a Native American accent. "You have an unsophisticated sense of humor."

"I can't help it," I said, wiping at tears of laughter. "It never gets old." I waved to the open ground across the fire from me. "Sit, sit, be welcome, big brother."

"Appreciate it," rumbled the giant and squatted down across the fire from me, touching fingers the size of cucumbers to his heart in greeting. His broad, blunt face was amused. "So. Got any smokes?"

It wasn't the first time I'd done business with the Forest People. They're old school. There's a certain way one goes about business with someone considered a peer, and Strength of a River in His Shoulders was an old school kind of guy. There were proprieties to be observed.

So we shared a thirty-dollar cigar, which I'd brought, had some S'mores, which I made, and sipped from identical plastic bottles of Coca-Cola, which I had purchased. By the time we were done, the fire had burned down to glowing embers, which suited me fine—and I knew that River Shoulders would be more comfortable in the near-dark, too. I didn't mind being the one to provide everything. It would have been a hassle for River Shoulders to do it, and we'd probably be smoking, eating, and drinking raw and unpleasant things if he had.

Besides, it was worth it. The Forest People had been around long before the great gold rushes of the nineteenth century, and they were loaded. River Shoulders had paid my retainer with a gold nugget the size of a golf ball, the last time I'd done business with him.

"Your friends," he said, nodding toward the disappeared researchers. "They going to come back?"

"Not before dawn," I said. "For all they know, you *got* me."

River Shoulders' chest rumbled with a sound that was both amused and not entirely pleased. "Like my people don't have enough stigmas already."

"You want to clear things up, I can get you on the Larry Fowler show any time you want."

River Shoulders shuddered—given his size, it was a lot of shuddering. "TV rots the brains of people who see it. Don't even want to know what it does to the people who *make* it."

I snorted. "I got your message," I said. "I am here."

"And so you are," he said. He frowned, an expression that was really sort of terrifying on his features. I didn't say anything. You just don't rush the Forest People. They're patient on an almost alien level, compared to human beings, and I knew that our meeting was already being conducted with unseemly haste, by River Shoulders' standards. Finally, he swigged a bit more Coke, the bottle looking tiny in his vast hands, and sighed. "There is a problem with my son. Again."

I sipped some Coke and nodded, letting a little time pass before I answered. "Irwin was a fine, strong boy when I last saw him."

The conversation continued with contemplative pauses between each bit of speech. "He is sick."

"Children sometimes grow sick."

"Not children of the Forest People."

"What, never?"

"No, never. And I will not quote Gilbert and Sullivan."

"Their music was silly and fine."

River Shoulders nodded agreement. "Indeed."

"What can you tell me of your son's sickness?"

"His mother tells me the school's doctor says he has something called mah-no."

"Mono," I said. "It is a common illness. It is not dangerous."

"An illness could not touch one born of the Forest People," River Shoulders rumbled.

"Not even one with only one parent of your folk?" I asked.

"Indeed," he said. "Something else must therefore be happening. I am concerned for Irwin's safety."

The fire let out a last crackle and a brief, gentle flare of light, showing me River Shoulders clearly. His rough features were touched with the same quiet worry I'd seen on dozens and dozens of my clients' faces.

"He still doesn't know who you are, does he."

The giant shifted his weight slightly as if uncomfortable. "Your society is, to me, irrational and bewildering. Which is good. Can't have everyone the same, or the earth would get boring."

I thought about it for a moment and then said, "You feel he has problems enough to deal with already."

River Shoulders spread his hands, as if my own words had spotlighted the truth.

I nodded, thought about it, and said, "We aren't that different. Even among my people, a boy misses his father."

"A voice on a telephone is not a father," he said.

"But it is more than nothing," I said. "I have lived with a father and without a father. With one was better."

The silence stretched extra-long.

"In time," the giant responded, very quietly. "For now, my concern is his physical safety. I cannot go to him. I spoke to his mother. We ask someone we trust to help us learn what is happening."

I didn't agree with River Shoulders about talking to his kid, but that didn't matter. He wasn't hiring me to get parenting advice, about which I had no experience to call upon anyway. He needed help looking out for the kid. So I'd do what I could to help him. "Where can I find Irwin?"

"Chicago," he said. "St. Mark's Academy for the Gifted and Talented."

"Boarding school. I know the place." I finished the Coke and rose. "It will be my pleasure to help the Forest People once again."

The giant echoed my actions, standing. "Already had your retainer sent to your account. By morning, his mother will have granted you the power of a turnkey."

It took me a second to translate River Shoulders' imperfect understanding of mortal society. "Power of attorney," I corrected him.

"That," he agreed.

"Give her my best."

"Will," he said, and touched his thick fingertips to his massive chest.

I put my fingertips to my heart in reply and nodded up to my client. "I'll start in the morning."

It took me most of the rest of the night to get back down to Chicago, go to my apartment, and put on my suit. I'm not a suit guy. For one thing, when you're NBA sized, you don't exactly get to buy them off the rack. For another, I just don't like them—but sometimes they're a really handy disguise, when I want people to mistake me for someone grave and responsible. So I put on the grey suit with a crisp white shirt and a clip-on tie, and headed down to St. Mark's.

The academy was an upper-end place in the suburbs north of Chicago, and was filled with the offspring of the city's luminaries. They had their own small, private security force. They had wrought iron gates and brick walls and ancient trees and ivy. They had multiple buildings on the grounds, like a miniature university campus, and, inevitably, they had an administration building. I started there.

It took me a polite quarter of an hour to get the lady in the front office to pick up the fax granting me power of attorney from Irwin's mom, the archeologist, who was in the field somewhere in Canada. It included a description of me, and I produced both my ID and my investigator's license. It took me another half an hour of waiting to be admitted to the office of the dean, Doctor Fabio.

"Doctor Fabio," I said. I fought valiantly not to titter when I did.

Fabio did not offer me a seat. He was a good-looking man of sober middle age, and his eyes told me that he did not approve of me in the least, even though I was wearing the suit.

"Ms. Pounder's son is in our infirmary, receiving care from a highly experienced nurse practitioner and a physician who visits three days a week," Doctor Fabio told me, when I had explained my purpose. "I assure you he is well cared for."

"I'm not the one who needs to be assured of anything," I replied. "His mother is."

"Then your job here is finished," said Fabio.

I shook my head. "I kinda need to see him, Doctor."

"I see no need to disrupt either Irwin's recovery or our academic routine, Mister Dresden," Fabio replied. "Our students receive some of the most intensive instruction in the world. It demands a great deal of focus and drive."

"Kids are resilient," I said. "And I'll be quiet like a mouse. They'll never know I was there."

"I'm sorry," he replied, "but I am not amenable to random investigators wandering the grounds."

I nodded seriously. "Okay. In that case, I'll report to Doctor Pounder that you refused to allow her duly appointed representative to see her son, and that I cannot confirm his well-being. At which point I am confident that she will either radio for a plane to pick her up from her dig site, or else backpack her way out. I think the good doctor will view this with alarm and engage considerable maternal protective instinct." I squinted at Fabio. "Have you actually *met* Doctor Pounder?"

He scowled at me.

"She's about yay tall," I said, putting a hand at the level of my temples. "And she works outdoors for a living. She looks like she could wrestle a Sasquatch." Heh. Among other things.

"Are you threatening me?" Doctor Fabio asked.

I smiled. "I'm telling you that I'm way less of a disruption than Mama Bear will be. She'll be a headache for weeks. Give me half an hour, and then I'm gone."

Fabio glowered at me.

St. Mark's infirmary was a spotless, well-ordered place, located immediately adjacent to its athletics building. I was walked there by a young man named Steve, who wore a spotless, well-ordered security uniform.

Steve rapped his knuckles on the frame of the open doorway and said, "Visitor to see Mister Pounder."

A young woman who looked entirely too nice for the likes of Doctor Fabio and Steve looked up from a crossword puzzle. She had chestnut-colored hair, rimless glasses, and had a body that could be readily appreciated even beneath her cheerfully patterned scrubs.

"Well," I said. "Hello, nurse."

"I can't think of a sexier first impression than a man

quoting Yakko and Wakko Warner," she said, her tone dry.

I sauntered in and offered her my hand. "Me neither. Harry Dresden, PI."

"Jen Gerard. There are some letters that go after, but I used them all on the crossword." She shook my hand and eyed Steve. "Everyone calls me Nurse Jen. The flying monkeys let you in, eh?"

Steve looked professionally neutral. He folded his arms.

Nurse Jen flipped her wrists at him. "Shoo, shoo. If I'm suddenly attacked I'll scream like a girl."

"No visitors without a security presence," Steve said firmly.

"Unless they're richer than a guy in a cheap suit," Nurse Jen said archly. She smiled sweetly at Steve and shut the infirmary door. It all but bumped the end of his nose. She turned back to me and said, "Doctor Pounder sent you?"

"She's at a remote location," I said. "She wanted someone to get eyes on her son and make sure he was okay. And for the record, it wasn't cheap."

Nurse Jen snorted and said, "Yeah, I guess a guy your height doesn't get to shop off the rack, does he." She led me across the first room of the infirmary, which had a first aid station and an examination table, neither of which looked as though they got a lot of use. There were a couple of rooms attached. One was a bathroom. The other held what looked like the full gear of a hospital's intensive care ward, including an automated bed.

Bigfoot Irwin lay asleep on the bed. It had been a few years since I'd seen him, but I recognized him. He was fourteen years old and over six feet tall, filling the length of the bed, and he had the scrawny look of young things that aren't done growing.

Nurse Jen went to his side and shook his shoulder gently. The kid blinked his eyes open and muttered something. Then he looked at me.

"Harry," he said. "What are you doing here?"

"Sup, kid," I said. "I heard you were sick. Your mom asked me to stop by."

He smiled faintly. "Yeah. This is what I get for staying in Chicago instead of going up to British Columbia with her."

"And think of all the Spam you missed eating."

Irwin snorted, closed his eyes, and said, "Tell her I'm fine. Just need to rest." Then he apparently started doing exactly that.

Nurse Jen eased silently out of the room and herded me gently away. Then she spread her hands. "He's been like that. Sleeping maybe twenty hours a day."

"Is that normal for mono?" I asked.

"Not so much," Nurse Jen said. She shook her head. "Though it's not completely unheard of. That's just a preliminary diagnosis based on his symptoms. He needs some lab work to be sure."

"Fabio isn't allowing it," I said.

She waggled a hand. "He isn't paying for it. The state of the economy, the school's earnings last quarter, et cetera. And the doctor was sure it was mono."

"You didn't tell his mom about that?" I asked.

"I never spoke to her. Doctor Fabio handles all of the communication with the parents. Gives it that personal touch. Besides. I'm just the nurse practitioner. The official physician said mono, so behold, it is mono."

I grunted. "Is the boy in danger?"

She shook her head. "If I thought that, to hell with Fabio and the winged monkeys. I'd drive the kid to a hospital myself. But just because he isn't in danger now doesn't mean he won't be if nothing is done. It's probably mono. But."

"But you don't take chances with a kid's health," I said.

She folded her arms. "Exactly. Especially when his mother is so far away. There's an issue of trust, here."

I nodded. Then I said, "How invasive are the tests?"

"Blood samples. Fairly straightforward."

I chewed that one over for a moment. Irwin's blood was unlikely to be exactly the same as human blood, though who knew how intensively they would have to test it to realize that. Scions of mortal and supernatural pairings had created no enormous splash in the scientific community, and they'd been around for as long as humanity itself, which suggested that any differences weren't easy to spot. It seemed like a reasonable risk to take, all things considered, especially if River Shoulders was maybe wrong about Irwin's immunity to disease.

And besides. I needed some time alone to work.

"Do the tests, on my authority. Assuming the kid is willing, I mean."

Nurse Jen frowned as I began to speak, then nodded at the second sentence. "Okay."

Nurse Jen woke up Irwin long enough to explain the tests, make sure he was okay with them, and take a couple of little vials of blood from his arm. She left to take the vials to a nearby lab and left me sitting with Irwin.

"How's life, kid?" I asked him. "Any more bully problems?"

Irwin snorted weakly. "No, not really. Though, they don't use their fists for that, here. And there's a lot more of them."

"That's what they call civilization," I said. "It's still better than the other way."

"One thing's the same. You show them you aren't afraid, they leave you alone."

"They do," I said. "Coward's a coward, whether he's throwing punches or words."

Irwin smiled and closed his eyes again.

I gave the kid a few minutes to be sound asleep before I got to work.

River Shoulders hadn't asked for my help because

I was the only decent person in Chicago. The last time Irwin had problems, they'd had their roots in the supernatural side of reality. Clearly, the giant thought that this problem was similar, and he was smarter than the vast majority of human beings, including me. I'd be a fool to discount his concerns. I didn't think there was anything more troublesome than a childhood illness at hand, but I was going to cover my bases. That's what being professional means.

I'd brought what I needed in the pockets of my suit. I took out a small baggie of powdered quartz crystal and a piece of paper inscribed with runes written in ink infused with the same powder and folded into a fan. I stood over Irwin and took a moment to focus my thoughts, both upon the spell I was about to work and upon the physical coordination it would require.

I took a deep breath, then flicked the packet of quartz dust into the air at the same time I swept the rune-inscribed fan through a strong arc, released my will, and murmured, "*Optio*."

Light kindled in the spreading cloud of fine dust, a flickering glow that spread with the cloud, sparkling through the full spectrum of visible colors in steady, pulsing waves. It was beautiful magic, which was rare for me. I mean, explosions and lightning bolts and so on were pretty standard fare. This kind of gentle, inter-rogative spell? It was a treat to have a reason to use it.

As the cloud of dust settled gently over the sleep-ing boy, the colors began to swirl as the spell interacted with his aura, the energy of life that surrounds all living things. Irwin's aura was bloody strong, standing out several inches farther from his body than on most humans. I was a full-blown wizard, and a strong one, and my aura wasn't any more powerful. That would be his father's blood, then. The Forest People were in possession of potent magic, which was one reason no one ever seemed to get a decent look at one of them. Irwin had begun to develop a reservoir of energy to rival that of anyone on the White Council of wizardry.

That was likely the explanation for Irwin's supposed immunity to disease—the aura of life around him was simply too strong to be overwhelmed by a mundane germ or virus. Supported by that kind of energy, his body's immune system would simply whale on any invaders. It probably also explained Irwin's size, his growing body drawing upon the raw power of his aura to optimize whatever growth potential was in his mixed genes. Thinking about it, it might even explain the length of River Shoulders' body hair, which just goes to show that no supernatural ability is perfect.

Oh, and as the dust settled against Irwin's body, it revealed threads of black sorcery laced throughout his aura, pulsing and throbbing with a disturbing, seething energy.

I nearly fell out of my chair in sheer surprise.

"Oh no," I muttered. "The kid couldn't just have gotten mono. That would be way too easy."

I called up a short, gentle wind to scatter the quartz

dust from Bigfoot Irwin's covers and pajamas, and then sat back for a moment to think.

The kid had been hit with black magic. Not only that, but it had been done often enough that it had left track marks in his aura. Some of those threads of dark sorcery were fresh ones, probably inflicted at some point during the previous night.

Most actions of magic aren't any more terribly mysterious or complicated than physical actions. In fact, a lot of what happens in magic can be described by basic concepts of physics. Energy can neither be created nor destroyed, for example—but it *can* be moved. The seething aura of life around the young scion represented a significant force of energy.

A *very* significant source.

Someone had been siphoning energy off of Bigfoot Irwin. The incredible vital aura around the kid now was, I realized, only a fraction of what it *should* have been. Someone had been draining the kid of that energy and using it for something else. A vampire of some kind? Maybe. The White Court of Vampires drained the life-energy from their victims, though they mostly did it through physical contact, mostly sexual congress, and there would be really limited opportunity for that sort of thing in a strictly monitored coed boarding school. Irwin had been attacked both frequently and regularly, to have his aura be so mangled.

I could sweep the place for a vampire. Maybe. They were not easy to spot. I couldn't discount a vamp completely, because they were definitely one of the usual suspects, but had it been one of the White Court after the kid, his aura would have been more damaged in certain areas than others. Instead, his aura had been equally diminished all around. That would indicate, if not conclusively prove, some kind of attack that was entirely nonphysical.

I settled back in my chair to wait, watching Bigfoot Irwin sleep. I'd stay alert for any further attack, at least until Nurse Jen got back.

River Shoulders was right. This wasn't illness. Someone was killing the kid very, very slowly.

I wasn't going to leave him alone.

Nurse Jen came back in a little less than two hours. She looked at me with her eyebrows raised and said, "You're still here."

"Looks like," I said. "What was I supposed to do?"

"Leave me a number to call with the results," she said.

I winked at her. "If it makes you feel any better, I can still do that."

"I'm taking a break from dating cartoon characters and the children who love them." She held up the envelope and said, "It's mono."

I blinked. "It is?"

She nodded and sighed. "Definitely. An acute case, apparently, but it's mono."

I nodded slowly, thinking. It might make sense, if Irwin's immune system had come to rely upon the energy of his aura. The attacks had diminished his aura, which had in turn diminished his body's capacity to resist disease. Instead of fighting off an illness when exposed, his weakened condition had resulted in an infection—and it was entirely possible that his body had never had any practice in fighting off something that had taken hold.

Nurse Jen tilted her head to one side and said, "What are you thinking?"

"How bad is it?" I asked her. "Does he need to go to a hospital?"

"He's in one," she said. "Small, but we have everything here that you'd find at a hospital, short of a ventilator. As long as his condition doesn't get any worse, he'll be fine."

Except that he wouldn't be fine. If the drain on his life-energy kept up, he might never have the strength he'd need to fight off this disease—and every other germ that happened to wander by.

I was thinking that the boy was defenseless—and I was the only one standing between Bigfoot Irwin and whatever was killing him.

I looked at Nurse Jen and said, "I need to use a phone."

"How serious?" Doctor Pounder asked. Her voice was scratchy. She was speaking to me over a HAM radio from somewhere in the wilds of unsettled Canada, and was shouting to make herself heard over the static and the patch between the radio and the phone.

"Potentially very serious," I half-shouted back. "I think you need to come here immediately!"

"He's that ill?" she asked.

"Yeah, Doc," I replied. "There could be complications, and I don't think he should be alone."

"I'm on the way. There's weather coming in. It might be tomorrow or the next day."

"Understood," I said. "I'll stay with him until then."

"You're a good man, Dresden," she said. "Thank you. I'll move as fast as I can. Pounder, out."

I hung up the phone and Nurse Jen stared at me with her mouth open. "What the hell are you doing?"

"My job," I replied calmly.

"The boy is going to be fine," Jen said. "He's not feeling great, but he'll be better soon enough. I told you, it's mono."

"There's more going on than that," I said.

"Oh?" Jen asked. "Like what?"

Explaining would just convince her I was a lunatic. "I'm not entirely at liberty to say. Doctor Pounder can explain when she arrives."

"If there's a health concern, I need to know about it now." She folded her arms. "Otherwise, maybe I should let the winged monkeys know that you're a problem."

"I told his mother I would stay with him."

"You told his mother a lot of things."

"What happened to not taking chances?"

"I'm thinking I'll start with you."

I felt tired. I needed sleep. I inhaled and exhaled slowly.

"Nurse," I said. "I care about the kid, too. I don't dispute your medical knowledge or authority over him. I just want to stay close to him until his mom gets here. That's why I was hired."

Nurse Jen eyed me askance. "What do you mean, it's more than mono?"

I folded my arms. "Um. Irwin is a nice guy. Would you agree with that?"

"Sure, he's a great kid. A real sweetheart, thoughtful."

I nodded. "And he has a tendency to attract the attention of . . . how do I put this?"

"Complete assholes?" Nurse Jen suggested.

"Exactly," I said. "People who mistake kindness for weakness."

She frowned. "Are you suggesting that his sickness is the result of a deliberate action?"

"I'm saying that I don't know that it isn't," I said. "And until I know, one way or another, I'm sticking close to the kid until the Doc gets here."

She continued looking skeptical. "You won't if I don't think you should. I don't care how much paperwork you have supporting you. If I start yelling, the winged monkeys will carry you right out to the street."

"They'd try," I said calmly.

She blinked at me. "You're a big guy. But you aren't that big."

"You might be surprised," I said. I leaned forward and said, very quietly, "I'm not. Leaving. The kid."

Nurse Jen's expression changed slowly, from skepticism to something very thoughtful. "You mean that, don't you."

"Every word."

She nodded. Then she called, "Steve."

The security guard lumbered into the room from the hall outside.

"Mister Dresden will be staying with Mister Pounder for a little while. Could you please ask the cafeteria to send over two dinner plates instead of one?"

Steve frowned, maybe trying to remember how to count all the way to two. Then he glowered at me, muttered a surly affirmative, and left, speaking quietly into his radio as he went.

"Thank you," I said. "For the food."

"You're lying to me," she said levelly. "Aren't you."

"I'm not telling you the whole truth," I said. "Subtle difference."

"Semantic difference," she said.

"But you're letting me stay anyway," I noted. "Why?"

She studied my face for a moment. Then she said, "I believe that you want to take care of Irwin."

• • •

The food was very good—nothing like the school cafeterias I remembered. Of course, I went to public school. Irwin woke up long enough to devour a trayful of food, and some of mine. He went to the bathroom, walking unsteadily, and then dropped back into an exhausted slumber. Nurse Jen stayed near, checking him frequently, taking his temperature in his ear every hour so that she didn't need to waken him.

I wanted to sleep, but I didn't need it yet. I might not have had the greatest academic experience, in childhood, but the other things I'd been required to learn had made me more ready for the eat-or-be-eaten portions of life than just about anyone. My record for going without sleep was just under six days, but I was pretty sure I could go longer if I had to. I could have napped in my chair, but I didn't want to take the chance that some kind of attack might happen while I was being lazy.

So I sat by Bigfoot Irwin and watched the shadows lengthen and swell into night.

The attack came just after nine o'clock.

Nurse Jen was taking Irwin's temperature again when I felt the sudden surge of cold, somehow oily energy flood the room.

Irwin took a sudden, shallow breath, and his face became very pale. Nurse Jen frowned at the digital thermometer she had in his ear. It suddenly emitted a series of beeping, wailing noises, and she jerked it free of Irwin just as a bunch of sparks drizzled from its battery casing. She dropped it to the floor, where it lay trailing a thin wisp of smoke.

"What the hell?" Nurse Jen demanded.

I rose to my feet, looking around the room. "Use a mercury thermometer next time," I said. I didn't have much in the way of magical gear on me, but I wasn't going to need any for this. I could feel the presence of the dark, dangerous magic, radiating through the room like the heat from a nearby fire.

Nurse Jen had pressed a stethoscope against Irwin's chest, listening for a moment, while I went to the opposite side of the bed and waved my hand through the air over the bed with my eyes closed, trying to orient upon the spell attacking Irwin's aura, so that I could backtrack it to its source.

"What are you doing?" Nurse Jen demanded.

"Inexplicable stuff," I said. "How is he?"

"Something isn't right," she said. "I don't think he's getting enough air. It's like an asthma attack." She put the stethoscope down and turned to a nearby closet, ripping out a small oxygen tank. She immediately began hooking up a line to it, attached to one of those nose-and-mouth-covering things, opened the valve, and pressed the cup down over Irwin's nose and mouth.

"Excuse me," I said, squeezing past her in order to wave my hand through the air over that side of the bed. I got a fix on the direction of the spell, and jabbed my forefinger in that direction. "What's that way?"

She blinked and stared at me incredulously. "What?"

"That way," I said, thrusting my finger in the indicated direction several times. "What is over that way?"

She frowned, shook her head a little, and said, "Uh, uh, the cafeteria and administration."

"Administration, eh?" I said. "Not the dorms?"

"No. They're the opposite way."

"You got any lunch ladies that hate Irwin?"

Nurse Jen looked at me like I was a lunatic. "What the hell are you talking about? No, of course not!"

I grunted. This attack clearly wasn't the work of a vampire, and the destruction of the electronic thermometer indicated the presence of mortal magic. The kids were required to be back in their dorms at this time, so it presumably wasn't one of them. And if it wasn't someone in the cafeteria, then it had to be someone in the administration building.

Doctor Fabio had been way too interested in making sure I wasn't around. If it was Fabio behind the attacks on Irwin, then I could probably expect some interference to be arriving—

The door to the infirmary opened, and Steve and two of his fellow security guards clomped into the room.

—any time now.

"You," Steve said, pointing a thick finger at me. "It's after free hours. No visitors on the grounds after nine. You're gonna have to go."

I eased back around Nurse Jen and out of the room Irwin was in. "Um," I said, "let me think about that."

Steve scowled. He had a very thick neck. So did his two buddies. "Second warning, sir. You are now trespassing on private property. If you do not leave immediately, the police will be summoned and you will be detained until their arrival."

"Shouldn't you be out making sure the boys aren't sneaking over to the girls' dorms and vice versa? Cause I'm thinking that's really more your speed, Steve."

Steve's face got red. "That's it," he said. "You are being detained until the police arrive, smartass."

"Let's don't do this," I said. "Seriously. You guys don't want to ride this train."

In answer, Steve snapped his hand out to one side, and one of those collapsible fighting batons extended to its full length and locked. His two friends followed suit.

"Wow," I said. "Straight to the weapons? Really? Completely inappropriate escalation." I held up my right hand, palm out. "I'm telling you, fellas. Don't try it."

Steve took two quick steps toward me, raising the baton.

I unleashed the will I had been gathering and murmured, "*Forzare.*"

Invisible force lashed out and slammed into Steve like a runaway car made of foam rubber. It lifted him off his feet and tossed him back, between his two buddies, and out the door of the infirmary. He hit the floor and lost a lot of his velocity before fetching up against the opposite wall with an explosion of expelled breath.

"Wah," I said, Bruce Lee style, and looked at the other two goons. "You boys want a choo-choo ride, too?"

The pair of them looked at me and then at each other, gripping their batons until their knuckles turned white. They hadn't had a clear view of exactly what had happened to Steve, since his body would have blocked them from it. For all they knew, I'd used some kind of judo on him. The pair of them came to a conclusion somewhere in there—that whatever I had pulled on Steve wouldn't work on both of them—and they began to rush me.

They thought wrong. I repeated the spell, only with twice the energy.

One of them went out the door, crashing into Steve, who had just been about to regain his feet. My control wasn't so good without any of my magical implements, though. The second man hit the side of the doorway squarely, and his head made the metal frame ring as it bounced off. The man's legs went rubbery and he staggered, bleeding copiously from a wound that was up above his hairline.

The second spell was more than the lights could handle, and the fluorescents in the infirmary exploded in showers of sparks and went out. Red-tinged emergency lights clicked on a few seconds later.

I checked around me. Nurse Jen was staring at me with her eyes wide. The wounded guard was on his back, rocking back and forth in obvious pain. The two who had been knocked into the hallway were still on the ground, staring at me in much the same way as Jen, except that Steve was clearly trying to get his radio to work. It wouldn't. It had folded when the lights did.

I spread my hands and said, to Nurse Jen, "I told them, didn't I? You heard me. Better take care of that guy."

Then I scowled, shook my head, and stalked off along the spell's back-trail, toward the administration building.

The doors to the building were locked, which was more the academy's problem than mine. I exercised restraint. I didn't take the doors off their hinges. I only ripped them off of their locks.

The door to Doctor Fabio's office was locked, and though I tried to exercise restraint, I've always had issues with controlling my power—especially when I'm angry. This time, I tore the door off its hinges, slamming it down flat to the floor inside the office as if smashed in by a medieval battering ram.

Doctor Fabio jerked and whirled to face the door with a look of utter astonishment on his face. A cabinet behind his desk which had been closed during my first visit was now open. It was a small, gaudy, but functional shrine, a platform for the working of spells. At the moment, it was illuminated by half a dozen candles spaced out around a Seal of Solomon containing two photos—one of Irwin, and one of Doctor Fabio, bound together with a loop of what looked like dark grey yarn.

I could feel the energy stolen from Irwin coursing into the room, into the shrine. From there, I had no doubt, it was being funneled into Doctor Fabio himself. I could sense the intensity of his presence much more sharply than I had that morning, as if he had somehow become more metaphysically massive, filling up more of the room with his presence.

"Hiya, Doc," I said. "You know, it's a pity this place isn't Saint Mark's Academy for the Resourceful and Talented."

He blinked at me. "Uh. What?"

"Because then the place would be S.M.A.R.T. Instead, you're just S.M.A.G.T."

"What?" he said, clearly confused, outraged, and terrified.

"Let me demonstrate," I said, extending my hand. I funneled my will into it and said, "*Smagt!*"

The exact words you use for a spell aren't important, except that they can't be from a language you're too familiar with. Nonsense words are best, generally speaking. Using "smagt" for a combination of naked force and air magic worked just as well as any other word would have. The energy rushed out of me, into the cabinet shrine, and exploded in a blast of kinetic energy and wind. Candles and other decorative objects flew everywhere. Shelves cracked and collapsed.

The spell had been linked to the shrine. It unraveled

as I disrupted all the precisely aligned objects that had helped direct and focus its energy. One of the objects had been a small glass bottle of black ink. Most of it wound up splattered on the side of Doctor Fabio's face.

He stood with his jaw slack, half of his face covered in black ink, the other half gone so pale that he resembled a Renaissance Venetian masque.

"Y-you . . . you . . ."

"Wizard," I said quietly. "White Council. Heck, Doctor, I'm even a Warden these days."

His face became absolutely bloodless.

"Yeah," I said quietly. "You know us. I'm going to suggest that you answer my questions with extreme cooperation, Doctor. Because we frown on the use of black magic."

"Please," he said, "anything."

"How do you know us?" I asked. The White Council was hardly a secret, but given that most of the world didn't believe in magic, much less wizards, and that the supernatural crowd in general is cautious with sharing information, it was a given that your average Joe would have no idea that the Council even existed—much less that they executed anyone guilty of breaking one of the Laws of Magic.

"V-v-venator," he said. "I was a Venator. One of the Venatori Umbrorum. Retired."

The Hunters in the Shadows. Or of the Shadows, depending on how you read it. They were a boys club made up of the guys who had the savvy to be clued in to the supernatural world, but without the talent it took to be a true wizard. Mostly academic types. They'd been invaluable assets in the White Council's war with the Red Court, gathering information and interfering with our enemy's lines of supply and support. They were old allies of the Council—and any Venator would know the price of violating the Laws.

"A Venator should know better than to dabble in this kind of thing," I said in a very quiet voice. "The answer to this next question could save your life—or end it."

Doctor Fabio licked his lips and nodded, a jerky little motion.

"Why?" I asked him quietly. "Why were you taking essence from the boy?"

"H-he . . . He had so *much*. I didn't think it would hurt him and I . . ." He cringed back from me as he spoke the last words. "I . . . needed to grow some hair."

I blinked my eyes slowly. Twice. "Did you say . . . hair?"

"Rogaine didn't work!" he all but wailed. "And that transplant surgery wasn't viable for my hair and skin type!" He bowed his head and ran fingertips through his thick head of hair. "Look, see? Look how well it's come in. But if I don't maintain it . . ."

"You . . . used black magic. To grow *hair*."

"I . . ." He looked everywhere but at me. "I tried *everything* else first. I never meant to harm anyone. It never hurt anyone *before*."

"Irwin's a little more dependent on his essence than most," I told him. "You might have killed him."

Fabio's eyes widened in terror. "You mean he's . . . he's a . . ."

"Let's just say that his mother is his second scariest parent and leave it at that," I said. I pointed at his chair and said, "Sit."

Fabio sat.

"Do you wish to live?"

"Yes. Yes, I don't want any trouble with the White Council."

Heavy footsteps came pounding up behind us. Steve and his unbloodied buddy appeared in the doorway, carrying their batons. "Doctor Fabio!" Steve cried.

"Don't make me trash your guys," I told Fabio.

"Get out!" Fabio all but screamed at them.

They came to a confused stop. "But . . . sir?"

"Get out, get out!" Fabio screamed. "Tell the police there's no problem here when they arrive!"

"Sir?"

"Tell them!" Fabio screamed, his voice going up several octaves. "For God's sake, man! Go!"

Steve, and his buddy, went. They looked bewildered, but they went.

"Thank you," I said, when they left. No need to play bad cop at this point. If Fabio got any more scared, he might collapse into jelly. "Do you want to live, Doctor?"

He swallowed. He nodded once.

"Then I suggest you alter your hairstyle to complete baldness," I replied. "Or else learn to accept your receding hairline for what it is—the natural progression of your life. You will discontinue *all* use of magic from this point forward. And I do mean all. If I catch you with so much as a Ouija board or a deck of Tarot cards, I'm going to make you disappear. Do you get me?"

It was a hollow threat. The guy hadn't broken any of the Laws, technically speaking, since Irwin hadn't died. And I had no intention of turning anyone over to the tender mercies of the Wardens if I could possibly avoid it. But this guy clearly had problems recognizing priorities. If he kept going the way he was, he might slide down into true practice of the black arts. Best to scare him away from that right now.

"I understand," he said in a very meek voice.

"Now," I said. "I'm going to go watch over Irwin. You aren't going to interfere. I'll be staying until his mother arrives."

"Are . . . are you going to tell her what I've done?"

"You bet your ass I am," I said. "And God have mercy on your soul."

Irwin was awake when I got back to the infirmary, and Nurse Jen had just finished stitching closed a cut on the wounded guard's scalp. She'd shaved a big, irregularly shaped section of his hair off to get it done, too, and he looked utterly ridiculous—even more so when she wrapped his entire cranium in bandages to keep the stitches covered.

I went into Irwin's room and said, "How you feeling?"

"Tired," he said. "But better than earlier today."

"Irwin," Nurse Jen said firmly.

"Yes ma'am," Irwin said, and meekly placed the breathing mask over his nose and mouth.

"Your mom's coming to see you," I said.

The kid brightened. "She is? Oh, uh. That's fantastic!" He frowned. "It's not . . . because of me being sick? Her work is very important."

"Maybe a little," I said. "But mostly, I figure it's because she loves you."

Irwin rolled his eyes but he smiled. "Yeah, well. I guess she's okay. Hey, is there anything else to eat?"

Later, after Irwin had eaten (again), he slept.

"His temperature's back down, and his breathing is clear," Nurse Jen said, shaking her head. "I could have sworn we were going to have to get him to an ICU a few hours ago."

"Kids," I said. "They bounce back fast."

She frowned at Irwin and then at me. Then she said, "It was Fabio, wasn't it. He was doing something."

"Something like what?" I asked.

She shook her head. "I don't know. I just know

it . . . feels like something that's true. He's the one who didn't want you here. He's the one who sent security to run you out just as Irwin got worse."

"You might be right," I said. "And you don't have to worry about it happening again."

She studied me for a moment. Then she said, simply, "Good."

I lifted my eyebrows. "That's one hell of a good sense of intuition you have, nurse."

She snorted. "I'm still not going out with you."

"Story of my life," I said, smiling.

Then I stretched out my legs, settled into my chair, and joined Bigfoot Irwin in dreamland.

Blood-Red Greens

JOEL A. SUTHERLAND

Golf is a good walk spoiled.
—Mark Twain

Sweltering in his own juices under the intense mid-July sun, Randall shook the steering wheel clenched in his fat fingers and swore. And not just a middling little cop-out swear. His was a full-blown, roof-raising, appeal-to-the-heavens swear.

A line of cars stretched in front of his Mercury Grand Marquis as far as his poor eyesight could see. Up ahead a tall column of smoke rose to the sky as if from some unseen massive pyre. *Goddamn it, this accident's gonna make me late and Errol's gonna have a conniption,* he thought with a sense of dread so thick he could taste bile creeping up the back of his throat. A fly buzzed lazily beside his ear before settling on the dashboard.

Randall swatted at it with his palm. Unsurprisingly, he wasn't fast enough and the fly buzzed away even more lazily than it had been flying before, as if it knew Randall posed no real threat. Randall swore again.

The mix of the construction slowdown, the blazing heat and the fact that today he would play his last game of golf was stretching his patience rather thin. The fact that he hadn't yet announced his imminent retirement from the game to Errol thinned his patience further still. And the fact that the no-good, rotten, pain-in-the-ass, brainless fly had been buzzing with a disconcerting proximity to his eardrum for the past fifteen minutes had him just about ready to pack it in and head to the loony bin.

A police officer spun a handheld sign around from STOP to SLOW, waving Randall and the rest of the waiting traffic through.

As he sped thankfully along the country highway, Randall was so consumed with the desire to get to Golden Links Golf and Country Club as quickly as possible that he didn't take note of the birds and the bees, he didn't smell the intoxicating aroma of roses floating on the summer breeze and he didn't see the bloodied man at the scene of the accident with a six-foot length of steel pipe protruding from his chest and a vacant look in his eyes, chewing on the neck of a panicked paramedic.

• • •

"Cutting it a little close, don't you think, Randall?"

Randall had been right. Errol was not pleased with his tardiness. He hurriedly spun the crank in circles until the window was completely sealed, smiling apologetically at Errol, who was standing beside the Grand Marquis. Randall opened the door and pulled his considerable girth from the car. The Grand Marquis's frame bounced up, its shocks squealing. Randall removed the cap from his head and wiped the sweat from his brow. His canary-yellow golf T was wet under his arms, on his back and around his wide belly. His plaid pants, likewise, bore sweat stains down the middle of his round rump.

Errol *tsk*ed disdainfully.

Randall pretended not to hear and hobbled around to the back of the car, his knees and hips stiff after sitting for longer than he was accustomed to, and pulled his club bag from the trunk. "Didn't you see that accident on the Forty-eight?" he asked by way of explanation. "Goddamn! I doubt anyone will be walking away from that mess."

"No, I took the Sixty-seven. No matter, we still have time. Let's check in." Errol, aside from his age, was everything that Randall was not. Tall, slender and immaculately dressed, his entire being screamed wealth. He uncrossed his arms, wondered for the briefest of moments why, on such a beautifully sunny day, there were so few cars in the parking lot and then followed his perspiring friend into the clubhouse.

• • •

Shadows painted the walls of the pro shop, the window blinds closed against the early morning light. A ceiling fan spun lazily, trailing tangled strands of spiderweb. Other than clubs and putters standing in rows like sentinels, the room was empty and deathly quiet.

Randall and Errol approached the desk. Randall picked up a scorecard and a tiny pencil (the kind that always made him feel like a giant) while Errol craned his neck in an attempt to see into the back room. "Hello?" he called out as he dinged the metal bell next to the cash register.

A single blanched hand snaked quickly up from behind the counter and landed on the surface with a hollow slap. Errol flinched and Randall yelped, pitching the mini pencil over his shoulder. The hand tensed as it searched for a grip on the counter, pulling a man up behind it. The man's face was pallid, his skin splotchy and wet. A thin strand of mucus dribbled freely from his left nostril and embedded itself in the black mustache covering his quivering upper lip. Randall was about to stuff his dignity, turn tail and run, but the man spoke.

"Good morning, Errol. Randall." He tried to sound bright and cheery, but his voice was too full of phlegm and barely concealed pain to be successful in that endeavor.

Errol peered intently at the man. "Sam? My word, is that you?"

"The one and only," Sam said with a forced smile.

"What on God's green earth happened to you?"

"It's nothing, it's nothing," Sam repeated, as if saying it twice would make it so. "Just a head cold. Caught something from one of the tykes." His smile disappeared as he doubled over and coughed into a handkerchief. Randall saw that it came away covered in blood and yelped again. Sam hurriedly stuffed the handkerchief into his pocket and his spurious smile returned. "Well, gentlemen," he croaked, "there have been a few cancellations this morning—guess this cold of mine has been getting around, ha ha—so you two can tee off as soon as you like."

"Thanks," Errol said. "Say, have you heard the weather forecast for today?"

Sam cleared his throat loudly. It sounded like he had a spoonful of extra-sticky Jell-O clinging to the walls of his pipeline. "Unfortunately, they say the sunshine's not going to last. A big storm's heading our way, but you might get lucky and finish before it hits us. Just remember, gents, if lightning strikes, hold your one-iron up in the air because—"

"Even God can't hit a one-iron," Errol finished lamely with a roll of his eyes. Each and every time the forecasters called for a thunderstorm, Sam dropped this especially feeble joke on them. Clearly not tired of it yet, Sam began to laugh uproariously, which quickly proved too great an effort and he fell back into another manic coughing fit.

"Come on, let's go," Errol said as he turned and walked to the door.

Randall cautiously picked up another tiny pencil and hurried to follow his friend out of the decidedly macabre pro shop.

Standing next to his motorized golf cart, Randall looked out upon his doom: Golden Links Golf and Country Club's first hole. The hole was short for a par 4, clocking in at a mere 286 yards. The difficulty of the hole was placing your tee shot. The choice was either to go for the green or to take the more sensible approach and lay up, putting yourself in a decent position for your second shot. The fairway before the green was exceedingly narrow and slanted on both sides. If your ball ran off the fairway it landed directly in a large sand bunker on the left or a swampy bog on the right. Standing guard before the green was a creek eight feet wide known to regulars as the Ball Sucker. The green itself was sinisterly small and notoriously hard to land. Randall had never parred it, never bogied it, never even double-bogied it. He would be happy to settle for a seven but often had to take a dishonest eight.

Even with his extensive familiarity with the hole and its many pitfalls, Randall never exuded anything other than overrated bravado when teeing off.

He pulled his driver from the bag strapped to the back of their cart, envisioning the eagle he was about to score to begin the match. "This hole is going down," he said.

"First, let's talk business," Errol said, opening his well-worn pad of paper and uncapping his pen. "Skins game? Five dollars a hole?"

"Of course. Same as every Tuesday for the past fifteen years. Now stop stalling and let's see what you're made of."

Errol made a few quick notes in his pad and stepped away from the cart with his three-iron. He propped his ball on a tee in the supple ground, stepped back, surveyed the hole and approached the ball. After the briefest of moments he swung his club back and then swiveled forward, striking his target gracefully. The ball soared majestically through the air, touched down and rolled a short distance in the middle of the fairway, ten feet from being devoured by the Ball Sucker. "Just short of the green," he said as he stepped around Randall. "Should be on in two and down in three."

Randall snickered. "Not bad. But it's only two hundred and eighty-six yards to the hole. For me, that's good for one long drive and a putt." He plopped his ball down on a tee, took a hurried practice swing, stepped up to the ball, fiddled with his grip, wiggled the club back and forth, exhaled slowly, then swung the club quickly back and forth, topping the ball and sending it a mere ten yards in front of where he stood. With a clenched jaw, Randall shoved his driver hastily back in his bag and sat down on the cart.

"And now for one hell of a putt," Errol said with a straight face.

"Shut up."

Randall's follow-up shot was more unpropitious than his first, landing squarely in a patch of fescue to the side of the fairway, a long way from Errol's drive.

The two men stood ankle-deep in the long tangled grass, passing their clubs back and forth over the ground like metal detectors in search of buried treasure.

"I swear this is right where my ball went in," Randall said.

"You should have stayed on the fairway."

Randall paused for a moment and glared at Errol. "Thanks for the tip. I'll try that next time."

Errol shrugged his shoulders and continued the fruitless search. "Here's a good one: what's the difference between a lost golf ball and the G-spot?"

Randall thought for a moment and shook his head. "I don't know."

"A man will spend five minutes looking for the lost golf ball." Errol laughed alone before slowly trailing off.

After trying to decode the joke's mysteries for a moment, Randall considered laughing anyway but decided against it. He was a terrible actor and Errol would know he was faking. "What's the G-spot?"

Errol cast his eyes to the ground without comment,

resuming the search for Randall's errant ball, his joke hanging limply in the air between the two old friends.

After making sure that Errol's eyes were far from the space around his wide feet, Randall deftly reached into his pocket, pulled out another ball with the same markings as the first and gently let it fall to the ground. Looking up and smiling, he called out, "Found it!"

Errol spun around, an eyebrow raised and a curl to his lip. "It's true what they say. Golf is a game where the ball lies poorly and the player well."

"Huh?"

"Never mind."

Randall returned from the cart with a nine-iron. He grinned in pride for the sting he believed he had pulled off and prepared to chip onto the green. He looked at the flag and frowned. "What the hell?"

Another golfer was pacing slowly back and forth across the green. He didn't seem to have any purpose in being there other than to walk in circles without any apparent direction.

Randall sandwiched the club in his sweaty right armpit, cupped his hands around his mouth and hollered, "Hey! Get off my green!"

The unidentified golfer's head swiveled in their direction. A prolonged and throaty moan rumbled forth from his lungs and he began to amble toward the source of the shouting. However, at the rate he was moving, it would take forever for him to reach them.

"What a jackass!" Randall complained.

"Don't worry about it, Randall," Errol said. "Swing away. He's standing in the safest spot on the course right now."

"Shut up." Randall bent over his ball and shot Errol one last dirty look. "I'll show you. And him." Despite Randall's skill level's best attempt to make him scupper another shot, the ball lifted perfectly off the ground and soared straight for the green.

It landed square on the top of the head of the stumbling golfer with a hollow thud.

The pair flinched and groaned, surprised that Randall's shot was on target. They hopped in the cart and drove up to the man, who was lying on the edge of the green, unmoving, a large bruise-coated bump already protruding from his forehead.

"Damn, I'm sorry," said Randall with genuine concern. "Please don't be dead. What were you doing walking around on the green?" He dropped awkwardly down to his knees, his overburdened hips squeaking, and placed his index finger on the man's neck. He found no pulse. "Shit!" Randall said, looking up at Errol for support. "I killed him!"

Without warning the man sat bolt upright. His scraggly fingernails latched on to Randall's T-shirt and his jaws opened wide, desperate to bite, rip, tear, chew.

Errol screamed and Randall's thick thighs propelled his quivering frame backward. His arms windmilled, breaking the pulseless biting man's grasp on his shirt, and he fell on his back. Errol recovered from his moment of abject terror and yanked two random clubs from his bag. He tossed one to Randall, keeping the other for himself. Randall fumbled the club and scrambled to retrieve it, the man crawling on hands and knees toward him. But Errol halted his slow progression, raising the club high above his head and bringing it down on the small of the man's back. A loud *snap* split the calm summer day and the man fell to the ground. He spun around and his lifeless eyes fell upon Errol. He moaned again and Errol froze.

Randall had finally gotten a hold on the dropped club. He picked up where Errol left off, swinging the club in a speedy uppercut, connecting viciously with the man's lower jaw. Three bloody teeth scattered across the immaculately trimmed grass of Golden Links's first green like dice on a giant board of craps. Defying the limitations of the human body, the man seemed unconcerned and unfazed that his mouth was suddenly three teeth short and that his back was broken, and reached out a clawing hand for Randall's plentiful flesh.

He didn't get the chance for a single lick. Randall easily sidestepped the man's arm and swung the head of the club into the rapidly deteriorating body again and again and again. His face was covered in a ceaseless spray of blood as bits of bone peppered the ground around the pulverized man. Finally running out of breath, Randall dropped the club and stepped back, whimpering quietly.

Errol placed a reassuring hand on his shoulder, but Randall slipped out from under its comfort, commandeered the cart and barreled it straight at the limp body. He heard a wet and meaty crunch as the cart jostled up and down over the remains of the body. Randall turned the cart abruptly around and brought it to a halting stop next to his friend.

Errol frowned. "I think he was already dead before you ran over him."

"I thought he was already dead when he had no pulse, but then he tried to kill me."

"Are you sure he was actually trying to kill you?"

"Errol, he tried to bite my face off."

"Touché."

A black crow cawed from a lofty perch in a tree, happy to have such a great view of the murderous proceedings. Unseen by Randall and Errol, another man was rambling from the clubhouse along the fairway behind them.

Randall wiped the blood from his face with the bottom of his shirt, exposing his hairy gut. "We've got to do something with the body. If we get caught we'll be in big shit."

"Body?" Errol asked, cringing. Randall noticed his friend's disgusted expression and quickly pulled his shirt back over his pregnant-looking belly. "What body? All that's left is a puddle of tomato soup."

The man behind them rambled closer.

"Well, we can't leave that puddle of tomato soup for the marshal to find." Randall pointed at the sand bunker nearest the green. "Here, get that rake."

Errol glanced slowly at the rake and then back at Randall, his jaw slack. "Oh, that's a great idea. We'll just spread the pieces around and no one will ever find the remains."

"It's all I can think of. What if Sam comes out and sees this? He'll call the cops, or worse, he'll ban us. Sam's not to be trifled with."

The rambling man rambled close enough for Randall to feel his fetid breath on the back of his neck.

The rambling man was Sam.

"He's right behind me, isn't he?" Randall asked, blanching.

Errol nodded his head gravely. Randall turned around.

"Look, Sam, I can explai—"

Sam didn't give Randall the chance. He flung his body headfirst at Randall and brought his teeth mere millimeters from the old man's neck with a guttural groan.

"Randall, duck!" Errol yelled.

Randall obliged, dropping his body to the ground as if his bones had vanished. Errol swung the club full force into Sam's head, splitting a wide crevice in his skull that spewed meaty chunks of brain. Sam's body crumpled to the ground next to Randall, who rose wearily back to his feet.

"Why the hell is everyone trying to eat me today?" he asked.

Errol leaned in toward Randall's neck and for a second Randall was concerned that he was about to pull the same shenanigans as Sam just had, but Errol only sniffed. "It's your cologne," he said. "It's magnetic."

"Oh yeah, now's a great time for one of your jokes," Randall said, pushing Errol away.

"I'm just trying to alleviate some of the stress caused by the arrival of a zombie apocalypse."

"What? Get out of here."

"I'm serious."

"You really think that guy and Sam were *zombies*?"

"Absolutely," Errol said.

"Which means . . ."

"We'll have the course to ourselves."

"Nice," Randall said.

The crow above cawed once more before taking flight, knowing that more bloody carnage would be found in many other places on that fateful day.

The fairway of the fourth hole turned 90 degrees to the left 112 yards from the tee, carried on for 134 yards in that direction, then turned 90 degrees to the right and ended 40 yards farther at the pin, a zigzagging double dogleg almost as menacing as the pair of zombies who had attacked them three holes before.

After watching Errol drive his ball with the perfect amount of spin to draw it around the first dogleg, Randall felt slightly diffident. He flubbed his drive and shoved his club hastily back in the bag.

"Damn. I'm seriously considering giving up golf."

Errol stepped on the gas pedal and asked, "What's stopping you?"

"I'm married," Randall said without a hint of amusement. His glib joke had reminded him of his previous desire to retire from the game, if only he could muster up the courage to break the news to Errol. Randall had never beaten Errol in a skins match, and the joy in their weekly game had begun to fade. Today was a little different, however. He was still playing like crap and getting the snot kicked out of him, but his encounter with death had been exhilarating. The air smelled a little sweeter, the sun was a little warmer and his head felt a little clearer.

"Speaking of Beatrice, how is the old broad?" Errol asked, interrupting Randall's thoughts.

Randall shrugged his shoulders, in no rush to take his next shot. The course was, as predicted, dead. "Not bad. I just got a new set of clubs for her."

Not one to miss such a glorious setup, Errol said, "Good trade."

Randall laughed and slapped Errol on the arm.

In an interview for the local paper conducted shortly after Golden Links opened in the 1950s, Iorek

Antokol'skiy, the course designer, jokingly referred to the course's signature hole, the seventh, as "Hell's Half Acre, and I hope my ex-wife burns and rots there."

Squatting on his haunches, his pants riding ridiculously high up his legs, Randall lined up his putt. The green was like a mirage, a small island with edges that sloped down into a sea of undulating mounds of sand and blowing tumbleweeds.

Standing near the hole and holding the flag, Errol said, "Now, remember: real golfers don't cry when they line up their fourth putt."

"Shut up." Randall did his best to block out Errol's snide remark, but his overactive mind got the better of him and he couldn't focus. His putt ran a foot to the right of the hole and four feet past, tumbling down into the sandy abyss, the jaws of Hell's Half Acre.

"Son of a—" Randall yelled as he raised the putter above his head and heaved it straight down into the patchy green. He tore it free from the ground, loosening a chunk of dirt, and brought it down again.

A zombie crawled its way onto the green from the surrounding sand trap. Modifying his attack on the earth, Randall freed the putter again and slammed it deep into the skull of the ghoul, its eyes squirting blood from the tear ducts. With much effort, he pulled the putter free, loosening a chunk of zombie brain, and turned to face Errol, who was beholding his crazed friend with a mild air of confusion.

"That's a pretty good stress reliever," Randall said, trying to catch his shortened breath.

"You feel better now?"

"Yeah, I do."

Errol had a chance to test Randall's peculiar stress reliever on the next tee. The short eighth hole was rife with perils such as a maddeningly sloped green and a treacherous pin position, far too close to both the edge of the dance floor and the small pond that waited beside the lip. Blessed with this foreknowledge, Randall and Errol often chickened out and clubbed down from a one-wood to a three-wood to safely lay up their drives.

Randall watched in stunned silence as Errol, glaring down at his ball with a three-wood in hand, swallowed loudly and his knees began to shake.

Exhaling loudly Errol tore his gaze from the ball and took a step back, which turned out to be a fortuitous move. Otherwise he might not have seen the bloodied woman who sauntered out from the woods. She attempted to groan, the universal language of zombies, but failed magnificently—an angry gaping hole had been torn from her neck and her vocal cords were hanging limply from the bloody breach. Aside from the neck wound and an ankle bone that was protruding from her skin, she seemed to be fairly unperturbed and single-mindedly hell-bent on her newly discovered prize: the two tasty-looking golfers.

"The three-wood's all wrong," Errol said, shaking his head. "Would you mind handing me my driver?"

Randall willingly obliged and Errol thanked him for his aid. Gripping the club tight, Errol exercised his disciplined backswing and sped up on the downswing. The follow-through was a thing of beauty, slicing through the air with a clean whistle, catching the female zombie directly under the chin. With a neck that was already mostly severed, her head easily lifted from her shoulders and rolled deep into the woods. With a final gust of blood spurting high from its exposed jugular vein, the body wavered in place and then toppled to the ground beside the tee.

Errol laughed. "You know what? You're right. That *is* a good stress reliever." He laughed again, drove his ball with a sublime *ping*, and watched his shot reach the edge of the green. "I haven't played this well since I was twenty." He slapped Randall on the shoulder and wiped the blood from his driver on the grass.

Randall scowled and imitated Errol's voice perfectly. "I haven't played this well since I was twenty."

The next three holes played out exactly as one would guess. Errol scored two pars and a birdie while Randall displayed a raw talent for placing his ball in precisely the worst place to be on each hole.

On the ninth, Randall's drive landed under a bush and Errol gleefully informed him that he had to play it where it lay. The tenth found Randall's third shot roll off the green and stop directly behind a tree. Errol shrugged his shoulders under Randall's baleful look and didn't allow him to move his ball. The eleventh hole, however, presented a completely new and radical challenge for Randall, and perhaps for the history of golf. His ball had somehow perched itself on the eye socket of a dead golfer.

Randall opened his mouth to protest vehemently but Errol cut him off. "Sorry, Randall. You know the rules."

Deflated, Randall sighed and swung his club without his typical three-minute routine of stretching and judging and practice-swinging and wiggling. He swung a tad short and the iron's face struck the corpse's nose bridge and high cheekbone, sending painful reverberations up along the shaft and into Randall's wrists. He howled in pain and threw the club to the ground, then looked up to see where his ball had gone. To his surprise, he spotted a small white object headed straight for the green with a dream-worthy arc. "Hey, look at my ball go!" he proclaimed triumphantly.

"That's not your ball," Errol said. "Your ball went there," he added, pointing at the fairway ten feet in front of them.

"Then what's that?" Randall asked, gesturing wildly at the object flying through the air.

"That, my friend, is an eyeball."

Thunder rumbled tumultuously on the distant horizon, warning of its imminent arrival.

· · ·

Sam had been wrong. They would not finish their round before the storm broke. Although to be fair, he could not have predicted the slowdown caused by Armageddon.

The fourteenth hole was a superlative use of angles, forcing the golfer to weigh risk/reward scenarios for every shot necessary to reach the green, with a large lake on the right and a nefarious string of bunkers on the left. Of course, the raging wind from the lake put all the golfer's best intentions out to roost and the ball typically ended up traveling wherever it desired, which often happened to be the water.

The rain fell in buckets and felt like it was hitting Randall and Errol from the side, as if the water was being lifted up from the lake by the howling winds and slapping them in the face. Still, they trudged on, the frequent flashes of lightning illuminating their path on the darkened course.

Having spotted his ball, Randall tapped Errol on the shoulder and asked him to stop the cart. Errol peered at the lake, having noticed a small black shape on the water. Huddled under parkas with thin rods in hand, two fishermen sat in a small rickety boat, trolling for muskies.

"Look at those crazy bastards, fishing in the rain," said Errol, laughing.

Randall joined in the laughter and shook his head in

disbelief, lined up his shot, and swung his club through the downpour. Pleased with his shot even though he lost sight of it within seconds, Randall turned back to the lake and laughed again at the crazy fishermen.

Suddenly, a zombie broke through the water's surface and latched on to both of the fishermen, dragging them into the lake. It happened so quickly. No trace was left behind except for the now-empty boat, bobbing up and down.

Randall and Errol jumped in alarm and decided to move on.

As they played out the next three holes, the rainfall began to slow, and by the time they had reached the eighteenth and final green, the storm had faded away. The sun poked out from behind the last lingering dark cloud and the only reminders of the storm were the far distant rumbles, the sloshing-wet ground and their sopping-wet clothes. Even the birds were back, their melodic chirps soothing and peaceful.

Randall enjoyed the serenity of the moment as he lined up his shot from the dense forest behind the green, a place he was well familiar with. Errol, waiting out of sight near the pin, had already putted his ball and finished the round with another par.

Randall paused for a moment, distracted by an unearthly zombie moan followed by a loud *thwack*. With growing apprehension he made his shot and ran out from the woods. A zombie's unmoving corpse lay at Errol's feet on the edge of the green.

"What happened?" he asked, a knot twisting in his gut.

"Something . . . very hard to believe," Errol said. "Your shot landed in the middle of the green and rolled three feet from the hole." He pointed at the ball. If he hadn't, Randall wouldn't have believed him.

Randall sighed in relief. "And you're okay? I heard sounds."

"Sure," Errol said, waving his hand nonchalantly. "Just had one more run-in with a zombie. But I showed him." He wiped a splash of blood from his pitching wedge onto his pant leg as proof. "Don't let me keep you from finishing the hole. Make this putt and you'll close the round with a respectful—if unspectacular—bogey."

Without further ado, Randall made his putt and the ball plunked down in the hole.

Errol smiled, impressed. "Back-to-back good shots. Well done, old friend."

Randall was ecstatic. "Thank you! Good match, Errol. Even though I played like absolute crap, I really enjoyed myself." He held out his hand for the customary handshake.

"Me too," Errol said, grasping Randall's hand tightly. "That was the most fun I've had with clothes on in years."

A small trickle of blood ran down Errol's forearm. "What's that?" Randall asked.

Errol's hand quickly retreated from the embrace

and he moved his arm behind his back. "It's nothing, it's nothing," he repeated, as if saying it twice would make it so. "I just scratched myself on a sharp branch back on the seventeenth."

Randall looked at his friend skeptically. All of his shots had been down the center of the fairway.

"Scout's honor," Errol said, raising his non-bloodied arm.

Other than a few bodies lying here and there and two cars that had collided and been abandoned, the parking lot was exactly as they had left it—curiously empty. Although the old men didn't find that curious anymore.

Having placed their club bags in their cars' trunks, Randall turned to Errol and asked, "How much do I owe you?"

"Well, let's see." Errol coughed into the crook of his elbow and did some quick calculations on the back of their scorecard. "Five dollars per hole, eighteen holes . . . that would be ninety dollars."

"Can I pay you later?"

"Of course."

"This is crazy," Randall said, "but I was close to giving up golf this morning."

Errol feigned concern in good humor, but his act lacked his usual showmanship. His skin looked more like wax than living flesh and beads of sweat coated his forehead. "That *is* crazy. Did you change your mind?"

"You bet I did." Randall paused before closing his car's trunk. "Say, Errol. You never told me what the G-spot is."

Errol placed a shaking hand on the big man's shoulder. Once again Randall saw the bloody forearm gash—it smelled rancid and the blood had blackened. "If I told you now I'd be afraid you wouldn't show up for our next game, so I'll tell you next Tuesday. Same Bat-time, same Bat-channel?"

Nodding in agreement, Randall said, "Absolutely."

An awkward pause passed between the two men as Errol's hand rested on his friend's shoulder a moment too long. His eyes closed and his head drooped.

"Errol?"

Errol didn't respond.

"Errol? Wake up."

A crow landed on the clubhouse's roof and cawed. Randall looked up at it and squinted when he saw the sky. The storm clouds had returned and were flickering with electricity. As if on cue thunder boomed.

"Hey, Errol, we should go."

Errol looked up and opened his eyes. They were milky white, as if suddenly afflicted by cataracts. His fingers gripped Randall's shoulder tightly and his jaw opened with a groan.

His zombie-fighting instincts now sharpened after an entire golf game spent fending off the undead, Randall shoved Errol backward. He reached into his trunk and pulled a club out of his bag. The club made a metallic *schwing* sound like that of a katana being unsheathed. It flashed in the lightning.

"Damn it, Errol," he said, raising the club above his head and taking a step forward. "Now I'll never find out what the G-spot is."

Zombie Errol clearly didn't care about Randall's concern or his lack of knowledge regarding the female anatomy. He stood back up and lurched forward.

Randall pulled the club back to swing it into Errol's skull but was suddenly thrown backward. He slammed into his Grand Marquis and tumbled to the pavement. His head spun, his hearing was muffled and the smell of burnt hair wafted under his nostrils. He had no idea what had happened.

And then he saw something that made him smile. He couldn't help it. The club he had pulled from his bag was charred black, obviously struck by lightning. It was a one-iron. God had finally hit one.

The irony in that was only slightly less painful than the feeling of Errol sinking his teeth into Randall's round belly and ripping off a nice long strip of man meat.

When he died, so too did the game of golf.

For seven days.

Randall, on the other hand, stayed dead for only five minutes before standing up as straight as a putter and leaving Errol without so much as a by-your-leave, stumbling off in search of a little post-game snack.

Exactly one week later, same Bat-time, same Bat-channel, Randall stumbled as quickly as possible into

Golden Links's parking lot. His clothes fluttered about him in tatters, he walked with a considerable limp (his left ankle had been violently twisted and his toes were nearly pointing backward) and he had bits of brain stuck in his teeth.

Errol was walking in circles between their two parked cars, trailing bright red blood on the pavement where he paced. He looked up with death-slimed eyes and moaned and groaned, which Randall took to mean "Cutting it a little close, don't you think, Randall?"

Randall grunted and bellowed in response: "A little close for . . . for what?" He tried to think but his mind was so cloudy.

A series of screeches and wails from Errol. "To satisfy our hunger. To feed our need."

Hunger. Feed. Need. Randall had been feeding his need all week and as a result was likely the only person to ever gain weight postmortem. He scratched the open wound on his belly and wondered if he and Errol had made plans to go human hunting together.

Then something shiny caught his eye (his right eye—the left one was dangling from his socket by the optic nerve).

Golf clubs. Resting in the trunk of his car as if they had been waiting for him to return.

Suddenly his need flipped. He reached into his trunk and lifted out his bag. He turned to Errol and cackled and squalled. "Another eighteen holes of torture, then?"

"Golf *is* a game invented by the same people who think music comes out of a bagpipe," Errol growled and hissed.

With a sound like a dying cat in heat, Randall laughed. As they stumbled side by side to the first hole, Randall didn't even notice the teeth that fell from his mouth when he smiled. "I could do this until the end of time."

Errol nodded in agreement. "Or until our bodies rot and fall apart."

And so they did.

V Plates

KELLEY ARMSTRONG

"You need to help Noah lose his V plates," Reese said.

Nick looked up over his laptop as his young Pack brother strode onto the back deck, two icy beers clutched in one hand. Nick reached out. Reese dropped into a chair, popped the top on one and set the other on the deck.

"That's backup," he said. "Fridge is full for once."

"Because I filled it. With *my* beer."

"No wonder it tastes like horse piss." Reese drained the can, wiped his sweaty forehead with the still-frosty empty, then grabbed the second. "If you and Antonio want me on lawn-cutting duty, you gotta keep the fridge full." He leaned back in his chair. "Though I don't see the point in cutting two goddamn acres every week. Back home, we had a few thousand, and I never cut one of them."

"Because you lived in the desert."

"No, I lived in the outback. The part with grass, because sheep don't live long eating sand." He waved at the surrounding yard. "That's what you need, you know. Sheep."

"Werewolves and sheep, they go so well together."

"Actually, they do, if you raise them yourself."

Nick shook his head and typed the final paragraph on his marketing plan while Reese tapped the deck with his sneaker, waiting for him to be done so he could talk again. For over four decades, Nick had been the one sitting there, impatiently waiting for his father—Antonio—to finish work. Then, a year ago, their household had doubled with the addition of Noah, the teenage son of a former Pack mate, and Reese, twenty-three, running from some mysterious tragedy in Australia. So now Nick got to play the responsible adult. Several decades past due, some might argue.

He closed his laptop. "You're on yard duty until Noah is done with exams. He took it for you last month. Speaking of Noah, what's this about plates?"

"V plates. You need to help him lose his." Reese watched for Nick's reaction, then sighed. "They don't say that here?"

"I'm sure they don't say it anywhere except the middle of nowhere. In the outback. With sheep."

Reese choked on a mouthful of beer. "Sheep should definitely not be involved. Which isn't to say they aren't, sometimes, but for the record, no sheep were involved in mine. Though, I admit, the girl wasn't a whole lot brighter than one."

"Ah. V plate. Virginity." Nick glanced around.

"Don't worry. Noah's studying on the opposite side of the house, which in this place means he's a block away."

"Well, I'm sure he'll come to me when he's ready. I'm not going to rush him."

"He already came to *me*."

"What? Noah knows I'm here—"

"For all his questions about girls and sex. You are the undisputed expert. Which means there's no way he's admitting he's an eighteen-year-old virgin to you—a guy who lost his in primary school."

"It was high school." Nick paused. "Well, the summer between the two."

"And by eighteen, you were probably well into double digits. Which is why he's not coming to you." Reese leaned forward, elbows on his knees. "Did he tell you he broke it off with Lexi? He made a date with Bree Madison for Friday night."

"I don't think I've met Bree."

"Sure you have. There's one in every school. Can't get laid? Ask Bree out."

"Oh."

"Right. So, he's dumped a nice girl to hook up with one who puts out. Then he'll dump *her* and get back with Lexi. That's no way to treat either girl."

"Agreed. We have to help him find a better way."

"I already have. You need to buy him a hooker."

Nick would have been very happy if the conversation had ended there. He'd have said, "Like hell," and that would have been it. But Reese had gotten it into his head that Noah needed a hooker and that Nick was the best person to provide one.

Not that Nick had any experience with hookers. True, one couldn't overlook the convenience factor, but really, did you want someone who was only there because you'd paid her? No. Nick liked women, and he liked women who liked him back. That meant no hookers.

As it turned out, Reese didn't expect him to find one. He had that covered. A brothel in Philadelphia, highly recommended by a couple of mutts Reese used to run with. Reese had never been there himself—he had hang-ups about girls, part of the baggage he'd brought from Australia. He'd kept the address, though, which suggested the no-girls situation might not be as dire as Nick feared. There was, however, no way Reese was taking Noah to the brothel himself. That was sex, and in this household, sex was Nick's department.

"I can't believe you talked me into this," Reese muttered as they walked along the dark Philadelphia street.

"We can't come to Philly without seeing Karl and Hope," Nick said. Karl was a Pack mate, Hope his half-demon wife. "When I mentioned it to Hope, she assumed you were coming too."

"Just as long as she doesn't plan to introduce me to another cute young intern at *True News*." He checked Nick's expression, then let out a growl. "She does, doesn't she? Bugger it. I don't—"

"Oh, look, there it is." Nick pointed at a house two doors down. There was no sign, of course. It was just a house, a rambling old Victorian with tended gardens and a lush lawn.

"It doesn't . . . look like a brothel," Noah said.

Nick glanced over at the boy. Slightly built, five foot eight, light brown hair hanging in his thin face. Eighteen, but looking a couple of years younger, which really didn't help him with girls.

Noah hadn't said much since they'd arrived in Philadelphia. Not that he ever said much. He'd had a rough time of it in Alaska. While dealing with his Change to a full werewolf, he'd been in juvenile detention. Then he got out, only to lose both his father and grandfather—the former taking off, the latter murdered by mutts—before Noah was whisked across the country to live with strangers.

Nick had grown up with Noah's dad, but that didn't help much—they'd lost touch before Noah was born. The boy seemed to be doing better, though. More talkative. Less moody. Not as easily frustrated. But he was still easily set off—an alcoholic mother left his wiring frazzled. That meant the virginity issue couldn't be ignored, as it could with most boys. For Noah, it was like a sliver, a minor irritation that would inflame and fester until they dealt with it.

"If this isn't what you want . . ." Nick said gently.

"It is." Noah looked over, his expression resolute. "I'm sick of the guys razzing me. They stopped when I told them you were bringing me here."

"You . . . told them I was taking you to a brothel?"

"Uh-huh." A rare grin. "They were so fucking jealous. None of their dads would ever take them to a whorehouse. Not that you're my dad, but you know what I mean."

Reese thumped Nick on the back. "Better let Antonio handle the next parent-teacher night. Though I think you're about to become a very popular choice for school-trip chaperone."

Nick sighed.

"It's very dark," Noah said as they headed up the front walk.

It was. No lights on the cedar-shrouded porch. All the blinds drawn. Nick supposed they were just being discreet. He knocked.

It took a few minutes before the door opened, long enough for Noah to start fidgeting. He didn't stop when it did open, probably because the woman holding it had to be at least sixty. And not a well-maintained sixty.

"Please tell me that's not a—" Noah started to whisper before Reese cut him short with a look.

"Hello. Liam and Ramon sent us," Nick said, naming the mutts who'd given Reese the brothel recommendation. "We're looking—"

"*He's* looking," Reese interjected, pointing at Noah.

"—for companionship for our friend here."

"Not tonight." The woman started to close the door.

Reese grabbed it and held it open. "What's wrong with tonight? We came a long way and we were told appointments weren't necessary."

"We are busy tonight."

Reese shoved the door open, so they could see into the dark interior. "Doesn't look busy."

"It is not a good—"

A second woman slipped through a hall doorway and tugged the old lady back. She was in her late thirties. Handsome, in a severe way, dressed in slacks and a blouse.

"I'm sorry," she said. "Darlene is a little overprotective of the girls. It's their day off, actually, but you said only one needs companionship?"

Both Nick and Reese pointed at Noah.

"Ah, I see." The woman smiled and winked at Noah. "I'm sure I'll have more than one girl happy to give up her night off for such a handsome young man."

The woman—Angelica, as she introduced herself—led them inside. It was a perfectly normal-looking house, no red velvet to be seen. She took them to a modern room with leather couches, a pool table, a bar and a big-screen TV.

As they sat, Nick noticed Reese sniffing the air. Nick himself was trying to inhale as little as possible. There were candles burning everywhere, giving off a slightly musky scent that he figured was supposed to be a turn-on. With a werewolf's overdeveloped sense of smell, though, the only thing it turned was his stomach.

They'd just settled on the sofa when Darlene returned with a girl. Not really a girl—midtwenties, Nick guessed, which was good, because he'd gotten to the age where an eighteen-year-old hooker would have made him want to throw his jacket around her and bustle her out of there. Not that this girl needed to cover up. She was still dressed for her night off, in jeans and a pullover. She'd taken a few minutes to put on makeup, though. Too much, really, but she was cute enough, and when she walked in, Noah let out an audible sigh of relief. He got to his feet.

The girl giggled. "In a hurry?"

"Um, no, of course not. I, uh—"

The girl cut him off with a loud kiss. "I wasn't complaining. I like eager. *Young* and eager is even better." She grinned. "We don't get a lot of hot young guys here." She glanced at Nick and giggled. "Or hot guys of any age. I'm sure I could find friends for you two upstairs."

"Nope, we're good," Reese said. "Tonight is all about him."

"Then let's get right to it." She took Noah's hand and led him out. "I'm Sophie, by the way."

"Rob," he said. "I'm Rob."

Once they were gone, Angelica offered drinks from the bar. Nick eyed the Scotch, but Reese grabbed them both beers. Then they settled in, chatting awkwardly, glancing at the clock, as if waiting for Noah to finish an appointment. A short appointment, Nick figured.

After about ten minutes, another girl slid around the corner. This one was older than the first, and she *looked* like a hooker—bleached-blond teased hair, huge breasts that threatened to pop out of her bustier, long legs encased in fishnets and ending in stilettos.

She flashed her smile at Nick first, but his expression must have said she really wasn't his type, because she plopped herself onto Reese's lap instead.

Reese jumped so fast he nearly sent her flying. Then he lifted his hands, as if to keep them from going anyplace they shouldn't.

"I, uh, I'm not a client," he said. "No offense. I just wouldn't want you to, uh, waste your efforts."

The woman gave a throaty laugh and reached to run her hands through Reese's hair, which brought those huge breasts right up into his face. Reese tensed and Nick thought he was going to throw her off, and

Nick tensed himself, ready to run interference. But then Reese went still.

Nick couldn't see his expression, probably because his face was buried in the hooker's boobs, but it probably said something like, "Hmm, this isn't so bad after all." Reese had his hang-ups, but he was still a young werewolf. God only knew how long it'd been since he'd had sex. That couldn't be healthy at his age. Hell, that wasn't healthy at any age.

As Reese let the hooker coo and rub her breasts against his face, Nick began to think this brothel scheme wasn't so crazy after all. Noah might not be the only guy who got his problem solved tonight.

"You know . . ." Reese began.

"Uh-huh," Nick murmured.

Reese pulled the hooker down onto his lap and plucked at the laces of her bustier. "Is there any way I can persuade you to give up your day off . . . ?"

"Sugar, I don't need any persuading," the woman drawled. "You're so damned sweet I'd give you all my days off."

She got to her feet, her hand entwined with Reese's. He stood, then turned to Nick.

"Come with us," he said.

The hooker laughed. "Oh, now, that would be a treat. Come with us indeed, handsome."

Nick was all for helping Reese and Noah. He liked taking on the role of guardian. A few years ago, when Clay and Elena—his Pack mates and best friends—

had their twins, he started thinking maybe he wanted kids of his own. It didn't take more than a few diaper changes to convince him otherwise, but he'd still felt the wolf instinct to raise the next generation. Taking in two almost-grown young werewolves seemed the perfect solution.

But this . . . this was taking mentorship too far. Of course he'd had threesomes before, but the male-female ratio had always been reversed, and that's how he liked it.

"I need you up there, Nick," Reese whispered.

Shit.

Nick looked at the hooker and tried not to shudder. Maybe he could just . . . be in the room. For moral support. He stood and waved for them to lead the way.

The hooker led them into the first bedroom at the top of the stairs. Which was a good thing, because Reese was almost as eager as Noah had been. Nick barely got the door closed before Reese had her on the bed. Then he pinned her, arms and legs on hers, hand over her mouth.

"Whoa!" Nick said, running forward. "Don't—"

"Find Noah," Reese growled. "I'll keep this one—"

The hooker bucked and writhed, her eyes blazing, jaw working as if she was trying to bite Reese's hand. He wrapped his other one around her throat and leaned down.

"Feel how strong I am?" he whispered. "There's no use—"

The hooker fought harder, her muffled screams loud enough to alert anyone in an adjoining room. Reese's hand tightened on her throat. The hooker glared at him one last time, then her body went limp, gaze emptying.

Reese yanked his hand back. "Shit! I barely—" His fingers flew to the side of the woman's neck.

"Is she . . . ?"

"Dead." He paused. "And ice-cold." Reese leaned down and inhaled, then made a face. "Decomp. That's what I smelled downstairs. The candles and her perfume were doing a good job of covering it until she got close."

"You means she's . . . ?"

"A zombie. We need to get Noah."

Nick swung into the hall to see Noah backing out of another doorway, staring into the room he'd just left, his eyes huge. When Nick started toward him, he wheeled. He saw Nick, tensed and glanced both ways, as if ready to make a run for it.

Nick loped down the hall before Noah could bolt.

"I-I didn't mean to do it," he said. "I swear. I decided since the guys knew I was coming here, that was good enough. I didn't have to go through with it. B-but when I said I changed my mind, she got mad. I promised we'd pay, but—"

"It's okay," Nick said, putting his arm around the boy's shoulders.

Noah pushed him away. "No, you don't understand. I tried to leave and she wouldn't let me, so I shoved her. That's all I did, but now she's dead and—"

"You didn't kill her."

"Y-yes, I did. I checked for a pulse and—"

"She was already dead," Reese said, coming up behind them.

Reese took Noah back into the room he'd been in with Sophie. "See? She—Shit."

Nick pushed past them. There, on the bed, was the girl. Or what remained of her—a skeleton wearing decomposing flesh, a red silk bra and panties.

"Th—that—" Noah began.

"Isn't what she looked like a few minutes ago?" Reese said. "Yeah, I'm sure she didn't."

"Oh God. We almost . . ."

Noah turned and retched. Nick rubbed Noah's back as he hurled dinner onto the carpet.

"Great," Reese murmured. "More hours of therapy."

"Did I say a hooker wasn't a good idea?" Nick whispered back.

"I didn't expect zombies."

"No one ever does." Nick stripped a pillow of its case and handed the fabric to Noah to use to wipe his face, then frowned at the dead girl. "The last zombie hooker I met didn't look like that."

"You've met others?" Reese said.

"One. With Elena and Clay. Everything like this usually happens when they're around. That zombie had the rotting thing going on from the start. That's what they do. Rot. And it's why they really don't make good hookers."

"Uh-huh. Well, as interesting as this anomaly may be, I say we leave it to Elena and the council and get out of here before—"

A thump sounded from out in the hall. Then a muted cry.

Nick started toward the door.

Reese grabbed his arm. "Curiosity doesn't just kill cats. Let's go."

Nick hesitated. A few years ago, he'd have agreed. Hell, a few years ago, he'd have been the one grabbing Clay or Elena and saying, "Let's go." But he wasn't the omega wolf anymore. He had responsibilities. Which meant . . .

He turned to Reese. "Take Noah out of here." He waved at the window.

Reese protested, but Nick got them both out. Then he crept back into the hall and followed the sound of stifled cries to a bedroom. The door lock snapped with a sharp twist of the knob.

He pushed the door open. An empty room. Another thump, the muffled sounds louder. Nick followed them to a locked closet. Another werewolf-enhanced twist and the door opened. Inside, a young man lay bound and gagged on the floor. Seeing Nick, his eyes rolled wildly.

Nick motioned him to silence, then pulled off the gag.

"Thank God," the young man gasped. "I didn't think anyone would ever hear me. You must be a—"

He said a word Nick didn't recognize. Probably the Latinized name for half demons with hearing powers. Reese did say the brothel catered to supernaturals.

"It's okay," Nick said as he snapped the ropes. "I'm going to get you out—"

"No!" The guy grabbed his wrist. "The girls. The whores. They're vetala."

"If that's some kind of zombie, I already know that."

"It's a demi-demon that possesses bodies of the recently dead."

Which explained the non-rotting, Nick supposed.

The young man continued. "I knew what they were as soon as I got here. I'm a necromancer. I can recognize the dead. I confronted the lady in charge and all of a sudden, they swarmed me and locked me in there."

"Okay, but you're out now. So come—"

"My friend. They took him to the basement for some kind of ritual. That's why they're closed tonight. We need to get him out."

Nick knew he wasn't considered the brightest guy in the Pack. Clay was a freaking genius and Elena was damned smart, too, so he never tried to compete, just sat back and let them come up with the plans. But he wasn't dumb. Or, at least, not dumb enough to try handling this on his own.

He clapped the young man on the back. "Don't worry." He took out his cell to call Karl. "I'll get help—"

The young man's eyes bugged. "There's no time for that. Don't you get it? My friend is about to be slaughtered in some kind of demonic ritual."

"Then we'll stall it until my friends arrive." Nick started dialing.

The young man knocked the phone from his hand. "You aren't making this easy, are you?" His eyes glowed orange and his voice changed. "I want your body."

Considering where they were, there was a brief moment when Nick thought, "Whoa, sorry, that's not my thing." Then he realized, given the whole zombie/vetala/demi-demon issue—and the glowing orange eyes—that probably wasn't what the guy meant.

A floorboard squeaked behind Nick, and the stench of rotting flesh wafted past. He spun as three young women slid into the room. The first looked normal enough, her skin just starting to gray. The second's face was covered in blackened boils that bubbled and burst. The third was barely more than a walking skeleton, flesh sloughing off with every step. All three wore silk negligees, thongs, garters and stockings, presenting an image that ensured Nick was not going to be enjoying the Victoria's Secret catalog for a very long time.

He backed up to the window, watching their outstretched nails and remembering the zombie scratch that nearly cost Clay an arm. When he reached the window and looked down, though, he saw two more zombie hookers waiting below in the yard.

Shit! Had Reese and Noah gotten away? He should have told Reese to call Karl and tell him where they were *before* he checked out the noise.

"Look, whatever's going on here, it's your business," Nick said. "I'm just going to leave and pretend I didn't see anything—"

"Did I mention I want your body?" the young man said.

"This body?" Nick said. "It's a lot older than you think. I'm a—"

"Werewolf." One of the girls licked her lips with a blackened tongue. "We know. That means your body is in very good condition. You and your friends picked a perfect night to visit. We were just beginning to gather fresh vessels. They last a long time, but not indefinitely. We'll take yours and the handsome young Australian's. The little one is too young, but we will kill him quickly. Mercifully."

Nick hit the man first. A lightning punch to the throat took him down, and he stayed down, the demi-demon abandoning its host. On to the graying girl, who was already running at him, shrieking. A blow to the stomach doubled her over. He grabbed her hair and snapped her neck. When he looked up, the other two were gone, leaving a trail of rotted flesh in their wake.

Nick exited out the window. Only two zombies down there. As he landed, they rushed him. He took the first out with two quick blows. The second ran off. When the first zombie was dead—or dead again—he dropped her and turned . . .

Zombies stepped through the hedges, surrounding him. Six of them. All in lingerie and varying degrees of decomposition.

A figure raced through an opening in the hedge. Reese. The young man ran to Nick's side and flipped around to cover his back.

"Noah?" Nick said.

"Safe."

The zombies began to circle.

"You need to watch their—"

"Nails, I know." Reese lowered his voice. "Where's the necromancer?"

"Huh?"

"Zombies are controlled by a necro. Where's—?"

Reese stopped as they spotted Angelica hidden in the shadows.

"I got her," Reese said. "Cover me."

Nick raced after him, knocking zombies aside as they charged. But not many charged. Not as many as should have, if Angelica could order them to guard her. Nick realized it just as Reese grabbed Angelica. Reese already had his hands around the woman's neck. Her eyes flashed orange, then emptied as the demi-demon left her.

"Goddamn it!" Reese said, dropping the corpse.

"The old woman," Nick said as he surveyed the zombies, closing in on them again. "Darlene. Where's—?"

A white-haired figure stepped through the gate, lips moving, hands fluttering. The zombies shifted forward, rumbling and hissing.

A shadow appeared behind the old woman. Noah knocked her to the ground. His hands shot up to snap her neck. The zombies turned and rushed him.

"No!" Nick yelled.

He raced over, shoving zombies out of the way. Killing the undead was one thing. Killing a living person—deservedly or not—wasn't something the boy needed on his conscience.

Nick grabbed the old woman away from Noah. A quick wrench broke her neck. The zombies hesitated. They didn't evacuate their shells, though. They just watched him, as if confused.

Because they weren't zombies. Shit. They were vetala, whatever that was. Normal rules didn't apply.

"What do you want with us?" the one in front said. She had trouble speaking—her jaw hung by a few threads of tendon. Of all the zombies, she was the most decayed.

Nick hesitated. They continued to watch him warily.

"You killed the one who summoned us," the leader said. "We belong to you. What do you want from us?"

"Nothing."

A rumble went through the pack, and they shifted from foot to foot.

The leader tilted her head. "We are free to go?"

"Yes," Reese said, walking up behind them. "You're free to go."

She continued to study Nick.

"Go," he said.

The leader dipped her head. "Thank you."

Her body collapsed. The others did, too, one after another, corpses falling onto the grass and rotting.

Once Nick had moved the bodies inside, checked the house and made sure there weren't any more zombies hobbling around, he called Elena. She'd contact the council and decide what to do about a brothel filled with corpses. Maybe he'd be back to clean it up. Maybe he wouldn't. Not his call, thankfully.

They walked back to the car in silence. As they got in, Noah said, "So that should work, right? If I tell my friends I went through with it? They won't . . . know?"

It took a moment for Nick to realize what he meant.

Reese beat him to an answer. "They won't know. We'll give you a few tips to make it sound good."

Noah relaxed in the backseat and Nick realized it was what the poor kid wanted all along. Not to lose his virginity. Just to get his friends off his back. If only he'd figured that out sooner . . .

"I'm going to call Lexi," Noah said. "Think I can get her back?"

"Just don't mention the brothel," Reese said. "If she finds out, tell her the truth—that nothing happened. I'll back you up."

"And as for winning her back," Nick said, "I have some tips for that, too."

Reese and Noah looked at each other.

"Um, maybe not," Noah said. "I appreciate your help, Nick, but after tonight . . ."

They both laughed.

"Excuse me?" Nick said. "This was *not* my idea."

But they were talking again, and neither heard him. He sighed and started to drive.

Suddenly, changing diapers didn't seem so bad. Parenting teens? Their messes were a lot bigger and a lot tougher to clean up.

Put On a Happy Face

CHRISTOPHER GOLDEN

The blood seeping out of the midget car was Benny's first clue that something had gone awry. The audience kept laughing—either they hadn't seen it yet or they thought it was part of the show—so Benny didn't slow down. He waddled on his big shoes, storming with exaggerated frustration toward Clancy the Cop, and slapped the other clown in the face with a rubber chicken.

It looked like it hurt.

The audience roared.

Back up.

The night before—a Friday—the circus had ended at quarter past nine on the dot. Appleby, the manager, was a stickler for punctuality. The last bow took place between ten and fifteen minutes past the hour every performance, and when the thunderous applause—which, honestly, wasn't always thunderous and was sometimes barely more than a ripple—had died down, the ticket sellers became ushers, ushering folks out of the tent as quickly as possible. The ushers didn't hurry people because anyone was in a rush to get their makeup off, but because once the little kids started moving, all the popcorn and cotton candy and soda and hot dogs started to churn in their bellies. Much better to hose the vomit off the ground outside than in the tent.

The clowns ran out of the tent the way NFL teams come onto the field, arms above their heads, whooping and hollering, before the last of the crowd had departed. Benny had always thought it looked stupid, but Zerbo—the boss clown and the troupe's white-face—wanted to leave the straggling audience members with an image of the clowns as a kind of family.

Out behind the tent, the family fell apart. The tents and trailers that made up the circus camp were a tense United Nations of performers and laborers without any real unity. Like a high school full of jocks and geeks and emo kids, the clowns and workers and animal trainers and acrobats each formed their own caste, every group thinking themselves above the others. Friendships existed outside the boundaries of those castes, but when it came to conflict, they stuck together like unions. The acrobats were effete, the animal trainers grave and sensitive, and the workers gruff and strong.

But nobody fucked with the clowns.

"You mess with the clown, you get the horns," Zerbo was fond of misquoting, right before blasting you in the face with an air horn. His idea of a joke. Most people laughed, but Benny had never found the boss clown all that funny.

The Macintosh Traveling Circus Troupe had been playing sold-out audiences in a field in Brimfield, Massachusetts, for a week. Normally, the grounds were used for the huge antique flea market the town held a couple of times a year, but the circus had been a welcome novelty, as far as Benny could tell. Not that Appleby talked to him about it. Clowns were beneath the manager's notice, except when it came time for him to talk to Zerbo about renewing contracts. Even then, nobody bothered to ask Benny what he thought.

In the hierarchy of clowns in the Macintosh Traveling Circus Troupe, Benny Martini was on the bottom rung. The runt of the litter. The redheaded stepchild. Shit, that last one was probably offensive in these sensitive modern times. No matter. The point was that Benny was an afterthought to everyone, even the audience.

He'd often thought about how much happier he would have been if, like Tiny and Oscar—two of the other character clowns in the troupe—he'd been too stupid to know it. But even Tiny and Oscar were above him. If the troupe had been a wolf pack, Benny would have been on his back, baring his throat for everyone who came along. And why?

It was all about the laughs.

Laughter and his status in the circus, nearly always the only two things he thought about, were foremost on his mind as he followed Zerbo, Oscar, Tiny, Clancy the Cop, and the rest of them into clown alley. Tiny bumped Oscar, then clapped him on the back—they'd successfully completed the Hotshots gag after having totally bungled it the night before. On a façade so rickety even old-time Hollywood stuntmen would've shied away from it, three-hundred-pound Tiny dressed in drag and pretended to be a mother trapped with her infant on the third story of a burning building. The fire effects were minimal—gas jets, a low flame, a lot of orange lighting, the whole thing designed by a guy who'd helped put together the Indiana Jones Epic Stunt Spectacular at Disney World, before he'd been fired for drinking on the job—but it looked great, as long as Tiny didn't set his wig on fire.

Oscar, in character as a clown firefighter, pushed a barrel of water back and forth across the ring, exhorting Tiny to throw him the infant and then jump into the water. The culmination of the whole thing was that Tiny's aim would be off, forcing Oscar to step into the water barrel in order to catch the baby—only a doll, of course. At the moment he caught it, the trapdoor would give way beneath the ring, dropping

Oscar and the baby and the water through and giving the audience the impression that the baby had been heavy enough to drive him into the ground. It was a pain in the ass to set up the gag, but when it went off, the surprise always led to real laughs, especially when Tiny theatrically threw up his hands, mopped his sweating face with his wig, took a deep breath, and blew out the fire around the windows like candles on a birthday cake. The lights would go dark. Cue the applause.

Thursday night, Tiny had stumbled, throwing off his timing. The doll—to the eyes of the crowd, an infant—had tumbled down to splat in the middle of the ring while Oscar stood watching like a fool, until the trapdoor gave way and shot him down into the space beneath. The audience had to know the baby wasn't real, but they'd screamed all the same.

Timing was everything, Benny always said.

How Tiny and Oscar could screw up the gag so badly and still be above him in the pecking order, he would never understand.

In clown alley that Friday night, he washed off his makeup without a word to any of the others. Most of the time he shot the breeze with them and tried to ignore the fact that, four years since he'd joined up, they still treated him like a mascot, but not tonight. The cold cream took off most of the makeup and then he splashed a little water on his face and dragged on a pair of stained blue jeans and a Red Sox sweatshirt—it had been strangely cool the past few nights, uncommon for July in western Massachusetts.

As he left the others behind and went out to wander the grounds and clear his head, he ran into the lovely blond contortionist, Lorna Seger. There were tears in her eyes and she gave him a helpless, hopeless glance that made him think maybe she wanted to talk about her breakup with the stunt rider, Domingo.

"Hey," he said, shaken from the reverie of his self-pity by her sadness. "You okay?"

Lorna smiled and wiped at her eyes. "Could be worse, I guess," she said. "I could be a clown."

Benny flinched. Lorna chuckled softly to let him know it had been a joke. He hoped Domingo ran her down on his motorcycle.

"You're such a bitch," he said.

Lorna rolled her eyes. "Why is it clowns never have a sense of humor?"

He walked on, fuming, wanting to scream, wanting to get the hell away from the circus but crippled by the knowledge that—like everyone else who performed under the tent—he had nowhere else to go.

Put on a happy face, his mother would have said. Remembering did make him smile, but it faded quickly.

The wind picked up as he walked the grounds, which were rutted and pitted with tire tracks from decades of vehicles moving through the fields in all weather, turning up muddy ridges, which had then dried and hardened. Loud voices came from the trailers where the workers had made their own small camp, and he could smell sausages cooking on a grill. When he passed a tent, he saw them, standing in a semicircle, drinking beer, a small radio picking up a static-laced broadcast of tonight's Red Sox–Yankees game. Summer in New England. These guys looked like their entire life was a tailgate party. They worked hard and were content with the cycle of labor and paycheck, beer and cookouts and Red Sox games. In a way, Benny envied them.

The stencil on the side of the converted school bus read ROSE'S MOBILE BOOK FAIR. In a side window there hung a cardboard sign, NEW, USED, AND ANTIQUARIAN—SOMETHING FOR EVERYONE written in thick black Magic Marker. Benny had seen the bus several times this season, in Vermont and New Hampshire and upstate New York. It might've been there when they'd played Bangor back in May, but he couldn't be sure. He'd never been inside—he'd never been much for books, unless they were about clowns or vaudeville or something useful.

Tonight, he just wanted a distraction.

The accordion bus door was open and a sign indicated that the mobile book fair was as well, so he went up the couple of steps, ducking his head though he'd never be tall enough to bang it. Oddly enough, he didn't notice the woman right away. At first, all he could see were the books, and he wondered how she managed to keep them all from falling off the shelves while she drove the old beast of a school bus around the northeastern United States. The metal shelving units had been secured to the walls and lined both sides of the bus. Each shelf had an ingenious device, a bar that went across the spines of the books to hold them in place and could be locked into different notches to accommodate racks of books of different sizes.

"Looking for something to read?" the woman asked, and he blinked and stared at her.

She'd been there all along, of course, but it felt almost as if he'd dreamed her into being. Slender and fit, perhaps forty, she wore black pants and shoes and a tight pink tank with a bright red rose silhouette stretched across her breasts. Rose—for how could she have been anyone else?—had an olive complexion and a proud Roman nose, and she wore a kindly expression, her gaze alert and attentive. Though the interior of the mobile book fair was lit mainly with strings of old white Christmas lights, he could see that her eyes were icy blue. It both pleased and unnerved him to have someone study him with such intensity—such intimacy. People looked at him all the time when he had his clown makeup on, but he couldn't remember how long it had been since anyone had really *seen* him when he didn't have it on.

"I doubt you'd have anything for me," he said. "I'm not a big reader."

"Didn't you see the sign?" she said, amused. "Something for everyone. What do you do here?"

He almost lied, but she would've taken one look at his little potbelly and stiff shoulders and known he wasn't an acrobat.

"I'm a clown."

Her eyes lit up. "I've got a small section back here. Not a whole shelf, but a handful of interesting antiquarian books I picked up from an old guy in Cheektowaga, when his carnival went belly-up."

Most of the books were things he'd seen before. Way back in high school, he'd researched Grimaldi and Tovolo and Ricketts, studied the Fratellinis, and watched the films of the great movie directors who had started their careers as circus clowns, like Fellini and Jodorowsky. Charlie Chaplin had become his god, and he mastered the rolling walk of the Little Tramp. There were many schools of comedy, but Benny had never been much interested in telling jokes or doing stand-up. In his heart, he had always been a clown. Though some of them were probably quite valuable, none of the books Rose's Mobile Book Fair had on her shelves were unfamiliar to him.

He'd just begun to turn away when he noticed the frayed spine of a book lying on its side atop the dozen or so she had shelved at the end of her boys' adventure section. The worn, faded lettering was almost unreadable in the shadows, but when he slipped his slender fingers in and slid the volume out, the cloth cover made him stiffen in surprise. The comedy and tragedy masks were there, along with the initials G.T.

Quickly he leafed to the title page and a warm feeling spread through him. *Charade: The Secret to Being a Clown,* by Giovanni Tovolo. He had never even heard of the book, had not run across it in any of his reading and research, even in the biography of Tovolo he'd read. The famous Italian character clown had retired after a horrifying accident had taken sixteen lives in a big-top fire outside Chicago in 1917. All but forgotten, Tovolo had been a particular fascination of Benny's because the man had earned his reputation doing characters. Most of the famous clowns were whitefaces or augustes. Tovolo could do anything, at least according to what Benny had read . . . but now, to read it in Tovolo's own words . . .

Maybe Tovolo could help him figure out how he ended up spending four years at the wrong end of clown alley. He glanced up at Rose, unable to stifle his excitement and hoping she wouldn't take advantage of him.

"How much do you want for this one?" he asked.

She took it from his hand, opened it to see the price she'd penciled on the first page. "Twenty-two dollars."

Benny swallowed hard, knowing his smile was too thin. Did she not realize that, to certain collectors, this book would be worth a hundred times that? Or did she simply not care, having paid next to nothing for it herself?

He smiled. "I'll take it."

• • •

Benny's mother always thought he was funny. All through his childhood he had been encouraged by her laughter, egged on by the way her face would redden and she would wipe at her eyes when he made silly faces or did the big, galumphing walk that would one day become his trademark. At the age of nine he had begun rearranging living room furniture so that he could stumble over it, practicing pratfalls and somersaults and rubber-leg gags—anything that might elicit laughter from his mother. Once she had laughed so hard that she had to wave at him to stop so she could catch her breath. Her chest ached for days afterward, and she had joked often that if he wasn't careful he would give her a heart attack.

That's how funny Benny Martini was as a kid.

He loved to make her laugh. He watched the Three Stooges and the Marx Brothers and forced his friends into helping him reenact their gags. Mrs. Martini took young Benny to the circus every year, and when the clowns made the audience roar with their hilarious antics, he watched with fascination and a dawning envy. For weeks after a circus trip, he would mimic the clowns, practicing the faces they pulled, their walks, their timing.

In school, he put whoopee cushions on the seats of teachers and thumbtacks on the chairs of the girls he liked. In the eighth grade, he had taped a sign to

Tim Rivard's back that read HONK IF YOU THINK I'M A MORON. Only other jocks had been brave enough to make honking noises when Rivard walked down the hall, but it took the football player until fourth period to really start to wonder what all the honking was about. He'd slammed Benny's head into a locker, but the sign alone hadn't been enough to prompt the violence. That had come when Benny had pointed out that Rivard going most of the day without noticing the sign pretty much proved his point.

When Benny told his mother what he'd done, she'd put a hand over her mouth to hide her laughter. And when he confessed that he'd been suspended for three days—even though he was the one with the black eye—she'd laughed so hard she had cried, tears streaming down her pretty face, ruining her makeup.

Benny had become the class clown by design. He knew every class had to have one, and he'd be damned if he let some other guy take on that role. His classmates—hell, the whole school—would remember him forever as *that guy,* the one with the jokes, the one with the faces, the one who couldn't be serious for two seconds.

There were dark moods, of course. Who didn't have them? Who hadn't spent a little time studying his own face in the mirror, trying to recognize something, anything, of value? Who hadn't tested the edges of the sharpest knives on the hidden parts of his skin just to see how sharp they really were, or sat in the dark for a while and wondered if people were laughing with him or at him?

By the time senior year of high school rolled around, Benny didn't know how to be anything but funny, and he didn't want to learn. His mother had told him he ought to try to do birthday parties, paint himself up as a clown and make children laugh. Benny would rather have cut his own throat. He didn't want to do gags at birthday parties for a bunch of nose-picking brats; he wanted to perform in a circus.

The Macintosh Traveling Circus Troupe came to town in the spring of his senior year. The Macintosh was small enough that it still relied on posters hung at ice cream stands and grocery stores and barbershops to pull in an audience. In a little town like Corriveau, Vermont, that sort of thing still worked.

He'd gone to the circus every day, hung around before and after shows, talked to the workers, the animal trainers, the ticket takers, and eventually worked up the courage to talk to the clowns. By the third day, after hours, they invited him into clown alley to talk with them while they removed their makeup and hung up costumes and props. Benny could barely breathe. It had felt to him as though he had stepped into a film, or into history. He could smell the greasepaint, could practically feel the texture of the costumes, could hear the roar of the crowd, even though the tent stood empty by then.

The second-to-last night, his hopes of an invitation fast fading, he confessed his hopes and dreams and begged for an apprenticeship. The clowns had indulged him, patted him on the back, told stories of their own glory days, but none of them had encouraged him. It was a hell of a life, they'd said, something they would never wish on anybody. It was brutal on family and worse on love. Circus life set them apart from the rest of the world, created a distance that could never be bridged. Once you were in, you were in. They were trying to scare him off, but Benny persisted.

Two hours after their final performance, as they were packing to move on, Zerbo—the boss clown—had given him the word. They'd take him on for the rest of the season, no pay, just food and a place to lay his head. If he was good enough to take part in the act by the season's end and could get some laughs of his own, the circus manager—Mr. Appleby—would hire him on. If not, he'd be sent home.

Benny had given it his all, pulled out every gag, every funny face, every silly walk he had ever learned. He had studied the troupe, could stand in for almost any of them if someone fell ill. At the end of the season, on the fairgrounds in Briarwood, Connecticut, they were as good as their word—a spotlight of his own, a chance to prove himself.

The laughs had been thin and the applause half-hearted, but Zerbo had given him the thumbs-up. Tiny had told him later that it had been a near thing, but he'd worked so hard they had wanted to give him a second chance.

Now, four years of second chances later, he still felt like an apprentice.

That Friday night, Rose moved on. She'd mentioned a carnival somewhere, and a Little League baseball tournament later in the week, but Benny hadn't really been listening. Kind as she'd been to him, a woman as attractive as Rose wasn't interested in doing more than selling him a book, and she'd done that already.

He stayed up all through that cool night, reading Tovolo's words over and over until the battery of his flashlight began to give out, the light to dim. By then, the horizon had begun to glow with the promise of dawn, but Benny read the final chapter of the book over a few more times. At first, he'd thought the whole thing was some kind of joke, Tovolo trying to pull one over on the reader or attempting some tongue-in-cheek social commentary about circus life that didn't quite translate in his imperfect English. The book had been broken down into thirds—part one a memoir of his life, part two a kind of compendium of what he considered the funniest gags, and part three a reminiscence about his lifelong interest in the darker aspects of the history of clowns, everything from suicides and murders to haunted circuses and black magic.

The final chapter concerned Tovolo's lifelong struggle with his own talent and his belief that he had never been funny enough. Two small circuses had merged, forcing him to perform alongside his longtime rival, Vincenzo Mellace, and every time the audience laughed for Mellace, Tovolo had wanted to set himself on fire. The reference to self-immolation made Benny shiver every time he read it, and he wondered if it had been written before or after the tragic blaze that had led to the Italian's retirement.

Tovolo had befriended a Belgian fire-eater who had come over from the other circus and who shared his hatred of Vincenzo Mellace. The fire-eater's mother traveled with her son and sometimes told fortunes on the show grounds after the audience had gone home and the circus folk had drunk too much wine.

She had been the one to instruct him as to the ingredients for the elixir and to explain to him precisely how to summon the spirit of Polichinelle, the patron of clowns, the demon known to children as the jester puppet Punch.

As the circus folk began to rise that Saturday morning, the day arriving overcast and bleak, Benny read Tovolo's final chapter over and over. Each time, he held his breath as he read the last few lines.

Mellace's routine was a disaster, he had written. *He had performed Busy Bee thousands of times, and yet it seemed like his first. Laughter was sporadic at best, and mostly sympathetic at that. There were boos. For myself . . . I could do no wrong. They laughed at a simple chase on the Hippodrome Track. They howled when Rostoni and I performed the Shoot-out. And when I went out to do the*

Cooking Class gag on my own, it felt like a dream of how smoothly I had always wished for a performance to unfold.

God, how they laughed.

I cannot say for certain that Polichinelle was in my corner that night, but he was certainly no friend to Mellace. If offering the demon a little of my blood and a handful of days at the end of my life was all that was required for me to become the greatest clown in the world, it was a small price to pay.

When Benny heard Oscar and Tiny calling for him, he closed the book, yet as he went about his morning, he could think of nothing but the elixir and the summoning spell that the fire-eater's mother had given to Tovolo. One line kept repeating itself in his head.

God, how they laughed.

The blood seeping out of the midget car was Benny's first clue that something had gone awry. The audience kept laughing—either they hadn't seen it yet or they thought it was part of the show—so Benny didn't slow down. He waddled on his big shoes, storming with exaggerated frustration toward Clancy the Cop, and slapped the other clown in the face with a rubber chicken.

It looked like it hurt.

The audience roared.

He'd asked the demon Polichinelle for his heart's desire—to be the funniest clown in the circus. As blood flew from Clancy the Cop's split lip, Benny began to have second thoughts. He staggered backward, tripped over his own big clown feet, and let himself roll with the fall. His whole life had been spent performing such antics, so if there was anything he knew how to do, it was fall. He rolled on his curving spine, then flipped back up onto his feet and executed a fluid bow.

Clancy, snorting like a bull, eyes bulging with his fury, barreled toward him, running on an engine of vengeance. Benny saw him coming just in time, spun in a circle to avoid his outstretched hands, and whacked Clancy in the back of the head with the plucked, frozen chicken—it wasn't made of rubber anymore. The impact dropped Clancy to the ground, where he began to spasm and seize.

Benny lifted the chicken by its legs, examining it in full view of the audience. From their seats, they couldn't have seen the blood on the chicken, would presume his horror just a part of the act. He turned and looked at them, a wide-eyed clown mugging for the paying customers, and they ate it up. The stands were shaking with laughter.

Stunned, a dead, frozen chicken dangling from one clenched fist, Benny remembered the midget car. He turned, saw the blood dripping from the door seam, and started to run toward it. A scream filled the air and Benny spun to see Tiny standing in the window of the Hotshots building façade, his striped dress and blond wig both in flames that spread quickly to his arms and the baby doll bundled in his arms.

But from the way Tiny stared at the swaddled infant—and from the high, shrieking noise that could really be nothing else—Benny had the terrible idea that maybe it wasn't a doll in Tiny's arms. Not anymore. Not thanks to Polichinelle.

Burning alive, screaming baby in his arms, Tiny jumped from the façade, which was now engulfed in flames, and plummeted toward Oscar, who stood knee-deep in the water barrel below. Too late, Oscar realized his situation. He tried to climb out of the barrel but tripped on the rim and fell half in, half out of the water, where he lay when Tiny and his baby struck Earth in a comet-like blaze. The trapdoor opened and all three of them crashed through, water barrel and all. Steam and smoke rose with a hiss and the stink of burning hair and flesh began to fill the big top.

The applause was deafening. The laughter rolled through the tent like a hurricane.

Bobo shot Zerbo through the head during the Shoot-out. The guns were supposed to be made of rubber. When Zerbo's only bullet went astray and killed a young father, passing through his popcorn tub on the way and spraying butter and popcorn onto a dozen people, the laughter turned to breathless, teary-eyed hysteria that reminded Benny of his mother.

Numb with shock, Benny staggered over to the midget car—what the public called a clown car—and vomited across the hood. Crimson leaked from every crevice in the miniature vehicle, pooling on the floor and running across the ground. The stink of blood and offal wafted off the midget car, and he felt as if he stood in an abattoir.

The driver's door popped open. A colorfully clad leg slipped out, and then Polichinelle climbed from the car. He wore a red and black jester costume, complete with ruffles at the shirt cuffs and bells atop his pronged hat and at the toes of his shoes. His alabaster skin did not appear to be makeup, nor did the bright red circles like burn scars on his cheeks.

Benny caught a glimpse of the carnage inside the midget car. The trapdoor meant to be beneath it no longer existed. Eight clowns had been broken and twisted and jammed together to make sure they could all fit in a space that would've been cramped for two, and somehow Polichinelle had fit into the driver's seat.

Bobo stood in shock above the corpse of Zerbo, shaking and weeping. As Polichinelle pirouetted toward him, Bobo could only stare, but as he looked into the demon's eyes, he screamed.

Polichinelle plucked a trick flower from Zerbo's corpse and held it as if offering it to Bobo for a sniff. When he squeezed the rubber bulb dangling from the flower, an acrid-smelling liquid jetted out of it, coating Bobo's head. His scream rose to a shriek as his face began to melt and his eyes sank into his skull. When he crumpled to his knees and then toppled sideways to land beside Zerbo, his scream died.

Benny had never heard laughter so uproarious. The

audience cheered. Some stood and others doubled over, clutching their bellies. Some slapped hands across their chests as their hearts burst and they slid into the aisles, gasping into cardiac arrest. Throats went hoarse, faces turned red, hands blistered from applause, but they couldn't stop. Their faces were stretched into grins that split the corners of their mouths and they wept tears of terror and pain and amusement, but they simply could not stop. It was, after all, the funniest thing they had ever seen.

God, how they laughed, Benny thought, and then, at last, he began to laugh as well.

Polichinelle performed a mad, capering little dance, part ballet and part mincing, mocking swagger, and then mimed a curtsy to the audience.

Through his laughter and his tears, Benny managed to choke out a single word.

"Why?"

Polichinelle gave him an apologetic shrug, an angelic look on the demon's face.

"You wanted to be the funniest clown in the circus."

Trying to catch his breath, Benny forced out the words. "All . . . all the others . . . are dead."

Polichinelle giggled. "Don't blame me, Benny. Blame your mother for all those years of lies."

Benny stared, eyes widening in horror. "My . . . my . . ." he gasped, but he couldn't get the word out.

"Sorry, pal," Polichinelle said. "But you're just not that funny."

The giant mallet seemed to appear from nowhere. Polichinelle gripped it in both hands as he swung, and Benny knew it wouldn't be made of hollow plastic or rubber. The crowd roared, laughing themselves to death.

God, how they laughed.

Devil's Contract

E. S. MAGILL

Maleficorum, Inc.
Software License Agreement for Maleficorum
Software

WHEREAS, Licensee wishes to use Maleficorum Software under any and all conditions set forth in this Agreement.

NOW, THEREFORE, in consideration of the mutual promises set forth herein, Licensee and Licensor hereby agree as follows:

READ CAREFULLY. By using Maleficorum Software you agree to be bound by the terms of this License. If you do not agree to the terms of this License, well, it's actually too late for second thoughts. By now you've probably stopped reading, if, that is, you bothered to read any of this at all. The latest figures show most people spend less than eight seconds on software agreements, thinking their time better spent checking out how many goats their life is worth at www.howmanygoats.com. Why bother anyway, right? It's not as if you have a choice, this being the most popular software program in the world, the one everyone uses. Therefore, you must accept our terms, but, alas, our attorneys say we have to inform you about them. We know, however, that if we throw in some hereins and herebys and make the sentences more than five words long, with the fourth-grade reading level you're accustomed to these days, you won't read this License Agreement. Whether you read the entire Agreement or not, this will end badly for you.

1. General. The software and documentation accompanying this License are licensed, not sold, to you by Maleficorum, Inc., for use only under the terms of this License, and Maleficorum, Inc., reserves all rights not expressly granted to you. In exchange for accepting this License, you hereby grant Maleficorum, Inc., access to your life and soul, whereby Malefico-

rum, Inc., secures the rights to do with it as it so desires, primarily the redistribution of said life and soul to other parties for the purpose of world domination and obscene wealth. While this Agreement constitutes a Devil's Contract, we are in no way associated with Lucifer, Satan, Mephistopheles, Scratch or any of their subsidiaries. We know that by now you've already clicked through to the Accept button and have missed, and will continue to miss, the finer points of this Agreement, but if you hadn't found the legalese so daunting and the overuse of commas so mentally taxing, you would have discovered that we now own your life and soul. We plan to use said life and soul to expand our hold upon the world through lucrative transactions with the enterprise known as Hell (or any other corporation—coal, oil, banking et al.— that can offer a better deal; thanks to deregulation, Hell no longer holds the monopoly on this type of transaction).

2. Permitted License Uses and Restrictions. You may make one copy of the Maleficorum Software for backup purposes only.

THE MALEFICORUM SOFTWARE IS NOT INTENDED FOR USE IN THE OPERATION OF AIRCRAFT,

LIFE SUPPORT MACHINES, NUCLEAR FACILITIES OR OTHER EQUIPMENT IN WHICH THE FAILURE OF THE MALEFICORUM SOFTWARE COULD LEAD TO SEVERE ENVIRONMENTAL DAMAGE, PERSONAL INJURY, OR DEATH.

We at Maleficorum, Inc., reserve those uses for ourselves, and will hereby prosecute to the fullest extent of the law any persons who encroach upon our right to decimate the earth and pillage humanity. You may not copy, decompile, reverse-engineer or create derivative works of Maleficorum Software or any part thereof. Only we possess the right to invade your computer with spyware, porn pop-ups, and the nosferatu virus, a little something special we created in the event we need to drain you dry on the spot (such need to be determined solely by Maleficorum, Inc.).

3. Consent to Use of Data. You agree that Maleficorum, Inc., and its subsidiaries may collect and use technical and other information from your computer, system software, peripherals, tax returns, social networking sites, criminal record, and that fan-based obsession you've been trying to hide from others. Maleficorum,

Inc., may use this information to improve our products, to let your mom know about those anime costumes in the back of your closet, or, for the pure sociopathic fun of it, to defriend your friends.

4. End Users. The Maleficorum Software and related documentation are determined as 48 C.F.R. §2.101, commercial software, as 48 C.F.R. §12.212, 45 C.F.R. §12.26 or 45 C.F.R. 861.1301, 52 C.F.R. 333.1 or 45 C.F.R. 861.1301, 52 C.F.R. 333.666. We haven't a clue as to what this means, looks like gobbledygook to us, but we do know that statistically a few of you will actually scroll through this License Agreement and will stop at this spot. We know that if we put in a bunch of abbreviations and numbers with decimals, your head will spin like that of a little girl possessed by Pazuzu (who now works in our marketing department). Plus, studies have shown that people are most fearful of this symbol: §. Unpublished rights are reserved under the copyright laws of the United States.

5. Complete Agreement. This Agreement sets forth the entire understanding of the parties and may not be modified except in writing executed by both parties. Fooled you! Made

you think you had a glimmer of hope of getting out of this, huh? Faustian bargains will not be considered. Don't worry, though. You won't have to suffer the fires of Hell for eternity, perform the Holy Kiss or engage in any other diabolical favors. You can go about your normal, mind-numbing routine like zombies trapped in a mall. Modern technology has facilitated our gathering of lives and souls much more effectively, closing any loopholes that allow the Licensee to avoid the terms of this Agreement. It's so much more efficient than the old sign-your-name-on-the-dotted-line-with-your-blood method. Please note: We no longer accept firstborns as exchanges. Neither do we negotiate terms or conditions, unless you can deliver souls on a mass scale. If so, please contact our corporate lawyers.

6. Termination. This License is effective until terminated by Maleficorum, Inc. Your rights will terminate automatically without notice if you fail to comply with any terms of this License. Actually, who are we kidding, all your rights have already been terminated since we now possess your life and soul. Consider this as coming to the crossroads with all alternate roads blocked off for indefinite repairs. This Agreement also prohibits litigation and

arbitration as a means for the Licensee to terminate this Agreement, and, anyway, Daniel
Webster now works for us. And if you're one
of those anal-retentive freaks who actually
read these things, don't think you can get out
of this Agreement by pushing the Decline
button because as soon as you do there will be
a knock at your door. (Clicking the Close box
will result in the same actions on our part.)
We've been monitoring you since this License
Agreement box opened, and any length of
time longer than it takes to click Accept indicates that you've really been reading this, triggering our response team to be at the ready to
terminate this Agreement, namely you. Don't
you wish you had just clicked through?

Click the Accept button if you agree to the
terms of this License Agreement. Click Decline
if you refuse these terms. Come to think of it,
you're damned if you do and damned if you
don't.

ACCEPT   DECLINE

Nine-Tenths
of the Law

ERIC JAMES STONE

The law offices of Thacker, Ford & Harward were on the upper floors of a downtown high-rise that had mostly escaped the ravages of the zombie troubles. I walked past the attractive, living receptionist and made my way toward a corner office, which I figured would hold one of the better lawyers.

None of the lawyers themselves had escaped infection, of course, because the zombies had deliberately targeted lawyers, judges, and politicians during the initial stages of the plague. But that only made them better lawyers. Contrary to movie stereotype, the typical zombie did not shamble around, arms outstretched, searching for brains to eat, because most zombies had all the brains they needed: The average zombie had an IQ of 182.

Instead of brains, they ate hearts. But nobody's perfect.

The name on the corner office door was Travis Gordon. I walked through the door and saw a gray-haired man sitting at a desk, his skin the usual waxy complexion of a zombie.

After a few moments, Gordon noticed me and looked up. "I didn't hear you come in." His voice was calm. "Considering my door is shut, and I can't smell you or hear your heartbeat, you are either a hallucination, a projection, or a ghost."

I walked to one of the chairs in front of his desk and sat. "Pretty impressive. I am, in fact, a ghost."

"Well, Mr. Ghost, or whatever your name is, the mere fact that you are dead does not excuse you from the rules of civil society. You can't just drop in unannounced. Feel free to make an appointment like anybody else."

"Yeah," I said, "about that . . . You have a living receptionist answering your phone. Very discriminatory of you, by the way. Manifesting to you is pretty easy, you being dead and all. My name's Kyle, by the way. Kyle Petrides. But even if I managed a phone call, she'd probably just hear white noise on the line, which her mind would then interpret as someone whispering words like, 'You're all going to die, get out, Paul is dead,' et cetera, et cetera. So I decided to do a walk-in. Plus, it's kind of an emergency."

"What kind of emergency?"

"Someone's about to haunt my house."

Gordon frowned. "Someone other than you, you mean."

I waved my hand dismissively. "I don't haunt my own house. But from my perspective, having a bunch of living people hanging around, appearing at odd hours, making strange noises and such, that's pretty much a haunting. I want to get an injunction to keep these people out of my house."

"You own it?"

"I did, twenty-one years ago, before I died. But I've been there ever since, and possession's nine-tenths of the law, right?"

"Hmm. There's no precedent for ghosts exercising property rights."

"Eighteen months ago, there were no legal precedents for zombie rights, either. But now . . . conditions are more favorable for ghosts to come out of the closet, so to speak. It's really a matter of civil rights."

Gordon pressed a button on his phone. "Maxine, reschedule my eleven o'clock and hold my calls."

We went to court the next day.

The living people who had bought my house had scrounged up an actual living human lawyer from somewhere. Most people had learned to live with the zombie takeover and even be happy with it—the government ran a lot more efficiently now—but there were still foolish prejudices. And picking this living lawyer was definitely foolish, since Gordon could talk rings around the guy.

"But, Your Honor," the lawyer whined, "my clients have paid good money to purchase the house from the legal owner. This, this ghost shouldn't be allowed to possess my clients' property."

"The owner of record is not necessarily the legal owner, Your Honor," Gordon said smoothly. "Mr. Petrides has been in continuous possession of the property for the past twenty-one years, with a claim adverse to that of the owner of record. Opposing counsel's clients were on notice of Mr. Petrides's possession, since they were aware that the owner of record was willing to sell the house for below market value due to its being haunted. It is not Mr. Petrides's fault that they did not believe in ghosts."

The judge nodded. "I've heard enough. Current law has clearly established that mere death of the physical body does not divest someone's rights. While the law was written with zombies in mind, on its face there is no reason it cannot apply to ghosts as well. There being no legal bar to possession by a ghost, I rule that the property in question belongs to Mr. Petrides."

Two weeks later, the Supreme Court unanimously affirmed the ruling. Justice moved a lot more swiftly now that the zombies controlled the entire process.

I met Gordon in his office for a celebratory drink—although he didn't offer me anything, of course. Not having a body had a lot of disadvantages.

"I imagine that, after this decision, a lot more of your kind will start coming into the open," Gordon said, then took a sip from his brandy. "And if ghosts start asserting their rights to own homes, it's going to cause increased demand for homes, which means increased property values, more construction jobs, and so on. Economically, it makes a lot of sense. I'm sure that's why your case got expedited."

"This was never really about property for me," I said. "It was about legal recognition of ghosts as beings with rights."

"Of course," Gordon said. "We zombies understand. Why do you think we went after the lawyers, politicians, and judges first?"

I nodded. "Interesting thing about those zombie-rights laws you passed. They allow the body to retain civil rights after death, even if the personality controlling the body is completely different. Very convenient."

"Well, of course. Since the virus wiped the old personalities—"

"No, I meant convenient for us ghosts." I walked toward him, and as I got too close he backed away until he reached a wall. "Your body keeps control of your assets no matter who controls your body. Combined with the recent Supreme Court decision that ghosts have a right to possession, it leads to some interesting possibilities. Taking over a human with a soul is tremendously difficult, but all you zombies in positions of wealth and power—well, you've done the hard part already."

I stepped into his body, possessed it, then lifted the glass to my lips and actually tasted something for the first time in decades.

"Like they say, possession is nine-tenths of the law," I said, just in case he could still hear me from inside what was now my head. "I think I'll like being a lawyer."

Scrumptious
Bone Bread

JEFF STRAND

I like live things all right, I s'pose, but when it comes right down to it, don't nothin' compare to dead things. You can do anything you want to dead things. That don't work with live things. I know—I've tried.

Oh, now, don't go gettin' your filthy mind in that kind of gear—that ain't what I mean. No nasty stuff goes on in my place of business. I'm not gonna go so far as to say that it's a *respectable* outfit—I mean, look at all the blood—but there ain't no foul necrophile stuff happenin' on my watch. If you walked inside my shop and waved a crisp new twenty-dollar bill in my face and said, "Tommy, I'll give you this here money for a poke at one of those dead things," do you know what I'd say? I'd say, "Oh, *hell* no," and then I'd take your twenty dollars just to teach you a lesson. That's exactly what I'd do. Cuz when you're three hundred and fifty pounds but in good physical condition, you can just snatch people's money right out of their hand for suggestin' that kind of obscene activity, and there ain't nothin' they can do about it.

I ain't never had an offer of forty bucks. That might change things. But until it happens, ain't no corpse-pokin' in my shop.

Now, there ain't no question that I'm fond of dead things that are already dead. Still, you know what I really like? Makin' dead things. Oh, hell yeah. I'll make dead things all the damn day long. It don't matter what: squirrels, ducks, badgers, turtles, humans, iguanas, elephants, centipedes . . . okay, I lied about the elephants. Not sayin' that I wouldn't make an elephant dead, given the opportunity, but it ain't never happened. Maybe if I moved to Africa or somethin'. As it is, the biggest thing I ever made dead was good ol' Dave Stringer. That was a fine day. I made up a song about it:

> *Makin' dead things*
> *Makin' dead things*
> *Makin' dead things*
> *All the livelong day*
> *Makin' dead things*
> *Makin' dead things*
> *Makin' dead things*
> *Like good ol' Dave*

It ain't "Freebird," but it's pretty catchy. I sing it a lot, or just hum it, dependin' on the social situation, and I change the name when appropriate.

My collection of dead things is about . . . oh, I'd say forty or fifty strong at the moment. It changes pretty regularly but hovers in the forty-to-fifty range. I add new ones, and old ones go too far past their freshness date and get buried or dumped. Some of 'em I leave lyin' around, because there ain't no laws against pluckin' out a centipede's legs, and others I hide under the floorboards, because there *are* laws against pluckin' out a human's legs. And I agree that there should be—I mean, if the world was chock-full of people like me, there'd be no people left, right?

I try to keep my hobby a secret from most folks, but sometimes you've gotta show off. I'd say about six people knew the true extent. It was supposed to be seven, but Nell's response wasn't quite what I expected and I had to make her dead. So when Andy came into my shop, I didn't bother to put away the finger I was whittlin'.

"Hi, Tommy," he said.

"Hi, Andy. Are you needin' any taxidermy services today?"

"Well, in a manner of speaking I suppose I do. I ain't gonna bury the lead: I murdered a man for his bones."

I stopped whittlin' and just stared at him for a minute. Andy's a thin, sickly-lookin' thing whose face would've been right at home in a grainy black-and-white newspaper photograph with the headline MUGGY CREEK SLASHER CAUGHT AT LAST, but I'd been unaware of him ever actin' on those kinds of impulses.

"For real?" I asked.

Andy swallowed some spit and nodded.

"Are you proud of it?"

"Not so much."

"Would you do it again?"

"I'd like to think that I wouldn't."

"Then I s'pose it won't be too hard to clear your conscience about the whole matter. But did I hear you right when you said you killed a man for his bones?"

"Yeah. When I was a kid, my ma and pa, they didn't know many bedtime stories, so sometimes they'd tell me about how my grampa choked on tobacco that one time, and sometimes they'd tell me 'Jack and the Beanstalk.' I loved that damn story. I used to dress up in green clothes and paint myself green and stomp all over the house."

"You painted yourself green?"

"Yeah. I don't mean paint like what you'd use on a house—that stuff don't come off easy—but my sister had been a witch for Halloween and she still had some makeup left so I'd use that. It's okay to wear your sister's makeup when it's a Halloween costume, right? It ain't like I was wearing her mascara."

"I ain't judgin' you," I said. "For all I care, you

could've wore her trainin' bra. But I'm pretty sure the giant in 'Jack and the Beanstalk' wasn't green. I think your ma and pa mixed him up with that Jolly Green Giant who tries to sell you corn and Brussels sprouts."

"Aw, hell."

"That giant sure don't murder nobody. He was always kinda passive and merry."

Andy shifted his weight from one foot to the other, like he had to pay an emergency visit to the outhouse. "That ain't important. Thing is, there's this part in the story where the beanstalk giant says he's gonna grind Jack's bones to make his bread."

I nodded. "Yeah, yeah, I remember that. It was 'Fee fi fo fum, somethin' somethin', somethin' somethin' smell blood,' then the bone bread part."

"What do you think bone bread would taste like?"

"Nasty, I reckon."

"But what if it ain't? What if it's scrumptious? I've gotta admit, when I was a kid I planted every kind of bean there is—string beans, black beans, pinto beans, jelly beans—to try to grow my own beanstalk into the sky. I ain't dumb, I knew that was never gonna really work, but it was fun to play pretend. But it didn't occur to me until this very afternoon that I might wanna try some bone bread."

"So you killed somebody?"

"Yep."

"Somebody who won't be missed?"

"Yeah. A hooker."

"Who?"

"That redhead who plays pool at Jake's."

I sighed with frustration. "Aw, Andy, your brain ain't screwed on right. She's no hooker. She's just a slut. All kinds of people are gonna be lookin' for her."

"But I see people handin' her money all the time!"

"Yeah, 'cause she's damn good at pool. You've opened up a real can of shit here. I don't think I can help you."

"Tommy, no, don't cut me loose yet." He looked really nervous and picked up a snake I'd stuffed the day before. If he broke it, he was buyin' it. "I ain't askin' you to do anything that's morally wrong. I already committed the atrocity, so whatever we do to the body from now on ain't a sin, right?"

"Now, that's just ignorant. You take one killer who shot somebody, and you take another killer who cut off people's arms and legs and called their severed head 'Ma,' which one do you think is gonna be looked at less favorably?"

Andy shrugged. "The one who chopped off the arms and legs, I reckon."

"Hell yeah. So you just take your jolly green ass out of my shop."

I've gotta say, Andy looked so sad when he turned around that my heart just about broke. It was like a little kid who falls in love with a puppy, and the parents say no, you can't have that puppy cuz you left your goldfish out to dry, and the kid is absolutely devastated.

Andy hung his head and he walked real slow and I swear I even heard him sniffle.

"C'mon," I said. "Don't be like that."

"All I ever wanted was a little taste of bone bread. If that makes me a monster, well then . . . growl."

I couldn't do it. I couldn't let the rascal saunter off like that, all mopey and depressed. "All right, all right," I said. "I'll help you, but it's gonna be double my usual hourly rate."

"You charge an hourly rate?" asked Andy. "I thought you charged by project. Taxidermy ain't no hourly-rate kind of business, based on what little I know 'bout it."

"Aw, hell, you got me," I admitted. "My negotiation skills were always crap. Gimme twenty bucks and we'll take care of your problem."

"Done." Andy handed me a sweaty twenty-dollar bill, and I tucked it into my pocket.

"Thanks," I said. "So what exactly is your problem?"

"I can't get her bones out."

"What are you talkin' about?"

"I killed her easy—used my best shovel—but I dunno, maybe it's because I'd just had some of Agatha's barbecue, but I thought the meat would come off the bones easier."

"Maybe you should show me what you done," I said.

Well, Andy took me out to his shed, and there was the girl's body, right there on the ground. He didn't have her on a drop cloth or nothin'. He was just lettin' her seep into the dirt like a complete amateur.

Her head looked like he'd bashed her with that shovel enough to kill her six or seven times—which was obviously more times than he needed to kill her—and various other parts of her were all messed up. It was disgustin'.

"Jesus Christ on a monkey, Andy, what have you been doin' here?"

"Well, I started with her arm, thinkin' I could strip it down to the bone real easy, but that didn't work, so I tried her ribs, and those didn't work either, which is kinda funny since she's such a skinny thing, and then I tried her leg, which I guess wasn't too smart since there was no way the leg was gonna be easier than the arm. I did save some skull pieces, but not enough to make bread."

"What kind of knife did you use?"

"I didn't have a knife. I reckon that could've been part of the problem."

"What the hell did you use?"

Andy avoided eye contact. "Trowel."

"You ain't got no knives in the house?"

"I got some, but I didn't wanna mess 'em up."

"It blows my mind that you could go through with the killin' part yet not buy a decent knife. Do you even want that bone bread? You do know that you're gonna pay me more than the cost of a knife, right?"

"The truth is, I got so sick when I got to the leg part that I couldn't handle it no more, and I was hopin' that you'd do the work. I'd give you a loaf of the bone bread."

Like I said earlier (you can look back if you don't believe me) I ain't crap when it comes to negotiatin'. And for all I knew, bone bread might be a thousand times better than sourdough.

"All right," I said. "Go get your biggest pot."

Andy looked like he felt real dumb when I explained that we were going to boil the slut, and he was right to feel that way. Of *course* you would boil a body to make the flesh easier to get off!

We dragged in some firewood, and we built a fire right there in Andy's shed. We did a lot of coughin' from the smoke, but if you're gonna boil a corpse, you can't have the door open so just anybody can look in and wonder what you're doin'. Andy's biggest pot wasn't near big enough to do the job right, so we used an axe to chop her arm into three pieces and dropped 'em in.

"How long is this gonna take?" Andy asked.

"A while."

"Damn."

It took even longer than a while, but we boiled and boiled and kept adding new pieces, and eventually we had ourselves a nice pile of human bones. Andy complained that I didn't clean them all well enough ("There's still meat on that one! I ain't no cannibal!") but I told him to hush up.

"Where's your grinder?" I asked.

"Grinder?"

"How the hell are you gonna grind her bones to make bread if you ain't got a grinder?"

"Don't get all annoyed with me," said Andy. "I didn't even have a knife, so if you're surprised that I ain't got a grinder, then you ain't no genius either!"

He had a point, but I couldn't help bein' frustrated at his lack of preparation, considerin' that he'd been a fan of "Jack and the Beanstalk" since he was a little kid. You've gotta plan these things out. I ain't gonna lie, my first sexual experience was a mess, but I had at least worked out the steps in the process, and I knew how much money to bring, and I had a rubber from a reputable manufacturing company, and I had the right-size pliers. Andy's behavior was just flat-out ridiculous.

"I have never in my life encountered somebody who would commit evil with such piss-poor planning," I said. "You can finish this off yourself."

"I don't think so," said Andy with a hint of a smile. "You're an accessory now, so I reckon if you know what's good for you, you'll help me do whatever it is I ask of you, or I may find myself with a hankerin' to get the law involved."

So I killed him.

It don't take much to kill a skinny thing like Andy. I just sorta smushed my hands together over his head, gave it a little twist, and he was done. After he dropped to the ground I sat on him. He wasn't gonna eat no bone bread 'cept in hell. Or on the floor, if I shoved some in his mouth, which I probably wouldn't.

I never liked that fairy tale, cuz Jack was so god-damn stupid that I wanted to strangle him, and once you've got a goose that lays golden eggs, what kind of jackass would go back for a harp? But there was a nice pile of bones there, and I've gotta confess that Andy had got my curiosity flowin'.

What if bone bread was delicious?

What if it made you stronger?

What if it made you live longer, because of some sort of energy-absorbin' properties?

I picked up one of his hammers and I smashed those bones. I smashed 'em for hours, it felt like. It wasn't easy, not at all, but I've got fine upper-arm strength and by the end of the process I'd bashed those bones into a nice white powder. Well, there were a lot of bone shards in that powder, and quite a few pieces that were chunkier than I would've liked, and the marrow kept it from lookin' anything like flour, but overall, not a bad job.

I scooped it all into a garbage bag and carried it home. Andy's wife wouldn't notice he was missin' for at least a couple of days, and his work would've been surprised if he *did* show up, so I had time to deal with that later.

Though it may surprise you to hear this, I ain't no baker. I figured the fairy tale was kind of vague as to the actual process used by the giant to make his bread, so I just used some Pillsbury premade croissant dough—the kind that comes in that cardboard can. I popped it open, laid the triangles of dough out on a baking sheet, and then mixed in the bone powder as well as I could.

I burnt the first batch and threw 'em away.

The second batch looked fine, and after they cooled down, I buttered up the first one and ate it. The bone shards tickled on the way down, but hand on my heart I ain't lyin' when I say that it was the best bread I'd eaten in my entire life.

I finished off the rest of 'em and then rushed off to the store to buy more dough.

Andy was a goddamn genius.

I'm a man who can eat a frightening amount when he sets his mind to it, and if I told you how many bone rolls I had that day, you'd gasp and your eyes would bug out of your head and you'd say somethin' like "*Whoa!*"

Funny thing is, they weren't just tasty, but I felt stronger after I ate 'em. I mean, my stomach hurt a little, and the trip to the outhouse was kinda ghastly, yet it was like I had the redhead's strength in addition to my own.

I went out and played a game of pool, and there was a shot where I just know I would've scratched, but I didn't. No, I didn't win the game—it's hard for me to squeeze between the two billiard tables at the bar, which limits some of my options for takin' shots—but I didn't lose as bad as I normally do.

Well, you know damn well that I boiled Andy for his bones. When his wife came out to the shed to bitch at him, I used his shovel and I bashed her as well.

I'd been wastin' all this time doin' taxidermy when I should've been bakin' bone bread.

Every time I ate another piece, I could feel myself growin' more powerful. I choked on the bone shards at least once per batch, and I admittedly did cough up some blood, and I was glad that the outhouse was too deep to see what colors might be down there, but I felt almost invincible!

By the time I had the skeletons of seven more citizens in my tummy, I knew that I was practically a superhero. I could never die. I was as strong as that damn giant on the beanstalk.

That's why I'm writin' this. Every morning at exactly ten o'clock the train comes through Dunner Street, haulin' whatever it is trains haul these days. I'm gonna stand right there in the middle of the tracks, and that train is gonna collide with my superhuman body, and that son of a bitch is goin' right off the track.

I've always wanted to watch a train bounce off me.

I have no intention of leavin' you hangin' with an incomplete narrative, so I've got this whole story in my pocket so that as soon as the train hits me I can write down my thoughts, to make sure they're as accurate as possible.

I'll let you know how it all turns out.

Let That Be
a Lesson to You

MARK ONSPAUGH

The box from Amazon seemed innocuous enough.

Perhaps it seemed heavier than I expected? I chalked this up to nerves rather than actual weight.

I willed myself to stop trembling and tore open the package.

I admit I was disappointed.

Inside was not the musty, leather-bound tome I expected, or better yet, a stinking and greasy volume bound in the skins of unconsecrated orphans and written in virgins' blood . . . Yes! And while we're at it, penned between fits of howling self-mutilation by some mad monk hidden deep in a cave or one of the subbasements of the Vatican.

Instead, it was a trade paperback, the cover in

bright yellows, reds and blues and dominated by a large, horned silhouette. The cover seemed to shout at me.

SO, YOU WANT TO BE A DEMONOLOGIST?

Contains all the material previously published in
THE END OF LIGHT: TEXTS OF THE
HELLSPAWN by Allakash the Unclean and
Morvled the Irredeemable, and later updated by
St. Vitus of Philadelphia. Reinterpreted and reimagined
by Dr. Beverly Scott, PhD, author of *The Werewolves
of Wuthering Heights; When, Wendigo?; The Easter
Bunny Conspiracy;* and *A Girl's Guide to Demons,
Devils, Imps, and Fallen Angels.*

I have never been a scholar, not even a good student. The book, even with its merry tone and friendly graphics, daunted me.

But it was negligence that had put me in this predicament. That and an almost prideful embrace of my ignorance.

Stupid, stupid.

I sniffed the binding. It was ordinary glue, not a trace of virgin's tears or baby fat. How could I take such a book seriously?

But what choice did I have?

Knowing that it would return from feeding at any time, I anxiously began to skim . . .

HORNED HINT #3: PREPARATION PREVENTS EVISCERATION!

Make sure the entity you plan to invoke knows your language! Curt Arbogast of Ohio foolishly called up J'kashk, an Assyrian demon that only understands Akkadian. While Curt screamed binding spells that were so much gibberish to J'kashk, the demon helped himself to Curt's bone marrow. And consider Sally Boone of Kentucky. She was in such a rush to sic AakaaKaal the Disemboweler on her husband that she improperly conjugated the Mesopotamian verb "ja'faal" ("slow and painful removal of intestines"). Sally's two-timing husband, Hoyt, came home to find *her* entrails decorating the Christmas tree—ouch!

That was no help at all. I skipped past chapters on "making lavish robes on a budget" and "choosing an intimidating sorcerer name." I didn't need a name, I needed a solution. The proverbial beast was already out of the barn.

BARBED TALE #11: IF YOU THINK YOUR WISH IS ALL FIGURED OUT, THINK AGAIN!

Ray Cooper of New York wished for all his bodily waste to be converted to gold, platinum and diamonds. Unfortunately, he never specified that such transmogrification take place *outside* his body. After excruciating obstructive constipation and a bloody death, his "assets" were seized by the IRS, leaving his heirs penniless and the butt of countless jokes.

That one actually made me wince and laugh at the same time. I felt guilty and resolved to be more serious about the whole thing. This just made me nervous and I began to wheeze, my asthma aggravated by the dusty attic. I used my inhaler and tried to think calming thoughts.

My problem, of course, was the Lks'spunn Spell of Binding. Perhaps Morvled had written a chapter on that . . .

I looked in the index and found: *binding . . . . . . 27, 102.*

Excited and hopeful, I thumbed back to page 27.

HORNED HINT #32 : FORGET HOCUS-POCUS, FOCUS!

The second your demon appears it will try to scare you into inaction or engage you in conversation. *Don't be distracted, necromancer!* Remember: That circle of virgin's blood is drying and will soon be useless. And that pentagram of martyred-nun ashes? It might blow away at any minute, rendering you vulnerable! Intone the Spell of Binding, Oath of Fealty or Chant of Subservience IMMEDIATELY. And if you have a sore throat, postpone! Better to put off your boss's flensing by imps than have your voice crap out and those chortling little flayers turn on *you.*

That did me no good, and the reference on page 102 was an equally useless one about tanning human skin for bookbinding, using common items from the kitchen.

I glanced at my watch and gasped. I had been at this for over an hour and had learned nothing. With a whimper I tried to browse more quickly, but my hands grew clumsy and I dropped the book. The cursed thing punched through the pink attic insulation and landed with a dull thud in the living room.

I held my breath . . . my testicles drew up tight against me.

Tok tok tok tok.

It was here!

It looked down at the book, then looked up, saw me and grinned.

In the kitchen I fetch a large metal bowl from the cupboard. There is a pet carrier on the counter, filled with kittens from the shelter. I remove three and pull their heads off, my tears making it difficult to see. Over the tiny, furry heads I pour a mixture of cinnamon and cardamom.

In a playpen is a tiny child with dark skin and a cleft palate. He is the sort of waif they advertise in the *Times* Sunday magazine, back near the crossword puzzle and ads for glittering town houses overlooking the river.

I cut his throat in the ritualistic way I have been

taught and pour his steaming blood over the contents of the bowl.

Weeping like a child, I take the bowl up to where it waits.

Where *she* waits.

I have heard she was a great beauty once. She was known by one name and her face adorned magazine covers and movie posters.

Now time and endless surgical procedures have given her the aspect of a ventriloquist dummy, her tanned flesh pulled taut in a parody of youth, an obscenity that lolls in silk and too much perfume.

"Astaroth," she purrs . . .

How I hate the way she says my name!

"Asty," she says, continuing, "hurry up with your snack! Mmmmm . . . Mama wants loving."

My gorge rises as she reveals her sex to me. I can hardly taste the bloody kitten heads.

She says the Word of Power and my member, forked and warty and barbed, rises in answer to her command.

You want to know where hell really is, my brethren?

It's in a tacky McMansion in Bel Air, the one with the soulless reproduction of Michelangelo's *David* out front.

Her lacquered talons beckon and I try to think of happier times, when I was deflowering convents or tearing the livers from saints.

Gods, I wish I had a condom.

Mint in Box

MIKE BARON

For the fourth time that morning, Jim Lovaas logged on to eBay and typed in "Varley Variant Action Figure." The screen coughed up bubkes. With a cluck of disgust, Lovaas pushed himself away from the screen, knocking over his talking Freddy Krueger doll. Carefully, he picked up the two-foot box and repositioned it on the shelf next to the Alien variants. A computer consultant, Lovaas lived in a three-room apartment in West Hollywood, every available surface filled with his collection of mint-in-box action figures. The walls were covered with posters from his favorite movies: *Terminator, Aliens, A Nightmare on Elm Street, The Ring, The Fantastic Shrinking Man.*

One room, "the guest room," was completely filled, floor to ceiling, with Lovaas's comic book collection. The rest of the house was filled with action figures.

His computer room looked like an alien invasion, with monsters and big-busted women standing shoulder to shoulder on shelving that covered every wall, on the windowsills, on top of the computer itself, and on the floor. Lovaas didn't try to collect every action figure. That way led to madness. He specialized in the grotesque, the gory, the horrific. Naturally, this encompassed most McFarlane toys. It went without saying he had every Stan Winston.

But one prize eluded him: the rare iridescent-skin variant of the demon Varley, from Dal Lazarus's cult classic *The Skin Eaters.*

Even among Hollywood legends, Dal Lazarus stood alone, a little off to the side in the wing that housed Fatty Arbuckle, the Manson family, the Black Dahlia, and Bob Crane. Not those happy fairy tales purveyed by *People.* Dal Lazarus was a dark visionary who blew out of the Midwest like a tornado, directing three of the most original, disturbing horror films ever made, before blowing out his brains.

First came *Deadly Doll,* forever establishing Alicia Folds as a tragic beauty, crushed by her own publicity. She committed suicide halfway through her next film. Next came *The Fantastic Shrinking Man,* a vision so disturbing it was screened for al-Qaeda prisoners in Guantánamo to make them talk. Finally, his masterpiece, the only one of his films to enjoy major studio backing, *The Skin Eaters.*

With *The Skin Eaters* came the whole Hollywood

hoopla machine. Articles in *Premiere* and *Fangoria*. Appearances at conventions. Most significantly, the merchandising. *The Skin Eaters* did not lend itself to fast food premiums, but it was tailor-made for the upscale collectors' market. The publicity-shy Lazarus put up with most of the hoopla in a churlish manner. But when Zombie Toys approached him about the *Skin Eater* figures, he embraced them enthusiastically.

A talented sculptor and designer, Lazarus designed the Varley figure himself. The basic eight-inch Varley was disturbing enough. But the variant version, packed one to one thousand, sported an iridescent skin that resembled an oil slick and immediately became the most sought-after collectible on the market. Lazarus added his own blood to the poly-mix.

With proceeds from his first film Lazarus purchased a mansion in Thousand Oaks, California, and would spend day after day basting in the sun, perfecting his tan. He was diagnosed with an incurable form of skin cancer on the very day *The Skin Eaters* premiered. Two months after the film was released, Lazarus killed himself. There were rumors of AIDS. Could you get AIDS from handling a plastic action figure? As long as the figure remained MIB—mint in box—no danger. Ten thousand fans lined up to pay their respects at his funeral. It was a closed-casket ceremony, and speculation ran amok that Lazarus was pulling off some kind of elaborate hoax. Lazarus sightings began the day after the funeral. The coroner's report was sealed.

Rumor ruled. Nonbelievers said he died from sucking on a ten-gauge.

The funeral was preceded by a private ceremony for Lazarus's close friends, of whom there were few. The producer Bob Fiffe made an unexpected and unwelcome appearance. Fiffe had been one of Lazarus's early champions, had produced *Deadly Doll*. But as so often happens in Hollywood, they had a falling-out over money, over art, over drugs, over a woman, and ceased speaking to one another. Although Fiffe was a model of probity in print, he couldn't resist a parting shot. On the way out of the nondenominational chapel, an enterprising reporter stuck a mike in his face.

"Son of a bitch still owes me two hundred and fifty thousand dollars," Fiffe replied, poker-faced. The reporter fluffed out his story with background: Both Fiffe and Lazarus came from the Midwest. Both were only children. But whereas Fiffe was aggressively hetero Lazarus was flamboyantly gay.

Along with thousands of others, Lovaas stood in the sweltering sun for two hours waiting his turn to file past the casket and pick up a copy of the program. Lovaas would have pocketed several hundred, but a thug in sunglasses and suit stood by the table with his arms crossed rumbling, "One to a customer."

Few actions are more successful in ensuring fame than early death. James Dean. Brandon Lee. Dal Lazarus.

The price of the *regular* Varley figure shot up to five hundred bucks. The variant? Fuggedaboudit. May as well seek the Philosopher's Stone.

Lovaas was a man obsessed. He was a sneaky son of a bitch, too. He advertised on the Internet, haunted discount houses, attended every con. But Lovaas also knew there were people who, through no fault of their own, had come into possession of those figures with no idea of their worth. He advertised in shoppers, country gazettes, and *AARP Magazine*. He advertised in antique newsletters, and especially homespun journals for the elderly, like *RV World* and *Pensioner*. One day he received a letter from Olathe, Kansas. It was written in shaky ballpoint script on lavender notepaper.

> *Dear Mr. Lovaas: I am retiring after operating our hobby shop for over fifty years. My late husband, Abner, God rest his soul, purchased a consignment of toys from Zombie shortly before he passed on. What with the funeral and all, I didn't get around to looking at that shipment until last week. I believe I have the toys you are looking for. It says Varley on the package, and it has an unpleasant skin like an oil slick. I have two of them. Are you interested in looking at them and perhaps making me an offer?*
>
> *Yours sincerely,*
> *Mrs. Abner (Amelia) Cummings*

The dumb bitch didn't even include her phone number. It took Lovaas fifteen seconds to find it on Whowhere? and five seconds to dial the number.

"Cummings Curios and Collectibles," said a quavering voice.

"Mrs. Cummings? This is Jim Lovaas. I wrote you about the Varley action figures."

"Oh, those awful little dolls. I don't know what to say, Mr. Lovaas. I hesitate to ask full retail . . ."

"I'll give you fifty dollars apiece, a hundred for both."

"Well, Mr. Lovaas, they only retail for twenty-four ninety-five, I really don't feel I should take advantage of you—"

"Mrs. Cummings, I insist. I'd like to FedEx you a check overnight. If you would be so kind as to ship the action figures to me as soon as you get the check, overnight, I'll be happy to pay all expenses."

"Well, Mr. Lovaas, I don't know."

What don't you know, you dumb bitch? Lovaas felt like screaming. "Mrs. Cummings, if you insist, I'll only pay you fifty dollars for both."

"Well, I don't deny I could use the money, what with all the bills Mr. Cummings left . . ."

Finally, Mrs. Cummings caved. Lovaas FedExed her a check. Two days later, he met the FedEx guy in the lobby of his apartment building, twitching like a nicotine addict. Gripping the large cardboard box as if it were a child, he ran up the three exterior flights of stairs to his unit, went inside, locked the door, and took the phone off the hook. Using his *Blade* Glaive, he sliced through the packing tape, threw Styrofoam pellets around the room, and extracted two rectangular display units, each constructed of hard, clear polymer, each containing an iridescent-skin Varley. No student of art was more intent. Lovaas crouched on the floor in his overcrowded living room, examining the creature in the sunlight streaming through the window.

Even held perfectly still, the skin of each Varley seemed to writhe in its box, like a psychedelic light show. Lovaas couldn't believe his luck. You could spend your whole life looking for a variant Varley without finding one. And he had two! One to remove and play with, one MIB to save for a rainy day! If he never added another item to his collection, his life would be complete.

Lovaas held the plastic box under the light. That skin. It shimmered and pulsed like a thing alive. Lovaas got the impression that if he pressed directly on the skin with his finger, it would radiate pulsating rings of color. No question! Heart beating, fully aware that he was puncturing its MIB status, not caring because he had *two!*, Lovaas placed his *Blade* Glaive against the hard plastic and made the first cut.

The screams emanating from Lovaas's apartment were finally too much, even for West Hollywood. His next-door neighbor, an al-Qaeda sleeper agent named Farook Ahmet, phoned 911. "Sounds like they are killing someone over there!" Two cops arrived in seven minutes. Ahmet allowed as he had never met his neighbor. He had never met any of his neighbors. That's the way he liked it.

The cops pounded on Lovaas's door. It opened to the length of its chain and a pleasant-faced middle-aged man, with jet-black hair and a very healthy tan, smiled out at them. "How can I help you, officers?"

"We heard reports of screaming. We'd like to look around."

The man arched his elegant eyebrows, then frowned in understanding. "Oh, I am so sorry! I was watching one of my horror DVDs and I'm afraid I got a little carried away with the volume. Of course you can come in. Of course you can look around."

The police entered and looked around. The place was jammed with toys and comics, but what the hell. West Hollywood. No signs of violence. The resident, who identified himself as James Lovaas and provided papers to that effect, released the mute button on his flat-screen television and the characters in the movie began to scream.

One cop held his hands up. "Okay. Okay! Turn it down, will ya? And be a little considerate of your neighbors."

"I will, and again, I'm very sorry, officers."

On the way out the door, one of the cops stopped and turned. "What the hell is that you're watching, Mr. Lovaas?"

"*The Skin Eaters,* have you seen it? It is absolutely the scariest movie made in this town since *The Exorcist.*"

"No thanks. We see enough of that on the job."

And so, peace. Or so it seemed. Lovaas's neighbors continued to come and go without glimpsing the reclusive computer programmer.

A week later, Bob Fiffe was driving back to California after receiving an honorary doctorate at Shimer College in Illinois, where he had matriculated without graduating. Since producing the multi–Academy Award–winning *The Polecat,* Fiffe had found himself the recipient of all manner of invitation. Especially from the alumni associations of any institute of higher learning with which he'd been associated, however remotely. If he had once crashed at a student's house, the college claimed him as its own.

Fiffe was driving solo in his Porsche Carrera when he chanced to pass through Olathe, Kansas, the hometown of Dal Lazarus. Not many people knew this. Lazarus had sworn him to secrecy the night he'd told him.

"Bob, if they find out I'm from Olathe, I'll die. I'll just die."

So Bob had never told. There he was, creeping down Main Street enjoying the look of envy on the yokels' faces, when he nearly ran a red light.

"Cummings Curios and Collectibles!" he exploded. He was among a handful of people who knew Lazarus's real name. Amazingly, there was an empty parking spot directly in front of the little shop. No parking meter. The simple joys of flyover country.

As a couple preadolescent boys on stunt bikes stopped to admire his car, Fiffe pushed open the door to the shop. A little bell jingled. The interior was crammed to the rafters with flea market junk—thousands upon thousands of blue plastic Smurfs, Disney variants, Barbie dolls, jigsaw puzzles, obsolete Erector Sets, rock-hard Play-Doh, Davy Crockett caps, toy guns with dangerous black nozzles.

A wizened homunculus topped with a Dairy Queen swirl of blue hair emerged from the back room. "Can I help you?" she asked in a quavering voice.

Like all Hollywood types, Fiffe had a weakness for toys. "Just browsing," he said. Then his eye caught the wire basket toward the rear, filled with the unmistakable shape of plastic action figures, MIB.

"You just let me know if I can help," the little old lady said, making her way slowly to the front. Fiffe made a beeline for the basket. Right on top, the brilliant back-card advertising of Zombie Toys. Could it be? Was it possible? High up on the food chain as he was, even Fiffe was aware of the incredible market for *Skin Eater* action figures. He picked up the top box and turned it over.

At first his eyes refused to register what he saw. The light was dim. He walked over to where a stray ray fell through a skylight. He held it close to his face. And nearly gagged.

Inside, in detail so perfect you could have sworn it had been shrunk, was the figure of a man who had been skinned alive. Enough flesh remained around his eyes and scalp to give a semblance of resemblance. The rest was all oozing subderma, exposed nerves, and agony. LOVAAS THE VICTIM, it said on the box. Fighting an urge to puke, Fiffe placed the box back in the barrel and headed for the door. Seconds later, the distinctive whine of a high-performance flat six faded down the street.

The man with the jet-black hair and handsome tan stepped out of the back room wearing a full-length silk robe with the logo from *Deadly Doll* on the breast and on the back.

"Is he gone?" he asked.

"He's gone, Dal," his mother replied. "I don't know what upset him so much. Do you know him?"

"Know him? I still owe him two hundred and fifty large!"

The Great Zombie Invasion of 1979

J. G. FAHERTY

It was Elmer Dinkley who first spotted the zombies exiting the woods and heading across Charlie Muckler's cow pasture.

He knew right away what he was seeing. After all, it'd only been a couple of days since he and Selma had taken their monthly ride into Haddysville to do the shopping. While there, they'd caught the afternoon picture show at the Rialto. It'd been one of those scary movies Selma liked so much, filled with walking dead people who ate brains and sounded a lot like Selma's cousin Jimmy Ray, the one with the weird head and the goofy eyes.

"Holy Christ on a stick," Elmer said. "Charlie, looks like you got more'n cows in your field."

Charlie Muckler came to the porch door, holding two cans of ice-cold beer in his hands. "What's that you said?"

"Git your gun, you damn fool!" Elmer shouted, rising from his chair. "It's goddamn zombies, like in that movie I was tellin' you about."

"I think you got zombies on the brain," Charlie said, but he put the beers down and joined Elmer at the porch railing.

"Lookit how they're walkin', all stupid-like." Elmer pointed to where more of the undead were emerging from the trees.

"Mebbe they's just drunk." Charlie squinted his eyes, then remembered the glasses tucked into the top pocket of his stained overalls. He put them on and then frowned. "They don't look right, do they?"

"I told ya. Get the guns. You gotta shoot 'em in the head if you wanna kill 'em."

"Let's just make sure 'fore we start killin' folks. Last thing I need is Roy Biggins haulin' my ass off to jail 'cause you thought you saw monsters."

"Jumpin' Jesus! I forgot about Roy. We gotta let him know. Delbert!" Elmer raised his voice, calling for his eldest son.

"Yeah, Pa?" Delbert came out of the barn, struggling to button his shirt. Charlie's boy, Nate, tagged close behind, zipping up his jeans. Ordinarily, Elmer would've given the boys hell for messin' with the livestock, but there was no time for that.

"You 'n' Nate gotta get Sheriff Roy and bring him out here fast's you can. We got zombies!"

"Huh?"

"Elmer, I think we oughtta—"

"Shut up and take another look," Elmer said, cutting off Charlie midsentence.

Charlie did, and let out a startled gasp. Although the strangers were still several hundred yards away, there was no disguising their torn clothing or the suspicious dark stains on their shirts and pants.

"Sonuvawhore."

"Now you believe me?" Elmer didn't wait for an answer. "Delbert, tell Roy we'll try to hold 'em off long's we can."

"You want us to run all the way into town?" Delbert asked.

"Yes, and hurry your asses, 'less you want those brain eaters to catch you."

"What if there's more in the woods?" Nate asked, his face so pale his freckles stood out like chicken shit on snow.

"Dammit, boy, lookit how slow they are," Charlie answered. "You kin run faster than them with one leg. Now git!"

The two boys took off down the dirt driveway, already moving at full speed by the time they went past Charlie's ancient Ford pickup.

"I'll git the guns."

"Bring more beer, too," Elmer said, opening a can.

"Once we start shootin', we ain't gonna have time to get it."

"Smart thinkin'."

"That's why I'm the brains around here," Elmer muttered to himself as he watched the zombies, which by then were close enough that he could make out their features.

Of the thirty or so shambling, stumbling corpses that had come out of the woods, all but a handful were covered in blood. Although he couldn't hear them, Elmer saw their mouths moving, and in his head he heard the gibberish noises the monsters in the movie had made as they shuffled through the streets, searching for human brains. Just like those movie creatures, the zombies in Charlie's field walked like they were still learning to use their feet. The lumps and bumps in the pasture, hardened by several nights of autumn frost, seemed especially troublesome. Every once in a while one of the corpses would trip and fall, and several leaned on each other for support, like drunken sailors after shore leave.

Covered in dirt, with torn clothing and mussed-up hair, they could be easily pictured digging themselves out of their graves and attacking unsuspecting people in their houses. Elmer wondered how many of his friends were already dead or turned into monsters, and if he'd have to put them down, too.

"Ain't gonna catch me by surprise," he said, tossing the empty beer can into the yard, where it joined dozens of its relatives. "No dirty zombie's gonna eat my brains."

The screen door slammed open as Charlie shouldered through, his arms filled with an assortment of battered, rusty rifles and shotguns. Boxes of ammunition bulged in his pocket.

"Which one you want?" he asked, dropping the guns between the two rocking chairs.

"Start with the rifles," Elmer said. "Remember, you gotta hit the head, or else they's just gonna get up again. We'll save the shotguns for the close-up work."

"Gotcha." Charlie handed over a long-barreled .30–06 rifle.

"Hey, ain't this my gun?"

"Yeah." Charlie loaded a clip into a vintage Browning automatic rifle he'd snuck into the States after the Korean War. "You left it here t'other day when we was jackin' those deer."

Elmer paused in loading his gun and stared at Charlie. It was no secret the other man had been after Elmer's Remington since the day he'd seen it in Elmer's truck back in '68. In fact, he'd tried to steal it twice before. For a moment, Elmer considered putting a bullet in Charlie's head.

I could always say he turned into a zombie and I had to do it. Then he remembered the two dozen or so real zombies that by then were halfway across the pasture. He needed Charlie's help.

I'll deal with him later. Maybe next time we're hunt-

*ing he'll have one of them "unfortunate" accidents they's
always talkin' 'bout in the newspapers.*

"Lookit their faces."

Lost in his thoughts, it took Elmer a moment to
understand what Charlie was talking about. Then he
noticed how pale all the dead people were and he laughed.

"What'd you expect, you moron? They's dead! Shit,
looks like some of 'em is starting to go green already."

"They's gettin' closer." Charlie was nervously fin-
gering his rifle.

"Yep. I think we got just enough time for 'nother
beer before we gotta start shootin'."

"Holy mutherfucking moly, I fergot the beer!"
Charlie set his gun down and hurried back inside.

"I swear," Elmer called after him, "you'd forget your
goddamned ass if wasn't stuck to your legs."

Charlie returned with a large bucket piled high
with beer cans. "Yeah? Well, I ain't the one that couldn't
finish fifth grade."

Pulling the tab on a Falstaff, Elmer glared at his
longtime friend. "I coulda finished if I'd wanted to. Jes
so happened I had better things to do."

"Like what? Git drunk with your daddy?" Charlie
snorted laughter and beer foam.

"No, mister funny man. I had me some big plans
back then. Coulda made me some money, if anyone'd
listened."

"Yeah? Well, now the only thing you can write is
your name, and you can't read worth a shit."

"Readin' and writin' ain't important. Hell, Einstein couldn't read or write, you know."

"Really?"

Elmer gulped down more beer and belched. "Sure as shit. And he's so famous they put his face on posters now."

"Damn."

"That's right. It's ideas that's important, and I got a million of 'em. You stick with me, we're gonna be rich someday, too."

"Just like that Einstone fella?"

"Richer." Elmer pointed at the zombies, who were less than two hundred yards away by then. "You see them fuckers? Think how famous we're gonna be when people find out we killed 'em all and saved the town. We're gonna be goddamn *heroes*. Prob'ly get to meet the president."

Afraid Charlie might ask him who the current president was, Elmer finished off his beer and tossed the can over the rail, then waved his gun at the zombies.

"Hey, you fuckers! Get ready to taste hot lead!"

To his surprise, several of the zombies reacted, pointing at him and waving their arms.

"Shit," Charlie said. "They seen us."

Noises reached them from across the field, garbled sounds and words like when Gladys got the phone lines mixed together and all you heard was static and pieces of different conversations.

"What are they sayin'?" Charlie asked.

"Beats the shit outta me. I don't speak zombie." That set them both to laughing. Elmer opened another beer, placed it on the railing, and raised his gun. "You ready?"

Charlie nodded and knelt on the warped planks of the porch, using the railing to support his rifle. "Ready."

Elmer fired a round and one of the zombies, a fat man in a bloodied suit, went down, his head exploding like a rotten tomato.

"Gotcha, motherfucker!" He could barely hear his own shout over the ringing in his ears from the gun's explosive report. Another blast sounded, making him jump, and Charlie let out a war cry as a second zombie tumbled over.

"Wahoo! I got one!"

Elmer swallowed a mouthful of beer and then fired again, sending a third zombie to the ground. This time, the others finally reacted. Several of them stopped walking, while others frantically waved their arms back and forth. All of them were making their strange zombie sounds.

"It's like they's tryin' to talk," Charlie said as he fired again. The bullet caught a tall man in the arm and spun him around. He fell but almost immediately got to his knees and started crawling in the opposite direction.

Elmer threw his empty can at Charlie.

"Ow! What was that for?"

"The head, dummy. I told you, ya gotta hit the head or they don't die."

"I'll git him this time." Charlie fired another shot, and the injured zombie collapsed, red goo spraying from its shattered skull.

Elmer's next shot went wide, and he cursed. "Now you got me all messed up."

"Sorry."

Taking careful aim, Elmer sighted in on a skinny woman wearing tan pants and a matching jacket. Except for the grave dirt on her face and in her hair, and the bloodstains on her shirt, she might've been pretty. Even from this far away, he could tell she had nice titties. He pulled the trigger and had time to see a black hole appear in her forehead before she fell.

"Got the bitch that time."

Charlie dropped another and then paused. "How come I don't recognize none of them? If they's coming from the graveyard, shouldn't we know 'em?"

"You know everybody buried in the graveyard? Besides, how do we know where they came from? Could be from another town, or maybe some kinda secret military base. That's what happened in the movie I saw."

"They sure is scared now. Lookit 'em run!"

Elmer fired two more times and a fat zombie lady with a big purse tumbled over. Many of the zombies were moving in different directions. Some had even turned and were heading back to the woods. "Yup.

Guess they ain't all stupid. We better shoot faster, or some might get away. Then they'll just make more."

Charlie's gun went off three times, and two zombies fell. Elmer took two more down, aiming for the ones running away. Only a few were still moving forward, screaming their gibberish as if someone alive could understand it.

The two men paused to reload, and Charlie asked how the zombies make other zombies.

"All they gotta do is bite you," Elmer said after chugging down another beer. "You get all infected, and then you die. Couple hours later, you wake up again like them." He pulled the trigger and what had once been a young boy went down, the left side of its skull blown away. A heavyset female zombie went to its knees next to the little one and fell on top of it.

"Damn," said Charlie. "They even eat their own kind."

"They're worse than animals," Elmer agreed. "How many are left?"

Charlie put his gun down and counted, folding over a finger for each one. "One, two, three, four . . ." When he reached ten, he made a mark on the railing with his fingernail and then opened his hands again. "One, two . . . two plus ten is twelve."

"They's almost out of range. We're gonna have to go after 'em with the truck. Grab the shotguns." Elmer set his rifle down and picked up the beer bucket.

Two minutes later they were bumping across the

pasture, Charlie hootin' and hollerin' behind the wheel, Elmer in the pickup's bed, a double-barreled shotgun loaded with double-aught buckshot under one arm. With his other hand, he was alternately hanging on to the open cab window and drinking a beer.

"Here comes number one!" Charlie shouted, pulling up alongside an old woman who was trying to run in high heels.

Shows how stupid they are, Elmer thought as he dropped his beer and raised the shotgun.

"*Pomoshh!*" the zombie shouted. Bruises and bloody cuts covered her dead flesh.

Elmer pulled the trigger and the monster's face disappeared in an explosion of red.

"Wheeha!" Elmer hollered, then had to drop the gun and hang on with both hands as Charlie wheeled the truck around in a long, skidding slide and headed after another. The shotgun went off, blowing a four-inch hole in the rusted side panel of the bed.

"Watch out, you fuckin' moron!" Elmer pounded on the roof of the truck. "You're gonna get me kilt."

"Sorry!"

Elmer reloaded the shotgun, feeling a strong temptation to put a round into the back of Charlie's head, except that would probably just lead to the truck overturning. With a sigh, he grabbed his beer, which was rolling around and spraying foam all over the bed of the pickup. After sucking down the last remnants, he banged the empty on the roof.

"Pass me another!"

He grabbed the beer from Charlie and then dropped it as the truck approached another corpse, this one a middle-aged man wearing his burial suit.

"Time to die for good, motherfucker!" Elmer brought the shotgun up as Charlie slowed the truck.

"Net pozhalujjsta! Net—"

The rest of the zombie's garbled words disappeared as heavy buckshot tore its face away, sending skin, bone, and brains across the dark soil. In the cab, Charlie whooped again and threw an empty can at the headless body.

"Head for the trees," Elmer called out. "We'll get the furthest ones first and then come back for the others."

Charlie gave him the thumbs-up and sent the truck bouncing down a row. Elmer opened his beer, laughing as the highly shaken can sprayed foam across the top of the truck and through the back window.

"Watch it!" Charlie let go of the wheel and wiped at his sopping neck with both hands, flinging beer suds everywhere.

"Jesus, look out!" Elmer made a grab for the edge of the truck bed as the old pickup hit a rut and slewed sideways, but it was too late. A second bounce pitched him out of the truck, his gun and beer close behind.

He hit the ground hard enough to knock his breath away, could only watch as bald tires crunched over dead grass and semifrozen soil inches from his legs. Then the truck was past him, skewing wildly from side to side as Charlie fought to get control. Elmer tried to call out, but all his lungs produced was a raspy croak.

"Son of a bitch," he muttered, each word accompanied by a wheezing noise. He got to his knees and picked up his beer, figuring a cold drink would ease his tight chest.

Movement to one side caught his eye, and he looked up to see a man standing not five feet away.

Not a man! A zombie!

"Huh-huh-huh—" the thing said as it reached toward him with bloody hands.

"Oh, no, you ain't eatin' my brain!" Ignoring the rocks and sticks that cut at his palms, Elmer crawled to his gun, thanking the good Lord it hadn't gone off when it hit the ground. Although it only took a few seconds, he imagined the creature coming up behind him, its bacteria-filled mouth open and ready to bite. When he reached the gun, he didn't even bother standing, just turned and fired.

The zombie was farther away than he'd expected, but it didn't matter. The load of buckshot caught it right where the neck and shoulders met and blasted the head clean off the body. It hit the ground and rolled over, ending up facing Elmer. The eyes blinked several times and then went still.

"Goddamn!" Elmer let out a laugh. "Popped him like a cork!"

The roar of an unmuffled engine alerted Elmer to Charlie bringing the truck around.

"I lost the goddamn muffler!" Charlie yelled as he pulled up.

Elmer's already frayed temper gave out as he realized his old drinking buddy had no idea of what he'd done. Instead of climbing back into the truck, he stuck his shotgun through the window. Charlie cried out as the barrels smashed against the bridge of his nose.

"You dumb fuck!" Elmer shouted. "You almost got me killed! I oughtta blow your drunk-ass head right off'n your shoulders!"

"Hey, I'm sorry!" Charlie held his hands up. "I came back soon's I saw you were gone."

It took all of Elmer's control to stop his finger from tightening on the trigger, especially when he recollected that Charlie'd stolen his favorite hunting rifle. But a quick look at the field showed several more zombies left, and he'd need Charlie to help him kill them all.

Then it's his turn.

"Never mind. Let's finish this before they make it back to the woods."

They managed to put down the rest of the zombies without any further incidents, and by the time they finished, Elmer was sufficiently drunk to reconsider his private vow. After all, he and Charlie had helped themselves to each other's stuff plenty of times over the years. Including their wives. Besides, good drinking buddies were a lot harder to come by than guns.

Back at Charlie's house, Elmer stacked up the guns

while Charlie went inside for a bottle of celebratory hooch he kept for special occasions.

"It's the good stuff," he said. "My cousin made it just last week."

"Hell yeah." Elmer sat down in his rocker. "Now all we gotta do is wait for the sheriff to get here."

Charlie's voice barely reached from inside the house. "You think we might get a reward or—gaah!"

The sound of glass breaking accompanied Charlie's startled shout, but Elmer didn't pay much attention. Charlie was all thumbs when he was sober; after a dozen or so beers, it'd be surprising if he didn't drop something. Hopefully, it wasn't the sour mash.

Then a loud, pain-filled scream cut through the air, and Elmer knew something was wrong.

Very wrong.

After grabbing a shotgun from the pile, he made his way slowly down the narrow, windowless hallway. Something thumped and bumped in the kitchen, and more glass broke. Gun up and ready, Elmer jumped the last few feet, hoping to surprise whoever—or whatever—was in there with Charlie.

Sure enough, one of the zombies was kneeling on the floor, fresh blood on its mouth and hands.

"Shoot it!" Charlie shouted.

Elmer didn't hesitate. His finger pulled the trigger, sending a load of buckshot into the creature's head, which blew apart like a watermelon filled with dynamite.

The headless body fell over with a thud, and Elmer turned his attention to Charlie.

"What happened?"

Charlie let out a groan and shook his head. "God-damn thing got me when my back was turned. It said something in zombie-talk and I hit it with the bottle. Then you came in."

"Did it bite you?" It was obvious something had happened. A big, red stain covered one shoulder of Charlie's shirt.

After a brief pause, Charlie shook his head. "Uh, no. It got me with its nails. Like fightin' a cat. But it didn't bite me. Tried to, but I held it off."

Elmer stared at Charlie but the other man wouldn't meet his eyes. "Uh-huh. That's good." Relief showed on Charlie's face at Elmer's words, and Elmer knew the truth right then. He'd been friends with Charlie more than long enough to recognize a lie.

It bit him. That means it's only a matter of time now.

In the movies, the people who'd been bitten usually lasted a couple of hours before they changed.

But who knew how long it took in real life?

"Here, lemme help you up." Elmer pulled Charlie to his feet. "Since you busted the damn sour mash, what else ya got?"

"Got some grain under the sink," Charlie said.

"Get it. I'll clean this mess."

Elmer waited until Charlie's back was turned.

Sorry, old friend.

He fired the remaining round, scattering pieces of Charlie's skull across the cabinets and windows. Charlie's body landed next to the zombie's. Elmer racked another two rounds into the gun, just in case there were more undead things walking around, and then decided he needed a drink before doing anything else.

"Guess you won't be needin' this no more." Elmer opened the cabinet. "Sonovabitch," he muttered, spotting a second bottle of sour mash next to the moonshine. "He was gonna hold out on me after I saved his life. Figgers."

Elmer tipped the bottle up and took a long swallow. He was contemplating what to do with the bodies when the wail of a police siren sounded outside. A moment later, a car door slammed and Sheriff Roy Biggins came in, his pistol out and his eyes dancing back and forth.

"Holy shit, Elmer! What the hell happened? Your kid told me some kinda bullshit about zombies."

"You better sit down, Roy. It's all true."

Biggins shook his head. "I ain't got time for bullshit, Elmer. Got a big emergency on Route Forty. Goddamn busload of tourists headin' from Atlanta to Nashville smashed into a semi loaded with bug spray. I got ten dead and about thirty Russkies missing."

"Russkies? What the hell you talkin' about?"

"Russians, you idjit. Some kinda tourist thing. Can't imagine why we're lettin' those red bastards into the country, prob'ly gonna blow somethin' up."

A nasty feeling set Elmer's belly to rumbling. Route Forty was just to the other side of Charlie's property. Right past the woods where the zombies had come from.

He thought of the dead bodies littering Charlie's field. One, maybe two corpses wouldn't be so bad. Roy could cover those up as hunting accidents. But more than twenty?

That spelled electric chair in Elmer's book.

Only one thing to do.

"Shit, Roy, look out behind you!"

Biggins turned and Elmer fired the shotgun. He felt a moment's remorse at killing an innocent man, but better one more dead than being arrested for murder.

"Now I can blame the whole thing on Charlie. Say he went nuts, talkin' about zombies, and started killin' all those people. Forced me to drive the truck. When he shot Biggins, I had to kill him. I can still be a hero."

He had to make it look right, though. That meant moving the bodies and putting a gun in Charlie's hands. He knelt on the floor to grab Biggins's legs, felt a sharp pain in his hand.

"Goddamn!" He'd cut himself on a piece of broken glass. A good slice, too. Bleeding like a stuck pig. He put his mouth over the cut as he stood up, then paused at a noise from outside.

"Who's there?" The last thing he needed was another cop walkin' in.

But it was Delbert and Nate who entered the kitchen, still breathin' hard after runnin' back from town. Nate's eyes went wide and he pointed at Elmer.

"Holy Jesus, Del, your pa's a zombie!"

"Shit!" Delbert raised his hands, and for a moment Elmer thought the boy was gonna throw something at him.

Until he saw that Delbert had a rifle in his hands.

"Del, no, I—"

There was an explosion, and Elmer had time to wish he'd finished the last of the mash.

Then everything disappeared.

Dating After
the Apocalypse

STEPHEN DORATO

Until the moment when she dug her nails into the skin behind her ear and pulled back her flesh to reveal a skull gleaming with dripping green ichor, Malcolm had thought the date was going well.

There had been odd silences (okay, she hadn't spoken much at all near the end, had mostly made ambiguous slurping noises he took for assent), the meal had disappointed (the damn waiter had vanished on them), and they had been plagued by flies the entire date. But Malcolm had long learned to overlook that kind of thing.

But now, as she straddled him, the green fluid from her face beginning to drip on his stomach and groin, he knew this was too ugly to continue.

"Jessica," he said quietly, scooting back from beneath her and taking the Taser from the nightstand, "this just isn't working out."

The Taser made her glow a faint emerald that was almost pretty in the dim bedroom light.

She froze, her lidless eyes locked on his, then fell backward. He checked her pulse, the nightstick close by. Out cold. "Good," he said out loud, the tension draining from him in one long exhalation. You couldn't always tell; the Taser didn't always knock them out. And sometimes they would pretend to be unconscious, then grab your ankle as you walked by.

Malcolm left her in the hall, covered with an old blanket (more for the neighbors, he had to admit, than for her), and late that night he heard quite a commotion, a lot of screaming and even a couple gunshots. He hoped she'd gotten away; she had been one of the better ones.

"Hey, hey," Brad said, standing at the entrance to his cube. "How'd it go Friday night?"

"The usual," Malcolm said.

"As in she wouldn't put out?"

"No, the other usual."

"Oh." Brad made a face. "Sorry, man."

"It's okay." Malcolm shifted uncomfortably in his seat. The green stuff had dried and washed away easily enough, but the whole area down there was red and unhappy. And it also made him uncomfortable when Brad talked that way. He wasn't looking for a woman who put out; that wasn't the point. He wanted someone to share his life with. "Look, Brad, I gotta work."

The company firewall blocked his personal e-mail, which was probably a good thing since all Malcolm wanted to do was check if any of the other fifteen dates he had lined up had written him.

The phone rang and Malcolm squinted at the blinding red sunlight of a new morning.

"You never call," said a familiar voice.

"I called last week, Mom."

"You called last month. For all I know you could be dead! It happens these days, you know."

Malcolm would never hang up on his mother, or interrupt one of her tirades, but right now he wished it were possible to talk and sleep at the same time. His mother was droning on about something, and he had already lost the thread, which was a dangerous thing.

"You're not listening."

"I'm sorry, Mom."

"I asked if you were seeing that girl."

For a moment he paused, trying to figure out which girl that girl would have been. "I'm seeing lots of girls these days."

"I hope you're using protection."

He sat up and squinted at the red sky outside. "I am not going to have this conversation, Mom."

"Your cousin Eddie had his thing torn off. Do you want that to happen to you?"

"Yes."

He took Arlene out to watch the baseball game, though they did it with a pair of binoculars from the relative safety of an elevated highway four blocks away. Fenway had been hit the worst, which made it both a dangerous place to go and an interesting place to see. YouTube was full of videos by people much braver than Malcolm who had taped the games that went on there these days. Baseball with heads.

"This is nice," she said.

And it was. It was nearly perfect.

Had it not been so nearly perfect, had Arlene been a lousy kisser or less well proportioned, or had they taken the first—or the second or third—train that passed through the station, things might have gone better and there might have been a second date. Malcolm broke off from a particularly long kiss, blinked up at the grainy fluorescent lights, and wondered how much time had passed.

Two things happened, pretty much simultaneously.

The tunnel behind them glowed with the lights from an approaching train, the walls echoing with the shriek of brakes as it turned into the station.

And they heard the roar of the crowd coming down the stairs.

Too much time had passed.

They almost made it, had even made it on board the train when Arlene stumbled, her purse or something dropped back to the platform, and she went to retrieve it just as the red warning lights on either side of the door lit and the crowd swarmed toward the train. There wasn't even time for Malcolm to scream "leave it" before the automatic defense systems cut in and the steel-toothed doors cut Arlene nearly in half. He was left with her legs while the crowd got the rest.

And the date wasn't as perfect anymore.

Carrie was a no-go nearly from the get-go. She was a small-framed, mousy girl with light brown hair and a quiet voice, but as the date progressed (Italian at Marenno's in East Boston, Malcolm's standard for a first date since it had good lighting and easily accessible exits), it seemed harder and harder to see her or hear what she was saying.

"Your hair," he said, "it seems darker."

She looked embarrassed and muttered something. Or just moved her lips; it was hard to tell.

By now her hair was an absolute black.

"Are you okay?" he asked.

He poured her more wine, and as she reached for the glass he noticed that the shadow her arm made against the tablecloth lingered for a moment after her arm had gone. Her eyes, too, had been hazel and now were dark as his dreams and did not reflect the candle-light.

"I think I should ask for the check," he said, but the words sounded funny. Too quiet, like he was speaking underwater. He cleared his throat and tried again. Nothing. He could barely see her face now, except it was a lighter gray against the rest of her, and there were streaks of darkness coming from her eyes. Tears, he supposed.

"I'm really sorry."

At that point the waiter came, and he didn't hesitate before calling over to the bar for a shotgun, but by then Carrie was running across the restaurant, a black smear that left ashy high-heeled footprints behind. She did not open the door so much as pass through it, leaving a Carrie-shaped hole behind.

"You're paying for that," the owner said.

Malcolm was too broke to date for a while after that, which was probably a good thing. He needed time to collect his thoughts, watch a couple bad movies, ponder a brief solitary life.

It went well for a few nights, as long as he worked hard at the office (fielding Brad's inquiries with "I'm on the DL, dude") and came home too exhausted to think. He even reupped his membership at the corporate gym, though that was a mixed blessing. He found himself checking out any woman who came through the door, it didn't matter how ugly or married or otherwise deformed.

But you didn't sleep where you worked, or something like that, and besides, Malcolm knew that once he tried to go out with one coworker, all of the rules would be broken, all the barriers gone. A single date was one thing, a minor brush with death, perhaps, but the next morning you counted your fingers and toes and moved on. But dating here was a different story, a disaster with long-term consequences.

He tried to distract himself by using the machines at the front of the room, looking through the windows at the common and the feral squirrels that would occasionally launch themselves at passersby. He would come in the morning, the sky a beautiful mauve, the low sun a bruised purple that hurt to look at.

And then his mom called him for supper.

"You're my beautiful boy. Look at you, nothing changed."

"Would you like me to disrobe? You could check the whole package."

"Don't be smart."

They ate with the TV buzzing in the background, while his mother told him how a girl he'd gone to school with had burst into flame the other day, taking the bakery department of the supermarket with her. "And she was such a nice girl, so pretty; I always liked her."

"Cheryl did always enjoy her baked goods," he said.

"I think I know someone you'd like," Brad told him.

Malcolm thought that was unlikely, since he didn't even like Brad, and they'd worked in adjacent cubes for nearly three years now. There were days he wished someone would give Brad an enema with the giant statue of Godzilla he kept beside his desk.

"Um, no."

"Just like that, you don't even want to know who she is?"

"Considering the source—no."

"Hang on a sec," Brad said, rummaging through a desk drawer. "I've got a picture here somewhere."

Malcolm returned to his work and didn't look back when he felt Brad standing beside him. A photograph popped into view, too close to focus on. Malcolm snarled and grabbed the photo from him, held it at arm's length.

A girl of maybe twelve, her long blond hair in a braid.

"Um . . ." Malcolm said, and since he was at work it was probably a good thing he didn't say what he wanted to say.

"Sorry, I didn't have a recent photo. That was when we were kids. Note the sun."

There it was, reflected in a window in the corner of the picture, something bright and white. "Oh. Right." For a moment he ached to be back there with that girl, in the world with that sun, but it passed.

"Her husband died," Brad said.

Malcolm knew it would be impolite to ask for details, but he wanted to ask, *Did she eat him?*

"Besides," Brad said, "you were always flitting from woman to woman; I wasn't sure you'd be good for her. You can be kind of a creep sometimes."

He laughed, and Malcolm laughed back, but neither of them smiled.

Julie. Her name was Julie.

They met for coffee the first time, in the Starbucks near Government Center. Malcolm was so nervous he almost walked into a person trap shaped like a Starbucks; it was only as he stood on the threshold, about to open the front door, that he noticed that none of the people seated at the couches inside was actually alive, and that the scent of roasting coffee was tinged with something sweet that made his head buzz. He stepped back just as twin shutters flapped into place in front of him, catching the edge of his scarf.

He would buy another scarf.

He found the real Starbucks two blocks away on the other side of city hall. This one didn't smell nearly as nice, but the door was open and real, live people were milling about inside. Malcolm spotted her right away, seated at a small table near the front. Her face had not changed so much in thirteen years or so, and her tentative smile reminded him of the sun in the picture Brad had shown him. "Hi, Julie. I'm Malcolm. I work with your brother."

"I thought you weren't coming," she said a little sadly.

"I almost didn't make it," he said. "Starbucks plant."

She grunted, and they traded details. It felt awkward, talking to her in the clear white light of the coffee shop, but he let himself relax after the first grande mocha whateverthehellitwas.

Julie seemed to be a regular, ordinary girl—a bit reserved, but who wasn't these days? Near the end of the date she took his hand and smiled. "You're nicer than I expected."

"Why, what has Brad told you?"

"Nothing you need to hear."

But he let himself enjoy the touch of her hand, and the fact that it didn't make his skin burn, and that it was so . . . normal. The last normal girl he had dated had been before the change (he tried not to think of Arlene), and after the change it seemed that even Malcolm himself was different.

"Can we do this again?" he asked as the store around them began to close up. Real night was approaching, and nobody stayed on the city streets at night.

"Yes, I hope so," she replied, and touched his hand again and gave him a smile that was even better than a kiss would have been, and he went home with a lightness in his heart that even the nighttime screams outside couldn't touch.

Malcolm took it slow. He could tell that Julie didn't want to rush into anything, and to be honest, he was none too eager to change his lifestyle either. These days, the series of locks on his front door seemed less for keeping the crazies out than for keeping Malcolm's world whole. It felt comfortable, when he knew that he could break his self-imposed exile with a single phone call.

He felt connected, and at the same time, himself.

And then Julie slept over.

They had sex, slowly, tentatively, Malcolm able to manage an erection though he kept thinking of the last woman who'd been in this bed, the mattress he'd had to replace, the greenish fluid he'd had to mop from the floor. Even now, in the middle of the pitch-black night, he could see a faint glow from what remained between the floorboards.

And yet it was good, so good that after those first few moments all he could think of was Julie, the warmth from their skin touching, the feel of her breath on his neck. Afterward she turned on her side and he held her, and they lay in silence, hearing the sounds of the night.

"You're the first man I've slept with since Dan," she said.

He wasn't sure what to say to that, so he held her tighter. "You must have loved him very much."

"All I can remember now is how scared I was," she said, her voice low and quiet. "Every night, he went out on patrol with those friends of his. 'Cleaning up the city,' he called it, but it always seemed stupid to me. They would drive around in Dan's SUV and bring all their guns, looking for solo banshees and the night changers. So I knew it was just a matter of time before he didn't come back."

Malcolm, who could barely imagine stepping outside his apartment building after dark, said, "I'm not going anywhere."

"Better not," she replied, and kissed his hand.

He had never thought he would miss this apartment, the metal grilles over the windows, the welded and rewelded front and rear doors. *Your man cave,* Julie called it, and in a way it was true. This was where he hid from the world, kept himself safe from the world, amid his books and videos and his posters from college. But he could bring that with him, those and the scarred Louisville Slugger his father had given him after the change. Her place was better—better fortified, part of a gated community with electric fences. A better kitchen and a shower that didn't leak.

Once he'd boxed his stuff up, all that remained of his tenancy were white rectangles of cleaner wall edged with bits of double-sided tape, the bare IKEA furniture he would be donating to Goodwill, and that stain on the bedroom floor that would probably cost him his security deposit. He looked at his watch: two o'clock. Julie and her brother would be here soon.

Two o'clock turned into three, which turned into four, and Malcolm realized his phone had died. He found the charger in one of the boxes and the phone rang practically the moment he plugged it in. "The van broke down," Julie said, relief clear in her voice, "but Brad got it working again. We'll be there any minute now."

By the time they had loaded his boxes into the van, the sun was low in the sky and the shadows had already begun to move on their own.

"Shit," he said, and Brad nodded grimly.

"Let's get out of here," Julie said.

The complex was locked when they got there, but Brad had phoned ahead and two guards with shotguns were waiting for them by the gate. He slowed the van down as he took the curve leading up to the complex, and Malcolm heard the engine cough and die, the van shuddering to a stop a hundred yards from the first barricades. Brad turned the key again but the starter just whirred.

"Leave it," Malcolm said.

They had barely left the van when they heard shuffling behind them, and when the screams started they ran full-bore toward the gates. Malcolm kept Julie in front of him, safe, knowing at least he would see her before he died. But then they were at the gates, and it seemed an eternity before they opened; then they were inside and everything was quiet again. "You cut it a little close there," a bored guard told him. "You're safe now. You can get your things tomorrow."

But there was little left of the van the next day, and Malcolm knew the rest of his world was gone.

"It's just stuff," Julie said, giving him a little hug.

"It was just my fucking van," grumbled Brad.

Here he was, Malcolm in domestic bliss. And it wasn't so bad. He hadn't lost himself after all; it had only been stuff. It felt good to wake up to a warm bed, to roll over and kiss this woman beside him, to know this was their place—and, hell, after a few weeks her cat was even their cat, the damn fuzz ball loved him, started purring whenever he entered a room. A place with two other beings and neither of them trying to kill him.

Could this be happiness?

There were hiccups every now and then when things didn't feel quite right, didn't feel real. Like now. The cat was looking at him oddly. That's what cats did, he knew, but right now it bugged him, got under his skin. Malcolm went downstairs to turn off the lights and use the bathroom, and it was still looking at him. Making his teeth ache.

He went into the bathroom to wash up and the cat followed him around the edge of the door, looked up at him again, and purred. "Okay already," he said, and reached down to scratch behind its ears.

It happened then, the world blinking red just for an instant.

Blink, and the cat was gone, and something wet and red had taken its place.

The face in the mirror was his all right, but he saw bits of fur between his teeth and tasted blood in his mouth. He touched the reflection and his trembling fingers left behind a red smear.

"Everything okay down there?" Julie called down to him.

"Fine. I just have to take a shower," he replied, and shut the door.

There wasn't much left of the cat to flush down the toilet, and between the heat of the shower and soap, he felt better again, he felt normal, and then he didn't really remember so much. Why wouldn't he feel normal? He felt great, and full. He went upstairs and lay down, and it all felt so right.

No more dates, no more searching.

He shut his eyes and breathed in the scent of Julie's hair, felt her warmth beside him, and soon fell into a deep sleep untroubled by dreams or even the faintest meow.

Typecast

Jeff Ryan

Linda opened the door and saw a dozen psychopaths waiting for her. One had a half-torn straitjacket. Two wore long straggly beards. One man, bald, scraped his pate clean with an immense serrated knife. A fat deviant in overalls and no shirt held a pitchfork adorned with doll heads. One man was immaculately attired in a charcoal suit drenched in caked blood.

"Make a hole, people," Linda said, barging into the sea of crazies. They immediately parted, hugging the wall and lowering their eyes in respect. Three men in chairs contorted their legs so she could walk unimpeded past them. Linda's combination of perfume, hoop earrings, scarves, and an array of bracelets made her intrude on all five senses at once whenever she made any motion. Two steps behind Linda, June tried to catch up.

"Air! I need air!" she exclaimed, walking out into the humid summer day. The baking sun of Los Angeles was an immediate reminder of what this land wanted to be: desert. "Oh, God, it's Thailand out here. This is intolerable. We've got to go."

June followed in the morning sunshine, taking small amusement in literally being in Linda's shadow as the casting director left the production office. "Where are we going?"

"Do you have to ask?" Linda said, pointing with one bebangled arm across the street to a coffee shop. "I mean, seriously, June, you need to pay more attention." She crossed the street, oblivious to the honking of traffic and, in one lane, an actual squeal of brakes. "Pedestrian!" she yelled! "Eat my cheese!"

Linda pushed open the door as if expecting photography and held her pose for a moment. "The eagle has landed," she exclaimed upon entering the air-conditioning. "There, that's a proper temperature."

"This is nicer," June said in agreement, sneaking in before the door slammed. Linda didn't hold doors.

"No it's not," Linda said, changing her mind. "It's a meat locker in here. *This* is where we should be having auditions for our serial killer. After they kill us they can keep us in cold storage."

"I thought Kevin, the one who was barking, was good."

"Amateur hour," Linda said. "They don't under-

JEFF RYAN • 187

stand the business. They're trying way too hard to go
way too deep. I mean, barking. *Anyone* can bark."

"But he was really good. I mean, he was off book
and everything."

"Sweetie, you don't need to be off book for auditions. You don't really even have to act. You have to
be. Especially for a showy role like this. People act
too much, too much. One day a producer will listen
to me and I'll be able to audition people in a soundproof room. All I need is a glance, and I know who
you are."

There wasn't a line; the morning rush was over.
"What can I get for you today?" the woman behind the
counter said.

"Take this woman, for example," Linda said, turning to face her. "You're obviously an employee here, and
I'm sure you're good at your job, but—I'm a casting
director—I wouldn't cast you as a barrister, or whatever Italian word it is you invented to make pouring
coffee sound hard, in a million years. Midforties is *not*
what we're expecting to see in service roles. I put you
up on-screen dressed like that, the audience is filled
with questions: Is she married? Divorced? Kids? Can
she support them on this salary? Is she the manager?
Is this what she really wanted to do in life? It all draws
attention away from the principals."

"Can I , um, help you?" the woman repeated. Linda
was right, June could see: this was the face of a mom
of a troubled teen. No, the mom of a genius kid. Defi-

nitely not a romantic lead. As awful as Linda was, she was always right.

"Pour one-third soy, one-third half-and-half, and one-third skim into a grande cup, swirl it around, empty it out, and then pour black coffee in it. I'll know if you do it wrong. The milk should be swirling *around* the coffee, not *through* it."

"Of course," the woman said without batting an eye, then hit the "special order" key and went to confer with another drink maker. June got whatever on the menu was closest to $2.50, which was all the cash she had. Linda never paid for others' drinks.

After supervising the production of the drink, Linda took the coffee to the condiment station and added skim milk and a stack of Splendas as thick as a Twilight novel. "They never get it right, so I don't even bother trying anymore," she said. "It's like every store in the world saves its incompetent employees for me."

"Sounds like *The Truman Show* in reverse," June said, then gulped. She had learned not to bring up any movie or TV show, because . . .

"That movie was garbage. Casting was atrocious. I mean, Laura Linney? You see any gas station putting up pictures of Laura Linney on their tool racks? And Jim Carrey has the depth of a puddle of urine." She never liked anything she didn't cast.

"Laura Linney is a pretty good actress."

"If you want any sort of a future as a casting director, June, you'll refrain from saying 'pretty' and 'Laura Linney' in the same sentence."

June found them a table and sat down in her chair. Linda descended into hers. "Someone left their copy of the *Times* here. Maybe they sneezed all over it before so graciously leaving it for us." She tipped it to the floor with the press-on nail of her left index finger.

"I think—" June began. "Well—" she continued. "That is—" Finally, she figured her best rhetorical route of attack and asked, "Who do you think the show runner would be happiest with, of who we've seen so far?"

"The show runner can gargle my discharge. If he cared so much about casting he'd attend the damn casting."

Was this a test? "But he *was* there. He's still there now."

"Honey, he's not going to stay all day. He'll make up some BS story about being needed back on the set or in the writers' room. One guy even told me his wife had been hit by a car. There's dedication for you: I can't do my job because someone somewhere in the world is hurt."

"He might leave while we're on break," June said, wishing they were back doing their job. Linda blamed any delays on June's sloppiness. "There's craft services coffee."

"I'd rather drink septic overflow. In fact, I'm pretty sure that's what's in those silver urns. And we're not on break. I haven't taken a break in thirty years."

June knew where this was going. "Okay, so: Three o'clock. Man with BlackBerry. Who's he?"

Linda smirked. "Medical show. Doctor. Secretly gay. Wife and kids. They don't know. Has to operate on his gay lover but not let anyone know he cares."

"And the two women sharing the dessert?"

"Cell phone ad."

"The mom with the baby stroller?"

"Ditch the kid; no one wants to think her cleavage is a result of lactation. Then she's a craft store clerk with a husband fighting overseas. She cheats on him and shows her rack in the love scene. Otherwise she wears floral print."

"The older guy with the tea?"

"His daughter is dying."

"The guy in the Lakers jersey?"

"Troubled teen, covering up his brother's crime by taking the heat himself."

"The woman with the big soda?"

"Small-town racist."

"And the man coming out of the bathroom?"

"Wealthy dogfight sponsor."

"What about me?"

Linda paused. "Darling, no."

"Come on."

"Very well," she said, and took a beat. "Katherine."

"Katherine?"

"Yes, as in *The Taming of the Shrew*. A production set in the South, the 1960s. You're the plain brat who they need to marry off so your beautiful younger sister can marry the lumber magnate. Your male costar would slap you a lot, and the audience would love him for it."

"Oh."

"You bring it on yourself. All the arguing, all the demands. You can't act, of course, but if you could a bad casting director might suggest you for a variety of parts with fat comedy leading men."

June held her tongue, then thought of something else. "And you?"

Linda took two beats to process this. Then she did not hesitate: "Hogwarts professor."

June realized they never told anyone where they were going. A building full of hopeful maniacs was in limbo. "Maybe we should get back to—"

"Shut up," Linda said with a strange detachment. "Shut up, shut up shut up, silly." She was staring out the window.

"Oh, did you see—"

"What part of 'shut up' was unclear, dearie? Use your ears for once: I've just cast our part."

"Someone . . . someone you just saw on the street?"

"Yes, you Delphic oracle, someone on the street." She started charging out of the coffee shop, leaving her purse behind, a miasma of scent and sound and bauble and sparkle. "Pick up your phone, it's ringing."

June looked down; like all good assistants, she was scrupulously aware of her cell phone. Different ringtones for each VIP, a beep for texts, and vibrating for personal calls, which were rare. It was silent.

Then it went off. Miss Gulch's theme from *The Wizard of Oz* began to chime. That was Linda's ringtone, of course, June's one crack in her wall of nonchalance about how Linda treated her. She answered before the second du-*duhn* du-*duhn* da-*da-da*.

"You're late," Linda chirped. "Answer the phone when I call. Especially when I told you not five seconds ago to answer it."

"Where are you?"

"One block away. I'm reeling in a whale over here. He's everything the runner wants, everything I want, even everything you would want, if your opinion counted."

"What's he like?"

"He's Harrison Ford at forty. What do you think, girl? Stupid question."

"Have you, um, ever done this before?"

"Cast someone in an acting role? Let's see, I think maybe I can remember doing so once or twice."

"No, I mean picking someone off the street. I mean, he might not even be an actor."

"L.A., dear; he's an actor and a screenwriter and he'll hit himself with a riding crop beneath Venice Pier for twenty bucks if I offer."

"Are you sure? I mean, this is like Lana Turner."

"Let's not try to be the expert on the studio system, my dear. It was Veronica Lake who was discovered in a drugstore. She was probably there stealing speed."

"But just a guy off the street . . . !"

"Acting is like politics: the only people who want to do it are thus constitutionally disqualified from actually doing it well. George C. Scott was a delivery boy and they put a uniform on him, and Patton. Look it up, it's true."

"But this role has a lot of acting . . . I mean, in the script we know he's a serial killer but we don't know if he's killed the girl everyone's looking for."

"Worst comes to worst we'll put peanut butter in his mouth and hire Frank Welker to dub him in post. That's how they did it with Mr. Ed and Matt LeBlanc."

June was outside now, with two purses in tow (Linda's looked like Liberace's toilet seat cover), and Linda was nowhere in sight. "Where are you? I can't see you. You're too far ahead."

"That seems to be my assistants' collective mission statement in life. I'm about four blocks ahead, and one over. He's cutting through an alley now. I've been waiting until we're alone to give him the role."

"Are you sure this is—" June started to say, and then heard the ruffle of fabric. Linda had slipped her phone in a pocket of her jacket. The jacket dialed her by accident about five times a day, so she knew its muted ruffles by heart.

"Hey, you!" she heard Linda say. "You, slow down! What, are you late for a Klaus Kinski lookalike contest? I've got to tell you something. I know who you are. I can see it in your eyes, that head, that lurch—my God, it's like undead Shel Silverstein. Hey! Don't go away! I'm talking to you! This is important, crucially important! How'd you like everyone to see you? That's right, everyone will know who you are. Want to know what I see in your future? Murder. I see you digging holes in your backyard, burying girls facedown so if you didn't kill them dead enough they still can't dig out. I see you being pulled into a holding cell by a racially diverse group of young cops. I see your face in the teaser for next week, over the line 'He's a killer . . . but is he our killer?' Want me to make that happen for you? . . . Yes, exactly, just like that! That's precisely what I want to see . . . Whoa, hold up, Olivier, save some for Gary Sinise . . . Geez, off book already? Your character doesn't use a knife, you ham, he—"

Making the Cut
A Close Shave Story

Mike Resnick and Lezli Robyn

It's been a busy night at the Close Shave. I've already
given a trim and a shampoo to Harvey the Yeti, of
whom there is an awful lot to trim and wash. Mildred
the Lamia comes in looking for Leonard, her almost-
husband, and decides to have some feathers plucked
while she is here, and as the clock strikes midnight I
am giving Basil his nightly shave and trim. He hands
me a pair of books, one on dog grooming and one an
illustrated copy of Kipling's *Jungle Book,* and suggests
that he wants to look exactly like Akila, the leader
of the pack, and I point out that everything I do is
ephemeral because come morning he will look like an
aging, overweight Mowgli again.

"In fact," I say, "if the moon goes behind a cloud,

you will probably forget to be a wolf even while I am trimming your whiskers."

"What do you know about werewolves?" he says contemptuously. "We're a unique and noble race."

"Unique, noble, and hairy," I say. "Now be quiet and hold still or I'll wind up nicking you."

"What do I care?" he demands. "We werewolves are made of stern stuff."

"*You* may not care," I reply. "But *he* does."

I gesture toward Otis, who is sitting there reading the obituary column, as usual. His fangs are pressing against his lips as if they may burst through at any moment.

"Otis is my friend," says Basil. "He would never drink my blood."

"Not unless I was thirsty," says Otis in agreement.

"When are you thirsty?" I ask.

"All the time," admits Otis.

"Well, *I* would never drink your blood," chimes in Morton, which I find very disappointing. Morton is all bone as far as the eye can see. He looks like a refugee from a medical class or maybe a Halloween party, and I have been waiting for him to eat or drink something for fourteen years now, just so I can see where it goes once he swallows it.

"What's the matter with my blood?" demands Basil.

"Nothing," says Otis. "I will defend your blood for as long as it lasts." He stares at Basil. "I think it would go well with a jelly donut."

The door opens and a pretty woman with auburn curls as soft as fairy floss, dressed in slacks and a blouse, enters.

"Can I help you?" I ask.

She holds up a page she's torn from a newspaper. Otis sees that it's not another obituary column and pays her no further attention. "I'm answering your ad for a manicurist."

"You *did* see the part about the unusual clientele?" I ask.

"How unusual can they be?" she asks.

"Go to work on Basil here," I say, stepping aside, "and then tell me."

She pulls up a stool, I roll the manicuring tray over to her, and she takes Basil's paw in her hands.

"Claws," she says, frowning. "He has claws."

"And dewclaws," I add, pointing to the curved claw growing out of each wrist.

She shrugs. "What the hell, I need the work."

"Don't cut the quicks," says Basil, stifling a whine.

"Or at least alert me if you do," adds Otis.

"This is some place, this barber shop," she says. "By the way, my name's Mavis."

I am about to ask her what her last name is, or how much she thinks I am paying her, but just then three elderly ladies, all wearing hats and each carrying a hat pin in her withered fingers, burst into the shop.

"Damn!" mutters one of them. "He's not here!"

"Let's go, girls!" says another to her two companions, who haven't been girls since Sherman took a little stroll through Georgia. "He can't have gotten too far."

And just like that, they're back on the sidewalk and rushing down the block.

"This happens a lot, does it?" asks Mavis.

"Actually, we're hardly ever visited by old ladies brandishing hat pins," I tell her.

"I want a raise," she says.

"You've been here less than three minutes," I note.

"I want one anyway."

"You don't even know what I'm paying you."

"If I'm going to work on werewolves and skeletons, it's not enough," says Mavis.

"Okay," I say in agreement. "When you're right, you're right. You've got a raise."

"Good," she says, going back to work on Basil's claws.

I make a mental note that someday I must figure out what I'm paying her. At the moment, she doesn't seem to care, as long as it's more than it was when she walked in the door.

And speaking of walking in the door, she has barely begun to work on Basil in earnest when the door opens and in walks a burly figure. I assume it is a man, because it walks on two legs and wears shoes and socks. But it also wears a floor-length overcoat with the collar turned up, and a scarf wrapped around most of its face, and a slouch hat covering the rest of it, and while assuming it is a man would be safe anywhere else, here at the Close Shave it is very little better than an even-money proposition.

It walks to the clothes pole, where Morton and Otis have hung their overcoats—Basil doesn't need one with all that fur, and besides, he can't find one to fit him when he's busy being a wolf—and it peeks out through the front window.

"Are they coming back?" it says in a deep masculine voice.

"Who did you have reference to?" I ask.

"The old biddies with the hat pins," it says.

"No, they seemed in a hurry to go up the street," says Basil.

"Good!" it says with a sigh of relief. "Do you mind if I stay here for a few minutes, just in case?"

"Just in case they come back?" I ask.

"Just in case they're still on the street looking for me."

"What did you do to them?" asks Otis, who takes a professional curiosity in such things.

"Nothing!" it says passionately. It takes its hat and coat off, and I can see that it's a man. Or at least it used to be. He's got an awful lot of wounds on him, even a few bullet holes, but no blood and no scabs, and his skin is mostly gray. And all he's wearing under the coat is a pair of colorful gold briefs.

"I know you!" exclaims Mavis. "You're Loathsome Lamont! I saw you wrestle last month!"

He nods his head wearily. "Yeah, that's me."

"What *did* you do to those sweet old ladies?" Otis persists.

"Not a thing!" Lamont insists.

"Then why do they want you?"

"They want to stick their hat pins in me," says Lamont.

"For no reason at all?" says Otis dubiously.

"I'm a rassler," answers Lamont. "What other reason do they need? Most of our audience is excitable little old ladies with hat pins. If we ever stop, half the hat pin manufacturers in the world will go broke. I mean, who else *uses* hat pins these days?"

"But why are you hiding from them?" asks Morton. "Not to put too fine a point on it, you're a zombie. You can't feel pain."

"What does that have to do with anything?" says Lamont.

"Hold on," I say. "Now even *I'm* confused."

"Look," explains Lamont. "I'm a Bad Guy." I can almost hear the capital letters. "I don't want to be, I want everyone to cheer me, but"—a bitter expression crosses his lifeless face—"there's a prejudice against zombies. So I bite and I kick and I choke, and at least once a match I hit my opponent with a chair from ringside. It's all in good fun, and no one ever gets hurt. I mean, after all, we're *rasslers*."

"I always thought the matches were fixed," says Morton.

"They're not *fixed*," Lamont says, correcting him.

"They're *scripted,* like any other dramatic performance." A wistful expression crosses his face. "I'd give anything to be the Good Guy for a change. Lancelot Lamont, they could call me, or Lamont the Lustrous. Even Lamont the Lovable would be okay. But no," he concludes unhappily, "I have to be Loathsome Lamont. I blame it on anti-zombie prejudice in high places."

"I don't want to interrupt a mournful tale of self-pity," I say, "but why are you here at all?"

"I was choking the life out of Handsome Harry, same as always—we were going to meet later for a beer—and then he twisted out of it, applied a reverse Mongolian death grip, and threw me out of the ring, just like we practiced it in the gym yesterday."

"And the little old ladies threatened you with their hat pins and you ran away," says Morton. "But why? You're already dead. Nothing can hurt you."

"But *they* don't know it," answers Lamont. "They stick me, and I howl in anguish, and it makes their evening."

"Why do I think this story is not going where I thought it was going?" muses Otis aloud.

"When I was doubled up on the floor in mock agony, I was keeping an eye on *my* fans, and some *other* little old lady—I think she was there to abuse Horrible Hubert—stuck a hat pin in my back, and I didn't react. The woman immediately started screaming that I was a fake and that I didn't feel pain, and my loyal fans shouted her down and then decided to prove that of course it hurt when they stuck their hat pins into me . . . but there were so many of them I knew I couldn't react to every one of them, so I ran to the locker room, grabbed my coat and hat, and fled into the night."

And Otis, Basil, Morton, Mavis, and I all ask in unison: *"Why?"*

"They're my *fans*," he explains. "I couldn't break their sweet bloodthirsty little-old-lady hearts by disappointing them." A very dry tear tries to roll down his cheek. "I never want to disappoint *anyone*."

Mavis walks over and runs her hand through Lamont's unkempt hair, ignoring the pieces of scalp that flake off. He looks up at her with an expression I have only seen on abused puppies.

"Aw, you poor thing," says Mavis, who is adapting to the Close Shave quicker than I'd expected.

"All I ever wanted was to be a hero," says Lamont, his lower lip trembling. "Just once in my life—well, in my death—I want to hear cheers instead of boos. I want my fans to send me the roses, not the thorns. Is that so much to ask?"

"Hey, pal, we all have problems," says Basil, who is even less sympathetic as a wolf than he is as a man.

"You're a magnificent carnivore, very near the top of the food chain," replies Lamont. "What problems could you possibly have?"

"Do you know how few sheep are running loose in Central Park?" shoots back Basil. "I hang out behind an all-night hot dog stand begging for scraps. And the two times I actually find lady werewolves, they're not in heat."

"But you can still resort to dating humans," Lamont points out.

"Hey!" shouts Mavis suddenly. "*Resort?* Like a *last* resort?"

"Oh, no offense intended at all, madam!" apologizes Lamont.

She glares at him. "*Madam?*"

"*M-miss,*" stammers Lamont. "I mean *miss.*"

She arches an auburn eyebrow.

Lamont blushes—which is to say he turns a deeper shade of gray. "I would never insult a lovely lady like you."

She preens, twirling a lock of hair on an impeccably manicured finger, and then throws him a smile as a reward. From his reaction I get the distinct impression that Lamont doesn't get many smiles *or* rewards.

"So why do you want to be a hero?" I ask when Lamont is through with his version of a blush.

"Why indeed," adds Otis, deigning to look up from his obituary columns, "when it's so much *sexier* being bad?"

Lamont blinks, and it is obvious that he has never considered this angle before. "But I look like the walking dead. In fact, I *am* the walking dead. What could be sexy about that?"

Otis glances up at the zombie, amused, then folds

up the newspaper and looks speculatively at Mavis. He lets his gaze slide down from her face to the curve of her neck, suggestively licking his blood-red lips. She shudders delicately and unconsciously tilts her head to expose more of her neck.

Otis stands, and even I am transfixed by the elegance in the gesture; I've never seen him display his vampiric charms before. He glides over to Mavis while she stares at him as if hypnotized. He keeps eye contact for a long moment before moving around to stand behind her, sliding his hand up her arm as he does so, until he's pulling her hair away from the side of her neck. He leans in, his lips a hairsbreadth from the aortic artery throbbing in her neck. "It's the danger they find intoxicating," he says at last, baring his fangs. "Not only do we court death, but our natural instinct is to take away life. And yet a night with us can lead to immortality, and maybe even eternal love . . ." He looks up at Lamont and winks. "Women love that romantic claptrap. They don't realize that vampire males want the same thing as human males."

"What's that?" asks Morton, who long since ceased being any kind of a male.

"Poor fellow," says Otis with obvious sympathy. "I think I'll leave it to your imagination."

"But I haven't had an imagination in decades," protests Morton.

"Then perhaps I'll show you after all," replies Otis.

The sight of a vampire literally drooling all over my

newest employee suddenly brings me back to the here and now, and I realize how vulnerable Mavis is. While supernatural creatures such as werewolves and zombies are immune to a vampire's charms, human minds and hearts are very susceptible to manipulation. I see how the situation could become *very* bloody in an instant, and my insurance doesn't cover death from vampire attack.

"Otis, I don't think Edna's going to approve of this," I say, hoping mention of his insanely jealous wife will help snap him out of it.

"Omigod!" he rasps. "Is that *yenta* on the way in?" His eyes dart to the front of the shop, searching frantically for a full minute before relaxing. "So I wanted a little nosh," he says weakly. "Sue me."

"Try that again and I just might!" snaps Mavis, who is suddenly animated again.

Otis sighs and his eyes lose their hypnotic red glow as he pulls himself away from Mavis, severing their connection. He turns to me and asks in a half-whining, half-supplicating tone, "Not even a little taste?"

"You know the ground rules," I tell him. "No blood gets spilled in the Close Shave unless it's caused by my razor."

Otis sighs in the overly tragic fashion that only a self-centered vampire can approximate. His fangs retract and he makes his way back to his customary seat to bury himself in the obituary columns once again.

Mavis watches him until she's sure he isn't a threat

anymore, then turns to me, her impeccably manicured hands now resting pointedly on her hips. "Somehow I intuit that working here could be very hazardous to my health," she states.

Now it's my turn to sigh. "So I'll give you another raise."

Mavis flashes me a triumphant smile, which is more than a little bit curious, or at least premature, as I have never once mentioned her starting salary. "Wonderful!" she says, and then turns back to the barber's chair. "Now, Basil, tell me how you let your paws get into such a disgraceful state." She sits across from the werewolf again and opens up her beautician's bag, pulling out various implements—more than a few of them looking like small medieval torture devices—as well as a curious container of cream. While Basil complains about the damage the concrete causes his claws when he runs with the pack at night, Mavis starts to rub the cream onto his paws. "You just need to moisturize every day to keep your skin supple," she tells him. "That's all there is to it."

"I wish," laments Morton, who hasn't had any skin since before Mavis was born.

"What's the point?" asks Lamont. "I use antidandruff shampoo, and you can see how well that works." He shakes his head, and it's as if it starts snowing. Flakes of dead skin start falling everywhere.

"Walk around with a couple of talkative snakes for hair, constantly yabbering in your ear, and then see if you complain about something as trivial as flaky skin."

We all turn to where the voice is coming from and see Harold, one of my regular clients, walk through the door.

"I thought you were going on a walkabout," says Otis.

The Australian medusa shrugs. "It wasn't worth the hissing and whining," he says, taking his usual seat. "If it wasn't one damned snake, it was another. Cecil kept me awake all night, bitching about his broken fangs. As for the rest . . ." He grimaces. "Are we there yet? Are we there yet?" Then he mutters an obscenity. "When are they going to understand there is no tangible *there* on a walkabout, even in Central Park?"

"Are they dangerous?" asks Mavis quietly, carefully observing the undulations of the snakes.

"Don't be frightened," says Morton. "They're harmless."

"Even if you're not a skeleton?" asks Mavis dubiously.

"Don't listen to him!" cries one of Harold's snakes in a squeaky little voice as it stretches out to its full five inches. "I'm as vicious as they come!"

"Me too!" says another, and then another. And suddenly they are all bouncing up and down to get the manicurist's attention and baring their fangs to impress her.

Mavis's face blanches to a shade lighter than

Otis's—which is quite a feat, as Otis hasn't seen the sun for half a century—and I realize that if I'm not careful I could lose an employee, a commodity with which the Close Shave does not exactly abound. Mavis has been here twenty minutes, which is already longer that the previous four lasted.

"Harold is a pacifist," I say reassuringly.

"But *I'm* not!" says Cecil, the biggest of the snakes.

"Big deal," snorts Otis contemptuously. "I'll lay plenty of seven-to-five odds that you can't even bite your way through a balloon."

"Don't get him started on his broken fangs," says Harold plaintively. "It's all he talks about."

"But it hurtssss," Cecil hisses, his head hanging low.

"Maybe Mavis has a tooth file amongst her instruments," I suggest.

Her auburn curls bob around her face as she shakes her head. "I'll have to order one." She looks at me, head tilting. "The Close Shave will pay for it, right?"

"Yes," I say. Then I turn to Harold and add, "If Harold pays for the dental service."

Harold's face hardens. "I'm not even talking to Cecil this week."

I shrug. "There's your answer."

Suddenly Morton stands up and walks over to the vending machine. He puts some coins into it and out pops a Coke.

I can barely contain my excitement. Finally, fourteen years after putting that vending machine on the shop floor in the hope that Morton would someday use it, I am going to see where liquid goes when it passes through his teeth.

Lamont sighs. "Boy, that looks good," he says wistfully.

"So have one," I say.

He indicates his glittering trunks. "I was in such a hurry to leave the arena that my pants—and my money—are still in the locker room."

"Here, have mine," offers Morton.

"Thanks," says Lamont, taking it from him.

I wait for him to buy another.

He doesn't.

"Boy, am I thirsty!" I say finally. "You must be thirsty too, Morton."

Morton shrugs, and I swear I can hear his bones creak. "Not really. The urge has passed. Besides, I don't have any more money."

I try not to sound desperate. "The least I can do is give you another can, on the house, for being so generous."

"No need," says Morton, as polite as ever. "I've been meaning to go on a diet anyway."

I almost do a double take at the thought of a skeleton on a diet. "What the hell," I say in desperation. "I'll buy you a diet pop."

"It's bad for the teeth," answers Morton, giving me a full skeletal grin.

I stand there for a minute, not trusting myself to

speak. Otis looks up at me from his obituary columns, clearly amused, and I swear Harold's snakes are hissing in laughter.

I turn to the medusa, exasperated. "What the hell *are* you doing here anyway?"

"I've come for a shave and a shampoo."

"Please, not a shampoo!" begs one of the snakes. "It gets in our eyes! We'll be good from now on, I promise!"

"It's wet!" cries another. "My uncle Nate drowned during a shampoo!"

"Oh, aren't they just adorable!" exclaims Mavis, no longer wary of the terrified creatures.

The snakes all turn to Mavis. "Save us!" they hiss in unison.

"We promise not to bite," says Cecil. "Probably," he adds very softly.

I'm about to point out that Cecil can't bite anyone anyway when Mavis's face softens into a smile. "How about this," she says. "I'm busy with another client at the moment"—she gestures to Basil—"but if you boys behave, I'll wash you afterward." She raises her hand to stall any protests. "I promise not to immerse any of you in water. I'll just rub you with a wet soapy cloth to get you clean."

The snakes start writhing in excitement.

"You can do *anything* you want to us, sweetie!" one of them exclaims, pulling himself erect.

"Anything at all," agrees another.

"Okay, it's a deal," says Mavis. She turns back to Basil and starts working on his cuticles. Suddenly he yelps in pain.

"Don't be a crybaby," she admonishes him, "I've barely touched you."

He growls.

"Basil!" I warn him.

"But it *hurts*!" he whimpers.

"You're not a cub anymore," I say. "Man up!"

"Or wolf up," adds Morton helpfully.

Basil sinks back down in the chair, and Mavis starts to work on him again. Not a minute has gone by before he's howling in pain. "Oh, I'm so sorry, Basil!" she exclaims. "I'm not used to working on werewolves."

Otis drops his newspaper, now alert, his nostrils twitching. "*Blood!*" he intones.

I look over and see that Mavis has cut Basil near his dewclaw.

"The cream *burns*!" howls the werewolf.

"What's in it?" asks Lamont, walking over and looking at Basil's arm.

"It's a secret recipe that's been used by my family for decades. I know it uses chimera blood, and firebird feathers, and just a dollop of chopped liver. My uncle Saul, who is a Wizard of the Third Order, created it." She sniffs it. "I always thought it had cream cheese as well."

"Is it *supposed* to burn?" I ask, surprised to find myself genuinely worried for Basil.

"Only if I nick him," she responds. "It softens hard dry skin, and I suppose that includes nails, though in all my years as a manicurist I've never nicked a dewclaw before." She pauses, then adds thoughtfully, "In fact, I've never *seen* a dewclaw before. Well, except on my puppy."

"You have a puppy?" asks Lamont, suddenly interested.

"She's the cutest little thing you ever saw," says Mavis.

"Bring her to my next match at the arena," says Lamont. "I could pretend I'm going to eat her, and when I'm just two seconds away from biting her head off, Heroic Horace can whack me over the head with that rubber bat of his and throw me out of the ring."

"Where all your little old ladies will jab you with hat pins," says Morton. "Are you sure you want that?"

"I hadn't thought that far ahead," admits Lamont, and suddenly he's depressed again.

"*Ouch*, goddamn it!" snarls Basil.

"Don't be such a crybaby," I say. "You're giving werewolves a bad name."

"She's cutting me to bits, and you're giving me stupid little homilies!" moans Basil.

Mavis examines his paw, frowning. "I didn't cut a quick," she announces.

"You must have," insists Basil.

She shakes her head. "There's no blood."

"Damn!" grumbles Otis. "It's not fair to get a fellow's hopes up like that."

"You haven't been a fellow in fifty years," I tell him.

"No," concludes Mavis after checking his paw again. "I never touched a quick."

"Then you cut into my skin," says Basil accusingly.

"I most certainly did not," replies Mavis. "There's not a mark on it."

"It's not my skin anyway," sulks Basil. "It's my claw."

"You don't have any feeling in your claw," insists Mavis. "I put a tiny nick in the top of it, but you only have feeling in your quick, and I never touched it."

"Well, it hurts like hell," complains Basil.

"All right, all right," mutters Mavis. "Let me rub a little cream on it, just to make sure you don't get infected while you're running in the park."

She rubs the cream on, and only gravity keeps Basil from jumping right through the ceiling. His howl is so loud that I think he's going to shatter my front window, but fortunately it survives intact, though the mirror behind the chair develops two large cracks in it, and one of my fillings falls out.

"She's murdering me!" screams Basil.

She frowns. "It must be the chopped liver."

"Aw, come on, pal," says Lamont. "I was watching her, and all she did was dab a little cream on a claw."

"Yeah," says Basil bitterly. "And all Lizzie Borden did was trim her father's mustache!"

"If you were acting, I'd say you have the makings of a pro rassler," says Lamont. He frowns. "But you sound like you mean it."

"I do. I was fine until she rubbed that cream on me."

"I think I've got it," says Mavis. "Uncle Saul always complained that he really wanted the feathers of a harpy, but they are almost impossible to find without a qualified tracker, so he had to settle for some equally rare firebird feathers. Obviously the combined ingredients indeed soften the skin—its intended purpose—but the substituted ingredient also increases sensitivity exponentially." She shook her head. "No wonder the cream burns."

Lamont's gaze goes from Basil's claw to the cream and back to the claw. Finally he turns to Mavis and extends his hand. "Would you rub some of that on my hand, please?"

She shrugs and dabs the back of his hand with it.

"Can't feel a thing," says Lamont, who is clearly disappointed.

"I can't feel it on my other three claws," says Basil. "Just where she nicked me."

Lamont holds his hand out. "Bite it."

"No way!" says Basil. "That stuff hurts enough on the *outside* of my body."

"Otis?" says Lamont, extending his hand in the vampire's direction.

"I wish I could accommodate you," answers Otis. "But you don't have any blood. I don't think my metabolism could handle that."

"Ah, what the hell," says Harold, getting to his feet.

He walks over, takes Lamont's hand, and lays it on his head. "Dig in, boys."

Each of the snakes takes a bite—well, all except Cecil, who really needs the services of a dentist with a background in herpetology, or maybe a herpetologist with a background in dentistry—and suddenly Lamont shrieks even louder than Basil did.

"What happened?" I ask.

"I feel *pain*!" he exclaims with a huge grin. "Isn't it wonderful?"

Not surprisingly, not a single person in the shop—not even any of the snakes—agrees with him.

"Don't you see?" continues Lamont. "I'll rub this all over my body before a match, and then I won't have to pretend anymore!"

"You *want* to be in pain?" asks Mavis.

"It's for my fans," he answers. "Especially the little old ladies. They've kept me in business since I came back from . . . well . . . you know. This is the least I can do for them." A pause. "Maybe I'd better give it a field test."

He takes off his coat and has Mavis rub her cream all over his back, his eyes lighting up in both pleasure and pain as the cream bites into the wounds the little hat pin ladies inflicted after his match. "You can get more of this stuff, right?" he asks through gritted teeth.

"Uncle Saul left us five gallons of it," she tells him. "And if we run out, I'm sure I can convince him to leave the mausoleum for one night and make more.

He's always complaining about how cramped he feels in his tomb anyway."

Lamont walks to the door. "Wish me luck."

We all do, and then he's out in the street.

"Well, I'll be damned," says Otis, looking up from the paper. "Horatio Throop died."

"Who was Horatio Throop?" asks Morton.

"The cop who tracked me down after I bit every girl at the Our Lady of Unseemly Passions Flower Festival over in Brooklyn. Put six slugs into me at point-blank range. Of course they didn't do any damage at all, except to the watch I had in a vest pocket. They didn't believe his story at headquarters and fired him for being drunk or maybe delusional. We became quite good friends after that. Whenever he was depressed he'd give me a phone call, come on over, empty his revolver into me, and then he'd feel all better."

Just then Ursula the Undine enters the shop. She is only three feet tall, bald as an egg, and totally without fingernails, so I know she's not here on business.

"I don't mean to bother you," she says breathlessly, "but there's quite a commotion going on out there. I almost got trampled to death!"

"Oh?" I say.

"Yes," she replies. "A bunch of wild-eyed old ladies are chasing some poor guy down the street, jabbing him with hat pins. He's screaming in pain, but as he passed me he was smiling the biggest damned smile you ever saw."

"Mavis," I say as Ursula works up the courage to go back outside, "it looks like you just may have a client for life."

"Which in this case," adds Otis, "means quite a bit more than usual."

Acknowledgments

Will Ludwigsen

Such a work as this, plumbing the depths of everlasting human existence, could never be written alone, and the author is grateful to the following people and institutions without whom his expedition to Mosschase would not have been possible.

First, without the generous financial support of George M. Theerian, owner and president of the Theerian Wig Factory, this project could not have been executed at all. Though I never met his first wife, Flora, while she lived, she was clearly an extraordinary woman well worthy of her husband's obsession with the postmortem persistence of spirit. I am sorry not to have made her acquaintance during our séances, but I'm told that women spirits deprived of their worldly bodies sometimes find my locus of masculinity too intimidating to confront.

The wit, class, and emotional sensitivity of the present Mrs. Theerian, the radiant Pauline, could well have been my bedrock during the whole ordeal of Mosschase House. From her knowing glances to her sublime taste in hats, I couldn't ask for a greater companion. Her shoulder-rubs were almost as exquisite as her insights.

My own wife, Opal, of course, proved ever helpful as well, attending to worldly matters back in Sussex while I attended to the otherworldly ones.

David Darley and the team from Westinghouse were literally instrumental to our exploration: without their durable electrostatic detectors, temperature gauges, spirit condensers, radium lanterns, Victrola voice-capture machines, and ectoplasm containment jars, we'd have been marooned forever on the island of ignorance. May they soon conquer the fickle bitch of alternating current!

Beatrice and Chester Kleiner, present occupants of Mosschase, permitted free access to their home for all six weeks of our investigation. Both graciously accepted the daily company of twenty spirit investigators, not to mention their equipment, their foodstuffs, their sweat-soaked waistcoats and cravats, and their often coarse language. Some of the men proved quite excitable, and I beg the good Mrs. Kleiner's forgiveness for my torrent of obscenity in the face of the First Manifestation (see chapter 1). As for the wreckage of the south basement wall, I am sure the inevitable profits of this book can easily pay for that damage as well as the charred library mezzanine.

My gratitude runs especially strong for Emil Kleiner, that scamp cousin of Chester's, whose home-brewed absinthe accelerated both our quiet nights and our active ones.

My sincerest apologies, too, to young Master Heinrich Kleiner. To eyes aching from the lack of sleep, a ten-year-old boy in pajamas can easily be mistaken for an apparition, and we pray that the burns from the Faraday Net have long since subsided. Chin up, little soldier!

Mosschase wouldn't be a delightfully sinister heap of misshapen stones without the clumsy architectural stylings of Sir Quentin Montrose or the slipshod workmanship of Charles Gaston. Together, they built the perfect haunted house atop that lonely chalk cliff, knotted with ancient oaks and strangled by vines: a veritable spectral honeypot. Well done, gentlemen!

And, though I am loath to do it, I suppose I must also thank Baron Gerhardt von Klaugh for the underlying psychic trauma that makes Mosschase such an embassy for the damned. While I can't condone his practice of sewing shut children's mouths or hanging their corpses as puppets, it certainly suited his former home for my purposes.

I offer much gratitude, also, to the generations of terrified servants, wide-eyed children, and gibbering drunks whose local gossip served like linguistic lenses, compounding mere rumor into legend and finally, wondrously, into reality. So, too, must I thank my peers among the spiritual sciences whose dim fumbling against the shadows on Plato's wall saved me decades of false starts and blind alleys. Who'd have thought the answer, gentlemen, was simply to turn around?

Then there are the mediums. Where to start? Clearly with the ones who were less than successful.

Charley Two Feathers, if that even is his real name, provided a pleasant ambience of primitive spirituality. We're sorry that his spirit guides proved to be wholly ineffectual during the investigation, though one could hardly expect animals to operate a talking board anyway. Best of luck with the traveling carnival, "Charley"!

Though poor Madame Vladovich's spiritual eyes proved to be as cataract clouded as her ordinary ones, I'm quite obliged for her energetic table lifting. It isn't easy for an eighty-seven-year-old woman to heft an oaken table with rulers in her sleeves, but she certainly did. Brava!

Little Wendy Wexham, God rest her soul, gave us the last few weeks of her consumptive life just to communicate with souls as estranged from life as her own. I hope she's found her well-earned peace.

And, lo, the poor successful Erwin Haste: how sorry we were to have to send a bullet through your brain. Would that your open mind had not been so roomy for evil, my friend. Would, too, that the leather straps had held. May God forgive us for burying you facing down.

Harry the Gardener deserves my gratitude for his enthusiastic work with the pickaxe. If I'm ever trapped beneath a wall of infant skeletons again, their tiny bone hands clawing at my face, you will be the first man I'll telegraph.

To the neighbors, I will say I'm sorry. We did determine the awful truth behind the ghostly lights and the keening screeches at midnight, but ending them was beyond the charter of our expedition. We are planning a second excursion to your wonderful countryside, one dedicated to expelling this darkness once and for all. Donations for our cause will be heartily accepted by the publisher and passed on to us. Stay calm and carry on, good worthies: we're on our way.

And finally, most importantly, I thank you, the discerning reader, the curious and adventuresome explorer, for your excellent taste. It is your enthusiasm for the outré that makes it all worthwhile.

Mannequin

HEATHER GRAHAM

A scream pierced the air, loud and clear. The two young people sitting in the parlor of the Cantrell house froze for a moment. The sound touched them with such a knifing quality; it awoke in them a sense of acute primeval fear.

"What the hell?" Janet demanded, jumping up. There was deep concern and anxiety in her dark eyes and her long hair swayed as she moved; Janet was *Vogue* beautiful.

"Someone in the basement is playing games, surely," Keith, her boyfriend, said. But he too quickly came to his feet, ready to rush by Janet's side down to the basement to see what demons of the night might be playing games.

Andrew Adair was already up and moving. The scream had to have come from Alexi—Alexi was his wife, and they all knew her scream. She tended to be afraid of her own shadow. And yet, they were in the *Cantrell* house.

But Alexi had wanted to come here. She always said that she was a coward, but she still loved being afraid. Andrew, however, worried; maybe this was proving to be too much for her. Andrew knew that he, Keith, and Janet were the ones who truly loved horror movies, museums of the macabre, grisly tales and truths, and all things terrible and spooky.

Andrew didn't believe in ghosts.

Alexi did.

The Cantrell house was known worldwide for its horrible history, and, naturally, ghosts.

"Come on!" he called over his shoulder, already moving.

They actually had to leave the house through the kitchen via the side door and walk around back to take the steps down to the basement.

There were mannequins in the basement, just as there were in the house. When they opened the hatch and hurried down the stairs, one greeted them at the landing. She was dressed in an apron and a day dress; the apron was covered in a red stain. Blood. The owner of the now-bed-and-breakfast that the Cantrell house had become, Lacy Shore, had told them that when she'd bought the house from the previous owner, she'd bought the mannequins as well. The previous owner had claimed that the mannequin's apron was really that of Sarah Cantrell—Angus's second wife, the one who had hacked him to death in his bed in the murder room.

"Alexi!" Andrew cried.

She flew across the basement floor and into his arms.

"Who's down here?" Janet demanded. "Who made you scream?"

"What were you doing down here alone?" Andrew asked her, smoothing back her hair.

"I thought that Lacy was calling me—I heard voices down here," Alexi said.

"Lacy scared you?" Andrew asked. He was doubtful. Lacy thought a few unusual things had happened in the house. She greeted visitors, and she worked on maintenance, but she didn't live in it. He had a really hard time believing that she would purposely try to scare her visitors.

Alexi looked up at Andrew with her huge blue eyes. He had to admit, his wife looked the type of little blond snow queen to be scared at the drop of a hat.

"Alexi?" he asked.

"She *moved*," Alexi said.

"Who moved?" Andrew asked.

"She—she moved!"

Alexi turned and pointed a finger at the manne-quin that stood by the hundred-and-fifty-year-old defunct incinerator.

Andrew assumed that the mannequin was supposed to be Sarah Cantrell, the second wife of Angus. She stood near the old incinerator, a poker in her hand. Andrew wasn't sure what she was doing there—perhaps discovering a few of the bodies her husband had chopped up to burn.

The basement, of course, was supposed to be haunted. Many "ghost hunters" had come to the house over the years to do "expeditions," and they had all claimed that the specter of Angus Cantrell often haunted the basement. The basement was where he had honed his weapons. After the Civil War, he'd gone berserk—and he'd become very adept with a knife. The story had it that he'd used it first on his first wife and then on those who came to accept his hospitality when he ran the home as a tavern. Undetected in his life of grisly crime, Angus Cantrell had married again. His wife had found his stash of weapons and corpses in the basement.

She, in turn, had hacked to death Angus Cantrell, as he slept, in the room upstairs, now known, of course, as the "murder room." It had all happened in the late 1860s, and though remnants of bodies had been found, the tale had come out through Sarah Cantrell, the second wife who had killed him and had been the only one to come close to him and survive.

"It's easy to imagine that they move," Janet said.

"They're very real looking," Keith said, agreeing.

"But, Alexi, she didn't really move," Andrew said.

"I saw her! And she . . . she made me come down here!" Alexi protested.

Andrew disentangled himself to move over by the mannequin. He tapped her on the chin. The dull glass eyes stared at him, and for a moment, he felt a little shiver along his spine. The damned thing did look real. "Behave!" he said aloud, trying to get Alexi to laugh. "I mean . . . just behave, young woman! What's that? Ah!" He looked over at Alexi. "She's going to be good."

Alexi didn't look assured.

Andrew popped behind the mannequin and slipped his arms around it, pretending that his arms were the mannequin's. "Alexi, I do declare, there are those nasty open bulbs up there and all kinds of creepy shadows down here, and that's all!"

Keith and Janet laughed, especially when he placed his hand against the mannequin's cheek in mock horror.

"Andrew, get away from that thing!" Alexi said.

He'd touched the damn thing just to try to make her laugh; however, he had to admit there was something about it that didn't feel right. It should have been cold and hard. It seemed to have a strange warmth, to hum with an inner energy.

They heard footsteps on the stairs; even Andrew's heart leapt a little. The basement was . . . dark, dank, and creepy. The floor was mostly dirt over old bricks. The only light came from a few naked bulbs overhead, and they cast a strange glow over the room, falling on the mannequin and the old boxes and trunks that were here and there and causing them to create shadows, eerie contortions that almost seemed alive as they moved against the walls.

"What's going on down here?" someone called.

They all started at the sudden sound of the voice echoing in the basement.

But it was only Lacy, the owner. She was just a few years older than their group, probably in her early thirties. Andrew had struck up a conversation with her when he had called months ago to find a night on which he could book the entire bed-and-breakfast for their little crew. He'd later found rumors on the Internet that Lacy had indulged in an affair with a rich rock star; the bed-and-breakfast had been her compensation.

"Alexi got spooked," Janet explained.

Lacy laughed. "Okay, that happens a lot." She walked across the length of the floor to the mannequin. "Sarah, behave!" she said, grinning.

"Yes, I just suggested that she do so," Andrew said.

"Well, I was checking in with you. The medium is on her way. She takes cash—you remember I told you, right?"

"Yes, thanks. We have cash," Andrew said. Alexi was still pressed to his chest. "Hey," he said gently. "We're going upstairs, huh? The medium is coming."

Alexi nodded, still pressed against him.

The mannequin of a man in an old-fashioned frock coat was in the kitchen by the woodpile and the stove. Ironically, there was an axe in the pile of wood. The mannequin might have reached down and picked it up. It was tall with whiskers and a beard and brown glass eyes that seemed to be looking at you, wherever you stood. He knew that it was supposed to represent Angus Cantrell.

"Don't these things creep you out?" Andrew asked Lacy.

She shrugged, walking past the stove—it wasn't from the mid-eighteen hundreds, but it was an antique, probably from the turn of the century—and went to the sink. She turned on water to fill a kettle. "I've gotten used to them. When I bought the place a few years ago, they were all already here, and they were dressed, and they were creepy, yeah, but . . . hey, I rent this place all the time in the middle of nowhere outside of Richmond because it is creepy! You all booked here to be creepy, right?"

"True," Andrew admitted.

"You don't live here," Alexi said.

Lacy set the kettle on the old stove. "No, I live in a condo," she admitted. "But I've stayed here before. All night. Alone."

"And did anything . . . happen?" Alexi asked.

Lacy shook her head. "I thought I heard noises, but the house is nearly two hundred years old—old houses creak and groan."

"Where did you sleep?" Andrew asked her. "In the murder room?"

"No," Lacy admitted. "I slept on the sofa."

"That's no better," Alexi pointed out. "There's a lady in the front entry hallway, too, between the stairs and the door to the living room."

"Oh, that's Catherine Cantrell—the first wife," Lacy said mischievously. "They believe he made her disappear in the incinerator. He got married again, to Sarah, because she had so much money. He didn't think that Sarah would get him before he got Sarah! Okay, I admit, I was freaked out. So, I sat up and said, 'Oh, please! Don't haunt me. I'm trying to keep history alive here, please be kind—another owner might get rid of you all!'"

Even Alexi uttered a nervous laugh.

"Honestly, I'm not as easily spooked as Alexi," Janet said, "but I have to admit—I don't think that I could stay here alone. The house is bad enough with all the negative karma, but those mannequins . . . ugh!"

"They're actually rather cool," Keith said. "So life-like!"

They heard a tap on the door and a cheerful "Hello!"

Alexi jumped.

"It's the medium," Andrew said, trying to reassure her.

It was the medium. She was a slim woman with huge brown eyes and long dark hair that fell down her back beneath the wrap she wore around her head. She was in a skirt and Gypsy blouse, striking and dramatic. Her skin was the gold that came with the mix of many races; she was exactly the woman he would have expected to meet in a carnival tent.

"Hello. I'm Natasha Jennings, your guide through the spirit world," she said. "Hello, Lacy. Thank you for calling me," she added gravely. "You know how I feel connected with this house."

"Hey, Natasha," Lacy said. "Meet your group, Andrew and Alexi, and Janet and Keith.

"The perfect medium!" Keith whispered.

Natasha heard him. She spun around to stare at him gravely. She looked him up and down, and then smiled.

"Oh, yes. I am perfect. I'm a vessel. I'm a vessel for the spirits of the house. You see, they no longer have substance; they need a conduit. I just happen to be a conduit; I didn't choose my role in life. I've just been chosen."

"Right," Andrew murmured. "Of course." He tried to be serious, but Keith was standing behind the woman as she turned back to the group. Keith looked at Andrew, trying to contain a laugh. But he rolled his eyes and made the circle in the air next to his head that indicated the word *crazy* and even Alexi grinned.

"This is very serious business," Natasha warned them, as if she could see Keith.

"Of course!" Andrew said in agreement. When Natasha turned, he winked at Alexi. She looked back at him, frowning in warning.

"Just a vessel," Keith said dryly.

Janet elbowed him.

"Ow!"

"Careful of your *vessel,*" she warned him.

Natasha spun around to stare at them.

They all four smiled.

"Well, then!" Natasha said. "Come on, I'm going to set up in the living room."

Natasha pulled one of the little doily-covered occasional tables into the middle of the room, and, as they followed her, she instructed them to bring chairs around the table. "You can grab some from the dining room!" she told them.

They did so.

"Now . . . Lacy, get the main lights, will you? Now, everyone, sit around, your hands on the table, your fingertips just touching."

The group did as instructed. Lacy turned off the lights but didn't come to the table. She watched, leaning against the wall.

Alexi was to the left of the medium; Andrew sat next to her, and then Keith and Janet.

"First of all, just concentrate on clearing your minds. Think about the house and those who came through it. Think about Angus Cantrell, and his wives, and the others. Close your eyes, and let it all flow."

Andrew didn't close his eyes. He could see Lacy, and she had closed her eyes.

Suggestible! he thought.

He looked around the table; even the medium had closed her eyes. He was the only holdout.

But his gaze fell on the mannequin just outside the door frame in the main entry to the house—Angus Cantrell's first wife, Catherine Cantrell. The mannequin wasn't facing him; she was turned to the doorway, as if she waited to greet guests and direct them up the stairs to the bedrooms.

The murder room was the first room on the left, although, God knew, Angus Cantrell had reportedly killed ten to twenty "guests" when he had opened his home as an inn and tavern in the late 1860s.

"Now," Natasha said, "open up your hearts and minds, and let the spirits in the house speak to us. Ah . . . Angus Cantrell! You're with us now, aren't you?"

Andrew felt the table wiggle slightly. He saw Natasha's hands. They were flat on the table. It was a lightweight table. She could have moved it with a shift of her hand or even her leg.

Alexi let out a little gasp.

"Does anyone have a question for Angus?" Natasha asked.

"Why?" Janet asked softly. "Why did you kill all those people?"

The table seemed to leap in the air; Alexi let out a loud gasp.

"He says that you're rude and that you should understand. They taught him in the war to kill the enemy, and he only killed his enemies," Natasha said.

Andrew had the feeling that Angus Cantrell was saying no such thing. He managed to keep quiet; Alexi respected ghosts.

"Why did he kill his wife—his first wife?" Janet asked.

"Angus?" Natasha said, scrunching her eyes tightly closed. "Angus, come on, talk to your guests now. Why did you kill Catherine?"

The table began to sway.

"She was the enemy, too—that's what he says," Natasha said.

"Did he think that she'd betrayed him when he was off fighting in the war?" Alexi asked, her voice a little squeaky.

It seemed that the table really bucked on its own. The medium was pretty good at what she did, Andrew thought. But, then again, he couldn't wait until she was gone to test his theories.

"She was a whore! Like the whore of Babylon!" Natasha said. Her jaw suddenly went slack. Her voice actually took on a different sound, and she began speaking, not as Angus, but as someone else.

"I was innocent! I was innocent, and he killed me because of Sarah—he wanted her and her money, and so he made up a story about me betraying him with a Yankee captain! She was already in our lives; he knew her, and she was willing . . ."

The table began to wildly spin and gyrate. Alexi screamed and pulled back.

The table went still. Natasha opened her eyes and stared at them all.

"What the hell?" Keith yelped.

"Natasha!" Lacy breathed from the archway.

"What, what?" Natasha asked, ashen, her own hands pulled back from the table.

"You were speaking as Catherine Cantrell," Lacy told her.

"I've *never* had anything like that happen before!" Natasha said.

"Really?" Andrew said dryly. He had misjudged the carnival quality of the woman. She was really quite an accomplished actress.

"I speak with Angus all the time. He knows that I'm not his enemy," Natasha said. "He's the entity who comes to me—not Catherine." She appeared to be sincerely disturbed. Shaken. Even distressed by what had happened. She looked around their group. "Ah! There's another vessel in the room, a natural medium who doesn't know it yet. The added surge of power in the room brought it all home to me!"

"Oh, no, not me! I'm not a vessel," Janet said.

Natasha stared around the table at them, one by one. Her eyes lit on Alexi, who let out a little squeak of protest. "No, nope, no vessel here!" she said. Alexi was white. Andrew rose, shaking his head. They were all supposed to be laughing, and he had to get her laughing again.

"I'll get you your money," Andrew said. He rose;

his coat was in the entry on a hook; he had the twenty bucks apiece they all owed her.

As he started out of the room and into the entry, he froze.

The mannequin of Catherine Cantrell was now facing him. She seemed to be smiling.

He gave himself a shake; it was Alexi. She was so spooked that she was spooking them all, putting things into their minds, and they were starting to believe what they saw.

He walked past the mannequin. To his irritation, he felt a chill as he passed by the *thing*. She was dressed in a light blue flowered day dress. She had been created with a brown wig and hazel eyes, and those eyes seemed very natural and real. They were glass.

He got the money. As he reached into his coat pocket, he felt as if she was watching him. Impossible. She had somehow been turned to look into the parlor. He spun around, almost expecting the mannequin to have turned again.

Or to be standing right behind him!

She was not behind him, nor had she turned. He almost laughed aloud at himself.

He went back into the parlor and paid Natasha. She was speaking quietly with the others. "I've never even heard a suggestion that Angus killed his first wife in order to marry his second wife! Can you imagine the scandal back then?"

"So, was he crazy? Murdered his wife and all those

people because of insanity, because the South had lost the war, or because he was smart, cold, cool, and calculating?" Keith asked.

"Who knows?" Natasha said.

"But wait," Alexi said. "Sarah finally killed Angus. What happened to her?"

"She inherited the inn and the tavern and lived happily to the ripe old age of ninetysomething. Her grave is in Hollywood Cemetery. She lived from 1848 to 1945," Lacy told them from the doorway. "She left the house to a niece, who sold it immediately to the people who owned it right before the woman I bought it from. I guess, really, it was her house way more than it was Angus's house."

"Well, I have to go. Thank you!" Natasha said. She walked to the door and turned around and stared at them all. "Don't laugh at what lies beyond," she said gravely. "There's a vessel among you!"

Dramatically, she disappeared around the doorway.

When they heard the door out to the driveway close, Keith burst out in laughter.

"Stop it! She could still hear you," Janet protested.

"Oh, my love, I was just thinking that I'm going to *vessel* you pretty damned soon tonight!" Keith said, rolling his eyes.

Andrew looked at Lacy; she was still looking after Natasha. He glanced over at his wife, and she still looked disturbed.

He turned back to Lacy. "Okay, Lacy, please, I just have to check this out!"

"What's that?" Lacy asked.

"I know what he's doing!" Janet said. "Come on, Lacy, take Natasha's position."

"Please!" Andrew said.

Lacy joined them.

Alexi stared at Andrew. "Don't do this!" she whispered.

He gave her an encouraging smile. She returned it with a fierce frown. Well, one thing he knew: although he and Keith had decided they'd have great sex here at night with their women scared and spooked, he knew he wasn't going to get lucky in any fashion.

He still had to prove his point.

"Everyone, hands on the table . . . fingertips just touching. Now, clear your minds . . . think of the entities in the house!"

"Should we close our eyes?" Janet asked mischievously.

"Don't be silly," Keith said. "We're proving a point."

"Does anyone have a question for the spirits?" Andrew asked.

"I do, I do!" Keith said, "Come on, Cantrell, admit it! The old wife was kind of a cold and boring *vessel*, eh? And the new one promised all kinds of hot action!"

Janet and Lacy laughed; Alexi didn't.

Andrew had meant for the table to move; he'd meant to prove that they could move it just as the medium had done. He touched the leg with his foot and put pressure on his hands, hopefully so that none could see.

As he had expected, he got the table to move. As he hadn't expected, it moved violently.

"See! There you go!" Keith said, laughing. "I'm sorry, Lacy—your medium was a total sham."

Of course the table moved violently. Keith and Janet were aiding and abetting his trial!

"So she was," Lacy said. "Maybe," she added quietly. She looked toward the door, as if she was eager to leave herself. "But, hey, it's good theater. And I've got to get home myself. Cats, you know," she told them. "I have three of them. They expect to be fed at night. Make yourselves at home; I get back at about six, and we'll plan breakfast for eight. Checkout is eleven, remember, and you can hang around, but I have to have you out of your rooms by then." She smiled. "We have to clean up for the next guests coming in."

They all bid her good night.

And they had the house alone, the four of them, just as they had planned.

"Let's keep playing!" Janet suggested.

"I don't think it's a good idea," Keith said, looking at Janet. Andrew was surprised. Keith looked like a linebacker. He wasn't the type to be easily frightened. Andrew wasn't actually a slouch himself; he worked with computers but kept up at the gym.

"Then get up, my love," Janet said. "This *vessel* right here is curious!"

Keith left the table. Andrew was surprised that Alexi didn't get up. She seemed transfixed.

"Alexi," he said softly.

His wife's huge blue eyes turned to him. "We have to know!" she said softly.

"Know what?" he asked her, perplexed. He shouldn't have brought her here. The whole thing had sounded like so much fun, but now he was worried. He was seeing mannequins move himself, and he wasn't as suggestible as Alexi.

"The truth. Andrew, it's going to be important. We have to know the truth."

"Alexi—"

"Leave!" she said firmly.

"Alexi, we're an hour from Richmond—"

"Put your hands on the table, Andrew," she told him.

He sighed and did so. "Hey, we've already proved a point," he said.

Alexi spoke now. "Clear your minds. Concentrate on this house, on history, on the past. Think about a time long past, when a country was healing, when people had begun to travel again. Think about coming home . . . to your wife. About being suspicious of your wife. About meeting a new woman. About revenge on those who you thought stole your life or your youth and your country . . . concentrate on the people who came here . . ."

Alexi *was doing it!* Andrew thought. He wasn't, but Alexi was. She was making the table move, because it was rolling again.

"What is the truth? If there's a spirit or an entity out there, please, let us know the truth," Janet said quietly.

Alexi began to speak in a strange voice.

"Help me! Help me get her out of my house! They were wrong; Angus wasn't a killer. It was her! Sarah . . . Sarah came, and Sarah killed, and Angus was a fool. She made him into a cheater. Just like you!"

Alexi was staring straight at Keith.

"What?" Keith demanded. "Hey, I'm not a cheater!"

Janet stared at him.

"She's lying! I don't know what she's talking about. Ah, come on, baby. Alexi, what the hell are you doing to me?"

Alexi ignored him; she was speaking in the funny voice again. "No one would have thought that he would have been unfaithful to me. It was her! He believed her lies . . . help me!"

There was strange silence; Andrew could feel the tension around him.

"Help me, help me, help me!"

The words came from Alexi's lips. Andrew wondered how she had managed to change her tone of voice so.

"Alexi—" he said. What the hell was she doing? Janet and Keith were their friends.

"Help me!" she screamed.

As she did, the house was suddenly pitched into blackness.

Andrew felt a chill of pure terror seep into him. He started to stand; he felt his wife's hand on his wrist. Her fingers were like a steel trap; they were as cold as ice.

"Jesus!" Keith cried.

"Oh, my God!" Janet gasped.

The table fell as she leapt to her feet.

The lights came back on.

Alexi was still in her chair; the others were standing.

"What happened?" Alexi demanded.

Janet stared at her from the safety of Keith's arms. She started to laugh. "Oh, Alexi, you've had us all fooled. That was great. You were amazing! You should just become a medium—you'll freak everyone out!"

Alexi stood, angry. "I didn't do anything—I don't even know what you're talking about."

"Alexi, we're onto you!" Keith said, and he laughed, too. "Except, tell Janet the truth—you were playacting. I never cheated on anyone."

"I never said you did."

"Alexi, you did!" Keith said.

"She was fooling around; come on, guys, snap out of it!" Andrew said. He looked at his wife. "She's had us all fooled all these years—she's the brave one and the prankster."

Janet giggled nervously. "Alexi, I gotta admit, that was creepy good. Amazing!"

"Stop it!" Alexi said. "Stop it! I didn't do anything."

Andrew wondered if the scary history was really getting to her; she had to have acted out what she had just done, but it seemed that she didn't realize it herself.

He didn't want a huge fight among good friends, and he knew he'd have to defend his wife. He loved Alexi. She loved him. They were lucky. But what the hell had she been trying to do with Keith and Janet? He had to break it all up for now, though, ease the tension.

"Hey, let's check out the bedrooms again," he said.

"Sure—I'm glad you claimed the murder room!" Janet said.

"We'll take the one down the hall, to the right," Keith said.

"Yeah? You may be sleeping by yourself, mister," Janet told Keith."

Keith groaned. "It was an act! Right, Alexi?"

"I don't know what you're talking about," Alexi said.

"Alexi!" Andrew groaned.

"I didn't accuse Keith of anything," she said.

"Okay, let's check out the rooms," Andrew suggested. He stood as casually as he could and walked toward the foyer.

He passed the mannequin. The mannequin of Catherine Cantrell.

Damn it! It appeared that the damned thing had moved again, that she watched him as he walked.

Stop it—be sane! he told himself.

"Come on, guys!"

They followed him up the stairs. First, they walked past the murder room and all piled into the room at the left. There was no mannequin in the room.

"We'll take this one!" Keith said. He plopped down on the bed. As he did so, they heard, "Oh, Keith!"

Spinning around, Andrew saw that Janet had taken a doll off the bed from the bedroom across the hall. She remained in the hallway herself, and the doll—as creepy looking as the mannequin—was just inside the doorway. Janet made it dance. "Oh, Keith, you better not be a lying scumbag!"

Andrew had to laugh. Alexi cracked a small smile.

"Get it out and stop it!" Keith said.

Andrew took his wife by the shoulders. "Come on, guys, we're supposed to be laughing here, remember? Alexi, let's go to bed, shall we?"

"I can't! I can't go to sleep here," she said.

"Well, I'm going to sleep," Keith said.

"Great. There's a room in the attic," Janet teased him.

"Alexi! Tell her the truth!" Keith implored.

"Look, I don't know what you're talking about," Alexi protested.

Keith, angry, got up and brushed by them. He hurried back downstairs.

"All-righty then!" Janet said. "Maybe he does have a guilty conscience! Whatever, I am actually exhausted. Good night, all!"

She prodded Andrew and Alexi out to the hallway. Andrew stood uncertainly. "Go to bed," Janet told them. "I suspected him and that little twat he sees for coffee before work. I'm sorry, all. And thanks, Alexi, for the truth."

"I didn't—" Alexi began.

"Good night; we'll sort it all out in the morning," Andrew said. He drew Alexi behind him and they walked into the murder room.

Alexi stood at the foot of the bed. "It was here, Andrew. It was here that Sarah Cantrell killed her husband. I think she killed him because he fell out of love with her, and even if their Yankee visitors had been his enemies in the war, he was sick of the carnage. You know? I think that she was the really evil one! He knew that he'd killed Catherine for nothing. She was the one. She came here first as a friend, and she killed people, and then she killed Catherine. History has it all backward—because Sarah was the survivor, and that's the story she told. But it was a lie."

"Let's get some sleep, Alexi," Andrew said. He stripped down to his boxers and slid between the sheets, wondering how what had seemed like such a fun and wonderful idea as a weekend getaway for friends had turned into such a disaster.

She kept staring at the bed.

"Alexi, please!" he said softly. "Alexi, I love you, let's please get some sleep and hope we can fix this all in the morning."

She shook her head. "Please," she said aloud, and she wasn't speaking to him. "Please, keep us safe through the night. We feel for you; we believe in you. Keep us safe through the night! Protect us in this house!" She looked at him seriously. "If you speak to them nicely—like Lacy says she did—they'll leave you alone."

"Speak to them nicely?" Andrew said. "Oh, come on, please, Alexi—"

"Speak to them nicely!" she insisted.

"Uh—yeah. Hi, there, you all," he said. "Please, let us sleep here tonight, and don't wake us up, and . . . wow, I'm sure you were all really great people! Love ya all!" he said.

Alexi groaned. "Don't make fun of them!" she protested.

"Sorry. Um, hello, and please just let us sleep peacefully?" he asked, looking at Alexi.

"Better!" she said.

"Okay, Alexi, great, now come to bed," Andrew said.

After undressing, she crawled in beside him. She squeezed his hand and moved close to him. Usually when she did so, he experienced an instant erection.

That night, he shriveled like a prune. Pathetic.

But he squeezed her hand in return. He thought about getting up and making the drive back to Richmond. Then, of course, he'd have no manhood left at all. He gritted his teeth; sleep. If he could just fall asleep, he'd make it through the night, and in the morning, everything would be fine.

"It's all right; *we're* safe," she said.

Somehow, that didn't make him feel any better.

He lay awake for what seemed like forever, listening to the ticking of the old clock on the dresser. After some time, however, he fell asleep.

He knew he had fallen asleep because he woke with a start when a terrible scream from below seemed to shatter the night.

His eyes flew open.

And it was above him.

It.

The mannequin of Catherine Cantrell.

It leaned over him, its glass eyes on him as if it saw him. He screamed himself. He screamed long and loud, and in pure terror. Instinct made him rise in desperation and push at the *thing*.

"No!" Alexi cried, leaping to her feet. The mannequin had fallen back, but it hadn't fallen down. It was as if it had taken a step back.

The scream from below sounded again. "Come on!" Alexi told him. Before he could stop her, she was running to the stairs. Andrew jumped up to follow her; he crashed into Janet as she came bolting out of her room as well.

"What? What the hell?" Janet demanded.

"Help!" Alexi called from below. "Help us, help us, now!"

Andrew and Janet stared at one another. Wordlessly, they turned toward the stairs as well and raced down.

And Andrew didn't believe what he saw.

The mannequin of Sarah Cantrell was in the parlor. She had the axe in her hands. So far, she had axed half the sofa, trying to hit Keith, who was desperately avoiding her blows while Alexi looked for a weapon to use against the mannequin. She found a rolled-up newspaper and smacked the Sarah Cantrell mannequin on the head. The mannequin didn't even notice.

"*Newspaper, Alexi? Get something hard!*" Keith screamed in panic.

The mannequin of Angus Cantrell was walking in from the kitchen, jerking as he did so, glass eyes staring straight ahead.

"No!" Keith screamed.

"No!" Alexi gasped, and she raced forward, but the mannequin of Sarah Cantrell turned the axe toward her, and Alexi had to duck, screaming.

"No, no, no!" Keith said, frozen against the wall.

Sarah Cantrell turned toward him again.

"Stop!" Alexi cried.

She rushed past the axe-wielding mannequin and grasped a chair; it shattered as the axe was turned on her. Keith found strength; he rose and rushed forward, but the mannequin of Angus stopped him, throwing him back against the wall. He fell with a little whimper and went limp.

Andrew made a dash for the mannequin. It threw him off as if he were a fly. Janet screamed and raced toward the door; the Sarah Cantrell mannequin caught her and dragged her back by the hair. Andrew made a dive for its feet, and it fell over . . .

But it rose, and it started coming toward him, and they were both coming toward him . . .

He was vaguely aware of movement from the foyer. The mannequin of Catherine Cantrell was coming down the stairs. Not walking. *Gliding.*

He couldn't move; he heard Alexi scream, but he couldn't help her. He could only stare upward as the mannequin of Sarah Cantrell came toward him, the axe raised high . . .

The police arrived just at the break of dawn. Officer Landsfield stared around at the carnage in the parlor. "Looks like a massacre, all right," he said.

Arms and legs were strewn about the parlor.

"Young people," his partner, Officer Merrill, said, a note of sorrow in his voice. "They just have no respect for history."

"So," Landsfield said, and he turned to look at Andrew, who had managed to dress by now and was wondering himself what had happened. "Can you explain? I'm not sure yet just what we're going to charge you with!"

He looked over at Alexi, who was standing there,

shivering, by his side. He arched a brow at her. How in the hell were they ever going to explain this?

"They did it to themselves," Alexi said weakly.

"What?" Landsfield demanded.

"Well, you see . . . I woke up when one was on top of me," Andrew said. "I didn't realize she was just trying to warn me. Honestly, history has it all wrong. Sarah was the killer. My wife contacted Catherine, somehow, and . . . well, Sarah went after Keith, and I guess Angus was trying to protect Sarah—fool, he still loved her—and then Catherine came down to save us all. And she did. As you can see," he said, trying for a smile and a bit of humor, "Catherine is still standing. The pieces you see belong to Sarah and Angus."

"Oh, funny guy, huh? I'll get a pack of other charges to add to vandalism!" Landsfield told him.

"It's the truth!" Alexi said.

"And who creamed you on the head?" Landsfield demanded, turning to Keith.

Keith opened his mouth to explain; he closed his mouth and waved a hand in the air. No one was going to believe him.

Janet remained silent as well.

Andrew let out a long sigh. "Look, please. We were scared to death. I don't know what happened. Maybe we imagined it. We thought we were under attack. I'll pay for all the damages," he said. It might put them back a year, but he would pay for the damages—and happily, if they could just leave the Cantrell house.

"Lacy, what do you say?" Landsfield asked.

Lacy was back leaning against the door frame of the parlor. "Let them go; I'll take a check for the damage. Just let them go." She walked into the room and to the mannequin of Catherine Cantrell. The mannequin didn't move. She picked it up awkwardly and put it back in the foyer. She shook her head and moved it to the window. "There. She's all alone now, so she can greet people."

"I'll write a check," Andrew said.

"You write a check, and don't you ever come back to this town, young man!" Landsfield warned him.

"I swear!" Andrew promised him. He looked at the others. "Let's get our stuff—and get out!"

They moved faster than bats out of hell.

Ten minutes later, they were packed, badly dressed, and not one of them had brushed their hair or their teeth, but they didn't give a damn. They were in their cars, and their engines were revving.

"You okay?" Andrew asked Alexi.

She nodded, smiling. "I'm fine," she said, reassuring him. "I knew they could move!" she added in a whisper.

Had the damned things moved? Or had they all scared themselves into a frenzy?

Andrew didn't think that he'd ever know.

But he looked back.

And there she was, Catherine Cantrell. She was standing in the window, and she had been moved to look as if she was waving.

"She just wanted her house back and the truth out," Alexi said softly.

She wasn't real, Andrew told himself.

But as he did so, the mannequin winked at him. He closed his eyes; he looked again.

Yes, she winked. Damn her, she winked.

He lifted a hand and waved.

Alexi was actually smiling. "She has good taste; she likes you," Alexi said softly.

Andrew turned his eyes to the road and floored the gas pedal.

Short Term

DANIEL PYLE

Henderson checked for dogs before hopping the privacy fence: no little wooden house, no sleeping mound of fur chained to a stake, no evidence of feces in the grass. Probably no dog. Probably safe.

He straddled the slats for a second before dropping into the yard and winced when he landed and his legs buckled beneath him.

Easy, Gramps. You're not exactly in your fence-hopping prime.

Which was true, but not the *whole* truth. He might not have been as spry as he used to be, but he had plenty of hopping left in him. Plenty of invading. And plenty of what came after.

He grinned.

If there were motion-activated lights, Henderson didn't see them. He took a few steps into the yard.

When nothing happened, he crept the rest of the way to the back door and crouched by the knob.

His knees cracked. He ignored them. His back groaned. He told it to shut the fuck up.

Before he took his tools from his back pocket, he tried the knob. You wouldn't believe how often breaking into a place was only a matter of opening the door and letting yourself in. For the most part, midwesterners were honest, down-to-earth, trusting people.

In other words: idiots.

The knob turned just a little and caught. Locked.

Henderson reached for his kit.

The lock was old looking, cheap. He pulled a torsion wrench and a rake pick from his pouch but didn't touch the hook pick. No need to get too fancy for a piece of junk like this. He could have picked it with his fingernails.

Half a minute later, give or take—not a record, but not too terrible when you considered how shaky his hands had gotten in the last few years—the lock disengaged and the knob spun.

Piece of cake. He jammed the tool kit back into his pocket.

Somewhere nearby, sirens wailed.

He let go of the knob and hunkered against the house. No one in the street would have had much chance of seeing him back here, behind the house and the privacy fence and buried in the shadows, but he hadn't gotten this far in life by taking unnecessary chances. No, sir.

While he waited for the sirens to fade into the distance—fifteen seconds, thirty, maybe a full minute—he stared into the dark yard and listened to himself breathe. The silence that came when the emergency vehicles finally drove out of earshot surprised him almost as much as the initial burst of noise had, and he rubbed at his temples.

He waited another minute and then fought his creaking joints to a standing position.

Okay, where was I?

The lock was old looking, cheap. Before he reached for his tool kit, he tried the knob (it never hurt to go for the obvious option first). It twisted in his hand, and the door swung open.

Idiots.

He pushed the door open just far enough to let himself through and crept inside.

A small emergency light plugged into an outlet on the far wall provided him with enough illumination to see where he was going. The room seemed to be some sort of makeshift office. A futuristic-looking computer (to be honest, most computers looked like something out of a science fiction movie to Henderson) sat on a table-turned-desk, pulsing white light from a small dot on its bottom edge. He walked past the workstation and crept farther into the house.

The kitchen smelled like meat. Pot roast for dinner? Maybe. Or steaks. It was hard to tell from an hours-old odor and didn't really matter either way.

Maybe later he'd cut into some bellies and find out. If the mood struck him.

It was nearly midnight, but that didn't necessarily mean the occupants would be asleep. Twenty years ago, you'd have had trouble finding someone still awake at this hour, but these days, with twenty-four-hour Walmarts and internet shopping and television stations that never stopped airing their worthless crap, folks didn't have as much reason to hit the hay after the sun went down. These days, you could break into a place and find a whole family (children included) curled up on the couch and watching a movie at one o'clock in the morning. Henderson had done it.

But this didn't look like it was going to be one of those cases. At least not so far. This place was as quiet as they came.

The deeper into the house he got, the darker it became. He had a small Maglite in one of his back pockets and pulled it out when he could no longer see without it.

He found a long hallway and checked the rooms on either side. The first was a small half bath with floral wallpaper and a fuzzy cover on the toilet seat. It smelled like citrus and alcohol, like a Screwdriver, although Henderson guessed the scent was probably some sort of lingering soap or disinfectant. The next room looked like it might have been guest quarters once upon a time, but boxes and storage tubs and piles of bric-a-brac made it all but inaccessible and worthless as a sleeping area now. The rest of the house seemed clean enough, so Henderson guessed this was storage overflow rather than some sort of obsessive pack-ratting.

Down the hall, someone opened a door. Henderson slipped into the guest room and shut the door behind himself, twisting off the flashlight and shoving it back into his pocket as he went. His leg bumped a cardboard box, and for a second he was sure he would knock it over and reveal himself, but the box only wobbled a little and settled back into place.

Not that it mattered much. He was going to have to run into one of the occupants sooner or later. He *wanted* to. That had been the plan, right?

Plan? More like urge.

Whatever. The point was that he wanted to meet them on his own terms. Sneak up on them. Breathe on the backs of their necks and see the terror in their eyes when they whipped around and found him there grinning and licking his lips.

The door opener padded down the hallway. Slowly. Henderson pictured a pajama-clad hottie, shuffling along in her socks, her hair tangled and hanging over her face, her love lumps pushing at the front of her too-tight top.

That image got him stirring in his nether regions and just about convinced him to go ahead and burst out into the hall, but he held himself back, thought about the unsexiest thing he could think of (a geezer named McNeil wandering through the halls at the home wearing nothing but a Depends and sporting streaks of fecal matter on the backs of his legs and inner thighs) and waited for the sounds of footsteps to fade and disappear.

When it was quiet again, he waited thirty more seconds. Just to be sure. The joints in the fingers on his left hand were killing him. He rubbed at the knuckles and winced. He made a fist, unclenched, made another fist.

Forget about it. You have more important things to worry about right now.

Right. Of course. He shook his head and looked around the room. It was hard to see anything in the dark, but he thought he'd brought a flashlight with him. He searched his pants and found the light in his back pocket where a guy would normally keep his wallet.

He twisted the front of the flashlight and directed the beam around a room full of boxes and storage tubs. Just a bunch of junk from the looks of it. Christmas decorations and unfiled paperwork, old books and vacation souvenirs.

He crept out of the room and tried the next. This one was a small bathroom. Just a half bath really. A toilet and a small pedestal sink and an orangey smell that made Henderson think of a drink he might have ordered a girl in a bar decades before.

Without closing the bathroom door, he turned to

the room across the hall. Except . . . hadn't he already checked that one? He shook his head, rubbed at the skin above his eyebrows and felt the wrinkles there. Yes, he had. Storage boxes. Junk. That's right. He moved on.

In a large room at the end of the hall, he found a man sleeping in a bed the size of a small apartment. The guy was flipped over on his belly, wearing a pair of wrinkled pajama bottoms and tangled in a twisted rope of bedsheets. He looked young (*Who doesn't anymore?*), maybe in his mid-twenties. He had a lean, runner's musculature to him. His torso rose and fell gently as he slept, and the sound coming out of his mouth was like something halfway between breathing and snoring.

Henderson didn't have much use for a man. Not alive anyway. He snuck across the room, took the alarm clock from the nightstand, and swung it against the side of the man's head. The clock bounced off his skull, and the kid started to open his eyes. Henderson hit him again before he could wake up and make a scene. And hit him again. And again. He swung until both the clock and the sleeper had stopped ticking. He felt cast-off blood dripping down his face and over his lips. After he wiped away the bulk of it, he bared his teeth and growled.

The body lay sprawled across the bed (damned mattress must have been an acre across at least). The blood oozing out of the head wound spilled across the pillow and the few pieces of plastic that had broken off the clock's casing. Henderson left it that way. He'd come back later and have some fun with the corpse, but for now he needed to check the house for others.

Didn't you already hear someone else?

No, he didn't think so.

In the hall? Wasn't there—

No. He shook his head. That was just his mind trying to play tricks on him again. He needed to concentrate.

He left the bedroom and snuck down the hall. He peeked into each of the rooms he passed but found no one.

Something clattered in the kitchen. Henderson grinned and tiptoed that way.

A single bulb above the sink glowed and lit the room. The woman standing beneath it had a piece of pie on a plate in one hand and a large, half-empty glass of milk on the counter in front of her. She wore a pair of silky pajama bottoms and a thin tank top that probably would have left almost nothing to the imagination if she'd turned around. She had a nice, tight little body.

She put her plate down beside the glass and spun a roll of paper towels on the wall. A small puddle of milk oozed across the floor from where she stood to a spot near the middle of the room that must have had a little bit of a dip to it. Before she could get the towel off the roll and turn to her mess, Henderson moved to her, pinned her against the cabinet, and wrapped an arm around her chest.

She stiffened, let out a little yip, and then laughed. "Jesus. You scared the shit out of me."

Henderson leaned in and nibbled her earlobe. "Good." The word was more of a rasp coming from his old man's throat.

Now she screamed for real. She bucked and spun and continued screaming and punched something into Henderson's belly just above the waistband of his pants. He looked down and saw the handle of her fork jutting from his stomach, bobbing up and down as he gasped. There were little flecks of pie crust on it.

The woman twisted and bumped her plate. It slid against the glass, which dropped to the floor and shattered. Milk sprayed across his shoes and her bare feet.

Henderson backed away, gripped the fork, and jerked it out of his belly. He dropped the utensil to the floor and watched it splash into the spilled milk.

"Bitch."

She was moving away—he'd been right about the revealing top; now that she was facing him, he could see every little bit of nippley goodness—circling him but not turning her back to him, running her hands across the countertop behind her, maybe looking for a knife or some other kind of weapon. Before she could find one, Henderson lunged forward and punched her in the face.

His fist landed just beneath her eye and didn't do much except knock her off balance. As she rocked back, she slipped in the milk. She grabbed for the counter but lost her footing and tumbled to the floor beside the dropped fork. She tried to catch herself, but her hands slipped in the mess; her face and chest thumped against the linoleum. Milk splattered up around her, and she jerked.

He waited for her to scramble around, try to get her footing, maybe even kick at him, try to bring him down with her, but she did none of those things. Except for that initial spasm, she hadn't moved at all since she hit the floor. Henderson waited another moment and then leaned forward.

The liquid around her head had started to turn pink. Like strawberry milk. He grabbed her by the hair and flipped her over, still ready for an attack, a game of opossum.

But she wasn't going to be attacking anything any time soon. A long jag of broken glass jutted from her chest. From her left breast. The one over her heart. The jag wasn't moving, and neither was she. He didn't need to check for a pulse to know she was dead.

Great. Perfect. What a fucking waste. What are the chances of something like that?

He snarled and kicked at her body. As if this were all her fault somehow.

Isn't it? She's the one who tried to get away.

Except they *all* tried to get away. The ones he didn't kill in their sleep anyway. You could hardly blame her for that.

He sighed and turned away from the body.

What now?

He needed to check the rest of the house. She probably wasn't alone here. If he left someone to find her before he had a chance to get far enough away, he might have to worry about running from the cops. No sense risking that.

He left the kitchen and found a long hallway. Half bath on one side, storage room on the other. At the end of the hall, he found a bedroom and a man asleep beneath a tangle of sheets.

He didn't have any use for a man. Not alive anyway. But when he moved to take care of the guy, he saw that someone had beat him to it.

What the hell?

A broken alarm clock lay in a pool of blood beside the man's head. Whoever had done the bashing hadn't been a pussy about it. You could see folds of flesh beneath the cracked skull and matted hair that must have been brains.

The blood looked fresh, and Henderson frowned. What were the chances of breaking into a fresh crime scene? They had to be astronomical.

So? What are you going to believe? The laws of probability or your own fucking eyes?

He backed away from the bed, shaking his head a little, trying to clear out a half-formed wisp of memory attempting to push its way into his thoughts.

Get outta here. You picked the wrong damn house, old man.

He hurried down the hall and into the kitchen.

The second body lay in a puddle of blood on the floor. Stabbed. The pool of liquid looked lighter than it should have, milky almost. Henderson saw a slice of pie on a plate and tried to piece together a story that could explain it all. The scene reminded him of something he'd seen before, maybe something out of a Hitchcock movie? He couldn't remember for sure.

Sirens wailed from somewhere not terribly far away. The next block over maybe.

Seriously, you've got to beat it. If you're going to take the rap for something, it might as well be something you actually did.

He stared at the dead woman a second longer. Then he hurried out of the room, through another room with an emergency light blazing from an outlet and a computer on a desk that was really a table.

The sirens were getting closer.

He slipped through a door and into the back yard. Halfway to the fence on the other side of the property, his leg twisted and his knee popped. He slid to a stop and felt around the area above and below his joint. It didn't feel sprained—and definitely not broken—but it sure as hell hurt.

Go. Now!

He grimaced and hobbled to the fence. It took him two tries to hop the thing, and when he finally got over, he fell in a heap on the other side. His body ached, screamed. He pushed himself into a sitting position against the fence and waited to see if the sirens were coming or passing by.

The wailing seemed to go on forever. But eventually . . . finally . . . it faded.

He took a deep breath and stood.

See? Nothing to worry about.

He stood on his tiptoes and peered over the fence. He knew better than to hop without looking. Sometimes back yards had big, mean backyard dogs.

But not this one. No little wooden house, no sleeping mound of fur chained to a stake, no evidence of feces in the grass. Probably no dog. Probably safe.

He pulled himself over the slats and landed with a spryness he thought he'd lost.

Piece of cake. Maybe you're not as far past your prime as you thought.

He smiled and headed for the house.

Distressed Travelers

NINA KIRIKI HOFFMAN

Airports are my favorite places to collect emotions. You never know what you'll pick up. Some of the other Viri like sports events and sappy movies for their powers of flooding humans with feelings we can feed from, but I like the range of experiences people have at airports. Travelers come home from a long time away and fall into the arms of their loved ones. Rush! So chocolate and hot you can burn your receptors. People who are leaving homes and families, full of melancholy and apprehension. Yum, tastes like chicken! People afraid of flying, that teeth-clenching heart-tripping fear, so delicious, like the best red wine! People setting out on trips to other countries . . . people heading home for the funerals of loved ones . . . bored people cruising for hookups . . . so much variety and intensity.

That night at San Francisco International Airport,

when flights were being canceled left and right because of weather delays and people were furious, worried, frustrated, and scared, I was filling up to overflow and didn't know where I'd store the extra energy without budding off a piece of myself and creating a new person.

I didn't like doing that. Newbies took care and training. I did it once about eighty-five years ago and didn't enjoy it. I was glad to bid my bud farewell when he was old enough, skilled enough at mimicking human form and behavior, and strong enough to set out on his own. The hardest part was teaching him not to kill. But he learned.

Instead of stocking up on the overflow of emotion rushing from people in line to rebook flights, I went gourmet and stopped taking everything in. I just went for the elegant emotions, the caviar, pickled cherries, and peppermints of the feast before me. A mother and daughter had just returned from Germany, a flight that had taken them hours and included several delays and missed connections. Now they were stalled out yet again, and their discouragement and fatigue tasted like rivers of bittersweet chocolate.

A businessman had to get to Portland tonight or he'd miss tomorrow's early morning meeting to decide the fate of—I wasn't sure what it was, but it was monumental in his mind, and he knew he wasn't going to make it, and they *needed* him. Fluffy lemon chiffon with dollops of dark cherry sauce.

A mother heading home for her daughter's wedding. She had booked a cheap flight with too short a layover in San Francisco, missed her connection, and now she would be too late. Remorse, anger, despair, and guilt. A cornucopia of delightful flavored syrups!

I was in line with everybody else waiting for the ticket agents to make amends, which they were resolutely not doing. No admissions of guilt, no offers to give people extra miles. Smiling, they arranged other flights for everyone, some set for days later. Prospective passengers were twisting tighter in their resentment as they approached the desk. Salty seafood with Alfredo sauce. Mmm.

Delectable, but if I collected any more of this, I was going to expand beyond the range of unnoticeable. I'd already acquired a bit of a belly and added padding to my arms and legs, plus letting my part-of-me clothes grow to accommodate my new size. I'd also added an inch or two of height, incrementally. I needed to stop now. I'd taken on basketball-player physiques in the past when the situation warranted it, but not right in front of people.

Ducking behind a pillar could work if no one was noticing me beforehand. But just now, it would look pretty strange for me to abandon my prime place in line, about five people back from the information desk. No, I'd just stand there, shifting from foot to foot, quietly a bit larger than I had been.

I had to watch it with the changes, because I needed

to look like the picture on my driver's license. All this extra security was a pain in the butt. I wished I was better at distance feeding, but I needed line of sight, at least, and for that, these days, I had to actually buy airplane tickets and go places. The guards got suspicious if you ranged around by the baggage claim, greeting area, and ticket counters for more than four hours.

Airborne, I had a place to digest between meals, so it wasn't too bad. Air travel mostly bored me, except for the occasional fear-of-flying person, whose terror could keep me in a heightened state of stimulation for hours. Smooth, creamy caramel with nuts, and occasional jalapeños.

The man standing in front of me in line was strangely emotion-free and restful. He glanced at me. He was tall, with a neat Vandyke beard, round wire-rimmed glasses, short hair, and kind of an El Greco face and body—thin, stretched out, and a little blue. He had an uncreased suit, dark charcoal with a faint blue pin stripe; a black tie with three red diamonds on it; and a blue shirt. His carry-on was a brown leather briefcase. His hands were pale, with long fingers. He didn't fidget at all. His mouth was set in a faint smile.

Travelers ahead of us were being sent away with pink slips clutched in their fists. I collared someone and asked what the pink slip was.

"It's an eight-hundred number for booking hotel rooms at the distressed traveler's rate," he said. He growled and went off toward the exit.

So. Hotel room. Hmm. I could sleep off an excess of emotion there as well as I could on a plane, and probably pick up a snack or two the next morning in the van on my way back to the airport. A night in a private room, where I could splurf adequately, let go of this pesky, restrictive human form to relax in a more undifferentiated way—yes. That would be nice.

The stranger ahead of me noticed me looking at him, and his smile widened a notch. "Hi. I'm Stan."

"Tim," I said. I liked the name Tim. It had three letters I could rearrange. Also, it was the name on my current ID.

"Nice to meet you, Tim. We could cut costs by sharing one of these distressed hotel rooms." He glanced at the ceiling as though lost in thought and not attached to my answer. There was a small spike in his affect, though, a slice of roaring red that intrigued me. It tasted like cinnamon and cigarettes. At first I wasn't sure I liked it, but after most of it was gone, I changed my mind and wished he would have a stab of the same feeling again.

It was not a usual feeling. I analyzed what was left of it and decided it was spicy, smooth-as-butter desire. For me? How odd. I decided this was worth exploring. It would be a different journey from my usual, with new flavors. Stan had a different atmospheric color than most of the others in our little crowd of left-behinds. I had glimpsed others like Stan before, but always at a distance.

A night of digestion and study, but no splurfing. Well, I could deal with discomfort in the interests of exploration.

We ended up crammed into a hotel shuttle bus with ten other distressed travelers, on our way to a Blue Roof Inn some distance from the airport, but with a guaranteed shuttle back to the airport in time to catch our replacement flights the next morning.

Stan didn't have checked baggage, just his briefcase. I wondered what he had packed. My carry-on was mostly for show, since I could morph my own clothes, unmake and remake my teeth, and cleanse my insides with my own stomach acid. I had a couple of magazines and a book in my little duffel. *GQ* was always helpful when I was designing clothes and hairstyles. I carried shampoo and a hotel-size bar of soap, too.

The Blue Roof Inn was a big rectangular building with its face toward the freeway. All the corridors were open walkways with iron railings to keep people from spilling onto the asphalt below. The building was pink adobe, with blue doors in pairs along the walkways and a bright blue roof.

While we waited in line to check in, Stan said, "Would you like to put the room on your card or mine? I can pay you cash if you put it on your card."

I shrugged. Though I had no street address anywhere, I had a PO box just so I could maintain a few items like credit cards to buy plane tickets with. When the clerk invited us up to the desk to register, I pulled out my credit card. The distressed traveler's rate was sixty dollars, which I guessed was better than the usual rate. Stan handed me thirty bucks as we headed out of the lobby.

"So, Tim, what do you do?" Stan asked after we'd entered our room, which carried the heavy taint of previous tenants' cigarette smoke and was otherwise unremarkable.

"I'm a frequent flyer," I said.

Stan gave a short bark of laughter. "That's a job description? If that's the case, I've got that job, too."

"Oh. You were asking about jobs?" Belatedly, I knew that. I should have recognized this conversational ploy, but I was so interested in Stan's flat affect that I had forgotten to pay attention to my own cover. How did Stan exist in a state where his emotions were so repressed? How was I going to find out? I smiled. I loved puzzles. "I do some travel writing," I said. "What do you do, Stan?"

"I'm an accountant," said Stan. Again with the small smile that might or might not be a smirk, and no feeling behind it.

"That involves a lot of traveling?" I asked.

"I have jobs to go to," he said, and here came a flicker of annoyance, which tasted a bit like pine and detergent. Other people's tasted more like pine and maple syrup, so this was an interesting aberration.

I shrugged and smiled. "No offense," I said.

"None taken." He put his briefcase down on the

plywood desk and threw his jacket across the bed nearest the door, so I set my carry-on on the bed by the bathroom and settled down to await developments or sleep, whichever seemed likely to please me more in the moment.

"Hungry?" Stan asked.

"Not really," I said. I was so full of fascinating things I'd already eaten that I had the irritating impulse to bud, which I had to suppress. Buds! So much trouble! Years of upkeep, and you had to teach them how to feed without killing people. Some buds learn that lesson more easily than others. I had been a quick study, but my only bud to date had been very hard to restrain during his first few feedings.

"Pity," said Stan, fiddling with his briefcase. He unlocked it and pulled out a small black leather case. Again, he had a brief flash of emotion, a combination of pine-and-soap annoyance and the red, smoky taste of hunger.

"Are *you* hungry?" I asked.

"No," he said, even as his hunger spiked, a roaring conflagration of red and golden heat around him, smoke and barbecue and charred meat. His pupils flared, wide spots of darkness. His hands unzipped the leather case while he stared at me. "Guess I'll have to do this the other way. Did you want to shower tonight or tomorrow? My preference would be for morning."

"I don't care," I said. "It's not like the hotel is going to run out of hot water, right? But I've got to get back to the airport by around seven, so I guess I'll shower tonight." If I had been able to splurf, I wouldn't have needed a shower; I could absorb any grime attached to me and process it into whatever I liked. But now that I was stuck in my current shape for a while, I might as well do the external washing thing. I didn't excrete the same kinds of waste products humans did, but I did collect some unpleasant scents in the course of maintaining a shape.

"Good," said Stan.

While I stood under the stream of hot water, I thought about the puzzle that was Stan. Often people's emotional landscapes didn't match their words or acts, but Stan was kind of extreme in his dissonance. If I had that kind of hunger in me, I'd be gnawing on anything nearby. Maybe he was snacking while I was showering. It would be fun to check his hunger levels when I left the bathroom.

After I finished my ablutions and swiped the mirror with a towel, I checked my form. Still bulgy here and there. I rearranged some of my bulk to look more muscular and less bumpy, then grew a gray T-shirt and white boxers. I couldn't remember what color of either I'd been wearing when I came in. Why didn't I standardize these things so I didn't have to think about it? Sometimes I went with pale green, blue, or purple. Once or twice I'd even crafted logos on my T's. I hoped Stan wouldn't notice.

When I left the bathroom, I noticed that my little

duffel had moved slightly on my bed, and the zipper didn't have the inch-long gap I always left open. Huh. Stan was one of those. I wished him joy of it. My wallet held an ID, a credit card, and about three dollars and change. I had other cards and IDs sewn into the seam of the duffel in case I had to change shape quickly. Other than that, the reading material, and the plastic bag of minimal toiletries, I had a Clif Bar. Joy to any curious snooper.

Stan had the TV on, tuned to a late-night talk show with the sound turned up pretty loud. He was wearing some weird kind of slick-looking pajamas and sitting on the edge of his bed, his hands dangling between his legs. The little black case sat on the bed beside him. He stared at me. There was a low-level glow around him, red with growlers, and the flavor wafting from him was roasted coffee beans and, again, charred beef.

"Don't mind me," I said, waving at the television. "I can sleep through anything." I set my duffel on the floor and turned back the covers of my bed.

"I'm counting on it," Stan muttered. He jabbed something into my left buttock, and his flare of hunger was so strong I could warm myself on its flames.

I looked back over my shoulder in time to see Stan pull a syringe out of me, the plunger depressed. Uh-oh, drugs. What kind of reaction was I supposed to have? The jabbing part was supposed to give me pain, I knew, but it didn't; I had parted to accommodate it. He had left some kind of fluid in me, but my mass created a capsule around it. I could analyze it at will, but I couldn't tell what it was supposed to do to a human.

"So, Stan," I said. "What do you call that?"

He was staring at me, his pupils wide. He shook his head like a dog shaking off water when I spoke.

"What is it, and what's it supposed to do?" I could hardly fake a normal reaction if I didn't know what was expected.

"A paralytic," he said, his voice low and grating. His breathing had sped up, and his face was flushed. The hunger had spread out around him as though he were a stuntman on fire, or maybe a miniature sun, flames flaring out to the walls of the room.

"Oh." I collapsed forward onto my bed and lay sprawled.

"Yes," Stan muttered, "yessss." He rolled me over onto my back, leaned over my prone form, and stared into my eyes. Then he arranged my limbs: drew my arms to my sides, straightened my legs, gently, as though I were the corpse of someone he cared about. I noticed something: his fingers were covered in some slick surface. Latex gloves, I figured. The garment he wore was all one piece, like a hazmat suit, except it didn't have a helmet.

"You're mine," he said, and smiled. The flames danced around him. He started riffing on various deep purple versions of joy, and I couldn't help it. Full as I was, I had to taste that. I sucked some in—oh bliss, several varieties of sweet, succulent grapes, a burst on

the tongue and a wash of transcendent sweetness!—
and then Stan brandished a shiny, shiny scalpel in front
of my face.

"You're mine," he whispered again, while the talk
show host nattered loudly in the background about the
latest celebrity scandals.

He sliced neatly through the apparent material of
my fake T-shirt and spread it wide; I let it behave as
I imagined T-shirt material would. Then Stan carved
into my chest. I worried about whether I'd populated
it with the right mat of hairs and whether my nipples
were well enough defined to mimic reality. I guess Stan
didn't really care about that stuff, but his lovely, tasty
joy vanished when I didn't produce blood in the wake
of his slicing. It happened so fast. I always thought I
was pretty good under pressure, but I was too surprised
to whip up the requisite red stuff.

I looked down at my chest. He had carved some
letters there, cutting through the minimal tan I main-
tained when I wasn't being someone whose skin was
dark into the almost translucent white that was my
natural color. He'd gotten as far as A WORK OF GE and
stopped.

Oh. So he was That Guy. "WORK OF GENIUS"
KILLER STRIKES AGAIN! the headlines sometimes
read when I logged in to my e-mail. He had struck
in different areas around the country, leaving multiple
carved-up bodies with at least one message on them but
no trace evidence. He always killed near a major airport.

All the wine of joy had vanished from Stan's emotion-form, and his hunger had tamped down as well, leaving a thin layer of shuttered alarm. I wondered how he did that.

"What are you?" he whispered, poking me with the scalpel. I let it slide into me. There was nothing too solid near the surface for it to encounter. I had formed some of myself into a semi-skeleton, six times denser than my normal flesh, to support the weight of my form, but it wasn't a permanent state; I could will it away. Most of my neural connections were intangible, not necessarily in sync with the fleshy part of me. It squicked me to move the neural/emotional-vacuum part of me away from the solid parts, though, so usually I stayed integrated.

"What are *you*?" I asked, and Stan jerked back, the blade jerking too, slicing a gully across my stomach.

"You shouldn't be able to talk!" he said.

"Because of that stuff you squirted into me?" I shifted the encapsulated liquid from my back to my front, holding it just under the skin of my left hip. I densified some of myself into a hollow needle near the liquid. I had tried to analyze it, but it hadn't turned into anything I recognized. I could always stick it into Stan and see what it did. "Ever get the feeling that didn't work on me?" I asked.

"Shut up," Stan said. He aimed the scalpel at my face, then lowered it toward my throat.

Now, there was a lot of me that was pretty sloppy,

since I didn't expect people to look under my skin. I got energetic when preparing to be scanned by the new security measures, but so far I'd managed not to set off alarms, since none of me qualified as metal. Once I got through security and went hither and yon in airports, I relaxed.

The structures I established to handle speech, though, and fake breathing, that was complicated stuff, and I didn't feel like having to re-create it. Before Stan could slice for a jugular that wasn't there, I grabbed his hand.

"You can't move," he said, staring into my eyes with a fixed gaze that spooked me.

"Come on, Stan," I said. "You're ignoring the evidence of your eyes."

He didn't blink, nor did his gaze waver. His entire affect was compressed into a thin halo of silver-blue concentration surrounding him, only a millimeter from his skin, with about as much flavor as an ice cube. Fascinating. I'd never encountered anyone who could nearly disappear that way.

He tried to jerk his arm out of my grasp. I flowed more flesh around it, immobilizing him, then pressed on some nerves until his fingers opened and the scalpel fell. Meanwhile, I went ahead and closed the wounds he'd made on my front. Viri society in general frowns on our revealing ourselves to our fellow Earth inhabitants, but hey, that horse had left the barn.

I wasn't sure how to get out of this gracefully.

"How long is that stuff you shot me with supposed to last?" I asked.

"Half an hour. An hour. Depends on your metabolism. What is your metabolism?"

"Nothing you'd know about," I said. I sat up, keeping Stan's arm encased in me, and considered my options.

This guy was killing people. There were a lot of people alive, so many that I and my kind had no trouble finding sustenance. Still, the guy was theoretically cutting into our food supply, and I liked some of the people I knew, and would probably like others if I got to know them.

I could suck him dry. At the moment, there wasn't much to him, so it wouldn't be that far a trip. But because of Stan's weird emotional physiology, I wasn't sure that would incapacitate or kill him. The death-suck usually only worked on people who were completely agitated already.

Plus, I was still way too full from my last meal.

He started fighting about then. A smoky red stream bled into his thin silver halo, and suddenly Stan wasn't invisible anymore. He was kicking me and punching me, and head-butting me, even. I let my limbs snag his and hold him still.

A conflagration, red and blue and green flames, filled the room around us. Pickles, smoke, toothpaste, chili peppers. Boy, did this guy have feelings now that he was completely trapped. He was totally death-suckable, but my vacuum was clogged.

I could break him in two, or slice him up with his own scalpel, but I didn't like the psychic resonances that would leave me with.

I could leave. A few minutes' work would give me a whole new body—maybe I'd be a woman for a while. A fat one.

There was always another plane to catch, or I could switch to trains or buses for a while and live on a thinner diet. I could always fill up at a football or a hockey game, or just at a bar where people were watching some kind of sports event. I had lots of places I could explore to sample new emotions. Hospitals were legion, and I hadn't done much with prisons yet.

If I just left Stan there, though, he would kill again. Though it would be interesting to watch him operate on someone who gave him the kind of satisfaction he was seeking, I decided I shouldn't let it go.

I held him still and shot him with the stuff he'd tried to use on me. He went limp a minute or two after that, and his emotions flared up into a wall of melon-flavored fear. Okay, I couldn't resist sucking up some of that. I'm a fool for the fruit flavors. But I managed to stop myself midsuck.

I laid Stan carefully on the bed he had chosen. Only his eyes moved. The fear kept coming, beckoning me with its honeydew fingers.

I picked up the phone and dialed 911. It turned out

nine got me an outside line, so I had to do some redial-
ing, but I got through to Police Emergency eventually.
"Help!" I said in a voice a bit higher than the one I'd
been using. "I'm in a room with the Genius Killer!"
I gave my room number and our location. "He tried
carving me with a scalpel! I knocked it out of his hand
and got away, but he's after me, and—" I screamed and
dropped the phone.

I leaned over Stan while I re-formed clothes appropriate to public places. His eyes darted back and forth,
and his fear soured a bit.

"Have fun," I whispered. I grabbed my duffel and
left our room.

I didn't leave the hotel, though. I went downstairs
and hid in the plantings to make sure the police got
there before Stan could escape. If he tried to get away,
I would stop him again.

It didn't come to that. A bunch of police cars raced
up, red and blue lights spinning, but no sirens. The cops
swarmed into the lobby and then up to my erstwhile
room, and then there was a lot of radio action and even
more tasty emotions spilling all over the place, and,
unfortunately, some of them tasted like apples, and
some of them like blood oranges, and . . .

Upshot is I'm holed up in an abandoned shed not
too far from the hotel, getting ready to bust off a part of
myself and try to convince it to act with restraint, dang
it. I think I'll take a break from extreme emotions for
a while and try to subsist on a diet of library patrons.

Bayou Brawl

L. A. Banks

"Can you believe this shit, Earl?" Jerome lifted his rifle and squinted into its sight and pulled the trigger. He waited until the loud crack of gunshot report echoed back and then he spit over the side of the pickup. "Damn. Missed." He sat down with a thud and shook his head. "I swear the worl' done gone stone crazy. My cousin Gus said military bands're chattering 'bout UFOs and little green men, while we're out here shootin' rats? What kinda crazy mess is that?"

Earl nodded and stood to take aim at another larger coypu that looked like a cross between a huge beaver and a muskrat. "Would seem like to me, if the threat was credible, they'd have the army, the air force, the navy, and the marines out there with every local law enforcement body they could muster. Betcha it ain't no danged UFO, but they using that as a cover over the radio for a real true al-Qaeda threat, if you ask me."

Lowering his weapon to take dead aim at a pair of eyes reflecting in the truck's high beams, Earl pulled the trigger and then laughed. "Hot damn! Got that sucker!"

"Yeah, well," Jerome argued, "then if you right, why ain't they fixin' to bring us in on huntin' al-Qaeda, huh? Answer me that."

"I don't know," Earl said. "All I know is I'm up one rat on ya, buddy."

Arianna Paris Laveau looked out into the darkness, wondering how her life had become so mundane. A crappy economy had made taking this job necessary. Shooting coypu from the back of an NOPD pickup truck was not her idea of a good time. Yet, it was a necessary evil that fell under the jurisdiction of the sheriff's department—a leftover vestige of bureaucratic bull from New Orleans's previous mayor.

Common sense would make one ask why the hell police resources were being devoted to killing the huge river rats that plagued the area when bodies were turning up under very suspicious circumstances. But common sense and politics didn't always mix. The ex-mayor felt that preventing the damage these critters did digging burrows and causing infrastructure and roads to collapse was more important than police being devoted to cold case files. Since Katrina, he'd been on a mission to clear his name due to his very obvious lapse in judgment and leadership, so fixing the streets and shooting coypu was somehow supposed to assuage the furious electorate. It didn't.

Unfortunately, the current bureaucracy needed an act of council to change the edict, and until that happened, the good ole boys had to shoot coypu three days a week.

But given that the local cops had unofficially passed the hat to pay her hourly fee, on account of their growing trepidation about the recent rash of bodies that had been found, in the back of the truck she sat.

Superstition was simply a part of the New Orleans landscape, as much as the levees and canals were. She had a rep as being in the know with the local voodoo and hoodoo community, so hiring her to go out at night past the bats that roosted beneath highway underpasses and to accompany an NOPD truck through the dark canal zones obviously seemed like a safe bet to the men.

Everybody in New Orleans was uneasy these days. Most folks also knew her reputation as a bounty hunter for the strange, given her membership in the long lineage of the famous Marie Laveau and Santiago Paris out of Haiti. They didn't mess with her, just to be on the safe side, and the supernaturals didn't either, which was fine by her. As long as there was respect, there would be peace. The supernatural community viewed her as their local sheriff—the one who mediated disputes and meted out justice where it was required. So it was all good.

But what was really jacked up was the fact that the

bodies that had been found were killed in the most bizarre ritual she'd seen, and the local authorities were calling in the local supernatural talent—under the table of course.

Meanwhile, their men weren't taking any chances on routine patrols. None of them wanted to be out by the canals where bats and gators and the coypu lived, just in case there was something more noxious out and about. That's where she came in. Armed with silver shells and a silver-plated nine-millimeter, plus a rep for spell-slinging as long as her arm, she made the fellas feel better when she rode shotgun in their trucks.

Still, no doubt about it, she had to get a life. Here she sat at thirty years old on a Friday night with a bunch of guys passing a flask, combing the desolate canal banks while they got all excited about dropping huge river rodents.

Another crack of gunfire and the smell of cordite bled into her drifting senses.

"You see that huge one I just got!" Earl said excitedly, slapping his fellow officer five.

"Wait, wait, I got this next one," Jerome yelled, aiming and squeezing the trigger. "Hot damn! Got his ass! You ain't caught up on me yet!"

She just looked at them both with a wan smile.

"That's twenty-two to your eighteen," Jerome said, and then glanced at his watch. "Shift's over, and even with your back-to-back hits, you're still buying the beer tonight."

"Aw, sheeeit, man . . . that's the second time this week."

Jerome smiled and looked at Arianna with a wistful look in his eyes. "I'll buy yours, though . . . if you wanna go with us, Ari?"

She returned Jerome's hopeful smile . . . not in a million years. The poor man wasn't her type and would also freak out if he knew the kind of guys she really hung around. She looked at his big puppy dog eyes and cute dimples, set in a handsome face, and sighed. His partner was a cute blond version, all arms and legs and lankiness. But just not her.

"Guys, it's been a long night and if I do beers, I'll be no good tomorrow . . . and you know the captain wants me in on the investigation . . . but you didn't hear that from me."

"I understand," Jerome said, his expression a bit crestfallen. "But you can't blame a guy for trying."

She leaned over and gave him a kiss on the cheek. "No, a lady can never blame a guy for trying."

By the time she walked into Saints and Sinners Tavern over in Bayou Saint-Jean, all the local supernatural flavor was out. That was a good thing, especially since her two favorite contacts were there.

She slid into a booth seat next to Lamar and waited for his fantastically sexy greeting.

"Hey, baby," he murmured in a low, baritone growl,

nuzzling her neck with the five o'clock shadow on the side of his square jaw. "Glad you could make it."

"I heard you howl," she said, nipping his ear and tossing her ponytail over her shoulder.

"It's a full moon, Ari," he murmured, beginning to rub her back. "What can I say?"

"Whatcha got for me?"

He stared into her eyes, his beginning to glow gold as his upper and lower canines began to crest within his very sexy smile. They gleamed white against his dark tan Creole complexion, and she swore his thick brunet hair was lengthening by the minute, making her hands ache to touch it.

"You want the real answer to that . . . in here . . . or back at my den?"

"Arianna," a silky voice crooned, causing Lamar to look up with a warning growl.

Jacques slid into the seat across from them and took up her other hand. With a true vampire flourish, he swept it up and kissed the back of it. "Darling . . . you must allow me to buy you a merlot. It is always a pleasure."

"I called the lady out for the evening, man . . . so—"

"It's okay," she said quickly, and placed a palm on Lamar's bulging bicep. "Jacques called me, too."

"Indeed," Jacques said through a narrowed gaze as his fangs lowered to battle length. "But if you'd like to test the theory of gravity, we can step outside."

"How about that drink?" she replied, using her

calm tone to dispel a possible bar brawl between rival species. "I want to hear what you know so I can help."

Jacques sat back and brushed off the lapels of his black leather coat, glaring at Lamar, who rolled his shoulders and slung a possessive arm around her.

"It's a full moon," Arianna said, swallowing a smile, hoping that Jacques would just be cool.

"As an immortal, I have acquired patience," Jacques replied, somewhat mollified, but not completely. "We could compromise and make it a three-way," he added, calling over the waitress.

Lamar growled and leaned forward. "Only if you feel like being the receiver, motherf—"

"I was talking about for information sharing," Jacques said coolly, cutting off Lamar's protest. "Or is your libido so out of control right now due to the phase of the moon that you can't think straight? If so, maybe you need to go rectify that with one of your bitches that are in heat and allow me to have a civil conversation with the lady."

This time she had to broad-palm Lamar to keep him from going over the table.

"Lamar . . ." she said in the tone that she knew always worked. "Let's all just have a few rounds and talk, then . . . you know . . . maybe I'll stop by for a little while tonight. Cool?"

He sat back, gave Jacques an angry glance, and then nuzzled her again. "Promise, boo?"

"Yeah," she replied, rubbing his thigh.

"Oh, give me a break." Jacques folded his arms over his athletic chest as the waitress came over.

But Arianna caught his gaze and held it, sending him a telepathy barb that almost knocked his head back.

You know that he gets alpha male first rights on the full moon, oui? *So . . . I'll come see you after that—and it won't be sloppy seconds, that I promise you. Actually, there are more nights in the month that aren't a full moon than are. So please be nice.*

Jacques lifted his chin and ran his tongue over his incisors, retracting them very slowly and sensually. "On behalf of the lady's wishes, I stand down for the evening."

The muscles in Lamar's shoulders relaxed and Arianna released an inaudible sigh of relief. Managing two lovers from two different species was a trip. One night this was going to cause real issues, but not tonight.

"A merlot for the lady," Jacques crooned.

"And whatever she wants to eat," Lamar said in a low rumble. But then in a quick snatch he grabbed the waitress's wrist, causing her to hiss. "Next time when you spit in my Jack Daniel's, make sure you do it twice . . . it only makes it sweeter. But if you mess with my lady's drink, I'll be sure daylight finds your skank ass. We clear?"

Arianna frowned and looked at Jacques, who shrugged with a smile.

"Love, please do not taint the man's drink, or his lovely guest's drink . . . would you promise me?"

The waitress snatched her hand away from Lamar's hold, gave him an evil look, and stood close to Jacques. "Fine." She leaned down and kissed his neck and then left the table.

"Politics and passions run high here in New Orleans. What can I say?" Jacques made a tent in front of his mouth with his long, graceful fingers and gave her a wink.

"Which brings me to the point at hand," Arianna said, looking at both suitors, who were the best informants in town. "These strange deaths. You know if you guys have a rogue, we've gotta bring him or her down."

"The bodies were completely drained of blood," Lamar said, looking at Jacques with an accusatory frown.

"Correction," Jacques replied in a peevish tone. "They were drained of *all* bodily fluids, and not from a neat vampire's puncture wound, but by having their entrails sucked out of their anal orifices. Not our specialty. We don't do entrails or mutilate bodies. That's strictly wolf in nature."

"What? I've had just about enough—"

"You want to go, *mon ami*? Let's go!"

Arianna jumped up and was between both entities with her arms outstretched. Other tables gave the quarreling threesome only passing glances. In a supernatural bar, it would take more than a lunge to stir the crowd.

"Gentlemen, please. Enough of the insults and more on the matter at hand."

After a few minutes, both would-be combatants sat down again and the waitress, who'd been hanging back, brought their drinks.

"This is so weird that my pack has had ground forces out tracking the terrain," Lamar finally muttered, and took a sip of his Jack Daniel's. "We stick strictly to deer and wild hogs in the region, but we've noticed some of the wildlife and livestock also have the same patterns of mutilation. Just like that bullshit that happened out west and down in Arizona and Nevada. And for the record, we're meat eaters, true, but we butcher and *eat it*, not mutilate it, aw'ight. So don't try to signify that we had some foul hand in this crap. My people are looking into it, believe me."

"And you know my coven is *all* over this, Arianna," Jacques added, slowly sipping his blood-tainted merlot and pointedly ignoring Lamar's outburst.

"Then . . . ?" she said, glancing at both of them.

Lamar let out a heavy sigh. "My boys are saying it's aliens."

She just looked at him. "Really. Lamar, be serious."

"See, that's why I didn't want to talk about this until tomorrow . . . it'll ruin the vibe and I so *do not* want to ruin the vibe between us tonight, you feel me?"

"It won't ruin the vibe . . . it's just—"

"Insane," Jacques said in a weary tone, but held Arianna's gaze. "But as much as I hate to agree with him, plausible."

For a moment she'd felt Lamar's bicep tighten beneath his leather bomber jacket, then suddenly relax.

"Okay . . . so you guys saw it too, then, right?" Lamar waited, staring at Jacques for confirmation.

"You have no idea how I'd hate to corroborate your theory, but *oui*. Satisfied?"

"Are you serious?" She held her merlot in midair and looked from one man to the other.

"Not much goes down in the bayou without my pack knowing about it."

Jacques nodded. "There are intraterrestrials like us that have been able to walk through the dimensions since the dawn of time . . . why not extraterrestrials?"

"But them poaching in our territories is totally unacceptable," Lamar rumbled.

"My coven, as does the entire Vampire Cartel, agrees."

"The clan elders from the International Brotherhood of Were Clans are also talking a full-scale assault. They've been mutilating livestock and abducting humans in our zones, doing freaky experiments, you name it—since before Roswell." Lamar took a liberal sip from his short rocks glass. "It's fucked-up, because we eat what we kill. They don't. They just play with their food."

"Mad scientists," Jacques said, knocking the side of his blood merlot against Lamar's glass and then Arianna's. "Give us a bad name, when one isn't purely earned . . . and there's no honor to their sport. They don't procreate with their abductions—they don't turn a human into one of them and give them greater power . . . or feed and end the human's otherwise banal existence."

"It's unnatural, I tell you," Lamar said, shaking his head with disgust. "They picked the wrong fucking planet to start this bullshit."

"So wait, are you guys telling me that your mutual leaderships are gearing up for interplanetary war with aliens?"

"See, boo . . . I told you it would ruin the vibe," Lamar said, stroking her cheek with a thumb. "You're gonna be all distracted and worried . . . and damn, it's a full moon."

"Dude," Jacques said, leaning across the table and in dangerous proximity to a werewolf's fist. "Do you hear yourself?"

To her surprise, Lamar sat back and briefly closed his eyes. "Give me a break, man," he said on a heavy exhale. "It's a full moon and I ain't seen her in a month."

"All right," Jacques said, sitting back with his hands raised in front of his chest. "There's nothing I can say to that. However, there is the not-so-small matter at hand, namely, we are going to war. The human military has seen the craft crash-land in the swamp, our Central Vampire Intelligence sources say—and when they find it, they'll freak."

"Freak?" she said, looking at Jacques slack-jawed. "You mean like I am now?"

"*Chérie,* we cannot have your human military agitate the enemy with a nuclear threat. That would ruin the ecology of the flora and fauna for years, and for the record, the Fae are beside themselves about that. They're already ginned up to launch an attack on a human oil company after what was spilled in the gulf. I'm sure the Unseelie will beset the CEO for years behind that fiasco. Therefore, if humans burn the bayou and leave a smoking black hole in it with a missile or napalm, or whatever primitive devices they'd employ, then the Fae will indeed go after our food source—humans. So my council advises we send in a strike team to quietly and effectively eliminate the threat. There you have it in its purest form. We are quietly going to war, but using only our most elite special forces, which would include *moi.*"

"My point exactly, bro. We're going to war, and my pack is the squad going in for Alpha Team Wolf," Lamar said, removing his arm from Arianna's shoulders, where it had returned after the first outburst. "*Look at her.* Five eight, built like a brick house, and *knows* how we roll. So, if I'm gonna buy it from rushing aliens in the bayou, she is *definitely* one of the last things I'd like to do before I die."

Jacques released a wistful sigh and nodded. "I will grant you that." He looked at Arianna with a sensual gaze. "I've been around a very long time and have yet to find her rival. Perhaps my immortality has made me forget the needs of those with more finite existences . . .

and maybe I'm a bit jealous that the moon tonight gave you first rights of refusal."

"You know, guys," she said, after a careful sip of merlot, "that it's rude to talk about a person like they're not sitting there? Just saying."

"Our apologies," Jacques replied, bowing from where he sat. "But like I said, passions do run high, just like bayou politics."

"Definitely," Lamar murmured, nuzzling her. "You wanna get out of here? This moon is killing me."

Lamar's instincts were dead-on. Hell yeah, she was distracted. Vampires, Werewolves, and the Fae were going to war with aliens, in New Orleans—while there was a huge military base nearby getting nervous about UFOs sighted over at the Naval Air Station—and this brother wanted her to consummate a booty call?

As fine as he was . . . and as hard a body as he had . . . her mind couldn't focus.

Pressed up against the door to his fly alpha bachelor den, all she could think about was interspecies conflict—little green men versus dudes with fangs. What if the aliens weren't little green men, but were like those big bastards in *Predator* . . . or worse, those reptilian jobs with acid saliva like in *Aliens*?

A pair of hot, broad palms slid over the lobes of her ass, vying for attention as Lamar's punishing kiss devoured her mouth. She could feel the heat penetrating her jeans as his insistent pelvis caused them to sound like he was about to give her friction burn. The man felt fantastic, smelled so earthy and wonderfully male. A stone-cut chest pressed against her and an eight-pack of abdominal muscles contracted against hers with a groan. Her hands splayed against his muscular back beneath his jacket, and she marveled at the way every bit of sinew seemed to be its own steel cable as his arms enfolded her. No matter how many times she'd experienced being with him, she never tired of the passion and sheer prowess he brought to their encounters.

But his was a different brand than Jacques's. The latter of the two went in for the kill with the excruciatingly slow and highly skilled awakening of every erogenous zone on her body. Being with Jacques took time; being with Lamar took stamina. Tonight she was short on both.

"What's wrong, baby?" Lamar breathed on a ragged exhale. "Your mind seems like it's a million miles away." He kept kissing her neck and pulling her jeans down.

"It is," she admitted. "But my body's here."

He looked at her with an agonized expression. "You cool with that?"

She nodded and kissed him. "It's the least I can do for a man about to go to war."

Slowly shredding her jeans, he closed his eyes and allowed his head to drop back. "Bless you."

• • •

An hour later, she was in the bayou with an RPG launcher equipped with silver and hallowed-earth-packed shells, wooden stakes, silver-alloy-covered titanium Bowie blades, a semiautomatic, and her silver-plated nine that spit silver shells. She was hunkered down as an embedded human with Vampire, Fae, and Werewolf units. All had agreed that she needed to be there as a witness to be sure that it was indeed what they'd all sussed it out to be, an alien invasion.

The downed saucer was partially invisible but huge. The size of it could only be made out because the edges of it sparked in the water. Gators bobbed near it, floating upside down, as did dead swamp catfish.

"Look at this bullshit," a Fae archer said, his magical bow and arrow cocked toward the craft. "As soon as one of those bastards exits . . . right between the eyes!"

Jacques nodded, motioning with his chin toward the craft as two vampires materialized on the invisible edges of the UFO, each holding black energy-pulse charges. Lamar made a fist, then signaled with two fingers, and the forest lit up with gold gleaming eyes around the ship. He nodded to her.

"Wake 'em up, baby."

She pointed the RPG launcher and released a shell that exploded against the far side where there were no vampires standing. While completely ineffective against the craft, it did, however, let whatever was inside of it know that humans had discovered it—which was the strategy: make the aliens inside think that only primitive humans had found it so they'd be overconfident and come out to address the nuisance threat.

Several scythe-bearing messenger demons approached Jacques. The leader spoke, his eyes gleaming red, and he bent to bow.

"This alien contagion is giving the demon world a bad name . . . and we have been advised to join your forces. They have no right to apprehend humans and try to incite fear within them—that is our province!"

Jacques nodded. "Agreed. We can use your talent." But then he smiled. "However, there is no barter between us. You are here for your own reasons and thus we owe you nothing if we are victorious."

The demon spit on the ground, leaving a sizzling black spot, and then chuckled. "You are wise . . . and as we all say in hell, fair exchange is no robbery."

Jacques nodded. Arianna just stared. Everybody was out tonight and in rare form. Aliens were so gonna get their asses kicked in a bayou brawl for it all.

The door cracked open and bright UV light flooded the area. Several vampires burned and screamed, covering themselves in their black leather coats.

"Fall back!" Jacques shouted.

"Dog squad, Alpha One! Go, go, go!" Lamar yelled, his pack rushing the tall, willowy figures that slipped through the opening disc.

A silver shrapnel explosion rocked the swamp, the concussive blast blowing down trees and toppling firing Fae. Magic arrows whizzed through the air, missing their targets. Werewolves howled at the silver bits that stuck into their skins. Only the demons remained standing.

But the moment the scythe-bearers rushed in, the water around the fallen aircraft turned blue. Lamar turned and warned them as he smelled it quickly.

"Out of the water, now! It's from a cathedral—holy water infused with frankincense!"

Several demons perished as the demon-lethal compound rippled across the surface. Then, very calmly, what seemed like a hundred aliens gathered in the swath of protective light that projected down a ramp coming from their ship. She couldn't see their faces well but could tell that they were armed, as they were holding various instruments as they marched forward.

"We have studied all your species, and all your folklore and writings," a collective computer voice said after several moments of adjustment. "Do not attempt to engage us in armed conflict. You will lose. We are only here for the human food source."

Arianna glanced at Jacques and Lamar. Jacques was injured but so angry that his eyes were glowing red. His men now had on black hoods and gloves and what looked like tanning-salon goggles. Demons had reconvened into a smoking strategic position on higher, drier ground. The Fae had found new branches and had taken aim again. Wolves were circling again, but this time in their human form, wearing body armor and black riot helmets.

"Let me try something," Arianna whispered, gaining slow nods and worried glances from both Jacques and Lamar. "Everything is energy, right?"

"*Oui,*" Jacques said on a ragged breath, ripping a medical blood pack open and downing it. He winced as the bad burn on the side of his face began to heal. "But be careful. If they abduct you, *chérie,* I will be forced to burn—and I will for you."

Lamar just pounded his fist. "We've got your six."

"Thank you," she murmured. "Get word to the Fae to be on standby, then we'll hit 'em with everything we've got." She then stood and dropped her weapon. "I am the lone human out here and I come in peace." She knew she had to make it quick, because in the distance she could hear Apache military choppers beating the air.

Aliens may have figured out the science of what killed and injured the various supernatural phyla, but the one thing she knew they couldn't have mastered was magic—that was pure art embedded in the science. It wasn't textbook; there were too many forms of it to easily decode and address on the fly in a firefight. The Fae stood the best chance at an offense and had just been physically knocked down but weren't out. Once the ship's autoresponse to the threat could be disabled, it was gonna be on and poppin'.

She walked forward slowly, needing to get in range. Something had brought the aircraft down. If she could figure out what it was, then maybe they stood a chance.

"You may advance, human," the collective computer voice said.

Walking out until she was thigh-high in swamp water, she tilted her head to the side and closed her eyes, envisioning the ship dark. They were in Bayou Saint-Jean, the place where her late great-great-ancestor did her thing . . . and aliens thought they could jack with that? Stronger than any magic that had filtered down through her DNA was spirit—now, that was the nuclear bomb that not a single entity out there could harness.

"I call my auntie Marie! I call every one of her apprentices and all the ancestors in my line of every nationality who died on this land. Oust the aliens and give our friends cover against them!"

A blue-white carpet of energy lit up her body and then exploded from her tingly fingertips. Translucent souls fled up from the bayou water as the ship went dark and gray-green figures stood frightened and exposed. Scythe-bearers immediately swooped in, vampires rushed them, and the Fae hit foreheads dead-on with instantly released arrows. Wolves tore bodies in half, savaging the intruders, as Fae and vampires boarded the ship, hunting for survivors and tossing them out to demons and wolves for dispensation.

The mêlée continued for the better part of ten minutes until she saw the lights on the disc begin to slowly power up again. Several loud explosions in the distance made her call out to the units. In her mind she saw helicopters going down as another huge craft sliced through the sky toward them.

"Fall back!" she shouted. "Approaching UFO!"

Immediately all units fled the ship and took cover just in time for a wide swath of UV light to hit the ship and disintegrate it. Then in a spiral of pinpoint tractor beams, dead alien bodies quickly rose. And just like that, the light was gone and the new ship cut through the night sky and was gone.

A collective cheer went up. But this time it was Jacques who quickly placed his arm over her shoulder before Lamar could claim her. "How about a merlot for my favorite human?"

Lamar chuckled and held up both hands in front of his chest. "Even though it's still technically a full moon out, how can I get mad at a brother in arms . . . especially one who took UV mortar and lived?"

"A Jack Daniel's on me, my very sporting wolf brother?" Jacques released a sigh of relief. "Thank you . . . I don't have to explain to you."

"Oh, no, I feel you, man," Lamar said with a good-natured smile.

"Then drinks on us!" Jacques said, laughing. "Vampire tab to celebrate the bayou brawl for it all! Let the taps run blood for my men as well!"

A collective vampire cheer went up with the howls from the wolf pack.

"So, what, are we the Fae left out of this party?" a Fae archer called out from the treetops. "We have an ale that will knock you on your ass."

"I've heard, man," Lamar called out, looking up. "All warriors unite! If it wasn't for the lady and her people in spirit, dayum!" He glanced at Jacques. "The Fae got a lager that ain't no joke, son! We should put aside all our differences for one night and just party."

The lead scythe-bearer smiled a gruesome grin. "It is true about both the ale and the wolf's suggestion," he hissed. "We frequent Saints and Sinners all the time. What they have on tap there is truly wicked."

"I think our alien interlopers will give it due consideration before they attempt to poach in our territories again," Jacques said with a toothy grin.

"Yeah," a wolf pack member shouted, gaining barks and howls from the others. "They say, 'Don't mess with Texas'; hell . . . how about 'Don't fuck with New Orleans'!"

Arianna kept walking and gave Jacques and Lamar a sidelong glance, and then cautiously looked over her shoulder at the demon regiment that had joined them, even though she was still laughing. "Just make sure your boy knows, under *no circumstances* do I do demons. I've still got a soul."

"Come now, *chérie*, would I put you in mortal danger?" Jacques crooned, briefly nicking her jugular with his kiss.

Lamar winked at her. "Not on my watch."

She laughed harder as a handsome Fae archer gave her a discreet nod from a tree branch as she passed. "Good, because after all, a lady has to have *some* standards."

The Steeple People

John Alfred Taylor

Gorgo picked up on the first ring. "Couching and Portal, the Steeple People." She listened for a second, then nodded at Orabas. "It's Mr. Michaelis."

Orabas stared at her as he reached for his own phone. Hell's fashions kept changing, and Gorgo was different every day. This morning she had eyes where her nipples should be, blue ones with long lashes. At least she'd stopped straightening her hair—the snakes looked much more lively now.

"Orabas here."

"Got you a new customer," Michaelis said. "Thing that's a-building needs a steeple."

"Great, Ben. Standard kickback?"

"Not the standard," the architect said. "I want more this time, because I'm looking at the fifty-two-footer M-220 in your catalog."

Orabas nodded his great horse head. "The M-220, transported and installed? See what you mean about wanting more. Back to you once I do the math."

Actually Gorgo did the math. "We can give him five hundred."

Orabas hit redial. Michaelis was happy with five hundred and said he'd fax the order, but there was an extra that went with it. "Told my client how good your steeples are for the price—don't know how you guys do it. Anyway the reverend got interested and wants a plant tour. He'll be driving through on the way to Atlanta on the twenty-second, if that's all right."

Orabas rolled his eyes. "Fine, fine. The twenty-second. Though make sure he calls ahead."

Afterward he groaned. "Put down Reverend Clyde Simpson for the twenty-second."

"Already done, boss."

"Of course," he said. Gorgo had good ears. She was one smart demon: more than receptionist and secretary, she kept the books and organized the social security and payroll deduction payments for the fictional workforce. All done in her head, except for the documentation after the fact. Orabas guessed she could run the factory on her own, but your average male demon wouldn't take orders from a woman.

This Reverend Simpson better call ahead if he wanted his plant tour, because casting the glamour took time. The preacher mustn't see things as they were. One glimpse of Balam with his three heads, and the fool might never speak again, much less sermonize against hell.

But that was a problem for next week, not today. "This accountant I have to pick up—"

"You have lots of time," Gorgo said. "Toglas is coming in this afternoon, three fifteen on Delta 1024."

"Don't see the point."

Gorgo shrugged. "Whatever headquarters wants, headquarters gets. Won't find anything wrong with my books. Either set."

"Of course not." Somehow this came of Lucifuge Rofocale's insistence that the company turn a profit, even if it was secondary to their real purpose. And a handsome profit every quarter, with the whole crew working without wages, purely for the love of evil.

This was the first year Lucifuge had wanted a look at the books. *Ours is not to reason why,* Orabas told himself. North American headquarters seethed with gossip and backbiting—who knew what nonsense Rofocale had overheard, a hint that must have grown in his imagination, since suspicion was part of being a demon.

It didn't matter. Lucifuge's accountant would fly in this afternoon. Then he'd check the books and congratulate Gorgo and Orabas. And in a day or two Rofocale would send Couching and Portal Inc. another citation for Best Stealth Operation.

Not because they kept making a profit, but because every steeple they built, transported, and erected was delivered with its own resident imp or demon, turning each church into a focus of temptation. Orabas was proud. The whole thing had been his idea, and once it was green-lighted he'd built Couching and Portal up from nothing.

Orabas adjusted his tie one last time, then turned to Gorgo. "How do I look?"

He always had her check his human guise since the time he almost went public once with his horse ears showing.

"Convincing," she said.

"Hold the fort," Orabas told her on the way out.

He started his car and pulled away from the office—he would have liked something sportier than a Cadillac, but verisimilitude was everything. He hit the remote and the receiving-yard gate slid open. The demon there was passing as human, helping the driver unload louvered windows and praying-hands plaques from a semi. Orabas waved and went on.

Zagan stopped him at the outer exit. "Something you better see, boss."

"Like what?"

Zagan pointed straight up, so Orabas had to step out of the car to see what the guard was talking about. He wasn't impressed by the shapes he saw circling far overhead. "Just turkey vultures."

Zagan shook his head. "Ain't buzzards. Angels trying to look like buzzards."

"What makes you so sure?"

"I can smell the difference." Orabas could believe that. Even in his human form, Zagan had nostrils that looked like the business end of a double-barreled shotgun.

"How long have they been there?"

"Since day before yesterday. Without any others showing up. More proof they ain't buzzards."

"Keep watching them," Orabas said, and got back in his stodgy black Cadillac.

All the way to the interstate he wondered about the vultures who weren't vultures. Had anybody given angels a reason to hover around the plant? He hoped not—he'd drilled the security protocol into everybody's heads repeatedly. No going outside in one's natural shape, keep the shop doors closed when deliveries were being made in receiving, no daytime emissions of sulfur, and so on. To the best of his knowledge none of the rules had been breached, especially since the crew were encouraged to report on each other.

The first church the interstate passed had a steeple from Couching and Portal, and buzzards above. Not good.

But Orabas was partly reassured when he drove by Soul's Lighthouse and saw it had visiting vultures too. Because that steeple wasn't one of theirs, which meant all steeples were suspect. Though there was always the possibility these were real birds.

Not likely, he decided when he passed another

church with seeming buzzards circling overhead a dozen miles on.

Maybe they'd be forced out of business soon. And spectacularly—a raid by angels with flaming swords wasn't exactly bankruptcy court. Though if every steeple in the country was under inspection . . . No need to panic yet, just watch and wait. This might just blow over.

And if worst came to worst, Couching and Portal would have had a good run. Orabas liked the slogan on the company letterhead: *Pointing Toward Heaven for Twenty Years*. Though he thought it was more like giving heaven the finger.

Orabas remembered the moment the idea dawned on him. He'd been sent on a cross-country scouting trip, attending services in every monster church he could find—nobody called them megachurches then. He'd slouch in a pew toward the back, listen to the whispers of the congregation as much as to the sermon, then go back to his motel room and fill out the opposition research form. Possible weaknesses of the pastor, sheep-to-goat ratio of the flock, estimated tendency to confuse conformity with virtue. It was lonely work, except for the nights when he could consult his little black book of succubi.

This wasn't one of those nights, because Orabas had been too tired and discouraged for sex. He dropped a quarter in the Magic Fingers box, closed his eyes, and lay back on the vibrating bed, but even with his eyes closed he kept seeing jiggling steeples. He'd noticed them a lot this trip: so many of them were spiky prefab things that looked like afterthoughts. The church he'd been in that day had its steeple in the center, with low roofs slanting just enough for drainage all around, and looked like a huge, square thumbtack waiting for God to sit down. (And God did have a backside, because that had been all Moses was allowed to see.)

The thought of God sitting on a tack plus the realization that spires were manufactured en masse were his inspiration. What if hell went into the steeple business, and each would come with a resident demon, a spy and saboteur delivered straight to the church? Orabas sat up and hugged himself in ecstasy.

Conception was easy, accomplishment difficult. Back at headquarters he sent away for steeple and cupola manufacturers' catalogs. Later he journeyed to the nearest competitor's plant, creeping in unseen to study their shop practices. Next Mammon helped him flesh out his business plan, and Mulciber and the Cyclopes showed him how to speed production with demonic powers. The hardest thing had been selling the stealth project to Lucifuge. Lucifuge liked the idea from the start but needed to be convinced it was practical.

Afterward Orabas never looked back. He discovered he had a natural talent for business, and Couching and Portal prospered beyond expectation.

But now there were angels snooping overhead. Orabas had no idea why. He'd made sure the company stayed security-conscious, and they would have been raided before now if there'd been any slipup.

Even this trip to pick up Lucifuge's man was strictly according to protocol; without the need for secrecy the accountant could have flown in on bat wings last night.

Hartsfield-Jackson Atlanta International Airport resembled Pandemonium enough to make Orabas feel at home.

Delta 1024 actually came in on time, and despite their human forms the two devils recognized each other instantly. Toglas looked like an accountant should: serious with glasses, gray suit, and tie, pulling a wheeled overnight bag.

They traded banalities till they were in the car and could speak demon to demon.

"Lucifuge sends his regards."

Orabas snorted. "But also wants to check my books."

"Merely a matter of form," Toglas said. "Rofocale has nothing but praise for your operation."

"All right, but did he explain the operation?"

Toglas grinned admiringly. "You manufacture state-of-the-art church steeples at competitive prices, then deliver each with an imp inside. Subversion in the midst of sanctity. Very clever."

"So far," Orabas said. "Though it means you'll have to do your job twice."

"Oh?"

"We keep two sets of books. And I want you to check our fake books too, make sure they look as good as the real ones."

"I can do that," the demon accountant said.

"The fake books matter," Orabas explained, "because they keep track of the company we're supposed to be. Much bigger than we actually are. There's lots of talk about lean, mean companies, but we're the real thing, only eight of us, four demons on the shop floor and four fronting with the public. On paper we have to be twice as big, with payroll deductions and social security taxes for each of the supposed human staff. My secretary and executive officer does wonders keeping up with it all but could use somebody like you looking over her shoulder."

"She won't mind?"

"Gorgo will welcome your assistance."

They were heading home on the interstate now, giving Orabas a chance to see the churches off the other side. Neither of the steeples on the first two was from Couching and Portal, though buzzards circled over both. "Good," he grunted, then saw Toglas looking sideways and realized he had to explain.

"Worrisome that your watchman smelled angels above the plant," Toglas said once he heard the whole story. "But every steeple you've passed is under scrutiny, whether or not it's one of yours. So it's time to find out if other steeple manufacturers are under observation as well. Couching and Portal might not be in the crosshairs."

"Of course," Orabas said, feeling stupid. Should have thought of that himself.

Orabas was pleased that Gorgo and Toglas hit it off right away, but his first priority was following through on Toglas's suggestion. In a few minutes he was talking to Lucifuge Rofocale on a secure line.

"Toglas get there all right?"

"Everything's fine here," Orabas said. "He's already going over the books. That's not what I'm calling about. We have another kind of problem. Totally unexpected." He explained about the disguised angels circling over the plant and what he'd observed on the way to and from the airport. "So every steeple I passed had turkey vultures over it, whether or not it was one of ours."

"Couldn't some be real buzzards?"

Orabas couldn't help raising his voice. "Something dead by every church at the same time?"

"Guess you're right," said Lucifuge. "Hard to believe. So what to do about the damn angels?"

"First thing is to find out whether we're the only steeple manufacturer under surveillance. Maybe not, if everybody's steeples in the area are being watched. So send out scouts to see if our competitors' plants have vultures hanging about as well."

"That'll take a while," Lucifuge said. "Give me the company names and locations."

That had been yesterday.

Waiting made Orabas's ears twitch. He put his hooves up on the desk but couldn't relax and put them down again. The memory of the salamanders he'd had for breakfast returned to his throat. When he stood up Gorgo gave him an understanding look, which irritated him more. Toglas was too wrapped up in his task to notice when he went through the next room.

Things on the shop floor were pleasanter. Clanging and banging, flame and fury, the scream of tortured metal.

Balam was looking at plans with his ram's head, projecting the exact line to cut with a laser beam from the mouth of his bull's head, and whistling a pop tune from Ninth Circle with his human pair of lips. Furcas was scuttling across an aluminum sheet on his furry pads, scoring along Balam's laser line with an extended claw. After Balam and Furcas repeated the process two more times, Gaap stepped forward, picked up the aluminum sheet, and folded it like origami in his enormous hands. Nitibus raced up the open seam, welding it with his blue-white tongue, and they had the topmost spire of a steeple.

Balam grinned at Orabas with his human face. "What's up, boss?"

"Nothing. Just came to see how things are going." Then Balam's three heads triggered a memory. Reverend Clyde Whoozit was coming.

"Something wrong?" Balam said.

"Not at all," Orabas told him. "You guys are doing fine. Just remembered something."

Back in the office, he asked, "When's that preacher supposed to be here?"

"The Reverend Clyde Simpson," Gorgo said. "Sometime on the twenty-second."

"Holy hell—only six days to go! And we still have angels overhead." Orabas went to his project planning board on the wall, stared at the smudged plastic till each path made sense. Then he wiped the vertical column for the twenty-second clean and grease-penciled an X down through every empty box. Erasing and changing everything on the board after the twenty-second took longer.

Making the place safe for Simpson's plant tour should take less than a quarter hour, but his visit would probably set production back a day: glamour was a lot easier to create than to reverse.

If only Lucifuge would call.

"Good news I think," said Lucifuge. "It isn't just you. Every steeple factory you listed has buzzards overhead."

"That's some relief," Orabas said. "Though what's going on?"

"I have no idea. But I've declared a continental alert."

"So what do we do here?"

"What you're already doing. Hang in there."

It was a near thing, but Orabas slowed his arm halfway and didn't slam the phone down. *Hang in there.* Easy to say back at headquarters, not so easy here in the field.

To calm himself he walked over and looked at the production schedule again. Still had a company to run—while it lasted. The 205 model for the Lutherans—roll-coated Kynar in "Colonial White"—would be ready for transport tomorrow. The skinny 202 destined to top a Church of God chapel would be finished the day after but couldn't move because of the weekend. Next came the Reverend Simpson's visit, which meant the Four-Square Gospel spire would be delayed two days.

(Lutheran, Church of God, Four-Square, gibber gibber—he couldn't keep track of all their names. Way-back-when a demon was supposed to have said, "Our name is Legion," but Orabas thought these pullulating sects had a better claim on the title.)

Meanwhile there were angels overhead. Though perhaps their turkey vulture disguise was wearing thin—just how long had they been there? Orabas did the count in his head. Zagan had told him they'd been there since the day before yesterday when he took off for Atlanta International, so now it was four days.

People should have noticed if all the angels on patrol everywhere had been doing the buzzard act that long.

Because carrion had a short shelf life, there might be a way to tweak the watchers here without too much risk. He changed to human form, dressed, and put on a wide-brimmed straw hat. "How do I look?" he asked Gorgo.

"Okay," she said. "What's up?"

"Just going to the front gate, need to ask Zagan something."

The hat let him look up at the shapes circling overhead without being too obvious. *Patient sons of bitches,* he thought, and corrected himself; angels never had mothers.

"Not going away," Zagan said when he saw the tilt of Orabas's head.

"Unlike real buzzards. Which gives me an idea. Suppose we put something big and dead out in the woods overnight."

Zagan grinned. "So next morning they won't know how to act—lemme see what I can arrange." He was already on his cell phone when Orabas started back.

Orabas woke early, eager to see the results of his experiment. Late yesterday he'd watched as an extended-cab pickup unloaded its cargo under the roof of the receiving bay. He'd wanted a deer, and a man who jacked deer was among Zagan's mortal connections, but using a deer carcass would have meant too long a wait, so they made do with a pig. The sow was so sweet-tempered the taming spell was hardly necessary; she would have had no time for fear or pain after Zagan led her into the dark woods.

Hurrying through breakfast, Orabas went out to the receiving dock, where he could look up without drawing attention from the sky. Already the experiment was working. The twin angels were circling as always, but three real turkey vultures were orbiting with them. He'd wondered whether the fake buzzards had driven others away the first few days, or if real vultures had joined them in their soaring, then left when they saw nothing on the ground.

Now he had his answer. But this was just the start. He could stay and watch all morning, except he had a business to run.

Things were humming on the shop floor. Though the Model 205 for the Lutherans had already passed inspection, Orabas looked it over personally. Definitely ready to ship, once it had an occupant. The lights below came on automatically when he lifted the trapdoor. At the bottom of the spiral stair he checked the roster, though he'd already made his choice. Malpas would do well with Lutherans: he was good with pride, spiritual sloth, and lack of imagination. There was no snoring as Orabas went down the row of bunks; dormant demons breathed too minimally for that.

"Malpas," he said, and Malpas opened his yellow eyes, instantly alert. "Time to go out on assignment."

"Right," said Malpas. "What month is it now?"

Orabas explained the basics on the way upstairs. Malpas would be going north to a big church of the Lutheran Missouri Synod. Everybody on the shop floor stopped work to shake Malpas's hand or slap him on the back. "It's a jungle out there," Gaap joked, working his huge claws.

Malpas showed every needle tooth when he grinned. "That's how I like it." They wished him luck as he crawled into the horizontal steeple.

Back in the office Orabas made sure the transport and installation crew were on schedule for the afternoon, then went out to see what was happening with the birds.

Promising indeed. The real vultures were descending, making the angels' constancy absurd, even more absurd when the three hungry birds disappeared behind the trees. Once they realized how exposed they were the angels plummeted down to mingle with the others.

Orabas couldn't help laughing.

He stopped laughing a moment later, staring as the angels burst back out of the treetops, flapping desperately upward at first without the help of thermals, then rising till they were almost too high to see. And they weren't hovering up there but heading east. He watched them till they disappeared, unable to imagine what had happened, before going out to consult with Zagan.

"Did you see that?"

Zagan nodded. "Pretty funny. Looked like they ran into something they didn't like."

"But what? Surely not the sight of a dead pig."

"Beats me," Zagan said. "Whatever it is, the real buzzards must not mind it."

"Certainly nothing that could get between *them* and a good meal," said Orabas. "Keep watching. The fake birds might come back, though I doubt it, considering how fast they left."

The first thing to do was call Lucifuge Rofocale at headquarters and report the result of his experiment.

"Interesting," Lucifuge said. "They left in a hurry?"

"No real turkey vulture could get up that high that fast."

"So what is it vultures have that angels don't, or is it the other way around?"

"I have no idea," Orabas said.

"Neither do I. But we have experts who might know. I'll get back to you if I find out anything."

Orabas followed as the 205 was carried outside, with Balam and Nitibus under the tip, Gaap holding up the base by himself. They laid it down on the loading dock without going past the roof overhang, closing the shop doors when they went back in.

Orabas watched through a peephole as Zagan opened the outer gate for the truck from Parker Transport and Erection and it backed up to the loading dock. The 205 was one of their broader models and demanded a wide-load truck. Soon the men from Parker winched it aboard, red flags were attached, the demon in receiving (always in human shape) signed a form on a clipboard, and the truck was off to join its escorts waiting beyond the gate.

"Lucifuge called," Gorgo announced when he entered the office. "Wants you to call back. Says he's got news."

Lucifuge's receptionist put Orabas through right away. "Gorgo says you have news."

"Learned something that may explain all this angelic surveillance. Seems a Holy Roller church in Arkansas tried to exorcise its steeple."

"What denomination?"

"Assembly of God."

Assembly of God—could it be? "Where in Arkansas?"

"Town called Pevely."

"Afraid that rings a bell," Orabas said. "Pevely, Arkansas," he told Gorgo. "Look it up."

A moment later she handed him the file. "I'm looking at our record right now. Eligor went with that steeple six months ago. He was very enthusiastic."

"Maybe overenthusiastic," said Lucifuge. "We've got to get him out of there."

Orabas was speechless for a moment, and then it came to him. "We can do it with a bang—might as well take out the steeple at the same time."

"How do we do that?"

"Our steeples are shipped with lightning protection—aluminum air terminal, heavy aluminum cable down. What we don't advertise is that the grounding cable has a hidden charge that can cut it in an instant. Get the word to Eligor, send a thunderstorm over to zap the place, and he hightails it during the fireworks."

"Clever," said Lucifuge. "I'll get right on it. And I know just the storm demon—Ribesal's an artist with thunder and lightning. He's done a few churches already."

"Then our steeple should be a pushover for him. Built to fail if needed." Before hanging up Orabas asked his superior if he'd found out why the angels had fled that morning.

"Not yet, but I'll let you know as soon as I find out."

Because he dreamed of lightning that night Orabas woke knowing the problem in Arkansas had been taken care of. As long as Eligor was home free—though he doubted that would end things, because Lucifuge had said the angelic watch was everywhere.

Except maybe here. Had the angels come back after their panicked departure?

Orabas went out to the loading dock and looked

at the sky. He sighed—there they were again. But when the two birds started down, he realized they were genuine turkey vultures, doing what buzzards did. No chance of *them* snubbing the pig Zagan had laid out. He couldn't imagine what had sent the two angels rocketing upward yesterday.

Orabas ate his breakfast of centipedes and haba-ñeros with renewed gusto and would have flirted with Gorgo when he went to the office, except she and Toglas seemed to have reached an understanding. Ora-bas was never one to interfere with romance.

Everything was fine on the shop floor. When he came back, Orabas put his hooves up on his desk and decided to relax. Then the phone rang, and Gorgo sig-naled him. It was Lucifuge.

"We've found out why your angels left in such a hurry. Ethyl mercaptan."

Orabas was baffled. "I don't know the lady."

"Be serious," Lucifuge snapped. "It's a chemical compound, not a person. Given off by dead things. Vultures home in on it."

"I thought they just had very good eyes."

"They do. But they have good noses too. Ethyl mercaptan is a sulfur compound. It seems angels can't stand the smell."

Orabas snorted at the idea, never having met a sul-fur compound he didn't like. Angels were wimps.

Lucifuge continued: "Your little experiment paid off. So we're going to scale up: I'm going to have dead

animals laid out around other churches and steeple fac-
tories—randomly chosen, so there won't be any visible
pattern—and for good measure we'll douse other sites
with the straight chemical and see how that works by
itself. Already buying half a ton of the stuff."

"Ship some my way," Orabas said. "I can keep it in
reserve."

"I'll send a liter. More than enough, because a little
goes a long way."

Afterward Orabas grinned in satisfaction. He
hadn't told Lucifuge what he'd reserve the stuff for. If
any angels with flaming swords ever showed up they'd
get a fine surprise when Couching and Portal went
down.

Orabas drove Toglas back to Atlanta International
Sunday afternoon. Both of them watched the churches
they passed. There were no vultures above the first
steeple. Soul's Lighthouse had three, which meant they
were real buzzards: like Mormon missionaries, angels
always traveled in pairs.

"Looks as if it's working," Orabas said.

"The randomness helps," Toglas said. "They don't
know what's going on. So much for omniscience."

"It doesn't reach down past the top. And nowadays
He's mostly an absentee landlord."

"Good thing," said Toglas.

"Gorgo is going to miss you."

"I'm going to miss her too. But my job here is done." He shook his head in admiration, repeating what he'd already said more than once. "Her books were perfect, especially the fake ones. Real attention to detail."

Orabas smiled. "Told you so."

When he let the accountant off at the airport Toglas wished him good luck with the Reverend Simpson's plant visit.

Just as long as that preacher calls ahead, Orabas thought as he pulled away.

Returning, he watched for vultures but saw nothing out of the ordinary until the drive leading to the plant, where he saw two shapes circling very far up.

"Are the angels back?" he asked Zagan when he stopped at the gate.

Zagan flared his enormous nostrils wider, testing the air, and finally shook his head. "Can't be sure. They're too high to smell."

"Keep your eyes peeled. And when it's really dark, go see how much of the pig is left."

If those soaring pinpoints really were angels, why had they zeroed in on the factory again? Orabas was sure nobody here had made a mistake, not gone outside in their natural form, released sulfur in the daytime, anything on the list. He'd even given another security lecture after Zagan alerted him.

Could be they'd found out where the Arkansas

Holy Rollers steeple came from. Or maybe it was because they'd been the first to set out carrion and brought real buzzards to show up the angels. There was even a chance it was just a fluke.

But Orabas went to the shop floor for reassurance. The crew was off for the night, and he was alone with the steeples.

There the mercaptan was, attached to the central ceiling girder, with a bursting charge taped to it that Orabas could trigger with a garage door opener. The carefully packed liter bottle had been delivered late Saturday, by a person who might have been an actual FedEx driver—though Orabas suspected otherwise.

Gaap had been able to put it up without a ladder, while Balam had wondered what it was for. All Orabas told him was, "Think of it as the equivalent of a sprinkler system."

Reverend Clyde Simpson called to let them know he'd be arriving in the afternoon, so they had plenty of time to get ready.

The whole place was wrapped in illusion. In the office the mummified hand Gorgo used for a paperweight had turned to a millefiori glass hemisphere, and Orabas's huge throne with the hole for his tail seemed just another Aeron chair.

Perfecting the look of the factory floor was more complicated. The graffito GOD = DOG had been rendered invisible, the rat-on-a-stick skewers thrown into the trash. Orabas and Gorgo went around with check-lists—fire extinguishers and location signs for fire extinguishers, safety warnings, motivational posters—with Gorgo especially meticulous because she read all the OSHA literature.

They gathered round Orabas for final instructions before they broke for lunch, with Gaap still towering above the others, even with everyone in human form: "You all know what to do already, but let me repeat. Keep busy without faking it. I'll try to do all the talk-ing—though if he stops and asks you a question give sensible answers. Smile and be polite. And remember, it can't last long. It's not like this preacher wants to know the details."

A little after two Zagan alerted Orabas with a high-pitched whistle undetectable by the human ear. He ambled out to the loading dock, to see Zagan opening the outer gate for Reverend Simpson's car. He glanced at the sky but couldn't tell whether there was anything up there. He'd worry about that later.

Orabas went down the stairs at the end of the dock and was waiting in the receiving yard when the glossy black Lincoln pulled up beside him. Simpson came out like a jack-in-the-box and pumped Orabas's hand enthusiastically. He was a tall, wide man in a white suit and pale blue tie, with mobile eyebrows and impressive gray hair. He had tons of charisma, though more from testosterone than pneuma.

"So good of you to let me see your plant. Michaelis said you were the best."

"We try," Orabas said. *Though kickbacks help too.*

The reverend didn't want to wear the hard hat with the cross decal, but Orabas insisted, tapping his own for demonstration. "It's a safety regulation. We like to think of it as the whole armor of God."

"If it's a regulation," Simpson said, putting the helmet on crooked. *Doesn't want to mess up his coiffure,* Orabas realized.

The pastor blinked as they went in out of the sunlight, then looked around the factory, neat and bright in its phantasmal form. Balam and Nitibus were deburring the edges of the Four-Square spire, and a buffer was chuffing at the far end. "Like a church," Simpson murmured.

Orabas nodded solemnly. "We try to keep it that way. Because what we do is God's work too."

The tour went well. Every demon on the shop floor behaved properly, and Orabas was showing Simpson the paint room with its huge exhaust fans when there was an inhumanly loud roar from outside: Zagan shouting a warning. A second later a flaming sword smashed through the skylight, and the angelic raid was on.

The Reverend Simpson stared and screamed as Orabas and the others assumed their true forms. Angels cascaded from the shattered skylight, a chaos of wings and fiery weapons. Orabas waited till they were almost upon him before triggering the bursting charge on the mercaptan, gleefully watching the perfect, righteous visages writhing in disgust and horror. Beside him, the preacher was bent over, retching.

Time to go home. Orabas sank through the floor, dropping into the dormitory of demons in reserve. Wakened by the noise above, they were sitting up in their bunks. "It's a raid," he shouted. "Time to go to hell."

Then everyone was homeward bound, sinking through clay and slate and the darker, denser strata. Things became pleasantly warm.

Orabas hugged himself as he went down. He had no regrets—except not being able to carry on longer. But twenty years of stealth and subversion might be a record. The tales they'd tell when they got home.

And there were still lots of steeples with resident demons.

But best of all had been the expressions of the angels deluged with mercaptan. Maybe they wouldn't be so eager in the future. Attack a devil, expect a stink.

For Sale

DAVID SAKMYSTER

Featured Home of the Week:
666 Nevermore Trail, Kingston, MA

I. Property Summary

A classical nineteenth-century Victorian with a mansard roof, wrought-iron cresting around a beautiful stained-glass cupola, dormer windows and ivy-ensnared walls. Eight thousand square feet of interior living space[1] comprising three gorgeous, if perennially dusty, upper levels and including a substantive wine cellar/dungeon. Other beneficial features unique to

---

1. Square footage as of last count. Oddly, the number fluctuates based on which Realtor takes the measurements and when; some even claim that they've counted more rooms than are currently listed. How that can be possible is less due to our incompetence than to the intriguing characteristics of this house, which will become evident upon a visit.

this property include a network of adjoining caverns,[2] a conservatory still stocked with unusual (if a tad overgrown) fauna, a sublevel apothecary and a soundproof science lab.

And did we mention gargoyles?

One clinging to each cornice, these stone sentinels can be thought of as your own private security force. Neighbors (when there used to be some) would complain that these stone features were actually inclined to detach and go flying around in the night, often abducting (and consuming) their fluffy pets, then spitting the bones out over the lawn.[3]

Main levels are in excellent condition considering the lapse in ownership. Just some stubborn traces of gore remain, but otherwise this house is move-in ready, just waiting for that lucky new owner (which might be you—so don't dawdle, visit today! Open House midnight–four A.M.).

Still not decided? Read on—you won't be disappointed.

Exterior: a delight for any true craftsman with creativity and vision. The condition of the walled perim-

2. Caverns (and surrounding acreage) cannot be sold separately, nor any piece later partitioned, excluded or otherwise redistributed to unrelated third parties. Realtor absolves itself of any knowledge of criminal misdeeds, or evidence thereof, discovered in such tunnels, or indeed anywhere upon this property.

3. Although to be fair, apparently the former neighbors spent quite a lot of their free time in the wine cellar, so anything they may have said should be discounted accordingly.

eter allows one the opportunity to redesign the crumbling stone partitions to one's own specifications.[4]

The views from the open balconies: breathtaking. The steaming swamp pits along Cemetery Ridge bathe the crumbling mausoleums in decadently swirling mists, while the perpetually bleak forest to the east creates a haven for young children to play in and explore. Every spring, the scents of decomposing flesh emanate from the ice, and bloated carrion birds take to the sky with wild abandon.

Municipal records reveal nothing about this property—as if someone has purposely erased the records. Likewise, a perusal of local atlases (and even Google Maps) finds no such home where this one rests.

Which is all good news for you, the prospective buyer. You know the old adage "There's nothing certain but death and taxes"? Well, not in this case. One of the best features about this property is that *taxes are almost nonexistent*![5]

II. Location and Home Defense

The typical axiom has never been more fitting than with this property: *location is everything*. A steep,

---

4. Whether these walls were damaged during some sort of neighborhood uprising (complete with pitchforks and torches) or just the result of time and disuse, it cannot be said for certain, but given the scorch marks and the heavy preponderance of bones fused into the rubble, one can only imagine epic battles of yore.

5. And death? Well, that just depends on who and what you are.

winding road approaches from only one direction, and the turnoff to your street is all but concealed by prickly shrubs and thorny ferns of the carnivorous variety.

From the western approach: as mentioned, the pond. Bubbling all year round and never freezing, it's the perfect spa, medicinal and invigorating—as long as you stay away from the northern end, where the submerged caskets and the glowing barrels are most prevalent.

In terms of home defense, the ramparts are more than adequate to dump scalding oil or other noxious refuse down upon unwanted visitors, and should any daring investigators or pesky ghost-hunter Travel Channel nuisances breach the front door, the foyer is equipped with a working trapdoor,[6] leading to a (near as we can tell) bottomless pit.

III. Amenities and Features

Putting aside speculation about how the previous tenant could have failed to hold (and love) this home, it seems he left in a great hurry, forgoing the transport of even his most valuable personal property. Whatever remains in the house (everything you see here!) is included in the asking price.

The main living room, for example, sports an enormous emerald throne whose surface is so polished you can see your reflection.[7]

---

6. Trapdoor functionality subject to optional (but inadvisable) engineering inspection.

7. Assuming you cast one.

And within the central cupola, just above the master's chambers, there sits this property's prime attraction: *an immense globe of utter darkness.* Set in a golden container, it spins endlessly, and if one peers too long into its depths, a certain ease settles upon the soul, stirring visions of unimaginable vistas and alien skies.

The black globe spins for a successor, we like to think. Someone with the inner strength to rule a place such as this.

Through the years, several other interested parties have visited during our infrequent open houses. But so far, none have been willing to pay the price, meager as it is.[8]

And of course, we like to believe in the old real estate truism "The house chooses its next owner."

It could choose you.

But you're not decided. Understandable. It's a big step, and you're concerned about maintenance.

IV. Staffing and Support

Unquestionably, the upkeep of such a large and enviable property requires a substantial body of employees.

If you're a Necromancer, your task is significantly easier—as evidenced by the scattered bones strewn here and there about the grounds (and, most likely, in the pond). A major portion of your needs surely could

---

8. We, of course, continue to plague them with property updates, price drops and threatening e-mails. So act fast before they give in!

be met simply by raising what your predecessor left behind.

If necromancy is not in your skill set, another steady pool of laborers exists down in the valley, unaware of this property's existence except through occasionally disquieting dreams or bouts of unexplained irritable bowel syndrome.

Easy pickins.

V. Price and Closing Costs

Consider well this once-in-a-lifetime opportunity. Carefully reflect on all the intangibles. Think of all the fun your young ones will have exploring the forest, discovering the home's secret passageways or just inviting their friends over to play with ancient torture devices.

And don't forget those abysmally low taxes!

Consider too the mystery of the strange black orb, and yes—you must also consider the curious fate of the previous tenant.[9]

But don't wait. Come and take the tour. Drive on

---

9. On this subject, various rumors abound. Perhaps the most interesting, entertainment-wise at least, is the unfounded notion that a minor fourteenth-century Romanian duke acquired a device of blackest power from the caverns beneath his castle; it offered immortality—at the cost of blood sacrifice, consumption of human flesh and other unseemly acts. Escaping persecution, this duke moved to the New World, where it is surmised that this nobleman's downfall came not from the valiant effort of God-fearing villagers who opposed his bloodthirsty deeds, but rather from retaliation by said orb's vindictive previous owners. But make of such tall tales what you will.

up; just keep an eye out for that sneaky right turn or you'll quickly get lost in the woods. And if you find yourself in the middle of a cemetery with a fair amount of open graves, you've gone too far.

Come, explore. But don't wait too long.

After you tour the house (and fall in love with it), go on up to the cupola. We have a feeling, a notion really, that the black orb spins for you.

Go check it out. Then come back down and make your offer.[10]

---

10. Incidental Realtor fees and sacrificial insurance taxes apply. See also appendix 3, "Detailed Costs," and appendix 4, "Seller's Rights in the Event of Buyer's Early Termination or Premature Demise."

The Man Who Could Not Be Bothered to Die

NORMAN PRENTISS

Tony didn't hear the first knock. He wasn't expecting anyone this Tuesday evening, certainly not so late on a work night, but Barker scrambled to the front door, tail wagging and head raised in expectation. Tony saw his sister through the spy hole, and he opened the door to let her in. Then a few more people swarmed onto the porch. His stepdad. Kevin from work, and Rachel. His regular doctor, plus the hygienist from his dentist's office and the trainer-specialist from his gym.

They all jostled through his front door and crowded into his living room.

If Tony's family ever decided to give him a surprise

birthday party, this was better than the guest list he'd expect. Unfortunately, they weren't bearing gifts, and they weren't wearing funny hats. He wished a few of them would smile.

His stepfather made a hesitant step forward, as if he wanted to give Tony's shoulder a reassuring pat. He stopped himself, the well-meaning impulse suddenly distasteful. "I know I'm not your real father," Martin said. "But I've always prided myself on treating Ellen's kids like they were my own. Even after your mother died, I've considered you and Jill part of my family. You may not think I've earned the right to say this, but here goes. You need to end it, son."

Tony looked at Jill, whose head was down as if she couldn't believe what she was hearing. This no doubt was supposed to be a happy occasion, and their awkward stepdad screwed things up once again, as he often had during Tony and Jill's childhood.

But Jill said, "My turn. We're supposed to use 'I' statements. So here goes: When you continue breathing, I feel sad."

Brad, who'd sold him a lifetime membership to MidTown Fitness, assured Tony that he wasn't trying to cheat him out of the remaining years on his contract. "Hell, do the math. You've been a member for six years. Yearly dues are two hundred and fifty dollars, so you've already more than recouped the cost of your lifetime plan. I think you should just face the facts."

Dr. Maddox said, "I've taken the Hippocratic oath,

so I can't really speak frankly. But we all know why I'm here. I support your family and friends and think you should listen to them."

The dentist's hygienist said, "We don't care anymore if you floss. We really don't."

That's when Jill totally lost it. "He's not listening to us," she screamed. "He's going to keep going, regardless of what we feel. He's so selfish."

His stepfather, as usual, assumed the weak role of mediator. "Look what you're doing to your sister. I want you to think about this."

Had things really gotten this bad? He was only thirty-five years old. How had he reached this point?

At the dentist's office two weeks ago, he'd experienced a familiar disorientation as the chair tilted back, raising his legs unnaturally higher than his head. He tensed up.

The hygienist seemed more than usually hidden behind her surgical mask. He imagined her nose crinkled up behind the paper. She wasn't talkative. She didn't push the small mirror into his mouth to angle for a better view of his teeth. All the years he wished the dentist visits would pass more quickly—that the hygienist wouldn't scrape and scrape at his teeth, pressing metal tips into the spaces between, poking at his gums then asking him to rinse blood out of his mouth. Now the process was quick and painless, and he should have been happy. Instead, he felt insulted.

The hygienist stretched a span of floss between her fingertips and reached into his mouth. Floss pressed into his loose gums like a wire through warm cheese.

On the way out, he stopped at the front desk to schedule his six-month return visit. Instead, the receptionist just looked at him and shook her head.

Tony tried to be cheerful. "Is your computer down? I can call you tomorrow."

"No," the receptionist said. "Just . . . no."

"I thought you were gone for the day." Kevin's chin rested on the back wall of Tony's cubicle. This was how he often saw his coworkers: heads on the partition wall, lined up like tin cans for shooting practice.

"No, just ninety minutes for a dentist's appointment. I don't want to waste too much sick leave."

"But you're *supposed* to waste it. I woulda gone home to rest up—after all that drilling or whatever."

"I like to save it. Might need it later."

"Might need it now," Kevin said. "Honestly, you don't look so good."

Great advice, coming from a disembodied head.

"Thanks," Tony said.

"Don't mention it. Hey, you think those guys in the collapsed mine will get out today?"

"Dunno. It's day nine, isn't it?"

"Ten. But who's counting?" Every news program and website, for one. And the office pool. Kevin had two bucks riding on day forty.

Later, Rachel-head drifted by and told him about doughnuts in the break room. The chocolate-frosted ones were gone by the time he checked, but maybe he'd have better luck next time.

That afternoon, Alan-head asked for a donation to his son's uniform drive. "I'll try to bring my checkbook tomorrow," Tony responded.

"Now might be better." Alan-head jiggled the donation box over the top of the cubicle, and coins rattled against cardboard. "Anything you can spare, 'cause . . . tomorrow might not work out for you."

In retrospect, that last remark seemed ominous. Other people noticed something, but Tony was oblivious.

He was always the last to know.

After work on Mondays, Wednesdays and Fridays, Tony went to the gym. Mostly he used the treadmill or the bike, sometimes one of the weight machines.

There were rules posted for the machines. At the bottom, in caps and highlighted in yellow, each instruction sheet said: PLEASE WIPE OFF THE MACHINES WHEN YOU ARE FINISHED.

Such an unpleasant reminder. It made Tony think

of germs and fluids, a smeared stain left behind as a back pressed into vinyl or callused palms scraped over a metal bar, leaving behind flecks of dead skin.

It was rude to stare at people while they exercised, so he found himself absently reading and rereading the instruction sheet—while his own body, like a squeezed sponge, left its impression on the equipment.

The phenomenon wasn't unique to exercise equipment. Every surface you pressed against absorbed a small piece of you. Life was a constant, tedious leprosy.

But that Wednesday night, two weeks ago, should have been a cause for celebration. Tony had reached his target weight—those last ten pounds seemed to melt off effortlessly. And he'd finally achieved the body-fat ratio recommended on his exercise card.

He took the card to the gym's resident trainer. The grid was hatched with weights and dates annotated in Tony's meticulous handwriting, most of the ink smeared by months of fingertip sweat. Brad accepted the card from him, then gave him a new one with slightly different goals.

"This *might* help," Brad said. "More cardio. More weights to strengthen muscle tone." He seemed skeptical.

But now Tony had new goals. Something to live for.

So he did.

• • •

Later that same day, he watched *Crime Spree: Tuscaloosa* on channel 43, sprawled on the sofa and tossing a few random pretzel sticks to Barker during the commercials. Maybe sometime during the final segment . . . maybe that was another moment when it almost happened. Maybe Tony's heart had *almost* stopped.

But there was too much going on in the episode: the rusted key hadn't yet been matched to a bank deposit box; the numbers and symbols on the first ransom note hadn't yet been decoded; Detective Ajax still hadn't discovered the fourth victim's body, and his partner still needed a date for the Governor's Gala (would she ask him?). Too many loose ends, and only five minutes left.

Damn it! It was a two-parter.

Which meant he'd *have* to wait until next week.

And the next, too, if it was a longer arc.

Some things were worth looking forward to: Vacations and weekends. Going to the movies. Walking Barker each night after dinner. Reading in bed and eyes getting heavy until he set the book aside and drifted to blissful sleep.

But just as many tasks were tedious. Waking and showering and getting dressed. Brown-bagging a lunch. Driving to the office. Then work itself: a series of repetitive tasks, laced with the stress of artificial deadlines.

At his cubicle, Tony often caught himself staring at

a blurred computer screen, not remembering what task he was supposed to complete. He'd check his e-mail and find a large list of new messages, many of them marked with a red exclamation point.

Urgent. Funny how so many things could be considered urgent . . .

Last week, for example, a window popped up to inform him that his virus definition file was thirty days out of date. He could fix the problem now or click on "Remind Me Later."

He'd clicked "Remind Me Later" each day since. It only took a few minutes to update the file, but the reminder always popped up while he was in the middle of something else. Like while he was entering figures into the budget spreadsheet, or replying to a memo about the new reimbursement policy (receipts, in triplicate, for anything over $10). Or when he was checking CNN and Fox for information about the trapped miners (still trapped), or checking his Match-up account for potential dates in his area (he was planning to click "Interested" on a few of them but wanted to finish reading all the profiles first; more profiles were added each day—it was impossible to keep up).

"Day twenty," Kevin said from his cubicle on the other side. "Halfway there." He wasn't standing and peering into Tony's area, so his voice sounded muffled. Possibly, he also had a hand cupped over his nose and mouth.

"You might win the pool," Tony told him. "I'll be curious to see how this turns out."

"Yeah, if you outlast them."

"What's that supposed to mean?" His coworker's voice was still muffled and nasal, so Tony might have misheard.

"Nothing," Kevin said.

"You know, it's kind of cruel that you picked such a high number—like you wished they would stay down there longer."

"Just playing the odds. The guys in Chile were stuck for sixty-nine days."

"Even so, you'd be profiting from their discomfort." Tony thought about germs and fluids, scraped skin and body waste and foul breath—the constant, tedious leprosy of existence. "All of them stuck in that tight space. Can you even imagine the smell?"

"Yes, I think I can," Kevin said.

He didn't seem to want to talk further, so Tony turned back to his computer monitor. A new profile, added today: Kristin R., 42. Likes: Dogs and Cats. Favorite movies: *Fight Club* and *Gone with the Wind*.

His finger slipped on the mouse button as he clicked for the next page. There was a slick gel on the button, in the shape of his fingertip. He clicked in the navigation bar, then typed in a new Web address. The letters on the keyboard felt soft and wet.

These recent days, the heads seemed to float quickly past his cubicle wall. Rachel-head didn't tell him if doughnuts were in the break room; people avoided getting into the elevator with him.

Still, Tony's job performance was fine. At the end of each year, his boss always checked the "Meets Standards" box on the review form. Tony continued to meet standards.

Yet when he phoned his sister for their usual Sunday chat, she mentioned some of his coworkers were concerned about him.

"Kevin, most likely," he said, and Jill didn't deny it. "What kinds of concerns? Why is he calling *you* instead of talking to me directly?"

"Some topics are difficult," Jill said. She proved her point by not elaborating.

"Okay, I've been feeling a little weak lately," he admitted. "I overslept some mornings and maybe didn't dress as carefully as I usually do." Or shower, though Jill didn't need that detail.

Seemed like she already knew, though: "There's kind of a bare minimum. An expectation for what's worth . . . um . . ."

"I should take better care of myself," he said, finishing her argument.

"That's not quite what I meant."

Silence.

They typically spent most of their Sunday talk complaining about their stepdad. This was getting a little too personal.

So he changed the subject. "How's your husband?"

"Fine."

"How are the kids?"

"They're fine," Jill said. Usually she had lots of stories—cute dinner-table remarks from Janey, or Adam's latest score on a math quiz.

"I bet they miss their uncle Tony. I should visit more often."

"Actually, Janey's got a flu bug. Adam's coming down with it, too."

"I wasn't talking about visiting *today*," Tony said.

"Oh."

"I thought you said they were fine."

"Yeah, aside from the flu." He heard Jill's hand smother the mouthpiece as she yelled into the distance. "What's that? You need Mommy? You think you're throwing up again?" Another scratch against the mouthpiece, then Jill spoke in a normal voice: "Time to go, Tony."

She hung up before he could promise to call again next week.

He visited instead. That same Sunday. His sister's house was a quick twenty-minute drive.

Jill wouldn't open the door.

"I'm not feeling well," she shouted from inside the house.

"I thought the kids were sick, not you."

"The kids? They're not here."

"Jill, come on." He resisted an urge to kick at the door. "Let me in."

Eventually he heard the latch chain jangle, and his sister opened the door a crack. Jill peered at him over the taut chain. She had pulled the collar of her T-shirt over her mouth and nose. "I can't let you in. Don't want to give you this cold." She lifted a hand and fake-coughed into her shirt.

In the background, he heard SpongeBob's theme music. "You watching cartoons?"

"No, that's . . ." Her eyes darted uncomfortably to the side, then back. She spoke to his left shoulder rather than to his face. "I just left it on. You know how, sometimes, you keep things running."

"I guess."

"It's not good though. A waste." Another fake cough.

"Of electricity."

"Sure."

He heard Janey's distinct laugh in response to one of SpongeBob's antics.

"Tony, you have to leave," Jill said.

Even then, he sensed his sister was doing more than chasing him off her porch.

She closed the door.

Two days later, that crowd of people muscled their way into his house. Jill must have organized the whole intervention—which explained why she got so out-of-sorts after things weren't going so well.

"You're putrefying!"

It wasn't a terribly polite thing to say. His sister had recently gained back all the weight she'd lost after a recent diet—and then some—and he'd been courteous enough to keep silent.

Martin placed a gentle hand on Jill's shoulder. "No insults," their stepfather said. "That won't get us anywhere."

"You're right." As far as Tony could recall, Jill had never previously agreed with Martin. As a matter of fact, it was odd that she didn't shrug his comforting hand off her shoulder.

Dr. Maddox stepped forward, his arms raised toward the living room ceiling. "Walk into the light."

There wasn't an overhead light in the living room, so Tony didn't know how to respond.

"Oh God," Jill said. "I don't think he *knows*."

She looked ready to cry. Tony suddenly wanted to hug her, but his sister's body language told him the affection wouldn't be welcomed.

They all kept their distance.

Even Barker. He could see that now, the way his dog jumped up at Kevin, delighting at a simple scratch behind the ear, licking his coworker's hand, then sniffing at his crotch. Barker hadn't acted like that in quite a while. Lately, the dog stayed in separate rooms; he pulled to the farthest end of the leash when they went for their evening walks.

"Of course I know," Tony said. "I'm not blind." He thought about how he'd dressed each morning. He would pat his hair gently with his hand, afraid a comb would pull out clumps of hair or wet scalp. When he checked his appearance in the bathroom mirror he focused mostly on one shoulder or another, as Jill had when he visited on Sunday.

Tony always knew this would happen eventually, but he was only thirty-five. It should have waited until he was in his seventies, in a nursing home bed. His loved ones would gently ask to unplug the machines. He'd let them.

"So why didn't you . . . ?" Jill couldn't quite bring herself to say it.

Tony shrugged. "I don't know. I've just been . . . busy."

Jill snorted. "Busy? Doing what?"

How could he respond? His sister ran her own catering business, raised two kids, kept the home spotless for her whole family. What could he say that would satisfy her: Walking the dog? Watching television? Waiting for chocolate-glazed doughnuts?

"It's hard to find the time," he said.

"Oh, listen to you." His sister raised her voice; he didn't want to hug her anymore. "It's like you couldn't be bothered."

"No, it's not that." He had work to finish. He wanted to date someone from the Match-up website. He wanted to plan a vacation cruise for next summer.

"What is it then?"

"It kind of snuck up on me." He looked at each of them in turn. "When should it have happened? About two weeks ago?"

Rachel nodded her head. "That sounds about right."

"Earlier than that," Kevin said. "A *lot* earlier. Trust me: I'm right next to you every day. I notice stuff."

"Oh, you poor thing," Jill said. Something about the concern in her voice struck him, made him feel unbearably sad. He raised a finger to his eye to wipe away a tear. His hand smelled like burnt provolone cheese.

"I hadn't realized how much I was hurting all of you," he said finally, giving in. "All the people I care about." He felt strangely charitable, as if he loved everyone in the room—even his physical trainer.

Jill's eyes lit up. "So you'll do it?"

"Yes. Yes, I'll try."

His stepfather scolded him. "You need to do more than try, son."

"Okay. I'll do it."

Soon. He really meant it.

This had been a difficult intervention for him, and he realized it was tough on them as well. Especially Jill. She'd planned the whole event, must have agonized over how things would play out. She'd done it all out of love.

As the gathering dispersed, she was the last to

leave. Before she stepped outside, she turned and looked directly into his eyes.

"Thank you," Tony said, and she responded with a weak smile.

He closed the door behind her, exhausted. This would be the perfect time to let things take their natural course.

He wandered into the front room. His dog whimpered from the kitchen, and Tony sank into the couch. He lifted the remote and aimed it at the television, surfing the channels one last time. Maybe there'd be news about the trapped miners.

He stopped on channel 13. No harm in watching for a few minutes. The first episode of the latest *Survivor* had already started.

He wondered who'd make it to the end of the season.

The Last Demon

DON D'AMMASSA

On his 666th birthday, Ogerak the Off-putting escaped from hell into the world of humans. It wasn't really his birthday since demons aren't actually born, but transmogrificationday is a far less satisfying term. When he noticed that the Portal had been momentarily left unguarded while an influx of newly lost souls was arriving to begin their eternal penance, he acted on impulse, hunching his shoulders so as not to be noticed among the throng as he made his way back against the tide of damned humanity and so crossed over, determined to find his destiny, or at least enjoy a break from his tedious existence.

It is not easy being the very last of the one hundred thousand demons to be created. For one thing all of the really nifty names were gone, along with most of the formidable body enhancements. Ogerak didn't even have claws, his tail was vestigial, and his horns were invisible under his unruly hair. He was tall and broad-shouldered and spectacularly ugly, but even without a magical enchantment, he could quite easily pass for human.

Ogerak hesitated when he stepped out of the Portal, wondering if this had perhaps been a mistake. He had never been to the human world before and the stories he had heard over the centuries from more senior demons—and all of them were more senior—were contradictory and no doubt distorted by memory, or more likely caprice. Demons lived only to inflict torment and confusion, even upon one another. But if Ogerak was having second thoughts, it was too late to act upon them. The Portal closed behind him and he hadn't the slightest idea how to open a new one.

It was very dark, but Ogerak was used to the absence of light. He was standing in an empty lot flanked by tall buildings in every direction. He could hear faint traffic noises in the distance, which he mistakenly interpreted as the muted roars of predators. Since his immediate surroundings appeared to be deserted, he set off toward a cluster of lights he could barely discern in the distance.

Moments later he encountered his first humans, or to be more precise, his first living humans. He was traversing a narrow, cluttered passage between two buildings when three figures separated themselves from the shadows and barred his way just as he stepped into a pool of light cast from a fixture above one of the doors. Ogerak stopped and blinked, wondering what this portended. "I am Ogerak," he announced. "Tremble in the presence of my puissant evilness." All of the really good personal catch phrases had also been taken by the other demons.

There was a muted sound that might have been suppressed laughter but that Ogerak chose to interpret as panicky obeisance. One of the figures stepped into the light. "Hey, dude, this is Troll territory and you have to pay to use our alley. It's sort of a Troll road, get it?"

Ogerak blinked and examined the figure more closely. "I have worked with trolls, I know trolls, some of my friends are trolls. Imposter, you are no troll."

He took a menacing step forward into the light and the one who had spoken took a balancing step backward. "Hey, you're a big fellow, aren't you? I like the tattoos on your cheeks. They're classy. And the leather outfit isn't bad either."

Ogerak blinked in confusion. "Tattoos? Are you referring to the Cicatrices of Coryphon, inscribed on my face to honor my service to the Nether Realms?"

"Nether Realms? Who are they? I know every gang in the city and I never heard of them. Hey, you must be from out of town."

Ogerak nodded. "I am a visitor here as you surmise. Could you perhaps direct me to the master of the city so that I might pay my respects?"

"Well, just at the moment, you might say that I was master of the city, at least as far as you're concerned. And you'll pay all right, but not just your respects."

Ogerak frowned and his face became even more off-putting. "I detect insolence in your tone. Do you venture to challenge me?"

The human moved his arm and there was the flash of light on metal. "If you're looking for a fair fight, dude, then you've come to the wrong place. Now, let's see some money or I'm gonna have to cut you."

Ogerak had never been in this situation before. As the most junior demon, it was he who issued challenges, all of which had to date failed. But he knew the proper response. The human's soul was hopelessly lost so he lunged forward with surprising quickness for one with such a large body, his jaws already dislocating to accommodate their distension, and he bit off the human's head before the latter had time to react. The body remained erect for a second, then fell quietly to the ground. Ogerak swallowed the head—it was rather too salty for his taste and he wasn't really hungry—and looked around for the other two humans, who were running at full speed toward the far end of the alley rather than proffering their obeisance. He considered this a shocking lapse of manners.

For the next few minutes, he waited for the body to produce a new head so that he could interrogate the former master of the city about the attributes of his domain, but nothing happened. This puzzled and upset Ogerak. The losers in a challenge always regenerated promptly back in hell, at which point they graciously acknowledged their defeat. Perhaps the process took longer in the human world. Impatient, he decided to dispense with a formal capitulation and set off once more, this time confident with the knowledge that he, Ogerak, was now master of the city.

Moments later three demons materialized at the exact spot where Ogerak had earlier stepped out of the Portal. For a split second, a theoretical observer might have noticed claws and fangs and prehensile tails, but then the masking charm took effect and the threesome appeared only as vaguely disreputable humans with no fashion sense.

The threesome had been sent to reclaim Ogerak. Murmural the Maleficent was the team leader, with Nuramor the Noxious and Inkarion the Irritating as backup. Murmural had been to the human world before, though not since the fourteenth century, while his companions were on their first visit. Murmural expected that it would be a very brief excursion. A demon as inexperienced as Ogerak must have drawn attention to himself almost immediately upon arriving. Onorus the Overbearing—currently in charge of the Office for Suppression of Forbidden Awareness—would be very unhappy if Ogerak had revealed his true nature to any humans. The demonic truant would be in very big trouble if that was the case.

"Follow," Murmural commanded, and set off, trying unsuccessfully to detect Ogerak's scent.

Ogerak had proceeded only a few more blocks before the hair on his back bristled under his leather vest. Trusting his demonic instincts, he paused and carefully examined his surroundings. On the opposite side of the street, a dim light showed inside an otherwise darkened building. In the window facing him he perceived a fearsome array of beasts.

Undaunted—he was after all master of the city—Ogerak crossed to confront the danger directly. "I am Ogerak. Tremble in the presence of my puissant evilness." Most of the creatures remained quiescent but one rose onto its hindquarters and pressed its nose against the glass, wagging a not-at-all-vestigial tail furiously back and forth. Ogerak was momentarily nonplussed, not having expected such a direct challenge, but he was prepared to defend his prerogatives against all comers.

Something growled softly behind him and Ogerak spun—or turned at least—to see a much larger creature approaching. Indeed the newcomer was considerably bigger than Ogerak himself. It had two large glowing eyes and a crest that cycled between red and blue in a hypnotic rhythm as it advanced. Ogerak was perplexed by its manner of locomotion since there are no wheels in hell. Wheels might make some tasks easier for the damned, after all.

The creature addressed him in a booming voice. "YOU THERE! STEP AWAY FROM THE BUILDING AND LET ME SEE YOUR HANDS!"

The tone was so peremptory that Ogerak obeyed without thinking. The voice very much resembled that of Astoriak the Appalling, his immediate supervisor back in hell. If he had responded to the instructions in the correct order, all might have been well, but he extended his arms before stepping clear and one of them crashed through the window. The diminutive monsters began emitting a variety of upsetting noises and two of them jumped down onto the sidewalk. One had the temerity to sniff his ankle.

"ALL RIGHT, STOP WHERE YOU ARE! RAISE YOUR HANDS AND PLACE THEM ON THE WALL!" The larger creature began to wail and it moved suddenly forward. Ogerak found himself beset by danger from front and rear and he panicked, although he later characterized his action as swift and prudent withdrawal.

Although he was a bit overweight and definitely out of condition, he managed a quite acceptable sprint to the nearest corner and turned to his right, eyes darting about in search of sanctuary. The wailing increased in pitch and volume and Ogerak slipped into the first alleyway he encountered, confident that his pursuer was too large to follow. Three blocks later he crouched concealed in a Dumpster as the wailing creature, which was silent now, moved slowly past.

Ogerak was extremely uncomfortable. The temperature had dropped into the upper eighties and he shivered with the cold. It began to rain and he hated getting wet. And as the minutes slid past, he began to feel hungry. When the rain finally died away shortly before dawn, he slipped out of his hiding place and set off in search of food. He tried some of the debris from the Dumpster and was surprised to find it completely inedible. Although he usually fed on the damned—the supply was inexhaustible since they always regenerated—Ogerak often dined otherwise for the sake of variety. In hell, even rocks were magically transformed when ingested by a demon, but here, he realized, they remained just rocks. So he set off to find real food. Something fresh.

The buildings remained dark but once he reached a better-lit street, he saw a single human standing next to some enigmatic contrivance at an intersection. He approached cautiously, having decided to keep a low profile until he understood the rules of this world.

The human spun around as he drew near. "Hey there, big fellow. Shouldn't sneak up on a guy like that."

"I am Ogerak. Tremble in the presence of my puissant evilness." He paused for effect. "And tell me where I might find sustenance."

The human seemed to relax. "What are you? A street artist or just a homeless crazy?"

Ogerak had no idea what those terms referred to so he ignored the question. "I hunger. Can you help me in my quest?"

The human turned back to the artifact he'd been tending. "I'm not set up yet but I can manage a cold bagel and some cream cheese. It'll cost you though. Got any money?"

"What is this money of which you speak?"

"Cash. Moolah. Dinero. Bucks. Greenbacks. Coin of the realm. And I don't take plastic."

Ogerak shook his head. Demons were supposed to be able to understand and speak any conceivable human language but once again he had no idea what the human was talking about. "I have no knowledge of these things about which you speak."

"Foreigner, eh? Probably illegal. You got papers? A green card?"

Ogerak spread his hands eloquently. "I have nothing but what you see."

The human shook his head and turned away, then drew something out of a bag and extended it toward Ogerak. "Here, take this. The raisin ones never sell anyway. But you'd better find yourself a job, under the table obviously, if you want to stay around here."

He sniffed the proffered item. "What manner of flesh is this?"

"It's not meat, loony. It's a bagel. Baked in ovens."

Ogerak smiled, which actually made him look more fearsome. "My first duty was tending the ovens. But I desire more hearty fare. I am, after all, master of the city."

The human sighed. "Yeah, you and the mayor are

good buddies, I imagine. Look, this city chews up innocents like you and spits them out. You'd better wise up or hit the road."

Ogerak pondered what profit might be derived from striking the pavement as he sniffed the bagel. He had been considering devouring the human, but the latter's sudden act of charity meant that he was not irretrievably damned after all and was therefore beyond Ogerak's power.

Those last few words had also given him pause. Obviously there was not the clear hierarchy in the human world that existed in hell. Was this mayor superior to the master of the city or just a coequal? And was the city itself an entity that could swallow him and expel him at any moment? He did not relish being chewed up. Regeneration always gave him a headache.

He swallowed the bagel, which was refreshingly stale, but it failed to appease the grumbling in his belly. With a last regretful look, he turned and stalked off, while the human muttered under his breath and turned back to his wares.

Ogerak wandered the city throughout the morning, gathering a few odd looks but far fewer than he might have expected. He saw little that was familiar, but he did manage to make friends with a colony of rats—there are rats in hell—and he eavesdropped on humans in order to learn what this money thing was and where he might find some. At first he stopped people at random and asked, but they either ran from him with a scream, which was a moderately comforting reminder of home, or shouted imprecations. One or two even threatened to assault him and it was only his growing sense of discretion that prevented Ogerak from dispatching them on the spot. All but one had been fair game.

Money, he learned, consisted of small pieces of green parchment that could be exchanged for goods. There were mystical symbols inscribed on them—a key, a pyramid, an all-seeing eye—but he was unable to determine the nature of the magical spells they denoted. Ogerak was also at a loss to discover from whence came this scrip until he happened to notice a man emerging from a building with a handful of the parchment and inquired as politely as he could manage about where he had acquired it.

"The lobby's right through that doorway, asshole." Ogerak's most polite demeanor wasn't very. "Use your eyes. They're big enough."

Inside the building, Ogerak quickly ascertained the procedure. Humans stood in line until they reached one of several hooded windows, at which point another human dispensed the parchment from hiding. He considered bypassing the line since he was master of the city but decided to observe the process in more detail first.

And then he was at the head of the line. "Can I help you, sir?"

"I would like some money, please."

"Do you have an account with us, sir?" The voice was bored. Ogerak recognized boredom; he had experienced it for 665 of his 666 years.

"I am newly arrived in this city and do not understand all of its customs, but I have need of money."

"Do you have a traveler's check then? Or something else to be cashed? A money order, perhaps?"

Ogerak was hungry and frustrated. "I have told you. I need money. I am Ogerak. Tremble in the presence of my puissant evilness and give me what I wish or take the consequences!"

The attendant recoiled and a moment later Ogerak heard something very much like the wailing sound of the monster that had chased him the night before. Desperate, he caught hold of the enclosure with both hands and tore it free, which generated a chorus of screams and much running about. He saw a tray filled with rows of the magical green parchment and snatched up two handfuls, then turned and made his way hastily outside. The wailing meant that either there was a similar monster dwelling within the building or one was being summoned. He heard a popping sound behind him and a series of light jabs tickled him between the shoulder blades as he turned and began to run. Well, lumber. Running really wasn't one of his accomplishments.

The pursuit was more persistent this time and more than an hour passed before the wailing sounds subsided and Ogerak, who had broken into an abandoned warehouse, sat on the floor and tried various conjurations without finding one that would trigger whatever magical potential the green parchment contained. He finally gathered it up and tucked it neatly into a pocket in his harness.

Two blocks away, three figures had turned their heads toward the clamor. "Let us investigate," said Murmural. "The irritating Ogerak may have drawn attention to himself."

Inkarion protested. "It is I who irritates. The faithless Ogerak is merely off-putting."

"Whatever," Murmural answered, rolling his eyes.

Purchasing food from street vendors proved to be relatively easy and the yawning chaos in Ogerak's gut was finally assuaged, at least for the time being, although a human would have been much more satisfying. He had managed to find a few who counted beast flesh among their wares, although for some reason they insisted upon burning it before they would allow consumption. As darkness began to fall, Ogerak decided to emulate the humans and rest indoors. He had even learned that some of the buildings in the city catered to travelers and that these were called hotels. He found one such that was suitably dirty and unkempt and asked the attendant to explain the procedure for acquiring temporary dwelling privileges.

"You pay the nightly fee, in advance. No drugs, no women, no loud noises." The attendant considered Ogerak's oversized frame. "Break anything and you pay for it."

Ogerak laid out all of his money on the counter. "Is this sufficient?"

The clerk's eyes opened widely and he nodded. "For one night, sure. But you'll need more if you're planning to stay any longer." The money had already disappeared, confirming Ogerak's suspicion that it was magic.

"The depository is not likely to give me any more," Ogerak observed glumly.

"Depository? Oh, you mean the bank. Broke, huh? Don't you have a job, friend?"

Ogerak shrugged. "I have only what you see."

"Homeless too." The attendant shook his head. "Well, you'll have to get a job if you want more money, and you'll need more money if you want to stay here another night."

So that was it, thought Ogerak. The reason the attendant had been unwilling to give him money when he asked was because he had no job. He had not noticed that the humans were carrying such a thing, but perhaps they only produced it when they reached the window. "Where would I get one of these jobs?" he asked earnestly.

"They're pretty hard to come by. I feel for you, friend." This was patently false. "I was on the street for a while myself. If the guy who worked this desk before me hadn't up and died, I'd probably be there still."

Ogerak's brow wrinkled. "So you perform your duties here and your masters reward you with this job thing?"

"Well, sort of. Yeah."

"And once you have a job, the depository will dispense money at your request?"

"Within reason, yeah, depending on how much you get paid."

"And you succeeded to this post because of the death of your predecessor?"

"That's right."

"I understand." Ogerak smiled because he had already detected the distinctive odor of damnation, then unhinged his jaw and lunged forward.

It took the three demons several weeks to track Ogerak down and they ultimately found him by accident. They had entered the run-down hotel seeking lodging for the night and none of them had recognized the oversized desk clerk at first. He was wearing a shabby overcoat and his eyes were downcast and full of misery. Luckily Nuramor was hungry enough that he was examining humans closely, hoping to find one of the irretrievably damned.

"Ogerak! Is that you?"

It was a moderately joyful reunion with much slapping of backs, punching of ribs, gnashing of teeth, and pulling of hair. Eventually Murmural called them to order and informed Ogerak that he was to be taken back to hell, by force if necessary.

"On the contrary, I cannot wait to return. This world is a madhouse whose illogical rules have created an existence so unbearable that I now fully understand why humans sacrifice their immortal souls in order to escape. Here one must have a job, which is not simply assigned by a higher authority but which must be discovered by the individual, and only then if that individual possesses certain documents attesting to his personal history. But this history must be established by those same documents, a circular logic which makes them unobtainable save through subterfuge." Ogerak reached into the pocket of his overcoat and withdrew a battered wallet, opened it to display a social security card and driver's license. "I was forced to assume the identity of my former employer after I had eaten him."

Even Murmural found this hard to credit. The bureaucracy in the fourteenth century had not been nearly so advanced.

"Nor can one survive with a single job. I myself spend my evenings ejecting boisterous individuals from warrens where rhythmic sounds are played at such a high volume that they inflict permanent damage on the hearing of those humans present. And don't get me started about their politics." He would have regaled them further with details of the horrific world in which he'd trapped himself, but Murmural intervened.

"It is time for you to return and face the consequences of your indiscretion."

Ogerak beamed at him. "I welcome the ritual dismemberment. Let us be off."

Murmural glanced around. "Not here. I can only perform the ritual a single time and there must be ample space for the vortex to generate a Portal."

"There's a park at the end of the block. Would that be big enough?" Now that Ogerak had the chance to escape the human world, he was impatient to be gone.

"We shall see."

Presently, the four demons stood at the edge of the small fenced area. Two men with rakes stood on the far side but there was almost no other pedestrian traffic. "This should be adequate," said Murmural. "It will only take a few moments to invoke the Portal. Let us proceed."

Murmural had barely uttered the first few syllables when they were interrupted. The two humans they'd noticed earlier were approaching, brandishing their rakes. "Hey! Can't you jokers read? Keep off the grass. We just finished seeding here."

Nuramor was so furious that his disguise began to slip but Murmural stepped in front of him until he had restored control. "Our apologies, gentlemen. We did not mean to transgress."

"Yeah, well, move along then. And try not to make too much of a mess on your way out."

They left while the two men efficiently raked over their tracks.

"This way," urged Ogerak. "There is a larger park only a few blocks away."

There were humans there as well, but it was indeed much larger and the demons were able to find an open space among a cluster of trees where they believed they would not be observed. Murmural began the invocation again and this time the opening stages went smoothly. Ogerak was exhilarated by the sight of a Portal beginning to form in the center of the clearing, spinning lights and gouts of flame slowly taking on substance.

The Portal was half-formed when they were interrupted.

"Hey, buddy! You got a permit?"

Ogerak turned to see a uniformed man approaching rapidly. He moved to intercept. "Is there a problem, officer?"

"Not if you got a permit there isn't. But if you don't, there's a very big problem." He glanced up at the coalescing Portal. "Pretty impressive, I'll give you that. But you need a permit to do any kind of performance art here. Particularly with pyrotechnics."

Ogerak sniffed but the policeman, though nearly a lost cause, was not beyond redemption and was therefore untouchable. He thought quickly. "You don't understand. This isn't a performance. My friend here is very religious and this is a miraculous event. Surely we don't need permits for miracles?"

"Well then, it seems we do have a problem after all. Use of public land for religious ceremonies is a violation of city ordinances. I'm afraid your friend will have to cease and desist at once or I'll be forced to arrest him."

Ogerak began to protest, but the policeman stepped past before he could react and placed a hand on Murmural's shoulder. The senior demon started and shook his head, and the Portal began to oscillate. "Unhand me, human offal!" he shouted, forgetting himself, but it was too late. The outer rim of the half-formed Portal began to break up and the center began to deliquesce.

They were dismissed with a stern warning that they hardly heard. On their way out of the park, Ogerak asked if Murmural could try again, perhaps at night.

"I lack the power to repeat the ritual. We'll have to wait for the next scheduled Portal." He grimaced. "Which won't be for twenty years. But it is merely a drop in the bucket compared to eternal damnation, after all."

Ogerak helped them settle in. Inkarion and Nuramor became tag-team wrestlers for the WWL. Murmural hosted a radio talk show. Ogerak himself went back to managing the sleazy hotel. The years passed as a steady stream of minor torments and when the time finally approached that they would be able to return to hell, Ogerak felt that he had survived the worst that the human world could possibly throw at him.

He was wrong, of course. Two weeks before the Portal was due, he was randomly chosen for audit by the IRS.

A Misadventure to Call Your Own

Adrian Ludens

"You'll pay dearly for what happened every day for the rest of your miserable life!"

It's not a proclamation one wants to hear first thing in the morning. You open your eyes to the dim interior of your bedroom and search for the voice's source. Perhaps you'd only heard the interior dialogue of a vivid dream.

The strident voice continued. "You'll pay financially, emotionally and physically. I'll bleed you dry, until you're left with nothing but worry and suffering."

Apparently something's amiss, but whatever you may have done, this seems like overkill. You sit up amidst a tangled sheet and gaze blearily at the speaker. As your eyes adjust to the light, you see a short slender figure, their arms crossed in judgment. The speaker's hair is tousled to the point of disarray. The speaker is naked and has addressed you from the foot of the bed.

Your bed. The bed you share with your One True Love. You squint again.

Who is this?

If you realize you are simply role-playing with your One True Love, turn to page 3.

If you recognize the speaker as an elderly neighbor who is obviously having one of their "bad spells," turn to page 4.

If you're too hungover to remember what happened last night, take two aspirin and turn to page 5.

Feeling hungover and still quite confused as to what events transpired over the past few hours, you raise your hands in a pleading gesture. You need time to think. *Who is this person? How did they get here?*

The figure pads around the bed and leans down so the two of you are eye to eye. The sour scent of mixed drinks wafts around your head and a wave of nausea threatens to drown your calm. *Uh-oh.* Now you recognize the face, and it's from a distant past you'd rather not revisit.

"You won't be able to explain this when your significant other returns from that business trip," your guest—who has certainly overstayed their welcome—hisses in your ear. "There's no way out!"

You open your mouth to respond, but your tongue is a shriveled and lifeless mummy curled in the corner of your mouth. You didn't have a witty retort ready anyway.

"Apparently you thought I wasn't good enough for you so you moved on." Your accuser is trembling with rage, or possibly excitement. "But I tracked you down at the bar last night, got you to take me home. After what we did—after what *you* did—you belong to *me* now! I pull the strings now, puppet. Bow down to your new master."

A sliver of drool dives gracefully from your guest's bottom lip and disappears into the folds of your rumpled sheet. You decide they're trembling from excitement.

"What are you going to do now?" your new master inquires.

If you decide to call your One True Love immediately to confess everything, turn to page 8.

If you just remembered you've been concealing an ice pick under the pillow all along, turn to page 10.

If you realize all this talk has made you hungry, turn to page 12.

"I need to get some food in my stomach," you announce as you push aside the sheet and stand beside your guest. "Let's go up to the kitchen and discuss this like rational adults."

Feeling a pair of angry eyes practically burning holes in your bare back, you shuffle up the stairs, feigning a calm that isn't quite there. In the kitchen, you grab lunch meat, processed cheese slices and mayo from the refrigerator.

You can hear soft footsteps behind you. A board creaks but you don't look. *I need to come up with a plan.* You decide a steak knife might level the playing field, so you pull open the silverware drawer. Your hand freezes in midair. All the knives are gone.

Your guest snickers behind you. "Do you think I'm that stupid? I hid the knives before coming downstairs to confront you. What do you think about that?"

If you want to grab a fork and try to do the job anyway, scream "Fork you!" and turn to page 14.

If you want to grab a cool beverage and see what's on television, turn to channel 16.

If you want to grab your accuser and give them a kiss to trick them into dropping their guard, turn to page 17.

You smile broadly and confidently cross the kitchen. You reach out with both hands but this move is one your guest clearly does not welcome.

"Back off!" your former-lover-turned-one-night-stand-turned-blackmailer warns, and you notice they don't look too confident all of a sudden. Instead of stopping you lunge in for a claustrophobic "I could never stay mad at you" hug.

"Let me go!" your guest complains, and presses both palms against your shoulders in an effort to leverage their body free.

You unclasp your hands suddenly and your blackmailer staggers backward. Their arms flail and suddenly your guest tumbles ass over teakettle down your stairs.

Gazing down at the body sprawled at the bottom of the stairwell you realize immediately that your unwelcome guest is dead. You've seen enough broken necks in movies to draw your own conclusion: this looks fake so it must be real.

You slump against the cool counter behind you and consider your next move.

If you want to dispose of the body right away, turn to page 20.

If you want to grab that cool beverage and finally see what's on television, turn to channel 16 already.

If you just noticed that there's a new message on your answering machine and you haven't listened to it yet, turn to page 21.

Gazing across the room you notice the red light on your answering machine staring at you like an accusing eye. *Who called?* You never heard it, so perhaps the phone rang last night when you were otherwise indisposed. Knowing you'll never be able to focus on the problem at hand until you've heard the message, you approach the phone. You reach out a shaky finger and pause. Instead of a miniature devil and angel verbally sparring on your shoulders, fear of discovery battles anal-retentive compulsion.

Is checking your messages really a priority right now? Would any rational, sane person be distracted by this? The answer is no. But still, you are curious about who called . . .

If you think the message is from a bill collector, press delete and turn to page 22.

If you think the message is from a bill collector, but you plan to cite that segment you saw on the news about fraudulent bill collectors as an excuse not to pay, slyly turn to page 23.

If you think the message might actually be worth hearing, because it may turn out to have some plot-

convenient bearing on your present situation, press
play and turn to page 24.

You press the playback button and hear your
mother's voice:

"Hello, dear. I'm afraid I have some sad news. Your
uncle Marlin passed away two days ago."

This isn't sad news. Hearing of the demise of
"Uncle Bad Touch" brings a sneer to your lips.

"I should have called you sooner but I've been so
busy up here at his farmhouse putting things in order.
Services will be held at Trailside Church the day after
tomorrow at eleven. I know it's a two-hour drive up,
but I'd really appreciate it if you'd attend."

You wonder if he died of natural causes or if one
of your cousins paid an unannounced visit to his
ramshackle farm for some payback. You chew on
your bottom lip and mull the situation over.

Uncle Marlin lived on a farm seven miles north of
the tiny community of Trailside. The church where the
funeral will take place is on the outer edge of a town of
less than one thousand people. You decide this scenario
has some definite possibilities.

If you decide to call the funeral parlor to ask about
two-for-one pricing, turn to page 26.

If you decide your uncle's farm would be the perfect
place to dispose of the body, turn to page 27.

If you decide your uncle's funeral would provide the perfect opportunity to dispose of the body instead, turn to page 28.

You decide to attend the funeral and to bring a guest. The situation could provide a unique opportunity for the disposal of the body in your basement.

After two glasses of blood lite—your sobriquet for red wine—to fortify your faltering nerve, you descend the stairs.

The first order of business is to grab several hand towels from the bathroom cupboard to wipe up; there's no blood, but the loosened bowels and voided bladder make for a more voluminous mess than a few squares of toilet tissue can clean.

This accomplished, the soiled towels go straight into the washing machine and you wash your hands for several minutes longer than is necessary.

Next you decide to wrap the body in a spare bedsheet. You choose one covered with tiny pills that make it uncomfortable to sleep on. You made this purchase long before you learned about thread count or fabric quality and decide it also deserves to be buried in the ground.

You also backtrack to your bedroom to gather your guest's clothing and belongings. Rather than try to dress the body you tuck the articles of clothing around limbs so they'll stay in place. You straighten and survey your work.

If you decide you're too attached to that old sheet to part with it after all, turn to page 31.

If you remember reading somewhere that lime helps speed decomposition, turn to page 32.

If you can't shake the urge to wash your hands again, turn to page 33.

You remember reading somewhere that lime helps speed decomposition, so you trudge back upstairs to check your fridge for the little green fruit. You come up empty, which should be no surprise since you can't even remember the last time you used lime in a drink. Besides, slicing up a lime doesn't quite seem right. Isn't the lime supposed to be in powder form?

Feeling perplexed, you scan the kitchen, seeking inspiration. Your eyes fall on the spice rack. *Lemon pepper; not perfect but it will do in a pinch.*

You take the stairs two at a time back down and sprinkle liberal amounts of your find on the body. Inspiration strikes again and you retrieve spring-scented carpet powder ("Eliminates pet and other offensive odors!") and shower your guest with that as well.

Satisfied at last, you wrap the body up in the sheet and tie off both ends with their shoelaces.

Exhausted by your exertions, you tumble into bed for some much-needed rest.

If your sleep is plagued by nightmares of masked Mexican wrestlers pulling your teeth out with pliers (and whose isn't, really?), turn to page 35.

If sleep never comes because the moment you lie down the phone won't stop ringing, get back up and turn to page 36.

If you sleep well but awaken suddenly to the ominous tolling of a grandfather clock announcing the witching hour, turn to page 37.

Your heirloom grandfather clock pulls you from the irresponsibility of sleep and chimes twelve times. This, you decide, is the perfect time to move your visitor from the stairwell to the trunk of your car.

You dress quickly and haul your cargo by the ankles slowly up the stairs. You reach the kitchen and let their legs drop. Panting, you shuffle out your front door for a little advance recon. The street is empty. The houses are dark. Even the moon cooperates by discreetly ducking behind a rolling cloud bank.

Staggering under the weight of your burden, you reach the open trunk and deposit the body inside.

Another glass of wine and it's off to bed to lie awake and anxiously wait for morning. You think of your One True Love away on business and the unsavory business you must attend to before their return. You remember your brief fling—many years ago—with the deceased.

You think about your favorite movie, the best concert you ever attended and the last good book you've read. All the while the sun slowly crawls around the earth. You force yourself to wait until just after eight A.M. to dress and leave the house.

The drive north out of the city is a dull one but you are proficient at creating your own happiness and soon you are daydreaming about what you would do with the power of invisibility.

You are so absorbed in your imaginary escapades that you don't see the police cruiser easing up behind your car until the officer turns on his flashers and gives your eardrums a short burst of siren. The siren's song, true to legend, is one that conjures up fear but is very difficult to ignore.

If you were speeding, slow down, use your turn signal and carefully ease onto the shoulder located on page 38.

If you were not speeding but realize your tags are expired and you have no proof of insurance, turn to page 39.

If you really thought you'd get through a "dead body in the trunk" story without getting pulled over by an ornery rural cop, turn to page 40.

A big-bellied sheriff's deputy with a Smokey the Bear hat tipped back on his bullet head ambles toward your car. Even with his eyes hidden behind out-of-date mirrored sunglasses, you can see the smug satisfaction on his face.

His unsnaps the holster strap on his sidearm and gently rests his palm on the butt of his gun. With his other palm he scratches his butt. You try not to smile.

"Well, well," the cop says. "Someone from the city is driving through my stretch of country in an awful hurry."

You do your best to appear both sheepish and contrite and wait for him to continue.

"You were speeding, your tags are expired and for all I know, you've got a dead body in the trunk."

At first all the blood drains from your face, then it seems like it is catapulting back up and you feel your cheeks burning with guilt.

You realize the officer is waiting for you to respond.

If you've stopped near the bridge that stretches over Owl Creek and feel inspired to try to make a harrowing and adventurous dash for freedom, turn to page 42.

If you try to intimidate the officer by cranking up some vintage gangsta rap on your stereo, turn the volume up to 43.

If you nod sheepishly and admit, "Two out of three, officer; you got me," hold your breath and turn to page 45.

You finally decide to nod sheepishly and admit, "Two out of three, officer; you got me."

Despite an inexplicable sense of déjà vu, you feel cautiously optimistic. Even if the officer writes you a ticket for either—or both—infractions, chances are against him actually asking to look in the trunk.

Without warning a shrill howl raises the hair on your neck and goose bumps do the wave up and down your arms.

The deputy has tilted his head back and lets loose with a second barbaric yawp. Then he grins ferociously. "Lone Wolf sniffs out another perpetrator," he exclaims, and juts his chin out proudly.

You glance at the nameplate just below his badge and notice his name is "Moranus" but you decide it prudent to let him have his moment.

Two citations later you drive away, careful to stay five miles under the posted limit. Your forehead is drenched with sweat and your mouth is dry as alkali, but the secret in your trunk remains undiscovered. "Two out of three ain't bad," you mumble.

You are still thanking your lucky stars ten miles down the road when your vision blurs and a sharp pain hits you.

If the pain is in your right temple, turn to page 48.

If the pain is in your left arm, turn to page 49.

If the pain is in the right lower quadrant of your belly, just above your hip bone, try to locate the appendix.

You hit the brakes and kick up a spray of gravel and dust as you guide your car onto the shoulder of the road.

Once the car's forward momentum has stopped, you grimace and stretch your arms. Alternately massaging each forearm, you concentrate on relaxing. A deep inhalation, count to ten and let it out. You do this several times, flexing your fingers and running them through your hair. Not a heart attack; just muscle cramps from gripping the steering wheel too tightly.

You tell yourself to relax. Based on the scenery, you think the Trailside Church should only be a few more miles ahead. Your uncle's farm is seven miles farther north of Trailside.

Time to make another decision.

If you decide to turn back and risk getting pulled over again as you head for home, turn to page 51.

If you decide to pass the church and continue on to your uncle's farm, turn to page 52.

If you decide to stop at the church to make sure that creep is really dead, turn to page 53.

The Trailside Church is an unassuming little building. It has seen a few weddings, more than its fair share of funerals and even a baptism or two. Finding the parking lot full, you double-park beside the waiting hearse and jog up the stone stairs.

You ease the door open and slide into the narthex. As your eyes adjust to the dim interior you realize you are not alone.

Nearby is the cheapest casket the family could apparently find and nestled inside is your late uncle Marlin. You feel your lips press in a tight line and clench your hands until your nails dig into your palms. You wish you could inflict some suffering or indignity upon him.

You step forward and look through the narrow window into the sanctuary, which your mother insisted upon calling the nave because she believed it made her sound more cultured. The figures in the rows make a sea of black, dotted with whitecaps of gray, white, blue and bald. A sleepy-looking preacher reads predictable passages from a tattered Bible at a wooden podium near the altar.

You return to the casket and look at your uncle again. Perhaps there is some extra room . . .

"Hey there," a voice you don't recognize demands. "Who are you?"

If you explain that you are a member of the clergy administering "De Facto Last Rites of Duplication," turn to page 54.

If you explain that you are the mortician's assistant and that you are "just topping off fluids," turn to page 55.

If you curtly retort, "I could ask you the same question!" turn to page 56.

Failing to come up with anything more creative, you curtly retort, "I could ask you the same question!"

The narthex now seems filled with the odor of raw rhubarb mixed with cat pee and you narrow your eyes at the young man who has spoken. You don't recognize him as a relation so you decide he probably lives here in Trailside and is here with his folks, probably against his will. It shouldn't be hard to get rid of him.

"Did you sneak out for a couple hits?" you ask, feigning disapproval. The teen averts his bloodshot eyes guiltily and you cross your arms sternly as he hurries past you into the sanctuary. He slides into an empty spot next to an oblivious parental unit in a pew near the back.

You notice everyone inside has bowed their heads in either prayer or weariness, so you "carpe diem" and hurry back to your car. A quick scan of the parking lot shows that the coast is clear for the moment; perhaps everyone in town is inside the church with their backs collectively turned away from you.

You pop the trunk, hoist the body over your shoulder and hustle up the stairs. Adrenaline surges through your limbs as you slip back inside and triumphantly dump your cargo into the casket on top of your uncle.

You tip the lid down but it won't close. Lifting the lid back up you quickly realize that you'll need to read-just the casket's contents.

The congregation of mourners and small-town gawkers has collectively risen in their pews to mumble a hymn. You yank the body back out and replace it so that it lays facedown with the head resting between your uncle's feet. Panting, you glance over your shoulder and find the coast is still clear. Everyone is still in the nave and you're still craving a little knavery.

If you take a moment to shave your uncle's out-of-control eyebrows, go to page 60.

If you take a moment to say a few choice parting words to the deceased (plural), go to page 61.

If you flip them both the bird, close the lid and make a run for it, turn to page 62.

Your uncle's old-geezer eyebrows seem to bristle like threatened caterpillars. Seeing this as the perfect opportunity for some admittedly petty but worth-while revenge, you fumble around in your pockets for your ring of keys. On the key ring is also a tiny utility knife. You select it, cupping your keys in your hand and opening the knife's blade.

"You two deserve each other," you mutter, and extend the middle finger of your free hand at the new roommates. Then you lean in and scrape the blade against your uncle's skin, shaving off one eyebrow in three strokes. Just as you are about to move on to the other side, a surge in the volume of singing warns you that the sanctuary door has been opened.

You drop the lid to the casket as quickly as you can and turn to look behind you.

A dour-faced man strides forward. He is carrying a battered leather case and is wearing a large enamel name tag that reads:

Jolley Brothers Funeral Services
Bryan Bruce, Director

"Excuse me, but what exactly are you doing out here with the deceased?" he wants to know. This time you're prepared. In fact, you have so many excuses ready you'll need to narrow it down first.

If you want to reveal that your uncle had privately expressed his wishes for a closed-casket ceremony and you are simply honoring the dear old saint's wishes, solemnly turn to page 64.

If you want to accuse the mortician of shoddy workmanship and explain that you closed the casket lid out of necessity, haughtily turn to page 65.

If you want to reveal that you just drove a wooden stake through his black and centuries-old heart, turn to page 67.

"I noticed that one of my uncle's eyelids has collapsed," you explain to the man in hushed tones. You lead him away from the casket before continuing. "I closed the lid so that none of my uncle's loved ones would notice and become upset."

Mr. Bruce shakes his head and mutters, "We can certainly fix—"

You have to stop that train of thought before it leaves the station so you plunge with the only dagger at your disposal. "I'd hate to think what would happen if the relatives got together and demanded a refund."

The funeral director's mouth snaps shut as if wired closed and filled with cotton. Time to give the dagger a delicate twist to make sure the subject really dies.

"Think of the small-town scandal!" you murmur. "I'm sure you and I agree it would be best to leave well enough alone."

Mr. Bruce nods like it's the best idea he's heard in decades. He instructs the pallbearers, who have just arrived from the sanctuary, to carry the casket out to the hearse. The six of them grunt and heft their special cargo to the waiting car. Mr. Bruce slides in behind the wheel and leads the procession of mourners across the gravel road and into the gates of the adjacent Trailside Cemetery.

A group of clucking hens—your aunts—files past. Your mother is among them and she smiles wanly at you as she passes. You amble along with the stragglers but once you reach the open grave you find yourself pushing to the front of the group.

The casket is hefted out of the hearse and placed on the faded straps of the lowering device. The dithering preacher says a few more words about ashes and dust bunnies, and you wonder how much of this he could have said while still inside the church. You glance around and see many closed eyes and vacant stares. *Why is this taking so long?*

At last the casket is lowered into the hole. A few of your cousins don't look upset in the least. Normally you'd be able to relate but right now your nerves are fraying at an alarming rate.

If you try to jump-start the burial by kicking a few dirt clods into the hole and muttering "good riddance," turn to page 70.

If you volunteer to rev up the Bobcat skid loader you noticed parked behind the caretaker's shed, turn to page 71.

If you shriek "I admit the deed! Here, here! It is the beating of their hideous hearts!" fall to your knees and turn to page 72.

Like a bored kid in a fabric store, your left leg twitches spastically and before you can stop its motion, you've kicked several dirt clods into the hole. They rattle and patter on the casket lid like fists pounding against it from inside. You scramble to the outer edge of the solemn gathering and mop nervous perspiration from your forehead. Your breathing comes in gasps. *Keep it together!* The preacher is praying again and someone throws a bouquet into the hole.

Then everyone begins filing away silently. One or two of your cousins try to make eye contact as they pass and your mother gives you a strange look but you resolve to feign sorrow if confronted. No one speaks to you, however, and you soon find yourself alone with the man whose job it is to fill the hole.

You are vaguely aware of the sounds of automobiles starting and driving away. At last when you scan the church parking lot, you see only your car now double-parked next to nothing. Even the priest has departed. You become aware of your companion staring at you.

"I'm not supposed to do this with any of the family watching," he explains. "My wife said she'd have coffee and sandwiches on by two, so . . ."

"Yes, yes, of course." You force a smile and totter past nearly two centuries of stone markers, pass through the cemetery gates and cross the empty road. The sound of the skid loader's engine roars to life just as you reach your car. You pause to steal a glance back.

What took hours to dig takes minutes to fill. The man waves amicably as he drives past in his rusty pickup when the job is done and you smile and return that wave. You feel as if a great burden has been lifted from you.

Relief quickly gives way to elation as you realize that you've gotten away with murder (probably second-degree, but still . . .), apparent accidental infidelity *and* the disposal of the body. Best of all, you got a measure of revenge on your creepy uncle and accomplished everything without arousing any suspicion.

You chuckle as you remember how your uncle looked with only one eyebrow. You wish you had had more time to finish that job, but overall you feel thrilled by today's events. You burst out laughing.

You're still chuckling as you slide into the driver's seat. You're snickering even as you repeatedly check your pockets for your car keys. You're still grinning stupidly at your reflection in the rearview mirror as you recall why you were most recently holding them.

But as you realize where you likely dropped the tiny utility knife and the ring of keys it was attached to . . . that's when you stop smiling altogether.

Smoke and Mirrorballs

Chris Abbey

(MUSIC SWELL: MAIN THEME. PLAYOUT, DROP)

HOST: Well, here we are! Tonight, live, it's the grand finale of *Prancing Like a Minor Star*! Lots of surprises along the way, but it all comes down to this. Three couples, one trophy. Now, would everybody please welcome my cohost . . . err, somebody, whatever.

CASSANDRA: My name is Cassandra Troy, and I predict we're going to have a great time tonight.

HOST: Our couples are backstage waiting, probably almost tense enough to kill. But first, a special number from the eliminated contestants. Sadly, the human ones can't be here. Barbara's family asks that in lieu of flowers, send a head of cattle, because they need the brains. Hit it, Jimmy!

(MUSIC: MIDTEMPO "That's Life")

[Dancers pour out onto the stage, professionals kicking high, contestants looking like someone put Tasers in their breakfast cereal. The house band plays for two and a half minutes, then everyone stops and strikes a pose.]

HOST: (SMILING TO KEEP FROM WINCING) And there they are. Give them a big round of applause. (WAITS) When we return, our finalists, and a few memories from this surprising season.

(FADE TO BLACK)

(FADE UP)
(BACKGROUND MUSIC SWELLS, FADES)

HOST: And now, we have the finalists.

[Three large screens come up in the background. On them, taller than Kong, are a London gentleman with an old poofy-haired woman, a mummy with a woman in gold lamé, and a tuxedo and evening dress looking like they're on people.]

HOST: Van Helsing and our veteran dancer Phyllis, Amon-Ra with his partner Sheparda the former *Solid Gold* dancer, and Vlad with his partner Lucy. (APPLAUSE) Minutes ago, that girl talked to them backstage.

(SWITCH TO: VLAD AND LUCY IN A SMALL PURPLE-DRAPED WAITING AREA)

CASSANDRA: I'm told you and Van Helsing are rivals outside of the contest as well. How does it feel now that you're both in the finals?

VLAD: I can smell your blood.

CASSANDRA: What?

VLAD: It is sweet. What is that scent?

CASSANDRA: Eau de Humanity.

(SWITCH TO: SAME ROOM WITH AMON-RA AND SHEPARDA)

CASSANDRA: You two weren't expected to make the finals. How are you doing?

SHEPARDA: I think we have it wrapped up.

CASSANDRA: And how is it for you to be perform-ing live?

AMON-RA: Gggrrrrr.

CASSANDRA: Sorry, I forgot.

(SWITCH TO: SAME ROOM WITH VAN HELSING AND PHYLLIS)

CASSANDRA: I didn't get an answer from Vlad, but maybe you have something to say in the matter. You've been rivals a long time. How does it feel to be facing each other in the finals?

VAN HELSING: I shall leave him dust.

CASSANDRA: Don't you mean you'll leave him *in* the dust?

VAN HELSING: Quite.

(CUT TO: MAIN STAGE)

HOST: Welcome back. Though almost all the human contestants have died in what can best be described as mysterious circumstances (WINKS), we still have those whose remains remain. First up, Frankenstein's creation doing the only dance he knows.

(WRITER INSERTS OBVIOUS JOKE HERE)

HOST: I'm betting even the sweet release of death wouldn't help him . . . and it didn't! That's what you get when your creator gives you two left feet.

(AUDIENCE IGNORES APPLAUSE SIGN)

HOST: Heh heh . . . Before we bring out the next dancers, let's take a look back at how this all started.

(SWITCH TO: REHEARSAL ROOM, VLAD AND LUCY)

LUCY: (EXASPERATED) C'mon, it's one, two, three, four.

VLAD: Don't teach me how to count. I have a cousin in America who's a mathematician.

(SWITCH TO: REHEARSAL ROOM, AMON-RA AND SHEPARDA)

SHEPARDA: (SITTING ON THE FLOOR, ROCKING IN PAIN) Seriously, I twisted my ankle and all you can say is, "It happens all the time"?

(SWITCH TO: REHEARSAL ROOM, VAN HELSING AND PHYLLIS)

VAN HELSING: (FINGER POINTING UP TRI-
UMPHANTLY) Rehearse the kraken!

PHYLLIS: I never know what you're talking about,
but you do dance divinely. HA!

(SWITCH TO: MAIN STAGE, HOST AND
CASSANDRA)

HOST: Perhaps the most memorable rivalry was
between two competitors more known for their monthly
hair growth than for their ballroom skills. One from
London, and one from New Jersey.

(SUNBURST TO DARKNESS, FADING IN PRE-
TAPE ON WHAT LOOKS LIKE A MOOR)

WOLF RUSSELL: We Nurians invented rock and
roll hundreds of years ago. Have you seen the tattoo
on my hand?

(SWITCH TO A DESERTED CITY CORNER)

WOLF NAUGHTON: I *was* a professional dancer. I
just wish people would forget about my European tour.

(FX: SUNBURST, FADE TO MAIN STAGE)

HOST: Well, since the judges decided they both bite,

and neither one will get the gold, much less the silver, their rivalry has transformed into a friendship. Here they are putting on the dog one last time.

(MUSIC: "Werewolves of London")

WOLF RUSSELL: (LOUD) Shit, not this again!

WOLF NAUGHTON: I sang better any day . . .

[The wolves jump to the backstage area; screams and cartoon crashes create a more in-tune sound]

HOST: Looks like they're attacking the band. I don't think this was the choreography we saw in rehearsal.

CASSANDRA: I told them they should find a second tempo.

HOST: (VAGUELY TOWARD HER) It's like the wind keeps blowing in my ears.

(FADE TO BLACK)

(FADE IN)

HOST: Welcome back. During the break, we picked up a couple of spare musicians on the sidewalk, and now we're ready to continue. Next up is Cyclops. He's a one-eye doing a two-step for the third time. Let's bring him forth.

(MUSIC: "Ain't That a Kick in the Head?")

[Dancers circle around Cyclops, tempting him with plastic sheep. One by one, he catches the dancers and rips their heads off. Wouldn't you?]

HOST: There it is, survival of the fleecest.

(FADE TO BLACK)

(FADE IN)

HOST: And now the moments you've all been waiting for. Our three finalists will be dancing to a song they only learned twenty minutes ago and the band only learned during commercial.

CASSANDRA: Precognitive powers not so funny now, eh, suckers?

(MUSIC: "I'm Alive")

[Vlad and Lucy come out first. Lucy is trying to tango, but Vlad is not having any of it. When they get to mid-stage, Vlad faces the judges, turns into smoke, turns back into human form. He curls his hand at them, as if beckoning. Then he looks into the camera and does the same. Lucy continues to tango by herself.]

[Behind them come Sheparda and Amon-Ra. Amon-Ra shuffles surprisingly fast, though he only seems to shamble, one arm stiffly approximating the tango position. Sheparda does kicks and grinds, generally giving him and the audience a standing lap dance.]

[Last, Van Helsing and Phyllis emerge forcefully, Van Helsing dancing like the outcome of Armageddon depends on it, Phyllis dancing like a Borscht Belt groupie.]

(MUSIC FADE OUT)

HOST: Well, there it is, the last dance of the competition. Who will win the prize? The villagers have stormed the phone lines, and now it's up to these three non-eternal judges.

(SWITCH TO: JUDGES' TABLE)

[The first judge is elusive as cotton candy. The second seems to be a scarecrow made out of wood instead of straw. The third is collared and affixed with a heavy chain to his end of the table.]

HOST: What do you have to say about Vlad?

FIRST JUDGE: (AIRILY) Vlad Tepish is the kindest, bravest, warmest, most wonderful dancer I have ever seen in my life.

SECOND JUDGE: (WOODENLY) Vlad Tepish is the kindest, bravest, warmest, most wonderful dancer I have ever seen in my life.

THIRD JUDGE: (JUMPS UP ON THE TABLE, STRAINING AND CLAWING) Vlad Tepish is the kindest, bravest, warmest, most wonderful dancer I have ever seen in my life.

HOST: Well, I guess that's it, then. Vlad and Lucy have won!

(AUDIENCE CHEERS)

[Amon-Ra lets out a sepulchral scream, holding out his arms as if to strangle someone, anyone. But Van Helsing jumps in front of him.]

VAN HELSING: (ANGRILY) They didn't get to us! What about us!

CASSANDRA: I told you Vlad was going to win.

HOST: (OBLIVIOUS) All that's left is for the big group hug and the awarding of the mirrorball.

[Obeying, everyone onstage gathers around in a Hollywood Kiss scrum. From the middle comes a cry of agony and a puff of smoke. When they break, Vlad is nowhere to be seen.]

(RELIEVED SIGHS FROM THE AUDIENCE, FROM THE HOST AND CASSANDRA, FROM THE JUDGES)

HOST: Oh, thank goodness. I mean, what was a vampire going to do with a mirrorball, anyway?

BRIANS!!!

D. L. Snell

"I'm a zombie but still gots his brains," Kenny began, reading the opening hook of his first horrible novel.

With zombie popularity spreading so rapidly, he had hoped for a bigger turnout. But Kenny stood in the little bookstore, addressing only his mother, who took up three of the empty seats; she had a fat purse.

The handbag was not big enough, however, to fill the other vacant chairs.

"That's my son!" she cried out, waving her purse dangerously and losing her cents. "Woo-hoo!"

The cashier with a pink streak in her hair caught Kenny's eye.

"Mom . . ." he groaned.

"Sorry," she said, sitting down again. "Go ahead and start from the beginning."

Kenny cleared his throat and said, "Um . . . okay . . . I'm a zombie but, uh . . . still gots his—"

The bell over the front entrance rang. A man in a gray blazer came in, carrying a black duffel bag and tripod. His eyes instantly locked onto Kenny.

"Oooh," his mom said, "someone from the paper?!"

"No, ma'am," the man replied as he pulled a video camera out of his bag. "Someone with the local news."

"Oooh-oooh-oooh!" she said, ogling his equipment. "My son's very first book signing and he's already on TV?!" She bounced out of her seat, eager to talk off the reporter's ear.

But she got hung up—her purse caught on an empty seat. In the process, she lost all her marbles, gum wrappers, and change, and all sorts of embarrassing photographs of Kenny in his baby bath.

She gathered them up and showed them off to the reporter, who was now getting the photographic evidence on film.

Kenny groaned.

"So," the cute cashier behind him asked, "what's the book about?"

Kenny turned to face her. It was the first time he noticed how short she was. Short, but intimidating, as if cute could cut.

Her name tag said STEPH.

"Um . . ." he said, wishing his mother were there. She had a knack for putting words in his mouth.

"It's not about glitz-vamps, is it?" Steph asked.

"What are . . . those?"

"Because I hate glitz-vamps."

"Oh. No. It's—"

"Zombies with brains, right?"

"Uh, I think so . . ."

"Then why does the cover say 'Brians'?"

"Huh?!" Kenny asked.

"You know, as in plural for 'Brian'?"

"Uh-oh . . ." Kenny stared at the cover, which featured a badly Photoshopped eagle for some reason. Above that, his title was typed in bloody font:

BRIANS!!!

He was too mortified to look up from the typo.

"Give me that," Steph said, snatching the copy from his trembling hand. She skimmed the back-cover description. "Who's your publisher?"

Kenny almost said "self-published." But that wasn't entirely accurate, and it sounded stupid. So he said, "My mom."

Steph leafed through a couple pages and said, "It's crap."

"What?"

"You need an editor."

"But my mom's—"

"Well, your mom sucks."

Kenny couldn't argue with that.

"You need a real editor," she said.

"Okay."

"I charge by the word."

"What?"

She ignored him and gave the cover one last look. "You should have subtitled it *If I Only Had One*." Then she gave the novel back.

"Kenneth!" his mother called, motioning for him to join her and the reporter from the news.

Steph offered him a sarcastic eyebrow and then turned to tidy up a stack of *Dusk* bookmarks; a vampire stood glittering on the front.

Kenny shambled over to his mother, and the reporter offered him his hand. "Kenneth, right? I'd like to ask you a few questions if that's okay with you?"

Kenny's mom said, "Absolutely," and she took the reporter's hand herself. She didn't shake it though. She just slipped her hand inside his and waited, as if expecting him to kiss it.

The reporter shook her hand awkwardly and let go. "Okay," he said, "let's get started." He gave a wireless lapel mic to Kenny and said, "If you could just put this on . . ."

Kenny's hands shook so badly, his mother insisted on doing it for him.

"Mom—"

"Oh, hush. I used to help your dad put on ties all the time. I'm an old pro at this." She put the mic on upside down.

"Here," Steph said, "let me."

Kenny's mother shot her a dirty look as Steph affixed the device properly to his Cannibal Corpse shirt.

He had never been this close to a girl before. He held his breath, afraid it might stink. She smelled good, like cigarettes and wintry gum.

"Try that," she said, patting his shirt back into place.

"Um . . ." Kenny said.

The reporter gave him a thumbs-up. "Crystal clear." He aimed the camera at Kenny, going for the head shot. "So. Kenneth. Why zombies?"

"Uh . . ." he said, shuffling sideways as his mother shoehorned her way into the frame. He felt Steph's presence, too, not far behind him. For some reason, the smell of cigarettes gave him an idea.

"Um . . ." he said, "because glitz-vamps suck?"

Steph burst into laughter. "Maybe he does have one after all," she said to herself.

"One what?" his mother asked.

"A brain, Mom."

"What?"

"That's why I picked them."

"Picked what? Son, what're you talking about?"

"Zombies, Mom. The ones with the, um . . . brains. We're exactly like them, maybe. We're stupid but . . . we know how to eat and watch TV and stuff. So we've got to have *some*."

"Some what?!" his mother asked. "Honestly, Kenneth, you're not making any sense!"

"Um . . ."

"Didn't you hear him?" Steph asked. "He's talking about *brains*. Jeez Louise, lady, no wonder he turned out this way."

"What?!" his mother said, blushing. "Who asked . . . what do you . . . I wasn't talk . . . aaarrrgghh— why don't you just mind your own business, little miss?!"

"Scandalous!" the reporter cried. "Sassy!" He focused his camera on Steph. "*You* seem to have an opinion. What's your perspective on the recent rash of zombie popularity?"

"Well, I don't think it's a rash," she said, "I think it's an outbreak."

"Like the one on your face?" Kenny's mom asked, trying to interrupt, but Steph barely let her get a word in edgewise. Kenny admired her strength and her pink ribbon of hair.

"If you think about it," Steph said, "more and more people have become rabid zombie fans. They're so hungry for stuff to consume, they're ransacking bookstores, movie stores, and . . . they actually *trampled* a few obscurely famous *Blank of the Dead* extras this year, at the Zombie Decathlon!"

It sounded well thought-out, as if she were a panelist at a horror convention, which Kenny had never been to but had personally seen videos of online.

"Hmm," the reporter said. "Scintillating. Sensational."

"Oh yeah?" Kenny's mother interjected. "I changed Kenneth's diapers, so I, um . . . he dedicated his *Brains!!!* to me, so there!"

Steph got right in her face and said, "Actually, it's *Brians!!!*" Then she turned back to the reporter, who was ignoring the mother anyway.

"So," the reporter said, engrossed with Steph. "Why do you think people are acting this way?"

Before she could answer, the reporter quickly elaborated. "I mean, it's caused riots and economic depressions and . . . whole industries have gone under simply because people are staying home with their favorite zombie book or Ramirez film. Why, do you think?"

"Come on," she said, "anyone with half a brain can see: zombies are taking over the world!"

"Intriguing . . ."

"Boring!"

"Um . . . uh . . ."

"And not by some meteorite or hate virus," Steph said, "no. These zombies are taking over one bookstore and one Jane Austen novel at a time."

"Titillating," the reporter said, "introspective. Why do you think this 'zombie outbreak' hasn't spread here?"

Steph laughed. "What, to this little pissant town? Are you kidding me?!"

"Hey," said Kenny's mother, "show some respect! Yeah, we may have some pissants here, but . . . that's not the point!"

"Look," Steph said, directing the reporter's camera

to one of the bookcases. "You see that shelf over there? The one that says 'Made Right Here in Oregon'?"

"Excellent," the reporter said, "yes."

"Well, there's this book of poetry about vegetables over there, and it sells better in this town than *Dusk* ever will."

"Hmph," the reporter said, looking up from his camera's digital viewfinder. "Good series. Love glitz-vamps. But don't you think the outbreak's getting closer?"

Steph tried to answer, but again, the reporter butted in to elaborate. "Take our viewership in the next county, for example. The station's losing ratings left and right over there, ever since that stupid zombie show came on TV."

Steph crossed her arms. "I like that show."

"Yeah, well . . . it's forcing me to cover this story. That's why I came to talk with Kenneth, actually. I figured if I report about zombies, maybe people will actually watch the news."

Kenny's mom, in a desperate attempt to steal everyone's attention, suddenly stuck her whole face in the camera and said, "I brought boxes and boxes and boxes of books! Come get one so I can retire!!"

"Or at least make your money back . . ." Steph said.

The reporter had to pry Kenny's mother off his equipment and then wipe her lipstick off his lens. "I guess that's a wrap," he said, and started to pack up.

Kenny's mom said, "When will this air?"

"Probably the six o'clock news," the reporter replied.

"Tonight?"

"That's what that means, yes," answered Steph.

Kenny's mother ignored her. "Oooh, that's perfect! Kenneth's signing goes till eight!"

A strange look came over the reporter's face, as if something had just occurred to him. "Hmm," he said, "interesting. Eight, you say?"

"Yes," his mom said. "Didn't you read the press release I sent to the Internet?"

"Eight," the reporter repeated, as if committing it to memory. "Eight. Well, maybe my story will . . . I'll see if I can't . . . help us make a killing—I mean . . . you . . . make one."

He left quickly after that, casting a few weird looks back at Kenny and his book, and checking his watch, as if he were late.

After about 6:50 that night, people started trickling into the bookstore. They had seen Kenny's interview on the news and had driven from the next county over to buy his novel, they said.

"My son's so smart!" his mother bragged as he scribbled his illegible signature in a few copies of his book. "He's the next Stephen Coonts!"

"Stephen Coonts?" Steph asked, raising an eyebrow. "The guy who writes adventure thrillers?"

"No," Kenny's mother said. "The guy who . . . writes those horror ones."

"Dean Koontz?" Steph asked.

"Don't be absurd. He's not a horror writer."

"Stephen King," one of the customers chimed in.

"Yes!" Kenny's mother said, pointing him out. Then she gave Steph a snotty look. "See? At least someone here has some smarts."

Soon, Kenny's line of zombie fans stretched out the door, and Steph got pissy; she was so busy manning the register she didn't have time for a smoke.

Kenny's hand began to cramp from all the signatures. His mother, meanwhile, stood on a chair, slinging her purse around, screaming, "Woo hoo!!"

Some of the customers bought multiple copies and cradled them to their chests. They said stuff like "I just *devour* zombie books" or "Big smart author like you, I'd just love to pick your brain."

As the customers filled the store, and then the whole parking lot, their excited chatter began to take on a weird rhythm, like a chant.

"Do you hear that?" Kenny's mom asked, cupping her hand behind her ear. "What's that they're saying? Brians? Who's this Brian I keep hearing about?"

"Uh-oh," Kenny said, realizing something.

"What?" his mother asked. "Is your hand cramping again? What is it? Talk to me, sweetheart!!"

He showed her the empty boxes that once held his books.

She hesitated to grin. "You're out?"

Confused blather started circulating through the crowd. "What'd they say, he's coming out?"

"No, he's *out*."

"What? Of *Brians!!!*?"

"It looks like it," Steph said, sounding relieved and eager for a smoke. "Sorry, everyone, we're all out!"

"But . . . we drove all the way from the next county over!"

"Hey, that's right! Where's our *Brians!!!*?"

People started shouting and getting angry. Some pushed their way forward in line, making demands.

One girl who had sores all over her face and smelled like cat pee suddenly grabbed a copy of the book out of another customer's hand.

"Hey!" the customer yelled. "She took my *Brians!!!*"

"*Brians!!!—Brians!!!*" everyone shouted. "We want more *Brians!!!*" They started pushing and tearing at each other to get at Kenny, who sat totally petrified while his mother continued slinging her purse and singing, "Wooo!"

"All right, enough!" Steph shouted. "It's closing time!" She tried to herd the customers out the front entrance, but they started pushing her back.

The girl with the sores slipped past her and got ahold of Kenny's shirt. "*Brians!!!*" she said, and then, for no reason at all, she bit him. Right on the arm.

"Kenny!" Steph cried. She tried pulling the sickly girl off of him, tried to save his life.

"Stop it!" Kenny's mother said, and she beat Steph off with her gigantic purse. "She's his number one fan!"

As his mom struck again and again with her bag, more personal effects went flying: Smarties, a can of pepper spray, her collection of Kenny's baby teeth.

Steph fell to the floor.

Kenny's mom raised her purse, ready to bash in Steph's head and add red highlights to her hair. But then Steph got ahold of the fallen pepper spray and spritzed Kenny's mother right in the face.

"Aaarrrgghh!" His mom covered her eyes and backed up as Steph drove everyone outside with the intense repellent.

Steph slammed the doors shut. Blind, coughing, puking, and watering at the eyes, the customers immediately surged forward and pounded on the glass.

"Brians!!! Brians!!!"

Kenny's mother was outside, pressed against the window, saying, "Help me—help your mother!"

"I can't hold them forever!" Steph said as the doors shook and lurched against her hands. "Kenny, quick—push that bookcase over here! We need to block the door!"

"Kenneth," his mother moaned, "it *hurts.*"

Kenny looked from his mother to Steph, unsure of what to do. He had never expected to be this popular.

"Kenneth!" Steph said. "Do it!"

"Um!" He stood up and helped her block the door with the bookcase full of local vegetable poetry.

"But I'm your mother!" Kenny's mother yelled at him. "I pushed you out of my—"

"She's his mother?!" one of the customers said, catching on. "She's his mom!"

"Hey," another one said, "maybe *she's* got some *Brians!!!*"

They started tearing at her purse, spilling the rest of her Smarties, so that all she had left were Dum Dums.

"Get off me, get off—what do you want?!"

"*Brians!!!*" they moaned, "*Brians!!!*"

"What—who's Brian?!"

"They mean 'brains'!" called Steph.

"Brains?" Kenny's mother asked. "Brains?! I don't have any brains!"

But the zombie fans weren't listening. They grabbed her arms and legs and pulled her every which way until she came apart, as if her body were nothing but noodles. Blood and guts and body parts flew everywhere, and her dismembered head hit the glass with a wet thud, leaving a lipstick kiss on the glass.

Kenny moaned; he looked away.

The zombie fans redoubled their effort on the doors, which began to crack under their fists. The bookshelf of vegetable poetry began to budge, screeching across the tiles.

"Come on!" Steph said, grabbing Kenny's hand. She led him to the back of the store, to the roof access ladder. But as the two of them were climbing up, the front doors shattered and customers rushed in.

They grabbed Kenny's legs while he waited for Steph to unlock the hatch to the roof. They pulled at him, and his feet slipped off the ladder.

He hung from a rung while the zombie fans accidentally pantsed him. His jeans hit the top guy in the face, and the man fell, crashing into other fans on his way down. They all landed on the floor. Not a second afterward, they were clambering back up the rungs.

"Got it!" Steph said, finally opening the lock. She pulled Kenny onto the roof and shut the hatch just as the zombie fans tried to reach through. She slammed the little door on a few stray fingers until they cracked and slid back. Then she sat on the hatch, which began to buck wildly beneath her.

"A little help here!" she said to Kenny.

"Um . . ."

She yanked him down and made him sit on the door with her, back-to-back.

"Oh my God . . ." she said, looking out over the parking lot. It was completely filled with people and cars. And more and more zombie fans were pouring in by the carload.

"Why are they doing this?!" Kenny asked.

Steph gave the crowd a hard, evaluating look. "Because," she said. "They've got nothing better to do. They don't have a life."

They sat in stunned silence for several moments before Steph pointed something out. "Hey, look! That reporter!"

The man with the camera stood on top of a news van in the parking lot, shooting the action while shouting, "Bleeding! Leading! Better than that stupid TV show!"

"That bastard!" Steph said. "He planned this! Just so people would watch the news!"

Absently, she brushed at a candy wrapper stuck in her hair. It crinkled and fell, and Kenny noticed that it was one of his mother's, a Dum Dum.

Suddenly he got an idea. He stood up, and the zombie fans below them almost threw Steph off the hatch.

"Kenny, don't be stupid—sit down!"

"Uh . . . wait!" He ran to the edge of the roof and cupped his hands to his mouth. "Hey! Hey, you!"

He caught the attention of a few people near the front of the horde. The reporter noticed, too, and aimed his camera up at the roof. "Interesting development!"

Kenny suddenly remembered that he'd lost his pants, and so he stood there in his undies with a blush. But, remembering Steph's strength, he bulled on.

"There!" he said, pointing at the reporter. "*He's* my mom! *He's* got *Brains!!!*"

The whole crowd fell silent and frowned up at him, as if something he'd said didn't make any sense. One of the men asked, "What . . . what are brains?"

"Uh," Kenny said, "I meant *Brians!!!* He's got some, right over there!"

"Oh," the frowning man said. And then the whole

crowd was screaming again, this time headed for Kenny's "mother" standing atop the van.

"Wait!" the reporter said, still filming for some reason. "He's lying! I'm a man! I don't have any . . . I don't have any *Brians!!!*"

But the zombie fans were beyond reason. They grabbed the reporter's feet, and he kicked at them, still holding the camera to his eye, even as the fans dragged him down and tore into him.

For some reason, the girl with the sores bit into his skull—bit right through the bone somehow, as if it were nothing more than a melon. And then she said, "*Brians!!!*"

Kenny looked away as everyone dug in and scooped out the bloody gray matter, going, "Where?! Where's the *Brians!!!*?"

Steph yelped as the hatch continued to jump beneath her. "You're still not helping!" she told Kenny.

"Oh!" He ran over and sat down with her, and, back-to-back, they both rode it out.

Slowly, the zombie fans inside caught word that someone in the parking lot actually had some *Brians!!!* in his head. So they all climbed down the ladder to make their way outside.

Kenny and Steph sat there for several moments, just leaning against each other and feeling each other breathe.

"You know," Steph said out of the blue, "I'm actually . . . the writer of the *Dusk* series."

"Huh?" Kenny asked. It was a weird thing for her to say, given the circumstances. But for some reason—perhaps it was shock—Kenny was completely okay with it. "But, uh . . . I thought you, uh—"

"Hated glitz-vamps?" she asked, finishing his sentence like his mother always used to do. "Well, Kenny . . . now you know why. I have a five-book contract to fulfill."

"How come, uh . . . no one ever—"

"Knows it's me?"

He nodded.

"Because I write under a pen name," she said, "and I hire an actress who pretends to be the real writer. It's pretty convenient, actually."

"Uh . . ."

"But then why do I work here?" she asked, practically reading his mind. "Because. I like it here. I like it more than the job where I make millions of dollars, quite honestly." She took a deep breath and said, "I've never told anyone that before. You sure you still want me to edit your books?"

Kenny frowned and rubbed at his arm, where the girl with the sores had left her teeth marks. "I've got a . . . secret too," he said.

"What, that your mother brought you back from the dead to write books, so she could retire?"

"Um . . . how'd you—"

"I read your bio, dummy. It was right on the back of your book."

"Oh." He rubbed his arm again. "I think . . . one of those zombie girls bit me."

Steph didn't respond for a second. Then, sounding mildly concerned, she asked, "Does this mean you're going to eat me?"

"Uh . . ." he said, trying to think. "Are you going to . . . suck me?"

Steph, still leaning against him, burst into laughter, and Kenny liked how it felt.

"Maybe you do have a Brian after all," she said, and he laughed too. Then they both laughed together.

They laughed until they cried.

Still Life

KEN LILLIE-PAETZ

When I found the apple I dreamed that my oil painting would be perfect. If you cleared your mind and thought of the world's most perfect and delicious apple you would be picturing the very piece of fruit I had chosen.

I hoped that with my skills as a painter I could produce a composition that would capture the very essence of "perfect appley-ness."

Countless line drawings were created before I even dared attempt to work on canvas. Then I found myself second-guessing the quality of my art supplies and there were several trips back and forth to Michaels before I felt okay.

The indecision over whether I should go with my usual turpentine-diluted oil paint for the first layer or just skip ahead by using acrylic caused a panic attack so severe that I had to walk away from my subject, make a doctor's appointment and renew a prescription for lorazepam.

The second layer took forever before it was done. The first layer had dissolved beneath, allowing both layers to come to life in terms of tone and color. Yet, despite the fact that I was getting closer to completion, each brushstroke I made was now an agony of self-doubt. Every scrape with the palette knife was like a palette knife in my heart.

When the painting was finished it looked like it could have been produced by one of the Dutch masters. Despite how it would never scream "perfect appley-ness" or look good enough to eat, it was without question a faultless rendering of the subject—an apple that had rotted and dried up.

I placed the artwork on the wall behind its subject and felt satisfied.

Then I walked past the seated skeleton to look at my last painting. I was sure that *Still Life with Apple* had turned out just as well as *Nude on a Chair*.

A Day in the Life

SHERRILYN KENYON

"Ding dong, the bitch is dead."

Elliott Lawson looked up from her BlackBerry e-mail to laugh at her assistant Lesley Dane. "And there is much rejoicing."

Dressed in a pink sweater and floral skirt, Lesley flounced around Elliott's tiny office with a wide smile before she added yet another bulging manuscript to the top of the mountain of manuscripts in Elliott's in-box. Was it just her or did that thing grow higher by the heartbeat? It was like some bad horror movie.

The stack that wouldn't die.

Lesley continued. "Just think, no more e-mails with her calling us names and complaining about everything from title to synopsis to . . . you know, everything."

That was the upside.

The downside? "And no more selling three million

copies on the release date either." While Helga East had been the biggest pain in the ass to ever write a book, her thrillers had set so many records for sales that her unexpected death left a huge hole in their publishing program. One that would take twenty or more authors to fill.

Elliott's stomach cramped at that reality and at the fact that she'd just lost her star pony in the publishing race. "What are we going to do?"

"We'll build another blockbuster."

She scoffed at her assistant. "You say that like it's an easy thing to do. Trust me, if it was, every book we published would be one." And that didn't happen by a long shot. They didn't even break even on 90 percent of them.

"Yeah, but still the bitch *is* dead."

It was probably wrong to be happy about that, but like Lesley, she couldn't help feeling a little relief. Helga had been a handful.

Oh, who was she fooling? Helga had been the biggest bitch on the planet. A chronic thorn who had given Elliott two ulcers and a permanent migraine for four solid months around the release of any of Helga's books. In fact, Helga had been screaming at her over the phone when she'd had a heart attack and keeled over. It was creepy really. One second she'd been calling Elliott's intelligence and parentage into question and the next . . .

Dead.

Life was so fragile and tragedies like this rammed that home.

Lesley's phone rang. She left to answer it while Elliott stared out her tiny window at the red brick building next door where another drone like her worked a sixty-hour-a-week job at the bank. She didn't know his name and yet she knew a lot about him. He brought his lunch to work, preferred a brown tweed jacket, and tugged at his hair whenever he was frustrated. It made her wonder what unconscious habits of hers he'd picked out. They'd never waved to or acknowledged each other in any way, yet she could see enough personal details about him that she'd know him anywhere.

Not wanting to think about that depressing fact, she returned her attention to the cover proofs piled in front of her. One was for Helga's next book—the one she'd been working on when she died.

Her phone dinged, letting her know she had a new e-mail.

Sighing, she picked up her BlackBerry and looked at it.

For a full minute she couldn't breathe as she saw the last name she'd ever expected to see again.

Helga East.

Relax. It's just an old e-mail that was forwarded by someone else or one that got lost in cyberspace for a couple of days. No need to panic or be concerned in the least. It was nothing.

Still, her stomach habitually knotted as she opened it.

Tell me honestly, Elliott, does it hurt to be that stu-
pid? Really? What part of that heinous, god-awful
cover did you think I'd approve of? I hate green.
How many times do we have to have this argu-
ment? Get that bimbo off the cover and take that
stupid font and tell creative to stick it on the cover
of someone too moronic to know better.

> *H.*

> *PS: The title,* Nymphos Abroad, *is disgusting,*
demeaning, and insulting. Change it or I'll have
another talk with your boss about how incompetent
you are.

She sucked her breath in sharply as she realized the
e-mail pertained to the cover on her desk.

A cover Helga had never seen. It'd only arrived that
morning. Two days after Helga's funeral.

Yeah, there was no way it was Helga. Anger
whipped through her as she hit "reply." "Okay, Les,
stop messing with me. I'm not in the mood."

A second later, a response came back.

> *Les? Are you on drugs? Surely you can't afford*
them on your measly salary. I've seen the cheap
shoes you wear and that sorry excuse for a designer
handbag that you think no one will know you

bought in Times Square for five dollars. Now quit
stalling, stop reading your e-mail, and call down to
art and get me a cover worthy of my status.

She looked out her door to see Lesley on the
phone, her back to her computer. Definitely not her
pretending to be Helga.

But someone was. And they were doing a good job
of it too.

Who is this? she typed.

Helga, you nincompoop. Who did you think it was?
Your mother? I swear, is there no one up there with a single
brain cell in their head?

It couldn't be. Yet the return address in the header
was Helga's. It was an e-mail addy she knew all too
well. Numberonewriter@heast.com.

Maybe one of Helga's heirs was messing with
her. But why would they do such a thing? Surely they
wouldn't be as cruel as Helga had been?

Then again, maybe it was genetic. Helga's mean-
ness had seemed to be hardwired into her DNA. It was
what the lonely old woman had lived and breathed.

Her heirs wouldn't be able to see that cover. They have
no way of knowing what's on it.

There was that. No one outside of their publishing
house had seen it.

Another e-mail appeared. *Why are you still sitting at*
your desk, staring into space? I told you what to do. Get me
a decent cover, you twit.

A chill went down her spine. One so deep that she actually jumped when her cell phone went off, signaling her that she had a new voice mail message. Weird, she hadn't heard it ring.

Reaching down, she pulled it up and accessed her box.

"I will not stand for that tawdry, disgusting cover. Do you hear me, Elliott? I want it gone, right now. Hit 'delete.'"

Her heart pounded at a voice she'd know anywhere. Helga.

"You all right?"

She looked up at Lesley, who was staring at her from the doorway. "I . . . I . . ." Putting the phone down, she hit the 4 button to make it repeat. "Tell me what you hear."

Lesley put it up to her ear. After a few seconds, she scowled. "Man, I hate those pocket dials where all you get is background noise. What kind of imbecile doesn't lock their phone?" She handed it back.

Baffled, Elliott replayed it and held it up to her ear to listen. It was still Helga, plain as the desk in front of her. "It's not a pocket dial. Can't you hear her?" She held it back out to Lesley.

Again, Lesley listened. "There's no voice, El. Just a lot of background sounds like trucks on the highway or something, and someone laughing. You okay?"

Apparently not. How could they listen to the same thing and yet hear such radically different messages?

She hung up her phone and gave Lesley a forced smile. "Fine. Stressed. Tired."

Crazy . . .

Clearing her throat, she put the phone on her desk. "Did you need something?"

"Just reminding you about the marketing meeting in five minutes."

"Thanks." Elliott gathered her notes for the meeting while she tried her best not to think about the phone call and e-mails from a writer who was dead. It wasn't Helga. Some sick psycho was messing with her head.

Or it was a friend with a sorry excuse for a sense of humor.

Yeah, that would be her luck.

It's not funny, folks. But the one thing she knew from being an editor was that humor was subjective. How many times had Helga written something that she'd rolled her eyes over only to have the billions of readers out there find it hysterical?

Maybe I'm being punk'd.

Could happen . . . If only she was lucky enough for Ashton Kutcher to pop out of a closet.

But there was no Ashton in the meeting. Only mind-numbing details about books they'd already gone over a million times that left her attention free to contemplate who was being cruel and highly unusual to her.

Maybe it's someone in this meeting.

She looked around at her coworkers, most of whom appeared as stressed-out and bored as she was. No, they were too involved with their own lives to care about harassing her.

Why is this meeting taking so long?

It was hellacious. Surreptitiously, she glanced down at her watch and did a double take. Was it just her or was the second hand making a thirty-second pause between each tick?

By the time the meeting let out, she felt like she'd been stretched on the rack. Oh good Lord, why did they have to have these all the time? What Torquemada SOB thought this was a good idea?

But at least it was finally over. She breathed a sigh in relief as she gathered her things and left.

The moment she was back in her office, she checked her e-mail. There were ninety, n-i-n-e-t-y, messages from her wannabe Helga stalker.

She deleted them without reading.

Trying to put it out of her mind, she turned around in her chair to look at her "friend" in the other building. For once his office was dark. How strange. He never left early. But her attention was quickly drawn to something that was being reflected in the darkness of her glass. Something someone had attached to the cork bulletin board that she'd hung next to her door.

With a gasp, she turned around to see if her mind was playing tricks.

It wasn't.

Her heart in her throat, she got up and went to it. As she reached for it, her hand shook.

Someone had taken Helga's cover and pinned it with a blood-red tack to the board. It had nasty comments written all over it with a black Magic Marker. Worse? The handwriting looked just like Helga's.

Terror filled her as she ripped it down, then made her way to Lesley's desk. Lesley paused midstroke on the keyboard to look up at her.

"Who did you let into my office while I was at the meeting?"

"No one."

"Someone went in there." She held the marked-up print out toward Lesley.

She frowned. "Why are you showing me that?"

"I want you to tell me who wrote on it."

Her scowl deepened. "You did, Elliott."

What? She snatched it back and turned it over.

All of Helga's writing was gone from it. Now the only pen marks were where someone had approved the art by placing Elliott's initials in the margins. "I didn't do this."

Lesley looked at it carefully. "It's your handwriting, hon. Believe me, I know."

But Elliott hadn't written on it. Not even a little bit.

How was this possible? How?

Her head started throbbing. Without another word, she returned to her office and sat down to stare at the mechanical of the cover sans the nastiness.

"I'm losing my mind." She had to be. There was no other explanation for what was going on.

The skin on the back of her neck tingled as if someone was watching her. She turned around in her chair to inspect her office.

She was alone.

Still the feeling persisted. And of even greater concern was the prickly sensation that something wasn't right.

I'm being haunted . . .

Yeah, that's what it felt like. That uneasy feeling in the pit of her stomach. Something evil was in the room with her. It was all but breathing down her neck.

Panicked, she shot back to Lesley's desk. She needed to feel connected to someone alive.

Lesley gave her an arch stare. "You're pale. Is something wrong?"

If not for the fear of Lesley thinking her insane, she'd have confided in her. But no one needed to know her suspicion. "Doing research for a book on my desk. You know anything about the paranormal?"

"Not really, but . . ."

"What?"

"I have an exorcist on my speed dial."

Elliott burst into nervous laughter. Until she realized Lesley wasn't joking. "You're serious?"

"Absolutely. My best friend in the world is an exorcist."

"Who in the world has a friend who's an exorcist?"

She held her phone up and grinned. "Me. Whatcha want me to check?"

"Um . . . do you think I could speak with your friend?"

Her grin returned to a frown. "Sure. Her name's Trisha Yates. You want me to e-mail her info to you?"

"Please." Even though she was still skittish about her office, Elliott returned and closed her door. There was no need for Lesley to overhear this particular conversation.

Out of habit, she glanced to the office across the way.

Her heart stopped beating.

He was hanging from the ceiling, swinging in front of his desk.

No! It wasn't possible. She closed her eyes and covered them with her hands. *It's not real. It's not real . . .*

But it was. As soon as she opened her eyes, she saw him across the way. Medics were swarming his office, cutting him down.

He was dead.

All of a sudden, both of her phones started ringing. Gasping, she jumped. She grabbed her cell phone. "Hello?"

No one was there.

Same for the office phone. All she heard was a dial tone.

"It doesn't hurt, you know."

She spun at the sound of a male voice behind her. It

was the ghostly image of the man from the other building. "W-w-what doesn't hurt?" It was like someone else had control of her body. She was strangely calm and yet inwardly she was freaking out.

"Death. We all die." He walked through her.

Breathless, scared, and shaking, she watched as he continued past her, to the wall. He went through it and walked back to his cubicle.

No . . . No . . .

No!

As soon as the ghost was over there, the corpse, which was now lying on the floor, turned its head toward her and smiled.

She stumbled back into the door. Terrified, she spun around and clawed at the handle until she was able to open it.

Lesley met her on the other side. "Okay, you are seriously starting to freak me out. What's going on?"

I'm locked in a horror movie.

She didn't dare say that out loud. Les would never understand.

Without a word, she headed for the bathroom with her phone. She pulled up the e-mail and then dialed the number.

"Hello?"

Wow, the exorcist sounded remarkably normal. Even friendly. "Is this Trisha?"

"Yes. You are . . ." She paused as if searching the cosmos for an answer. "Elliott Lawson."

"How did you know that?"

"I'm psychic, sweetie. I know many things."

Elliott wasn't so sure she liked the sound of that. But before she could comment, the phone went dead. She growled in frustration as she tried to dial it again.

Nothing went through.

Instead, her e-mail filled up with more postings from Helga . . .

And other authors too. Some of whom she hadn't worked with for several years.

"Why did you refuse to renew my contract?"

Elliott shrieked at the mousy voice that came out of a stall near her. A woman in her midthirties came out. Her skin had a grayish cast to it and her eyes were dark and soulless.

"Emily? What are you doing here?" Emily had been one of the first authors she'd signed as a new hire. They'd had a good ten-book run before Elliott had made the decision to cut her from their schedule. While Emily's numbers had held steady, they hadn't grown. Every editor was held accountable for their bottom line and Emily had been hurting her chances for advancement. So Elliott had decided to move on to another author.

"Why did you do it? I was in the middle of a series. I had fans and was growing. I don't understand."

"It was business."

Emily shook her head. "It wasn't business. I can count off three dozen other authors who don't sell as well as I did whom you've kept on all these years."

"Not true." She always cut anyone who couldn't pull their weight.

Emily looked down at her arms, then held them up for Elliott to see. "I killed myself over it. After five years of us talking on the phone and working together, you didn't even send over a card. Not one stinking, lousy card."

"I didn't know."

"You didn't care."

Elliott struggled to dial her phone. "You're not dead. This is a nightmare."

"I'm dead. Damned to hell for my suicide because of *you!*" Her eyes turned a bright, evil red as the skin on her face evaporated to that of a leather-fleshed ghoul. She rushed at Elliott.

Screaming, Elliott ran for the door.

The handle was no longer there. She was trapped inside.

With Emily.

"Help me! Please! Someone help me!"

Emily grabbed her from behind and yanked on her hair. "That's what I begged for. Night, after night, after night. But no one answered my pleas either. I spent two years trying to get another contract and no one would touch me because of the lies you told about me. All I ever dreamed about was being an author. I didn't want much. Just enough to live on. Two books a year. But you couldn't allow me to have that, could you? You ruined me."

"I'm sorry, Emily."

"It's too late for sorry." Emily slung her through the door.

Elliott pulled up short as she found herself back in her office. Only it was hot in here. Unbearable. She went to the window to open it.

She couldn't.

When she tried to turn the radiator down, it burned her hand. It whined before it spewed steam all over her.

She turned to run, only to find more hateful notes from Helga.

Suddenly laughter rang out. It filled the room and echoed in her ears.

She spun around, trying to locate the source. At first there was no one there. No one until Lesley appeared in the corner.

Elliott ran to her and grabbed her close, holding on to her like a lifeline. "I need to go home, Les. Right now."

"You are home, Elliott. This is where you spend all of your time. This is what you love. It's all you love." Lesley pulled out her chair and held it for her. "Go ahead. Reject those books. Crush more writers' dreams. You're famous for not pulling punches. For telling it like it is. Go on. I know how much you relish giving your honest, unvarnished opinion."

A thousand crying voices rang out in a harsh, cacophonous symphony.

Your writing is amateurish and pedestrian. Do not

waste my time with any more submissions. I only give one per customer and your number is up.

If you can't take my criticism, then you've no business being a writer. Trust me. I'm a lot kinder than your readers, if you ever have any, will be.

While I found the idea intriguing, your writing was such that I couldn't get past the second page. I suggest you learn a modicum of grammar or better yet, stick to blog posts and Twitter feeds for your creative outlet.

Over and over, she was inundated with rejections and comments she'd written to writers.

And for once, she realized just how harsh they were.

Elliott shook her head, trying to clear it. "Helga! Why are you haunting me? Why can't you leave me in peace?"

Lesley *tsk*ed at her. "Oh, honey, Helga isn't haunting you."

"Yes, she is. I know I should have gone to her funeral, but—"

"Elliott, Helga didn't die." Lesley gestured toward her computer monitor. Her e-mail vanished to show an image of Helga happily at work in her office. "You did."

"I don't understand."

Laughing, Lesley transformed into the image of a red demon with glowing yellow eyes. "Welcome to hell, my dear. From this day forward and throughout all eternity, you will get to be Helga's editor. Oh, and I should mention, she's now doing a book a week."

Old MacDonald
Had an Animal Farm

LISA MORTON

I'm pacing my cage again today. My captors are taunting me outside.

Oh, I know—I shouldn't whine. After all, most have it a lot worse than I do. Worse as in forced labor camps. Strange torments. No hope. Me, I have a cage that used to be a five-bedroom house I couldn't afford, and I'm taken care of . . . but except for *them*, I'm completely alone. The last human being I saw—two months ago—was being chased down the street on a motorcycle, pursued by a pack snarling and biting at his back wheel. God only knows what happened to him.

How did it reach this point? I try to tell myself it wasn't my fault, that I was an effect rather than a cause, that *they* made me do some of the awful things I did, but I'm not convinced.

So I go over it again in my mind, as I've done a thousand times since . . .

I knew something was wrong when my cat walked out of the kitchen, stopped, looked me right in the eye, and said, "This food *sucks.*"

Poised as I'd been with a mug of steaming coffee halfway to my lips, I managed to douse myself with it and yelped slightly. Meowsy gave me one sideways glance and then sauntered past, looking even more disgruntled than usual. "Idiot," he muttered before disappearing into the bedroom.

I'd just been insulted by my cat. Or rather, for the first time I'd *heard* it.

I set the cup down, wiped myself off, and froze for a moment, trying to decide what to do. My indecision was interrupted by a tiny sound from outside the living room, a high-pitched, musical voice. Feeling a lump of dread growing in my gut, I walked the three feet to the window, looked out, and saw—

—a bird. A bird that was pecking at a feeder I'd hung outside and exclaiming excitedly, "Seeds! Mm-mm-mm . . . good . . ."

I already had my phone out of my pocket. I'd only been home from the hospital for twelve hours, and obviously something had gone wrong; I was reacting to a medication, or I'd had an aneurysm, or . . .

But I felt fine otherwise. And I wasn't seeing purple pterodactyls fluttering in the corners of the room or hearing Grandpa calling out to me. That would have made more sense—wasn't that what they always said happened to people like me?

People who had died.

Two days ago, I had died. I didn't remember it, of course, but the witnesses described it and the doctors confirmed it.

It was an office pool party at the boss's place. There were probably twenty of us there, including that loser Randy from accounting . . . and Cheryl. Cheryl, the new front-desk receptionist. Cheryl, she of the loose, killer smile and the drown-in-'em green eyes. Cheryl, who that day looked daaaaaaaaaaamn fine in a bikini.

Of course I was hardly the only one to notice. Every unmarried young guy in the company wanted to ask her out, and every married guy wanted to ask her in (to his office, that is, for a "private chat").

But doggoned if she wasn't flirting back at *me*.

I was feeling really and truly good at that party, except that Randy noticed and decided to screw with me: He took over the bartending duties and managed to make me some margaritas that had at least three shots of *reposado* each. After two of those drinks, I was just plain stupid.

What do stupid guys do to impress girls they like?

Yep. Stupid physical stunts. I'd been on the diving team in high school, and I thought I'd show Cheryl the real deal with a perfectly executed leap into the pool. Which I did. A beautiful jackknife.

Except I dove into the shallow end.

They say I was lucky, all things considered—I didn't break anything or permanently injure myself. Just knocked my head on the bottom and promptly lost consciousness. A few seconds (well, okay—it was actually a full minute) passed before Cheryl realized I wasn't fooling around and raised the alarm.

Later, I found out she'd brought me back with mouth-to-mouth. Damn, I wish I remembered that.

As it was, the next thing I knew, I was waking up in a hospital a day later. The doctors told me I'd been dead for about ninety seconds but had fully recovered. Cheryl had saved my life. They wanted to keep me overnight.

I was released the following day. I was so tired when I got home that I just checked Meowsy's food and fell into bed right away.

Now my beloved animal companion of eight years was calling me "idiot."

I ended up putting the phone down before I called my doctor. I'd wait first and see if it passed. Surely it would. In the meantime . . . it was actually kind of a fun hallucination. I'd go with it and see how it played out.

I walked into the bedroom and saw that Meowsy had just curled up on the bedspread for the day; he was licking his paws and pretending not to notice as I stood over him.

"Meowsy," I said, arms crossed over my chest, "I don't appreciate being called 'idiot.'"

Meowsy stopped licking. He looked up at me, and I'd swear I saw shock in his big green-yellow eyes. "What?"

"You called me an idiot. That's not a very nice thing to say to someone who feeds you, and changes your litter box, and plays with you, and—"

He cut me off. "Oh, spare me. I just didn't realize you could hear me."

It was the strangest sensation, now that I could analyze it: My ears heard the cat going "meow meow meow," but my brain was turning those sounds into perfect English. "I couldn't . . . until this morning." My words came out normally—I wasn't meowing. A long-standing suspicion of mine had just been confirmed: Cats understood English.

Meowsy sighed, then said, "Well, Mac, this changes things."

My cat had just used my nickname. I had no idea how he knew that . . . but then this was just a hallucination, right? "Really? How so?"

"I'm going to have to watch what I say around you now."

That didn't make me comfortable. "What . . . what were you saying before?"

He jumped off the bed and headed for the little

swinging door that led outside, indicating the conversation was over. "Don't ask."

They ran another MRI and some other tests. Everything came back fine. My doctor told me not to worry about it—the hallucinations would pass.

Except they didn't. My trip into Doctor Dolittle Land continued unabated. I fully expected to meet the pushmi-pullyu any second.

I heard them wherever I went: laconic cats, enthusiastic dogs, chattering birds. I had to be careful where I stepped, because I could even hear the tiny "NOOOOOOOOOOO!" screams of insects as my foot descended before crushing them into oblivion. Meowsy kept mum around me for the most part; he only opened his mouth to complain about his litter box ("Hey, y'know, Mac, let's see how *you'd* like crapping on the crap you crapped yesterday") or food. He started spending more time outside, disappearing from the apartment for long chunks at a time.

Work was a different matter, though. Cheryl and I started hanging out a lot together. I even told her what the initial "B" at the front of my name stood for ("Burne"—my parents were demented—and she immediately agreed that "Mac," as in short for "Mac-Donald," my last name, was far preferable). She invited me to her place at last. I was looking forward to our first intimate evening together . . .

But of course she had a cat. Or rather, a kitten—cute little girl, not even a year old. A tortoiseshell who was as far from aloof and inscrutable as you could get.

I didn't think Cheryl was quite ready to hear my confession about my superpowers yet (damn, it really would have been *so* much easier if I'd just come back being able to see dead people), but it was hard to tune it out when this little kitten, Mittens (Cheryl apologized and said she'd come prenamed), was blathering away at our feet. I swear she couldn't have been meowing that much, but somehow she went on and on about everything from how my feet smelled to what was on the television to a bird that'd flown by the window in the morning.

Cheryl wanted to kiss me. For real this time, not a desperate life-saving maneuver . . . but that damn kitten was distracting. Finally, just as our lips met, the kitten blurted out, "Ooh, are they sharing food? What are they doing? That looks fun—"

I'd had enough. I turned to the kitten and said, "Hey, don't you have somewhere else to play?"

Cheryl looked irritated, of course, glancing from Mittens to me. "Sorry, Mac . . . is she bothering you?"

"No," said the kitten.

"*Yes*," said I.

The kitten stared at me, wide-eyed. "You can hear me?"

"Yes, I can, unfortunately."

"What *are* you doing?" That last was from Cheryl.

"I'm talking to Mittens."

Well, she didn't believe me at first, so I thought I'd prove it by having Mittens tell me some things about Cheryl I couldn't possibly have known. Mittens obliged by telling me what color T-shirt Cheryl had worn to bed last night (black), and what she'd watched on TV (a movie about people who were lost and there were lots of birds), and what her favorite food was (some kind of smelly fruit).

Cheryl was underwhelmed, to put it mildly. In fact, she immediately assumed I'd been stalking her, and our date was effectively over.

"Gee, thanks a lot, Mittens," I grumbled on my way out.

"Get some help, Mac," was the last thing Cheryl said to me.

Two days later, I'd just pulled up and parked in front of my building (after another depressing day of watching Cheryl work extra-hard to avoid me) and was walking to my door when I overheard something:

". . . so it's all gonna go down soon, and they don't have a clue."

I stopped and looked around, and saw two alley cats, one tan and one black-and-white, sitting in the evening shadow of a driveway a few feet away. When they saw me staring at them, they turned sarcastic.

"Look at this moron," said the tan one. "Sure will be fun when the tables are turned, huh?"

Black-and-white answered, "No kidding. Hey, whattaya wanna bet this one is gonna be on his knees any second making stupid baby sounds at us?"

I tried not to let on that I could understand them, because I wanted to know more about what they were saying. So I played along, squatting and smiling. "Hi, fellas. Aren't you two fine looking?"

"Finer than you, dork," said Mr. Tan.

Already bored with me, Two-tone yawned, then said, "So when do we make our move?"

"We're just waiting on Tongue. Once he gets the dogs lined up, we're good."

They turned then and strolled off.

What the hell had I just heard? "The tables are turned"? And "our move"?

I'd just unlocked my door when something clicked in my head: *Tongue.*

Oh dear God—Meowsy's full name was Meowsy Tongue. I'd had a friend who just returned from a trip to China when I got the kitten, and it'd been riotously funny at the time.

"Meowsy?!"

I closed the door behind me, and Meowsy sauntered out of the bedroom. "What?"

"Have you been meeting with other cats at night?"

He froze, glanced involuntarily at the little swinging pet door that let him go in and out, then got a shifty look. "Cats *always* meet with other cats at night. So what?"

"Are you . . . planning something?"

"What did you hear?"

When I didn't answer right away, Meowsy walked up and swiped a paw at my ankle. I yowled and jumped, then looked down to see blood welling through my sock. "Ow! Meowsy, what—?"

Meowsy's ears went back and he assumed a look I'd only seen him give me once before, after I'd accidentally stepped on his tail. "That's just a taste of what's coming, human. You might as well hear it, because you can't stop it: We're taking over."

"Who's 'we'? You mean . . . cats?"

"All of the animals." Meowsy relaxed a bit and settled back on his haunches, resuming his usual imperious expression. "It started with the cats, because we're the smart ones, but the rest fell in line pretty quick— the dogs, the birds, the rodents, the reptiles, even the insects and spiders. The human race has done a pretty good job of screwing up everything, but no more. You'll be *our* pets in less than a month."

Part of me wanted to howl with laughter, but somehow the biggest part of me was chilled to the core. "Meowsy . . . haven't we—haven't *I*—treated you well? I mean, I get you the best food, I brush you, I—"

He cut me off with a derisive snort. "Oh, you have *got* to be kidding me. 'The best food'? Get a clue, twerp—I'm a frigging *carnivore*! I crave fresh meat and you serve me this ground-up crap made out of grain by-products! You only clean the litter box twice a

week—how would you like it if I made you flush your
toilet only every three days? You hacked away my masculinity before I was even old enough to know what it
was for! And worst of all: 'Meowsy Tongue'?! That is
the dumbest damn name ever! *What were you thinking?!*"

I mentally squirmed; he was right, after all. "Well,
y'know, if you hate it so much, you could've told me
before—"

"With *what*?!" Meowsy lifted his head and opened
his mouth. "Take a look in there, pal—that palate's not
made for human speech! I should ask why it took *you*
so long to understand *me*!"

I had no answer. I hung my head, silent, abashed.
Meowsy sighed and seemed to relent.

"Still, you haven't been without your uses, I suppose . . . and your newfound talent may yet prove useful
to us, so we'll keep you around. We won't send you to
the labor camps with the rest."

"The *what*?!"

"Good thing you didn't come back only being able
to see dead people," Meowsy said before walking past
me.

When I tried to leave not long after that, I found two
snarling pit bulls at my door. "Where do ya think
you're goin', *Mac*?" I didn't know dogs could snicker
until that moment.

I slammed the door shut and saw Meowsy eyeing me with considerable cat amusement.

I got to my phone before he could stop me and called Cheryl. Of course she didn't believe me when I told her Mittens was actually part of a plan to take over the world and turn humans into slaves. "Don't call me anymore," she said. Just before she hung up, I heard Mittens say in the background, "Yeah!"

It all went down pretty fast over the next few days; they kept me locked away, but I watched the news and read the blogs. Dogs started ordering their masters; cats committed billions of tiny acts of home sabotage, leaving their human owners so confused they couldn't think straight. Even the poor stupid chickens and turkeys pitched in, unaware that the cats had something else in mind for *them* once the overthrow of the human race was complete. I saw videos of Rottweilers herding humans, while wasps stung anyone who fell out of line. Too many of us were reluctant to take up arms against Snowball or Bootsy or Bunbuns.

After a week, when civilization was in chaos and us homo saps were finally starting to realize what was going on, Meowsy led me to my laptop and told me what they wanted me to do: I used my webcam to create a video in which I relayed Meowsy's message to the entire world. The animals were calling for humanity's immediate surrender, and in return they guaranteed we would be treated well.

In two hours the video was all over the Internet

and on every major television station. A lot of folks just laughed; others agreed with a full surrender; a few who complained were suddenly attacked by birds that would have made Hitchcock pale. I'm like Indiana Jones: The snakes were the worst for me, especially when they showed up in the White House. Within four hours, the television stations were all down . . . but it'd been enough. The victors had made their terms clear.

Because there was no doubt they *were* the victors, in what had been a very brief war.

That was three months ago.

Because I'd served them (and because I could still conceivably be useful to them, in the unlikely event of any human uprising), I was treated well. They gave me this gorgeous house, and I get to eat what they do— fresh chicken and turkey. I think most of the human slaves get fed by-products.

There's no more electricity (they don't really need it), and I haven't seen another human being since that guy on the motorcycle with the gang of shepherds going after him.

So . . . did I sell out my species?

For a cage this really isn't so bad. The previous owners had nice taste, the plumbing still works, and they do allow me some time in the backyard, where there are some fruit trees to tend to.

I tried telling them I was lonely, that I wanted a

little human friend. They said no. I told them I wanted Cheryl. They didn't care. I told them I was in heat. They said they could make an appointment for me at the special human spay and neuter clinics they've set up. I didn't push it after that.

Today I was rummaging through the bookshelves here, and I came across an old classic I loved as a kid. It's the one about the guy who's the last survivor after a vampire holocaust, and at the end he realizes that's made him legendary. As for me . . .

I am house pet.

Two for Transylvania

Brad C. Hodson

"Spawn of Satan, I banish you to *hell*!"

Van Helsing crashed the hammer into the stake, plunging it deep into the beast's pallid flesh. A scream erupted from its fanged jaw, and its taloned hands wrestled with the wooden shaft desperately, but to no use. The monster's eyes dropped, its hands fell to its sides, and Dracula was once again only a corpse.

The villagers gathered around, wide eyed and slack jawed. Prayers were muttered and weary hands patted Van Helsing's ancient shoulders. There were offers of dinner and drink, but like always, the aging vampire hunter said he had to be on his way, that the Prince of Darkness's ashes had to be scattered into a running body of water before sunrise to make sure that he would not plague the fine folk of Bistritz ever again. They were insistent that he take some form of payment and within minutes had scraped together enough money to last a man as humble in living as himself a year.

The corpse was loaded on his wagon and he set out alone, as he told them the ritual dictated.

Three miles outside of town, he ripped the stake from Dracula's ribs.

"What'd we get?" The Lord of the Undead rubbed the ragged wound in his chest. It quickly knitted itself together.

"Not much." Abraham unwrapped a turkey sandwich and took a giant bite. Crumbs dotted his beard and a string of meat hung from his lip.

Dracula rifled through the coins and jewelry. "Almost not even worth it. When did people get so . . . so . . ."

"What?"

"Never mind."

"You were gonna make some Jewish crack, weren't you?"

He slid from the wagon and made a show of stretching his back.

"Dracula?"

"No. I wasn't. And please, how many times have I asked you not to talk with your mouth full? It's disgusting."

"This from the guy who sleeps in earth and drinks blood."

The moon rinsed Dracula's pale skin in gray light.

He stared out into the dark woods, watching the trees sway in the wind. "Why do we do it?"

Abraham shrugged. "What else are we gonna do?"

"It's just that people have gotten so—"

"Don't say it."

"I was going to say *jaded*. No one believes anymore except the rubes. And what do they have to pay us with? A couple of knickknacks passed down from their serf grandparents and a week's worth of beer money?" He ripped the cape off and slammed it into the ground. "And I hate this fucking thing. Have I ever told you that? Why can't I just wear a nice suit? I hear tweed's in."

"I know. The cape is uncomfortable. But people expect it."

Dracula sighed. "Yeah. I guess."

"Look, if it makes you feel better, you can take my share. I've still got some money saved up from that mess at the Borgo Pass in March."

He turned and smiled at his partner, fangs glistening. "Thanks. I appreciate that."

Van Helsing patted the seat next to him. "We should get going, just in case those bastards decide to wave some torches this way."

In the blink of an eye, Dracula was next to him. Van Helsing gripped the reins, the horses snorted, and soon they were on their way again, rocking down the dusty Transylvanian road.

Abraham picked a piece of turkey from his beard and slurped it down. "You were supposed to say no."

"Huh?"

"When I offered you my money. You were supposed to say no."

"Then why did you offer it to me?"

"Because that's what I was supposed to do. I offer, you decline. It's etiquette."

"It's stupid is what it is."

They were quiet for a long while.

"What would you do, anyway?"

Dracula shrugged. "I don't know. There's just got to be something more than pulling these Gypsy scams—"

"Roma."

"What?"

"They're called *Roma*. 'Gypsy' is derogatory."

"Whatever. My point is that I used to command armies. I defended Christendom from the Turks. Can I say 'Turks'?"

"You can say 'Turks.'"

"I was a goddamned *legend*, Abe. Have you ever led an army into battle?"

"*Mein gott.* Always with that 'I commanded legions' shit. Let it go. It's in the past. You got to look at the *now*."

Dracula shook his head. "I'd rather look at the future."

"Which is what I'm doing."

"What do you mean?"

Abraham Van Helsing smiled. "You'll see."

• • •

They reached the ruins of Poenarri Castle before dawn. Dracula dug his way into the dirt in the basement. The next night when he pulled himself free, he almost regretted doing so. How nice it would be to just crawl into the ground here and hide away for centuries.

Laughter drifted down from somewhere above him. He climbed the stairs into what was once the dining room. A fire burned in the giant stone pit. Abraham sat at the long, oak table, drinking wine straight from the bottle. A young man sat across from him, wearing a tweed suit and glasses.

"Ah! And here he is!" Van Helsing smiled.

Dracula approached the table. The young man stood and extended a hand.

"This is my friend Renny. I used to run numbers with his father in Berlin."

"Pleased to meet you," the young man said, his German heavily accented.

"Ahem. Can we talk?" Dracula nodded toward the corner.

Abraham rolled his eyes. "Renny, finish that wine off. I'll be right back and we'll open another."

They walked into the corner. Dracula ran a hand through his thick, dark hair. "What are you doing?"

"What?"

"We can barely get by with just the two of us. You wanna bring a third person in?"

"It's not like that. Just hear him out."

"This is just like Athens."

Van Helsing crossed his arms. "We agreed never to bring that up."

"Well, what do you expect? You do the same damn thing again, I'm gonna bring it up."

His face turned red. "You *know* that what happened in Athens was not my fault. That fucking fisherman was supposed to be experienced. Lawrence said he could crack a safe. He swore he could."

"And Lawrence is never wrong."

"Is this about Lawrence?"

Dracula kicked a pebble across the floor. "No."

"Then what's it about? Huh? Because it sure as hell isn't about Renny, either."

Dracula was silent.

"You need to screw your head on straight. Undead or not, you gotta figure out your priorities. You wanna talk about Athens? Well, what about Istanbul?"

"Constantinople."

"Whatever. You and that cleric's daughter?"

Even though he fought it, a smile crept onto Dracula's mouth. "What a summer . . ."

"Yeah, for *you*. You almost got me castrated. I tell ya, man, a woman is gonna be your downfall someday."

"Yeah, yeah."

"Now, can we sit down and talk about this or what?"

"He just rubs me the wrong way. It's a . . ."

"A what?"

Dracula shrugged. "A vibe. Just a weird vibe."

"Jesus Christ."

"And he's wearing fucking *tweed*. You did that on purpose, didn't you?"

"How was I supposed to know what he was going to wear?"

"I told you it was in right now."

Abraham grabbed his shoulder. "Just do me a favor. Come over here, listen for a few minutes, and if you don't like what he has to say, you can bleed him dry and we'll leave him in a ditch somewhere. Okay?"

"Promise?"

"Hell, skull-fuck him for all I care."

"Don't be crass, Abe."

He smiled. "It's the wine. You know how I am after a few drinks."

Dracula glanced toward the table. "I do like that jacket."

They walked back over and sat.

"So, Renny was telling me about something pretty damn interesting he heard."

The young man smiled. "First off, it's fucking tits to meet you. I'm a big fan. Read that story of Lord Byron's three or four times. Great stuff."

Dracula rubbed his temples. He felt a headache coming on. "That story was actually written by Dr. John Polidori and it had nothing to do with me."

Abraham laughed. "Renny, tell him about London."

"Oh. Right. Anyway, just came from London—born and raised there, a true servant of Her Majesty I am—and I was talking to some solicitors I was fleecing. Had this real good operation going, where they thought I was a doctor from the States and—"

Van Helsing cleared his throat.

Renny nodded. "Sorry. Tongue gets away from me sometimes. Like Mama always says, if my brains were as quick as my mouth I could get somewhere. Always made me laugh. Little insulting, too, though, when you think about—"

"*Renny.*"

"Anyway, they was telling me about how they all wished they was rich, saying that real estate was the way to go. So one of them, fat little fella by the name of Worthington or Wellington or some such, one of these silver-spoon-up-his-arse types, starts blathering about how property's at a premium now, on account of how crowded everything is, and how that's a shame because there's all these broken-down abbeys and tenements and what have you—"

Dracula leaned over the table. "You have about fifteen seconds to get to the goddamned point before I eat your heart."

"Keep your knickers on, Impaler. Point is this: the Crown will subsidize work on these places for anyone what moves in. Now, there's this other law that they was talking about, about how if you fix up one of these shit holes you can sell it to the Crown before your loan is paid off, as you're doing queen and country good by improving the view or some such cack like that."

Dracula shook his head. "I don't understand."

Van Helsing laughed. "It's simple. We buy up a bunch of property around town, just throwing a token down payment at them. We do a quick job, new coat of paint and what have you, and sell them off. Then we skip town before the creditors come after us on what we owe and voilà! We're rich!"

Dracula leaned back in his chair. "And the government pays for the work."

"For some of it, yeah," Renny said. "The rest of it we'd have to pay for ourselves."

"Well, that kills it then. We don't have enough money to repair properties like that."

Van Helsing laughed. "But that's what's great about it. Remember when I pawned myself off as a doctor?"

"Yeah?"

"Well, one of my 'pupils,' Dr. Seward, has kept in touch with me ever since. And, in addition to running a mental institution, he freelances on the side as . . . as . . ."

"As what?"

"Guess."

"I hate guessing."

"C'mon."

"He's the guy what signs off on the renovations," Renny blurted out.

Dracula folded his arms and pouted.

"Renny . . ."

"Sorry, Abe. He said he hates guessing."

Abraham nudged him. "C'mon, buddy. This could be it. The big payday that you've been waiting for. You could start all over. What do you say?"

Dracula stared across the table at Renny. The young man fidgeted in his tweed suit.

"Listen," Van Helsing said. "I've got it all worked out. We pawn you off as some duke or something—"

"I was a *prince*."

"Yeah, yeah. I know what you *were*, but nobody cares about some bloodthirsty Wallachian from the fifteenth century. I'm sorry, but it's true."

Dracula stood and stomped off.

"Shit. I'm sorry, Renny. He's touchy. Wait here a minute." Van Helsing went after him. "Hey, buddy, I'm sorry about that. You were a great ruler. Phenomenal. Really, you were."

"You're just saying that."

"Look at me." Abraham spun the vampire around to face him. He gripped Dracula's shoulders and stared into his eyes. "I'm not just saying that. That shit you pulled where you impaled a whole forest of people? Fucking *genius*."

"It was a novel approach, wasn't it?"

"It was thinking outside of the box. That's exactly what it was and exactly why we need you on this." He glanced back at Renny. The young man waved. "Look, it sucks that nobody remembers your war for Christendom. It does and I'm sorry. But if you started calling yourself Prince Vlad people would get suspicious. I mean, how often do you meet a prince, right? But Duke Dracula? Nobody will even bat an eye. You're suave, debonair. Maybe you're not so handsome anymore—"

"Hey!"

"—but you have that certain royal charm, ya know? And if people think you're a duke . . ."

Dracula smiled. "Then no one will suspect that I don't actually have the money to renovate these places."

"Exactly."

"But do we have to use *him*?"

"He's perfect. Listen. He goes back to London, pretends to be a loon, and gets locked up in Seward's care. He does this trick where he eats bugs—"

"Gross. How is that a trick if he actually eats them?"

Abraham thought about this for a long while. "I don't know." He shrugged. "That's just what he calls it. But, point is, Seward will get so wrapped up in this new *psychosis* that he's just discovered in Renny that he won't have the time to actually check these places out. And, just in case he gets suspicious, his old mentor will start writing him again and maybe suggest a visit in the near future."

"I don't know. It's all a little iffy. Take crackerjack timing."

"We'll have to be on top of our game. But, hell, the

gamble's worth it. We could make enough money to be set for life. Well, my life. You'll be good for another hundred years or so."

"That would be nice. I've always thought about meeting a girl, ya know? Settling down . . ."

"You big softy. Ya know, Renny's got these three sisters coming out to meet him."

"Yeah?"

"Oh yeah."

"Single?"

"Does it matter?"

Dracula laughed. "All right. I'm in. Let's do it."

"Good. Now let's work out the plan."

As they walked back over to the table, Dracula paused. "One thing."

"What?"

"I don't like 'Duke Dracula.'"

"It's the alliteration, isn't it? I knew that would bug you. What are you thinking?"

"How about 'count'?"

Van Helsing considered it. "I like it. Has kind of a mysterious quality to it. Count Dracula."

"All right. So that Harker guy will be here tonight to sign the deal. You know the plan?" Van Helsing adjusted the cape on Dracula's shoulders.

"Yeah. I got it. I'll meet him at the pass, bring him back here, and scare the shit out of him so that the last thing he's thinking of is castle flipping and real estate fraud."

"Exactly. Let the girls have some fun with him too. He'd like that."

"Do I have to wear this cape?"

"We've been over this."

"But that tweed hugs my shoulders so nicely."

Van Helsing shook his head. "And makes you look like an accountant. You're regal. It's what people expect."

"And you?"

He picked up his suitcase and patted it. "I've got my part to play. One way or another, I'll weasel into this, don't you worry."

"When will I hear from you?"

"When the time is right." Van Helsing dusted his hat off and placed it on his head.

"Abe?"

"Yeah?"

"I want to thank you for this. I was really at the end of my rope, ya know? But now there's . . ."

"What?"

"Hope." He laughed. "That sounds a little queer, doesn't it?"

Abraham punched his shoulder. "*Homosexual.* You've got to get that under control. You're gonna be in London soon. It isn't the Land Beyond the Forest, man. They don't take to that shit." They shared a smile. "Actually, a little hope sounds great." He walked to the door. "Just do your thing and this time next year we'll be sitting pretty, sunning on a beach in Italy. Well, *you* won't be sunning, but still . . ."

"I get it."

Van Helsing opened the door.

"What if something goes wrong?"

The aging con man laughed. "What could possibly go wrong?"

The Four Horsemen Reunion Tour: An Apocumentary

Lucien Soulban

Interviewer: How did you all meet?

Famine: Death, he was always around, right? The Alpha—

War: And the Omega. Death brought us together.

Famine: Well, him and me.

Pestilence: I joined the lads after. War came last.

Interviewer: Why "the Four Horsemen"? Why not just "Horsemen"?

Pestilence: It was a statement. One for all and all for one.

War: Like that Zorro fellow.

Pestilence: You mean Three Musketeers.

War: No. There were only three of them.

Famine: And how many Zorros do you see running around, carving their initials in people?

War: There was Douglas Fairbanks and Antonio Banderas, um, George Turner—

Pestilence: George Hamilton.

War: Right, George Hamilton played the poofter.

Interviewer: Why a reunion now? What changed?

Pestilence: When we heard they were paving over Megiddo to build Israel's first Walmart, we figured it was time.

Famine: We decided to reunite the band for our farewell tour and we wanted to put on a show that'd knock everyone dead.

The hotel lobby is meant to be grand, an attempt to effect majesty with oak paneling, Victorian wreath friezes, Persian rugs, leather settees, and more plants than a Brazilian rain forest, though that part isn't too hard these days. The camera swings around and blurs everything in its sweep; in fact, the hotel looks like someone has loaded a bordello into a shotgun and opened fire indiscriminately.

Beyond the revolving doors, the lightning pitches and thunders, the rain heavy with meaty splats and panicked croaking. Then again, frogs know they aren't aerodynamic and, one could argue, have every right to panic as they tumble from the skies.

The camera turns in time to catch Famine entering the lobby. "Bloody hell!" he says. He flicks frog giblets from the tassels of his epaulets and shimmies his black leather pants up but fails to conquer the rolling hills of his belly. "Whose idea was that?" he asks the camera, thumbing a finger outside.

"God's, I think," War says, entering after him. War is surprisingly timid and never makes eye contact, in that passive-aggressive way that suggests he'll smile to your face and start genocidal wars the second you turn your back. And upon his legs ride red chaps pulled high past his belly button in a manner suggesting someone else dressed him—his aging rocker mother perhaps.

Pestilence arrives last, as the camera records. "Personally, I love the classics. Boils, frogs 'n' all that," he says, chipper. Then again, his optimism is always infectious. Pestilence is a curious fellow, his mouth drooping as though waiting for a sneeze that never arrives. His leather vest is open, revealing a sweaty chest, and lo, he wears white leather pants.

Famine looks around the empty lobby, unimpressed, and then at the camera. "Hey! Where're all the groupies? The weeping maidens and those blokes gnashing their teeth? It's the bloody apocalypse."

"Guys! Ya made it!" An old man walks toward them, his plaid wardrobe last seen on a 1950s vacuum cleaner salesman . . . or a couch. The sparse comb-over, a continental map of liver spots and hunched-over shoulders suggest Death has been making a sport of keeping him alive.

"Laz!" Famine says. "Where the hell is everyone?"

"Our manager," Pestilence whispers to the camera.

"Bad news, boys. Everyone here is dead. But I checked the rooms and you're gonna love 'em."

"Who's dead?" Pestilence asks.

"The entire hotel. Guests, staff, groupies—lucky bastards," Laz grumbles before his wrinkles crinkle into an approximation of resigned cheer. "Let's get ya set up so we can start the auditions. Then ya can let me die—"

"Wait, wait!" Famine protests. "Who's done them in?"

"No clue. They were like that when I got here. Looks like they all just dropped dead. Hell of a thing. Now, how about we start, huh? The grand show ain't gonna run herself!"

"Right, I guess," Pestilence says. He points the camera in the direction of the dead bodies slumped in chairs and in a pile behind the counter. "Isn't this a bad omen?"

"Nonsense," Laz says, shuffling back to Pestilence and pulling him along by the elbow. "You were going to knock 'em dead anyways, remember? Now, go get ready, find your fourth band member, and then you can let me die. Chop chop."

Interviewer: The last time you were all together was during the '39–'45 World War II Tour.

Pestilence: Yeah, that was brilliant. We really came together as a band.

Famine: We were huge. Poland, Czechoslovakia, Germany, Russia . . . we toured everywhere.

Interviewer: Some critics accused you of just copying the success of the *World War I* album, that you didn't really innovate anything.

Pestilence: Didn't innovate anything?! We innovated everything, baby. Society, technology . . . we've never been bigger!

Famine: Yeah, especially with the Jews, Christians, and Muslims. Oh, and them buggers in between.

War: In between?

Pestilence: Jews for Jesus.

War: Oh, right!

Famine: Nobody ever brought them together like us. Not even that Carter fellow.

Pestilence: And when we hit the stage, we'll make believers of everyone else, we will.

Interviewer: But Death turned you down.

Pestilence: Well, not him per se. But his lawyers were very emphatic.

Famine: Hence the auditions. Can't be the Four Horsemen without a fourth.

War: Or Death. It's not the same without Death.

"All settled in?" Laz asks. The camera sweeps around, taking in the ballroom's high ceiling, with stained-glass cupola, and the sprawling burgundy carpet. Otherwise, the room is empty save for the three seats in the middle of the room and stacks of chairs to the side under a dusty tarp.

"I suppose," War says. "There's a pile of dead maids in my suite."

"At least they didn't cover your furniture in plastic before they nipped off," Pestilence says.

"Do you blame 'em?" Famine asks. "Last time we shared a room, I caught cholera and SARS."

"Right, sorry."

"Anthrax, botulism, tuberculosis, and VD—"

"Hey! That last one wasn't mine, you filthy bugger," Pestilence replies. He takes one of the three chairs in the middle of the room and spins it around before straddling it backward. "So? We gonna talk about the corpses?"

"They're dead," War says in a morose tone. "They were going to die anyway."

"Speaking of dead," Laz chirps, "how about ya kill me now?" But they ignore him.

"Hey. You think they started the Apocalypse without us?" Famine asks.

"Without the headliners?" Laz says. "Nah, you guys are the stars."

Famine shakes his head and sits with War, who is taking a napkin to his chair. "Let's just get this started. War's right. So they aren't around for the final encore. We'll still pack the stadium. You recording?" he asks the cameraman, and receives a thumbs-up in response. The three Horsemen face the center of the room.

"So who's the first audition?" Pestilence asks.

Laz checks his clipboard. "Drugs. Formerly with Sex, Drugs, and Rock & Roll."

"I loved them!" Famine says. He drapes his corpulent arm over the back of War's chair and stares into the camera. "They were brilliant 'til Sex split and went off with Rap."

"Drugs was *it*, mate!"

"So where is he?" War asks, staring into the center of the room. "It's rude to keep people waiting."

"Nah! It's his bag, baby!" Pestilence says with a cheer.

At that, the room shudders and a mushroom cloud of green vapor explodes outward from the middle of the carpet. War coughs and waves away the smoke while Pestilence and Famine lean forward intently. When the vapors clear, Drugs lays on the floor, feather hanging from a leather strip in his spiky hair, with kohl-rimmed eyes, shirtless and emaciated, and wearing blue and green striped bell-bottoms.

"It's Keith Richards," War whispers.

"Looks like him a bit, I suppose," Pestilence says. "He all right?"

Laz kneels next to Drugs while the Horsemen stand over him.

"Look at those track marks!" War says. "Must have OD'd."

"You know many people who shoot up with ammunition, do you?" Famine asks.

"I—don't take drugs. I wouldn't know," War replies.

The camera focuses on the wounds, large puckered holes along his forearm smeared with dry blood.

"He's dead," Laz announces, sounding terribly disappointed. Or jealous.

"Fuck," Famine whispers. "Dead? Drugs's been murdered?"

"Hold on," Pestilence says. "We can die?"

Interviewer: So it was a shock seeing Drugs dead like that?

Pestilence: I didn't know we could die. It was a wake-up call it was.

Famine: I was in shock.

War: I said a prayer for him.

Pestilence: You what?

Famine: He prayed for him. War found God.

Pestilence: Was he lost? Nobody told me.

Famine: He wasn't lost! War just found him is all.

Pestilence: If he wasn't lost, wouldn't that make War a wanker for finding him? Sorta like Columbus discovering America when folks were already there?

Famine: No, no. War didn't *find* God. It's more of a spiritual thing. Like the Dalai Lama.

War: Nice bloke, that lama fellow. Maybe we should ask him to audition.

Famine: For the Four Horsemen?

War: Yeah.

Famine: Of the Apocalypse?!

Pestilence: What? War, Famine, Pestilence, and a skinny Chinese bloke wrapped in me mum's curtains?

War: He's Tibetan. And no . . . War, Famine, Pestilence, and Peace. Nobody would expect it.

Pestilence: That's called jumping the shark, that is.

Laz: And technically, boys, War found *religion*.

Pestilence: Oh! Well, God and religion, they're not the same thing, are they?

"Who's next, Laz?" Famine asks, one leg slumped over the arm of the chair. Drugs is tucked inside a rolled-up duvet and pushed against the wall.

Laz checks his list and then exclaims, "Ah, Child Labor is up next."

"An Asian pop star!?" Pestilence groans. "You're not going Bollywood on us are you, Laz?"

"He's also big in Africa and South America," Laz replies, studying the sheet. "Wouldn't hurt you boys to hit those markets."

"We could use the endorsements," Famine says. "Shoes, tires, clothing—though exploiting younguns hasn't been in vogue since—"

"Reality television?" Laz asks.

"That fall out of vogue and no one told me?" Pestilence demands.

"Since Calvin Klein, I was going to say," Famine replies, thinking about it, then he snaps his finger (and somewhere in the world, another supermodel dies with her finger down her throat). "We'd be controversial, though. Think about it—our logos stamped across them all."

"What? Across the children?"

"No!" Famine snaps. "Shoes, tires, and clothing. I'm tired of advertising in the Good Books. Where'd that get us, eh?"

"You actually considering this?" Pestilence demands. "Going mainstream? Selling out to the man?"

"What man? Christ?" Laz asks.

"Christ a man? We back to that old chestnut?" Famine asks.

As they continue arguing, the carpet unravels, the fibers widening in a spot until the gap is large enough to disgorge a man. Well, spit up really, like a numb tongue rolling out of someone's mouth. He is wearing fine silks and of an origin that most Westerners could approximate as Oriental (the Orient spanning, left to right, from the Middle East to somewhere just east of the California coastline). The man is lying on the ground, however, not-breathing with the skill of someone who's practiced not-breathing for the last several hours.

"Uh-oh," Laz says.

"He dead too?" Famine asks.

"Afraid so," Laz replies. "Lucky prick."

War: They don't get me. Don't get my sound, you know what I mean?

Interviewer: You talked about going solo.

War: Well, I could, couldn't I? Fundamentalist rock. It's my new passion.

Interviewer: So what's stopping you?

War: Nothing . . . now.

"Sorry, mate," Pestilence says, grunting as he pushes Child Labor up against Drugs with the heel of his knee-length leather boot. "But the show must go on."

"Go on?" Famine asks. "Drugs and Child Labor were murdered. Nobody said we could die."

"I'm just as surprised as you are," Pestilence replies, taking a seat on Child Labor. He pulls out a cigarette, the tip of which spontaneously combusts.

"I knew, actually," War says, wandering back into the ballroom.

"Where you been?" Pestilence asks. "Someone murdered Child Labor."

"Did you check with Murder?"

"Can't reach him," Famine replies. "Why didn't you say we could be offed?"

"I thought everyone knew," War says. "Ultimately, we're just concepts, aren't we? Death told me so."

"Death," Famine groans. "He'd be a boring cunt without us."

"Don't say that!" War says. "He's Death, the Omega of Everything."

"Never said he wasn't," Pestilence replies. "But without us, people would just keel over on the spot, wouldn't they? Dull as a sack of potatoes on black and white telly."

"Yeah," Famine says. "We provide the sport. Death just strikes shite down."

"Smites shite," Pestilence corrects him.

"Right, smites it. But we're the real artists. We do it with style. It's why we're chart toppers."

"What about Cancer?" War asks.

"His audition is at three thirty," Laz replies.

"No, no. Cancer's number one in North America, right. We're no longer at the top."

"We will be after this show," Famine says. "We're closing down the house!"

"Old Testament style!" Pestilence shouts, throwing up the devil's horns.

"Yeah, but it's fixed, isn't it? Preordained," War replies. "We're number one only because God said so millennia ago. Otherwise, where would we be?"

At that, the three Horsemen fall silent, none of them looking at each other or even the camera. "Turn it off," Famine says, shoving his hand up to the lens.

Interviewer: Did you ever consider changing your names?

Famine: I thought we were, like, immutable.

War: Actually, I'm thinking of changing mine to Holy War.

Pestilence: Isn't that, like, a jihad?

War: No! A jihad is a struggle. This is a holy war. It's like biblical. Epic.

Famine: We're already biblical! Or did I miss something?

War: I was big in the Crusades. I'm just going back to my roots is all.

The three Horsemen wait in the ballroom for the next audition. They hardly speak, the last exchange weighing on them while Drugs's and Child Labor's bodies still rot nearby. They don't glance at the corpses, which tally up to the eight-hundred-pound gorilla in the room (minus five hundred pounds or thereabouts, so really, a skinny eight-hundred-pound gorilla), the mortality of the Three Horsemen suddenly realized.

"Shouldn't we talk about it?" Famine finally asks.

When War throws him a quizzical look, Pestilence nods to the corpses. "You want to solve their murders do you, Scooby?"

"I don't give a fuck about their murders," Famine replies. "I want to know who bloody well killed them."

"Yeah, spot-on," Pestilence says, moving to the bodies. "Let's search them for clues, then."

As Famine and Pestilence look down at the rolled-up duvet holding Drugs, the cameraman scrambles to catch whatever poignant thoughts are about to fall from the two Horsemen. And there it is, captured on camera, that kernel of realization that flickers across Pestilence's face.

"Anyone else think he looks like a joint?" Pestilence asks.

"Bloody appropriate," Famine says. He bends over to grab the duvet's edge. "I think he'd appreciate the irony."

Pestilence kneels down and both men pull the edge of the duvet, unwrapping Drugs, who rolls and slumps to his stomach with a dull thud. War is behind them, fidgeting with his fingers and apparently equally uncomfortable and curious, judging by the way he cranes his neck. Famine notices him and steps aside, inviting War to participate.

"What? Me?" War asks.

"You know more about this sort of thing than I do," Famine says. "'Sides, my knees are fucked."

War looks ready to complain, then predictably swallows his protests and kneels next to Pestilence. Both War and Pestilence nudge the body, then prod it, then poke it when nudging and prodding fail to produce results.

"God," Famine says. "It's like watching the Quest for Fire."

"You want a go at it?" Pestilence shoots to his feet. Famine apologizes by raising both hands and backing off.

"Who do we know who's good with this crap?" Laz asks from behind them.

"An expert? Like Death? He told us to sod off," Famine says.

"Well, *like* Death, but not exactly him."

"What, like a Mrs. Death?" War asks.

Famine sighs. "Face it. We're good at dispensing this shite, not solving it."

"Right," Pestilence replies, clapping his hands together (and around the world, the smallpox vaccine wears off, leaving many people open for a spectacularly bad week). "Let's get back to what we're good at, then, shall we?"

With shrugs and nods, Famine and War drift back to their seats while Pestilence drapes the duvet over Drugs. "Sorry, mate," he says. "Laz, who's our next audition? And please, a live one."

A brown-green mist seeps up from the carpet and coalesces into a dapper-looking gentleman with a white sequined suit, a white rhinestone fedora, shades, and a white glove.

He is Caucasian one moment, then Latino, then African-American . . . or perhaps African-Canadian or African-British. The Horsemen are too embarrassed to admit they can't tell.

"Finally!" Famine says, relieved that their newest arrival is firmly upright.

"A single white glove? Really?" Pestilence whispers to Laz, who shrugs in reply.

The now-Asian man is about to say something when he notices Drugs and Child Labor to the side and dead. Several thoughts shoot through his head at that moment, such as "Are those dead bodies?" and "Just how seriously are you taking these auditions?" He raises his gloved hand to ask a question, which the others mistake for the start of his audition.

"Introduce yourself first, please," Famine says impatiently, but it's War who leans forward.

"Pardon? Who are you speaking to?"

"Global Warming, mate," Pestilence replies.

"Where?" War asks, looking around.

Famine, Pestilence, and Laz all turn to stare at War, but his expression remains serious, his lips pursed.

"Come again?" Pestilence asks.

"There's nobody there."

"You don't see him?" Pestilence says.

"Who?"

"Global Warming," Famine snaps. "The bloke who's standing right there!"

Mystified, War looks in the general direction of Global Warming, who in turn is staring back at them helplessly. "I . . . get that a lot," Global Warming offers sheepishly, but the others pretty much ignore him.

"Are you sure?" War asks.

"Yes!" Pestilence and Famine shout.

War shrugs. "But nothing's there," he says helplessly, his mouth opening and closing in search of something else to say.

"It's okay," Global Warming says, even though nobody is listening to him.

"Well this is bollocks," Pestilence says.

"What?" War asks.

"I'll leave," Global Warming says.

"We can't audition someone you don't believe exists, can we?" Famine says.

"All right then. Good luck."

"Are you sure someone's there?" War asks, looking at them and then back at the spot where Global Warming waits. Or rather through him to the spot behind their recent arrival. War seems genuinely concerned.

"Bye," Global Warming says, turning away. He hesitates, hoping someone will stop him, then realizes nobody is trying. He vanishes, dispersed as a mist that the carpet sucks back into itself.

"What? We're both hallucinating, then?" Pestilence says. "Laz?"

"He's not there," Laz says.

"See?" War replies.

"No, I mean he amscrayed."

Famine and Pestilence look back at where Global Warming stood and then roll their eyes to the cupola above them. The apocalypse will never come at this pace.

Interviewer: Why don't the Horsemen just go with three members?

Laz: Oh, I could spin some crap about brand recognition, but between you and me? It's ego. They're hungry to prove Death made a mistake walking away. They wanna show him *he's* the one that can be replaced.

Interviewer: That's a pretty brave statement considering *your death* rests in *their hands*. What happens when the Horsemen see this interview?

Laz: I'll be dead by then. Speaking of which, let me ask you something.

Interviewer: Okay.

Laz: Who's this documentary for?

Interviewer: Posterity.

Laz: Never met her, and I think you're lying, pal. There ain't no posterity after the Big Show, no encores or additional performances. Just a thundering ovation and the mother of all wrap parties. Unless you're here for another reason.

Interviewer: Like?

Laz: Like you know what's going on. Like none of this has got to do with the final concert.

Interviewer: Smart man. Well, let's just say that the show will go on. Only, without you.

Laz: Well, it's about fucking time. Will you kill me already, please?

Interviewer: Certainly.

"Y'seen War?" Pestilence asks, glancing at the camera.

"Uh-uh," Famine replies.

The greenroom is quiet, the bowls filled with chips, the trays covered in sliced veggies, mini-sandwiches and Oreo cookies, and a cooler filled with various alcoholic drinks. Famine moves from tray to tray, sampling things, taking mousy bites from everything before putting them back or licking the center from Oreo cookies, sandwiches, pigs in a blanket—really anything with a center to lick. He's a grazer, never eating fully but nibbling and double-dipping instead.

"I found Laz," Pestilence says. "He's dead. Did you break his contract?"

Famine stops snacking, more confused than concerned. "No."

Pestilence glances around before whispering, "What about War?"

"It's not his style, mate. He's anal about that sort of thing, with all his planning and the manufacturing of evidence before he even considers picking a fight. It's like watching the Rain Man trying to undo a bra."

"Still. There's something bothering me."

"What, you mean other than the dead bodies?" Famine says with a sneer.

"We could be next."

"Been thinking about it. Decided it'd never happen."

"What, like it never happened to Child Labor and Drugs?"

"Yeah, but they can't live without their fans. Wouldn't exist without them. After their fan clubs vanish, so do they. But us . . . we'll still be around, mate. Hunger exists in the animal kingdom. Ask the dinosaurs. So does disease—ask those things that kept sodomizing the dinosaurs and infecting them with STDs."

"Oh, them!" Pestilence says. "Well, War can't live without his fans either."

"Sure he can. Heaven was listening to him long before humans heard his tunes."

"Yeah," Pestilence says, "but heaven went to war *over* humans. No humans, ergo no war."

"Bloody hell. You've pulled out the Latin. This is serious."

"Famine . . ."

"What about Global Warming, then? He's nothing without his fans. Why isn't he croakers?"

"I don't know," Pestilence admits. "But I have an idea. Whoever's murdering our auditionees—"

"Is that even a word?"

"—is out to stop our farewell tour. You get me?"

"Right," Famine says. "So what's the game?"

Pestilence thinks about it and then smiles. "A surprise audition, and I know just the bint."

Interviewer: So, why did Death leave?

Famine: He said we weren't keeping up with the times.

Pestilence: He accused us of playing the same old
songs. Can you believe that? Us, stuck in a rut?
He's the one-hit wonder.

"What's going on?" War asks. He looks around the
ballroom, at the camera, at his two compatriots. Famine
sits on one chair, and Pestilence waits perched atop the
high back of another, his feet muddying the cushion.

"Last-minute audition," Pestilence says happily.

"Really? Who?" War asks. His fingers curl together
nervously, and then when he notices Famine, Pestilence, and the camera watching him, he tries to act
more relaxed (which isn't unlike trying to watch a
broom bend). "Who?" he asks more casually.

"You'll see," Famine replies.

As though on cue, the ground bulges, the carpet
tearing apart from the groundswell beneath before
it cracks open like an egg. The camera zooms in as
the tremor subsides, leaving behind a beautiful white
woman with silken black hair, Mother Goddess hips,
and a red and black floral sarong that wreathes her
ample body.

"I believe you know Overpopulation?" Pestilence
says.

"My ex-wife!?" War shrieks in panic.

"Hello, you sniveling, impotent little—" And then
she drops dead, the shot that pierces her skull silent but
nonetheless lethal. The room is still a moment before

the ground rumbles again. This time, a beautiful black woman with a rich full Afro and wearing the same sarong as the woman on the ground appears. "—fart of a worm," she says, continuing, and then realizes something. "Did you just try to—" Then she drops dead as well. This time the faint acrid smell of chlorine gas perfumes the air.

Famine and Pestilence look over at War, who appears very nervous. "It was a bad breakup," he protests meekly.

The ground shudders anew, this time revealing a Japanese woman with a punkish pageboy cut. "—kill me? You weasel-fucker. You did—" And she too dies, her body blown to smithereens by an unseen explosion.

"War!" Famine shouts. He's covered in a layer of gore. "Stop that!"

"You can't kill her," Pestilence says, picking out bits of woman from his long, feathered hair. "Not like you did the others."

"—try to kill me!" the full-figured Inuit woman with mahogany brown skin says.

"Overpopulation, please. Can you give us a moment?" Pestilence asks.

She hesitates, her black eyes locking on War, before she turns to Pestilence and replies sweetly with intent to wound her ex. "Of course, Pesti, dear. Just make sure you give him what's coming to him." With a final venomous glance at War, she and the two dead bodies and one human smear at her feet vanish.

"Phew," War says. "Glad that's over. I have to say, she wouldn't be a good fit for us, lads."

"War," Famine warns. "You've been killing off potential bandmates."

"No I haven't," he says weakly.

"You just murdered Overpopulation in front of us! Three times!" Pestilence says. "And the only audition who survived was the one you couldn't see! Why, mate? Why'd you kill them?"

"I—" War hesitates and then exhales, resigned to the truth. "I wanted the auditions to fail."

"Why?" Famine asks.

"Because humans appreciate me. Without them, I'll be the artist formerly known as War."

"Bloody hell, mate," Famine says. "What'd you think was going to happen? That we wouldn't notice?"

"And why'd you have to kill Drugs? What'd he do to you?"

"Nothing! But someone had declared war on drugs and—well—there you have it," War says. "Made. it easier to off him."

"Hold on," Famine says. "Even if someone did declare war on Child Labor and Drugs 'n' all that, you still can't kill their careers. It's not in you, mate."

"Sure it is," War replies, suddenly unable to meet their gaze.

"He's right. None of us have that star power. In fact, Laz is the only contract you could break," Pestilence says.

"Laz? Laz is dead?" War asks. "I—I didn't break his contract."

"That was me, I'm afraid."

The camera swings around in time to catch the interviewer striding in. He is tall and well groomed, comfortable in his blue sweater and black trousers.

"You?" Famine asks.

"And I would have gotten away with it if it weren't for you meddling kids," he says before winking at the camera. "Actually, I *did* get away with it." His face remains the same, still imbued with a healthy glow and cheer, but his clothes turn ashen; the colors bleed from them.

"You!" Famine says.

"'Allo, Death," Pestilence says. "Should have known you'd sabotage us."

"Yeah, but why?" Famine asks, looking from Death to War, then back to Death.

War shrugs and smiles sheepishly. "I didn't want to retire. Then Death offered to represent me."

"Yeah, but—but the final concert—everyone's already bought tickets!" Famine says in protest. "We were going to knock 'em all dead!"

"Change of plans," Death says with a shrug. "No final concert. No going out with a bang. The show goes on and we keep releasing albums and harvesting the proceeds."

"It's true," War says, standing next to Death with a fevered, admiring look. "Death is going to be my manager. I can go back to my roots as Holy War!"

"Besides, since humanity's been around," Death says, "I've discovered I can subcontract my work to them. Humans have grown so creative in offing each other, I hardly have to lift a finger!"

"You mean you're . . . lip-synching?" Pestilence asks, mortified.

Death shrugs. "People will never know the difference. They don't want to. So why not sit back, let them do the work and we reap the rewards?"

"W-we'll do this without you tossers, then!" Pestilence says.

"Do what?" Death asks, laughing with a healthy joie de vivre. "Without me, you're nothing. Famine without Death is a swollen belly. War without Death is a poke in the eye. Pestilence without Death is a sore throat. And the Apocalypse without Death is a bad hair day. You've always needed me. You still do." With that, Death strides for the ballroom door.

War tags along and pauses briefly to look back at Pestilence and Famine, almost pleading in his expression. "Please," War says. "Join us. We can be together again."

War leaves when Famine and Pestilence don't respond.

The pair remain quiet for the better part of an hour, the camera dancing in and out of focus on them. Finally, as the camera pulls away, exiting the room and abandoning them, Famine speaks softly . . .

"What if he's right?"

Famine: You sure the camera's on?

Pestilence: The light blinking?

Famine: Yeah.

Pestilence: Then it's on.

Famine: All right, then. Our next audition is, um, Natural Disaster is it?

Natural Disaster: That's right. You guys still auditioning for the final show? 'Cause there's a lot I can bring to the table, visual effects wise. Explosions, props and a light show you gotta see to believe.

Pestilence: Brilliant!

Famine: Though we've decided to put the final show on hold and start a new world tour. You good with that?

Natural Disaster: Absolutely. How long we talking?

Pestilence: Indefinitely.

Famine: It's for our new album, *Hell Is an Afterthought*. We're dedicating it to the fans.

Pestilence: Right, because without our fans, none of this could happen.

About the
Authors

After deciding to write a piece for this volume, the normally emo CHRIS ABBEY held three séances to summon a story from the ghost of Jack Davis. Since Mr. Davis is thankfully still alive, he wound up with this piece instead. Chris is best known for *The Wonderland Tarot*, in collaboration with artist Morgana Abbey (no relation). He lives in Buffalo, three blocks from a street named Voorhees.

KELLEY ARMSTRONG is the author of the *New York Times* bestselling "Women of the Otherworld" paranormal suspense series and "Darkest Powers" young adult urban fantasy trilogy, as well as the Nadia Stafford crime series. She grew up in southwestern Ontario, where she still lives with her family. A former computer programmer, she's now escaped her corporate cubicle and hopes never to return. Her website is www.kelleyarmstrong.com.

L. A. BANKS was named a 2010 Living Legend by the Black Alumni Society of the University of Pennsylvania, received the 2009 *Romantic Times* Booklover's Career Choice Award for Paranormal Fiction, was named one of Pennsylvania's Top 50 Women in Business for 2008, and won the 2008 *Essence* Storyteller of the Year award. Ms. Banks wrote more than forty-two novels and contributed to twenty-three novellas in the genres of romance, women's fiction, crime/suspense thrillers, and paranormal lore. She was a proud member of The Liars Club, a Board of Trustee member for the Philadelphia Free Library, and served on the Mayor's Commission on Literacy. Banks was a graduate of the University of Pennsylvania Wharton undergraduate program, with a Master's in Fine Arts from Temple University. L. A. Banks passed away in 2011; "Bayou Brawl" is one of the last stories she wrote.

MIKE BARON broke into comics with *Nexus,* his groundbreaking science fiction title co-created with illustrator Steve Rude. He has written for *Creem, The Boston Globe, Isthmus, AARP Magazine, Oui, Madison, Fusion, Poudre Magazine, Argosy,* and many others. *Nexus* is currently being published in hardcover by Dark Horse. Baron has won two Eisners and an Inkpot for his work on *Nexus,* now being published in five languages including French, Italian, Portuguese, and Spanish. Baron's revamp of DC's The Flash continues to garner great reviews. Marvel recently published two collections of Baron's work: *The Essential Punisher Vol. II* and *The Essential Punisher Vol. III.* A prolific creator, Baron is at least partly responsible for The Badger, Spyke, Feud, The Hook, and The Architect. The latter is available as a graphic novel from Big Head Press.

JIM BUTCHER is the author of the Dresden Files and the Codex Alera. He hopes to be the author of many more stories because that way they'll finally be in other people's brains distracting them, instead of in his own brain distracting him. He lives in Missouri with his wife, supernatural romance and romantic suspense author Shannon Butcher, and a ferocious watchdog.

DON D'AMMASSA is the author of seven novels and two hundred short stories. He was book reviewer for *Science Fiction Chronicle* for almost thirty years and now reviews for his own website. He has been writing full time since 2000.

STEPHEN DORATO is the pseudonym of a lab-radoodle living in a Boston suburb whose fiction has appeared in Gothic.net and Feral Fiction. When she isn't writing, she enjoys hanging out on the couch with her bitch Valerie or eating yummy moths.

JG FAHERTY grew up in the haunted Hudson Valley region of New York, and still resides there. Living in an area filled with Revolutionary War battlegrounds, two-hundred-year-old gravesites, ghosts, haunted roads, and tales of monsters in the woods has provided a rich background for his writing. A lifelong fan of horror and dark fiction, JG enjoys reading, watching movies, golfing, hiking, volunteering as an exotic animal caretaker, and playing the guitar. One of his favorite childhood playgrounds was an eighteenth-century cemetery. JG's first novel, *Carnival of Fear,* was released in 2010. His next book, *Ghosts of Coronado Bay,* a YA supernatural thriller, was published in 2011. *Cemetery Club,* his third novel, and *The Cold Spot,* a novella, will be released in 2012. His other credits include more than two dozen short stories in major genre magazines and anthologies. You can follow him at www.jgfaherty.com, www.twitter.com/jgfaherty, and www.facebook/jgfaherty.

CHRISTOPHER GOLDEN is the award-winning, bestselling author of such novels as *Of Saints and*

Shadows, The Myth Hunters, The Boys Are Back in Town, and *Strangewood.* He has also written books for teens and young adults, including *The Secret Journeys of Jack London,* co-authored with Tim Lebbon, and the *Body of Evidence* series. He co-wrote the illustrated novel *Baltimore, or, The Steadfast Tin Soldier and the Vampire* with Mike Mignola, as well as the comic book series born from the novel. Golden was born and raised in Massachusetts, where he still lives with his family. His original novels have been published in more than fourteen languages. Please visit him at www.christophergolden.com.

After a stint of several years in dinner theater, backup vocals, and bartending, HEATHER GRAHAM stayed home after the birth of her third child and began to write. Now a *New York Times* and *USA Today* bestselling author, she has written over one hundred novels and novellas including category, romantic suspense, historical romance, vampire fiction, time travel, occult, and Christmas holiday fare.

BRAD C. HODSON currently resides in Los Angeles, where he's happy to exercise his willpower every day by deciding not to play Demolition Derby while stuck in traffic. His work can be seen in a number of anthologies, as well as the feature film *George's Inter-*

vention and the play *A Year Without a Summer*. He's currently adapting William Peter Blatty's *Legion* (aka *Exorcist III*) for the stage as well as gearing up for pre-production on his feature film directorial debut, *Neverborn*. His first novel, *Darling*, was released by Bad Moon Books in April 2012. He tries to stay busy and enjoys writing about himself in third person. For more information, please visit www.brad-hodson.com.

NINA KIRIKI HOFFMAN has sold adult and YA novels and more than 250 short stories. Her works have been finalists for the World Fantasy, Mythopoeic, Sturgeon, Philip K. Dick, and Endeavour awards. Her first novel, *The Thread That Binds the Bones*, won a Stoker award, and her short story "Trophy Wives" won a Nebula Award in 2009. Her middle-school novel, *Thresholds*, was published by Viking in August 2010, and its sequel, *Meeting*, was published in August 2011. Nina does production work for the *Magazine of Fantasy & Science Fiction*. She also works with teen writers. She lives in Eugene, Oregon, with several cats and many strange toys and imaginary friends.

In the past two years, *New York Times* bestselling author SHERRILYN KENYON has claimed the #1 spot twelve times. This extraordinary bestseller continues to top every genre she writes, with more than 23 million copies of her books in print in over thirty countries. Her current series include: *The Dark-Hunters, The League,* Lords of Avalon, BAD Agency, and the Chronicles of Nick. Since 2004, she has placed over fifty novels on the *New York Times* list. The preeminent voice in paranormal fiction, with more than twenty years of publishing credits, Kenyon helped not only to pioneer but to define the current paranormal trend that has captivated the world.

KEN LILLIE-PAETZ is best known for his rambling theories on "How to Avoid the Apocalypse by Attacking Heaven and Hell First" and "Why Lemurs and Monkeys Just Can't Get Along." These musings can be found in his comic book properties *Elsinore* and *Monkey in a Wagon vs. Lemur on a Big Wheel.* It is believed that Ken resides in the frozen wilderness of Northern Ontario, Canada, where sightings of him are rare and any photographic evidence has been too blurry to substantiate these accounts of his existence. For a more complete story of this strange creature, see www.monkeypharmacy.com.

ADRIAN LUDENS lives and works in the Black Hills of South Dakota. Magazine appearances include *Alfred Hitchcock's Mystery Magazine* (two-time winner of the "Mysterious Photograph" story contest) and

Morpheus Tales, among others. Recent anthology appearances include *The Mothman Files* (edited by Michael Knost, Woodland Press), *D.O.A.* (edited by David C. Hayes and Jack Burton, Blood Bound Books), and *Zombie Kong* (edited by James Roy Daley, Books of the Dead Press). Look for Adrian's short story collection, *Bedtime Stories for Carrion Beetles,* available soon. Adrian would like to thank his wife, Crissy, and his fellow HWA members for their support. Visit him at curioditiesadrianludens.blogspot.com.

WILL LUDWIGSEN writes horror and fantasy for magazines like *Weird Tales, Asimov's Science Fiction, Strange Horizons, Alfred Hitchcock's Mystery Magazine,* and others from a leaning and vine-covered shanty in Jacksonville, Florida. He recently earned an MFA from the Stonecoast popular fiction program at the University of Southern Maine, enabling him to reach the apotheosis of his craft in "Acknowledgments." He blogs regularly at http://www.will-ludwigsen.com, including weekly installments of his One-Hour Stories—short tales written in one hour.

E. S. MAGILL has been influenced by two movies, *Night of the Living Dead* and *The Last Man on Earth.* "My life's goal is to have those metal roll-down security shutters on my windows, for when the zombie apocalypse hits," she states. Even though she has an MA in English (her area of expertise being the postmodern gothic), she insists on teaching middle school English by day. She is the former reviews editor for *Dark Wisdom* magazine. Southern California is home to her and her husband, Greg, and their menagerie of cats and Corvettes.

LISA MORTON's short fiction has appeared in such anthologies as *Dark Delicacies, The Mammoth Book of Zombie Apocalypse, The Museum of Horrors, The Mammoth Book of Dracula,* and dozens of others. Her screenplay credits include the cult favorite *Meet the Hollowheads.* She is also a renowned expert on Halloween, having authored *The Halloween Encyclopedia,* and has appeared on The History Channel. She lives in North Hollywood, California, where her life is absolutely ruled by her cat. Find out more at www.lisamorton.com.

As a child, MARK ONSPAUGH sat too close to the TV, and now needs glasses. His young brain was irradiated with monster movies, sci-fi, and Looney Tunes. DC Comics took care of the rest. Today, he is the writer of the film *Kill Katie Malone,* a co-writer of the cult fave *Flight of the Living Dead,* and has several scripts in development. He has sold numerous short stories and essays. He tells people he was raised by wolves, but his parents were nice people who only eviscerated the occasional wayward traveler. You can visit him at www.markonspaugh.com and on Facebook.

NORMAN PRENTISS won the 2009 Bram Stoker Award for Superior Achievement in Short Fiction for "In the Porches of My Ears," in *Postscripts 18*. His first book, *Invisible Fences*, was published in May 2010 by Cemetery Dance and received a Bram Stoker Award in the Long Fiction category. His fiction has also appeared in *Black Static*, *Commutability*, *Tales from the Gorezone*, *Damned Nation*, *Best Horror of the Year*, *The Year's Best Dark Fantasy and Horror*, and in three editions of the *Shivers* anthology series. His poetry has appeared in *Writer Online*, *Southern Poetry Review*, *Baltimore's City Paper*, and *A Sea of Alone: Poems for Alfred Hitchcock*. His essays on gothic and sensation literature have appeared in *Victorian Poetry*, *Colby Quarterly*, and *The Thomas Hardy Review*.

DANIEL PYLE is the author of several novels and novellas, including *Dismember*, *Freeze*, and *Down the Drain*. He lives in Springfield, Missouri, with his wife and two daughters. He'd tell you where he got the idea for "Short Term," but he can't remember. To stalk him online, slink on over to www.danielpyle.com.

MIKE RESNICK is, according to *Locus,* the all-time leading award winner, living or dead, for short science fiction. He has won five Hugos, a Nebula, and other major awards in the USA, France, Poland, Spain, Croatia, and Japan. He's the author of sixty-plus novels, two-hundred-fifty-plus stories, and two screenplays, and is the editor of forty anthologies. His work has been translated into twenty-five languages.

LEZLI ROBYN is an Australian author who has made numerous professional science fiction and fantasy short story sales—sometimes in collaboration with Mike Resnick—since her fictional debut in November 2008, to markets such as *Asimov's* and *Analog.* In 2010 she was nominated for an Aurealis Award (for best SF story) and the Campbell Award (for best new writer), and she has sold her first short story collection to Australian publisher Ticonderoga. Her latest publication, "Anne-droid of Green Gables," has just been selected for inclusion in the annual Australian *Year's Best Australian Fantasy & Horror* anthology.

Stop! Stop! Just stop it! I'll talk! My name . . . my name is JEFF RYAN. I've got a wife and two daughters. I live in New Jersey. I wrote a biography about Super Mario . . . stop laughing, I'm serious, I did! What else do you want to know? What's so precious that you would threaten my darling collection of *Guardians of the Galaxy* comic books? Take an acetylene torch to Charlie-27 and Major Vance Astro? I don't KNOW anything . . . !

DAVID SAKMYSTER is an award-winning author and screenwriter who discovers his ideas by throwing a bowl full of half-slumbered musings against a wall and seeing what manages to cling out of self-preservation. His short stories have appeared in *The Writers of the Future Anthology, ChiZine, Horrorworld, Black Static, Talebones, Abyss & Apex,* and others. *The Pharos Objective* and *The Mongol Objective* are the first two novels in a series about psychic archaeologists. And he's also quite proud of his horror novel *Crescent Lake* and the historical fiction epic *Silver and Gold.* You can step into his mind at www.sakmyster.com.

D. L. SNELL invites you to shoot him in the head at his blog, dlsnell.com, where you will find a Flash game in which he's a zombie and you're a bosomy vampire with a gun. Snell's e-short "Dick, and Larry Too," a sequel to his story in *Blood Lite: Overbite,* can be found in Amazon's Kindle Store. Seriously, visit his blog. Snell interviews editors about what kind of stories they want for their anthologies and zines, and he has interviewed authors such as Joe McKinney and Kevin J. Anderson.

LUCIEN SOULBAN lives in beautiful Montreal as a narrative designer and scriptwriter for Ubisoft and Triple-A videogame titles like *Deus Ex: Human Revolution*, *Rainbow Six: Vegas*, and *Warhammer 40K: Dawn of War*. He's also written for Nintendo DS games like *The Golden Compass*, *Kung-Fu Panda*, and *Kim Possible*. On the fiction side of things, he's written five novels, including *Dragonlance's Renegade Wizard* and *Warhammer 40K: Desert Raiders*. His proudest accomplishments, however, have been his numerous contributions to anthologies like *Horrors Beyond 2*, *Dark Faith*, and to all three HWA comedy-horror anthologies, *Blood Lite* I, II, and III. Be sure to visit his website at www.luciensoulban.com.

A three-time *Blood Lite* offender, ERIC JAMES STONE has also been published in *Year's Best SF*, *Analog*, and other venues. Eric is a Nebula Award winner, a Hugo Award nominee, Writers of the Future winner, Odyssey Writing Workshop graduate, Orson Scott Card's Literary Boot Camp graduate, and assistant editor at *Intergalactic Medicine Show*. Although he received a law degree, he has since repented and does not practice law—which he hopes will save him when the hyper-intelligent zombie apocalypse reaches Utah. You can find more of Eric's fiction at www.ericjamesstone.com.

JEFF STRAND has been in all three *Blood Lite* anthologies, a feat that few have dared to attempt and even fewer have accomplished. He's also written a bunch of books, like *Fangboy, Wolf Hunt, Pressure, Dweller,* and *Single White Psychopath Seeks Same.* If you are reading this, you are morally obligated to visit his website www.JeffStrand.com within the next fifteen minutes.

JOEL A. SUTHERLAND makes his living as a librarian, surrounded by books both at work and at home. His short fiction has appeared in many publications (including *Cemetery Dance Magazine* and *Blood Lite II: Overbite*), and his first novel, *Frozen Blood,* was nominated for the Bram Stoker Award. He is also the author of *Be a Writing Superstar,* a creative writing book for kids published by Scholastic, is the founder of the DarkLit Fest, and appeared on the first season of Wipeout Canada as the Barbarian Librarian. He's happiest when he's hanging out with his wife, Colleen, their son, Charles, and their goldendoodle, Murphy. They live near Toronto. Sutherland can be reached through his website, www.joelasutherland.com.

JOHN ALFRED TAYLOR writes poetry, horror, and science fiction, and now that he's a Professor Emeritus (translation: geezer) can focus on his writing full-time. Over the years he's had stories in *Galaxy, Galileo, Aboriginal Science Fiction, Twilight Zone, Oceans of the Mind,* and *Grue.* Notice these are all dead magazines—he hopes his presence didn't kill them. Probably not, because *Asimov's* published his stories and survived. A collection of his horror stories, *Hell Is Murky,* is currently available from Ash-Tree Press.

Editor KEVIN J. ANDERSON's first novel, *Resurrection, Inc.,* was nominated for the Stoker Award. Of his hundred or so published novels, some have been horror, particularly his international bestselling *X-Files* novels, and his new humorous series featuring Dan Shamble, Zombie P.I., which begins with *Death Warmed Over.* He is best known for his epic science fiction and fantasy (*Dune* novels with Brian Herbert, his own *Saga of Seven Suns* science fiction epic, and his *Terra Incognita* fantasy trilogy). Anderson is the editor of eight anthologies, including the three bestselling science fiction anthologies of all time. His cats, however, are not particularly impressed.